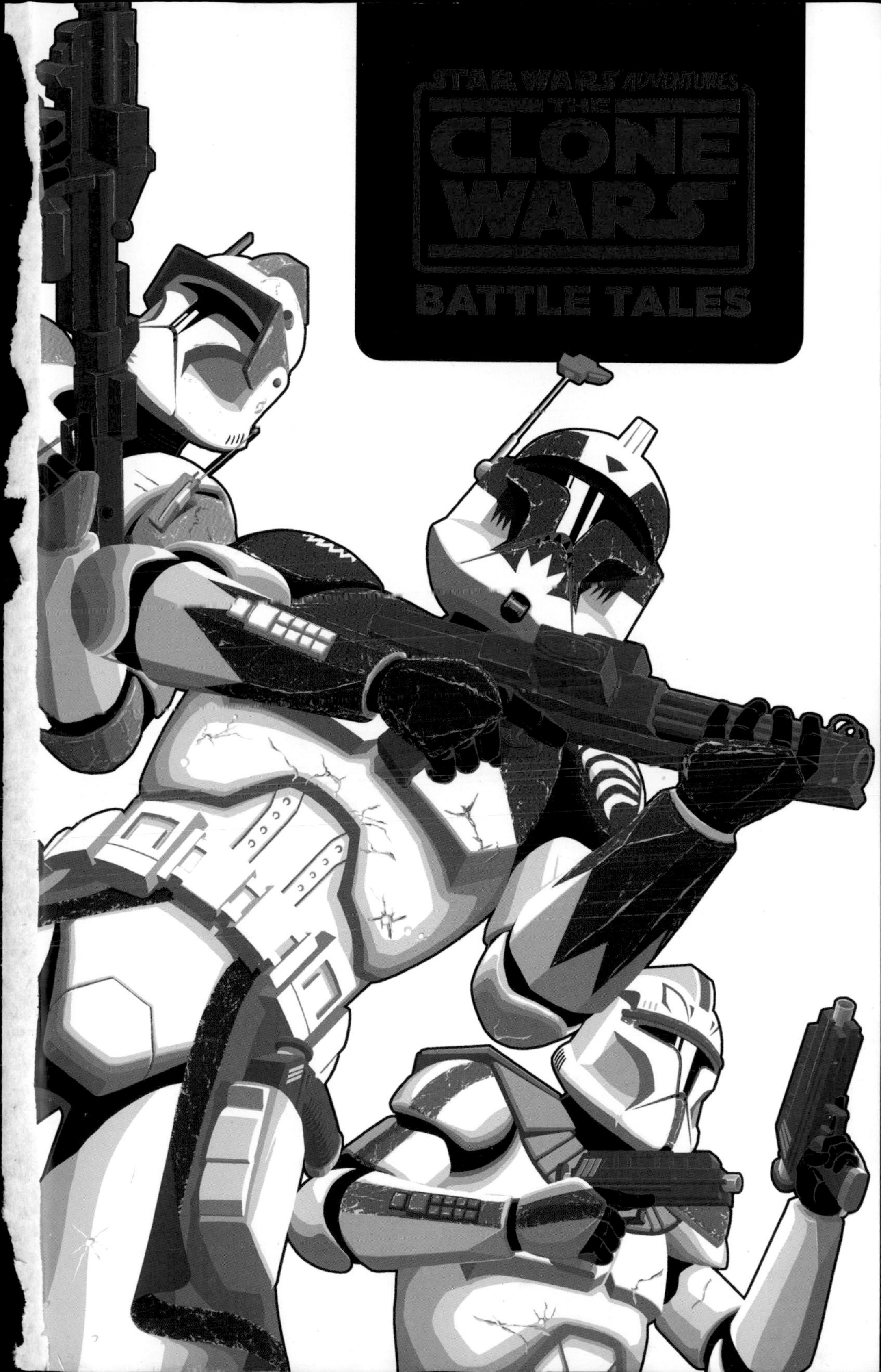
STAR WARS ADVENTURES
THE
CLONE WARS
BATTLE TALES

Facebook: **facebook.com/idwpublishing**
Twitter: **@idwpublishing**
YouTube: **youtube.com/idwpublishing**
Tumblr: **tumblr.idwpublishing.com**
Instagram: **instagram.com/idwpublishing**

ISBN: 978-1-68405-723-8   24 23 22 21   1 2 3 4

COVER ARTIST
DEREK CHARM

LETTERER
JAKE M. WOOD

SERIES EDITORS
ELIZABETH BREI
& DENTON J. TIPTON

Originally published as STAR WARS ADVENTURES: THE CLONE
WARS—BATTLE TALES issues #1–5.

SERIES EDITORIAL ASSISTANT
RILEY FARMER

Jerry Bennington, President
Nachie Marsham, Publisher
Cara Morrison, Chief Financial Officer
Matthew Ruzicka, Chief Accounting Officer
Rebekah Cahalin, EVP of Operations
John Barber, Editor-in-Chief
Justin Eisinger, Editorial Director, Graphic Novels & Collections
Scott Dunbier, Director, Special Projects
Blake Kobashigawa, VP of Sales
Anna Morrow, Sr Marketing Director
Tara McCrillis, Director of Design & Production
Mike Ford, Director of Operations
Shauna Monteforte, Manufacturing Operations Director

Ted Adams and Robbie Robbins, IDW Founders

COLLECTION EDITORS
ALONZO SIMON
& ZAC BOONE

COLLECTION DESIGNER
CLYDE GRAPA

Lucasfilm Credits:
Robert Simpson, Senior Editor
Michael Siglain, Creative Director
Phil Szostak, Lucasfilm Art Department
Matt Martin, Pablo Hidalgo, and
Emily Shkoukani, Story Group

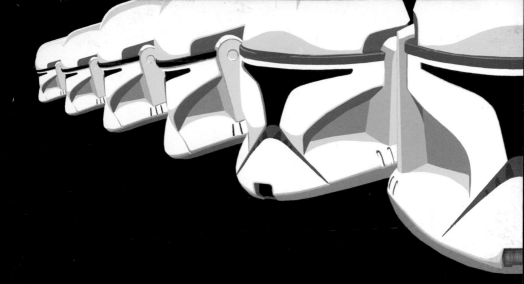

Writer: Michael Moreci

Chapter 1
Artists: Derek Charm, Arianna Florean, and Mario Del Pennino
Colorists: Luis Antonio Delgado and Valentina Taddeo

Chapter 2
Artists: Derek Charm and Megan Levens
Colorists: Luis Antonio Delgado and Charlie Kirchoff

Chapter 3
Artists: Derek Charm and Valentina Pinto
Colorists: Luis Antonio Delgado and Valentina Pinto
Layout Assistant: Davide Tinto

Chapter 4
Artists: Derek Charm and Davide Tinto
Colorists: Luis Antonio Delgado and Thomas Deer

Chapter 5
Artists: Derek Charm and Philip Murphy
Colorists: Luis Antonio Delgado and Rebecca Nalty

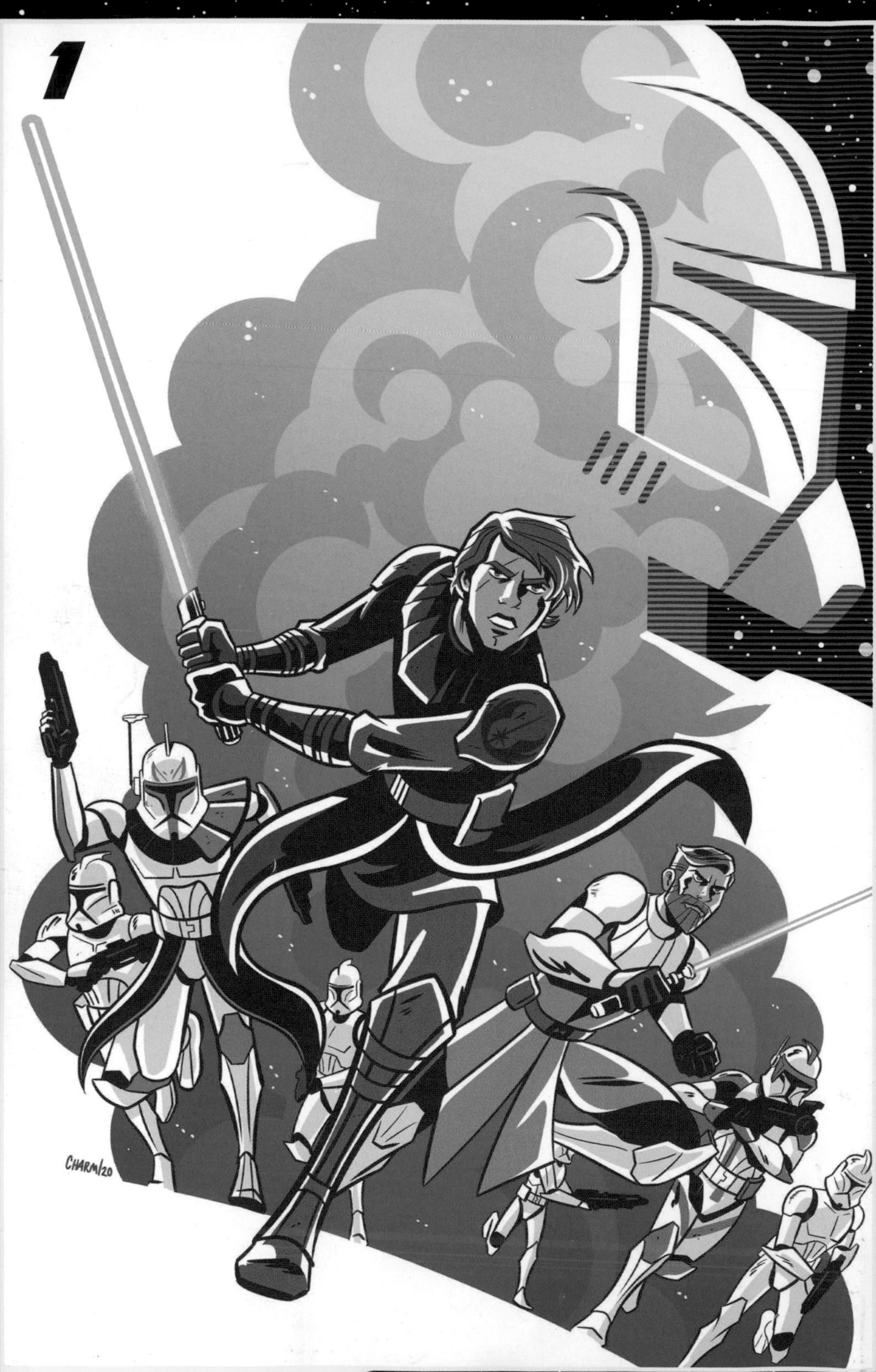
1
CHARM/20

Art by Derek Charm

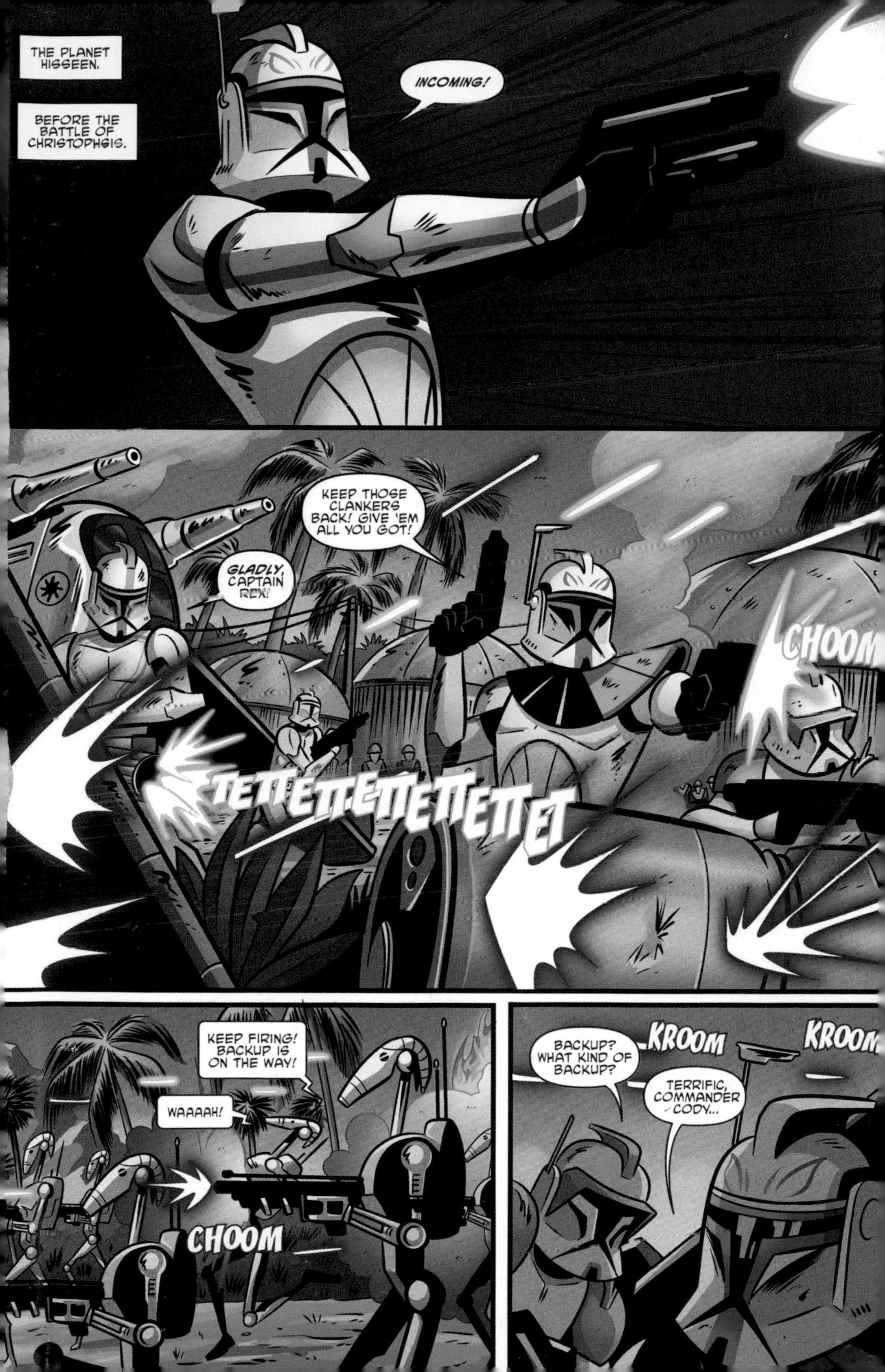
THE PLANET HISSEEN.
BEFORE THE BATTLE OF CHRISTOPHSIS.
INCOMING!
KEEP THOSE CLANKERS BACK! GIVE 'EM ALL YOU GOT!
GLADLY, CAPTAIN REX!
CHOOM
TETTETTETTETTETTETTET
KEEP FIRING! BACKUP IS ON THE WAY!
WAAAAH!
CHOOM
KROOM
KROOM
BACKUP? WHAT KIND OF BACKUP?
TERRIFIC, COMMANDER CODY...

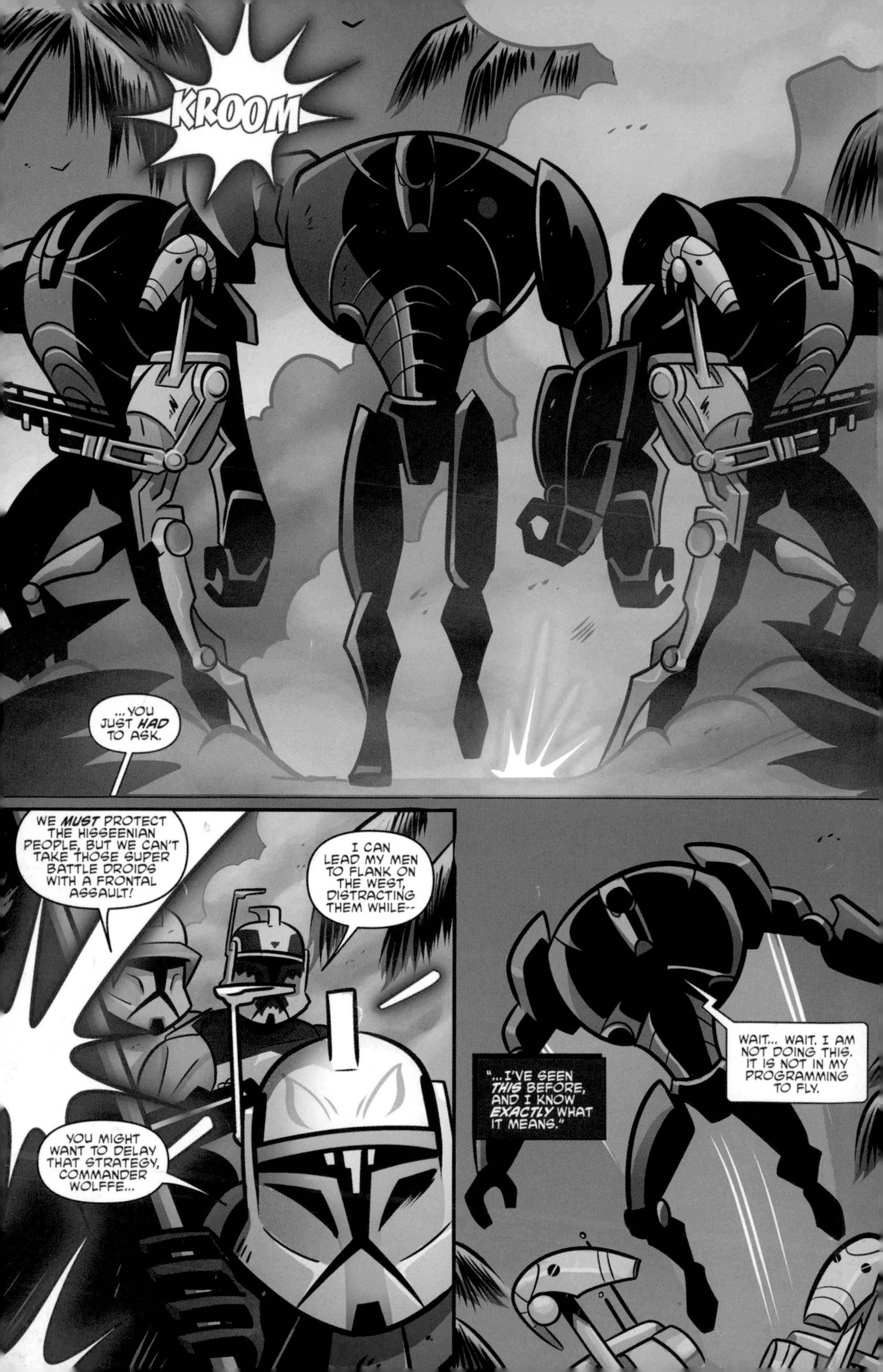
KROOM
...YOU JUST HAD TO ASK.
WE MUST PROTECT THE HISSEENIAN PEOPLE, BUT WE CAN'T TAKE THOSE SUPER BATTLE DROIDS WITH A FRONTAL ASSAULT!
I CAN LEAD MY MEN TO FLANK ON THE WEST, DISTRACTING THEM WHILE--
YOU MIGHT WANT TO DELAY THAT STRATEGY, COMMANDER WOLFFE...
"...I'VE SEEN THIS BEFORE, AND I KNOW EXACTLY WHAT IT MEANS."
WAIT... WAIT. I AM NOT DOING THIS. IT IS NOT IN MY PROGRAMMING TO FLY.

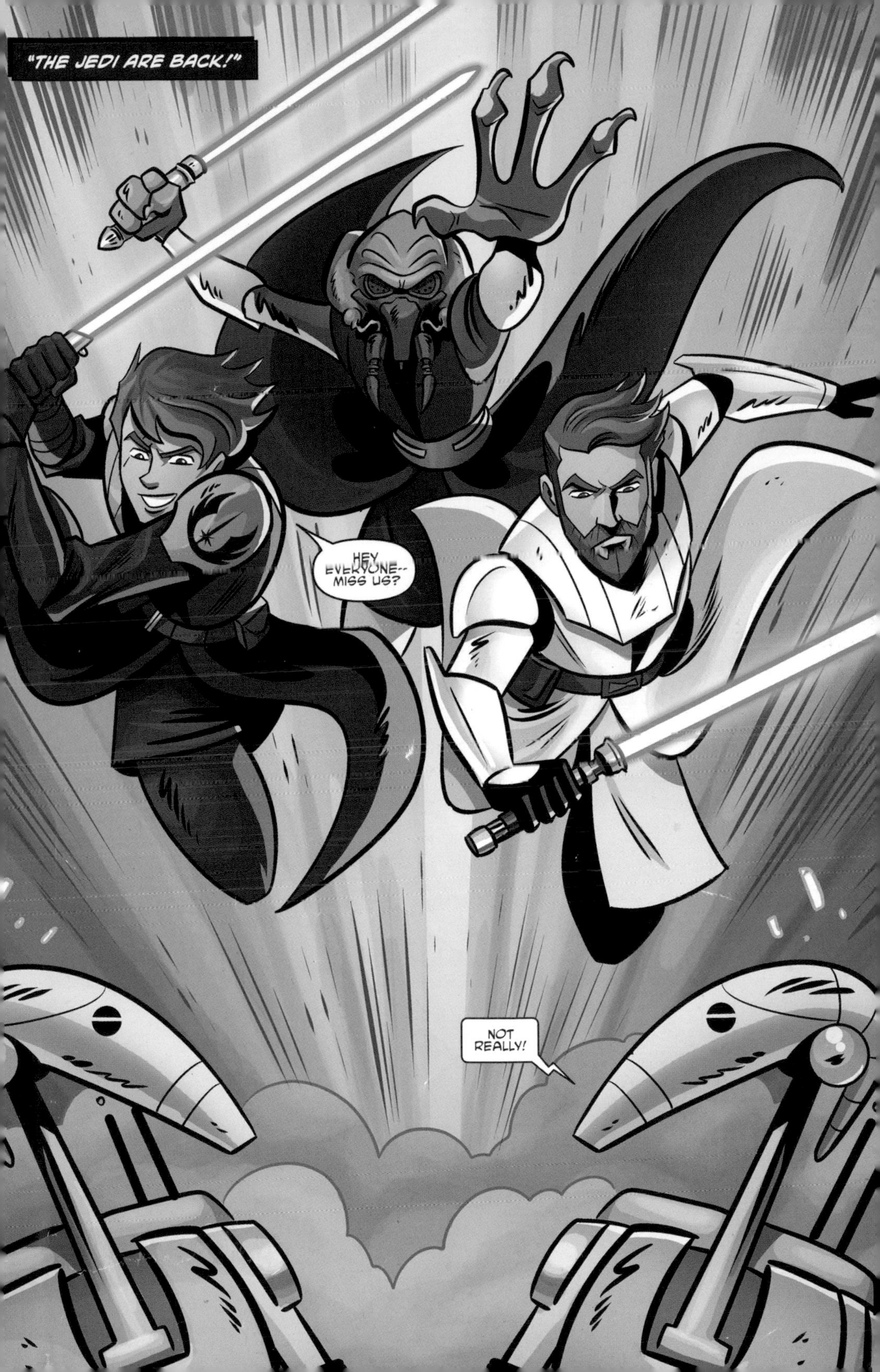
"THE JEDI ARE BACK!"
HEY EVERYONE-- MISS US?
NOT REALLY!

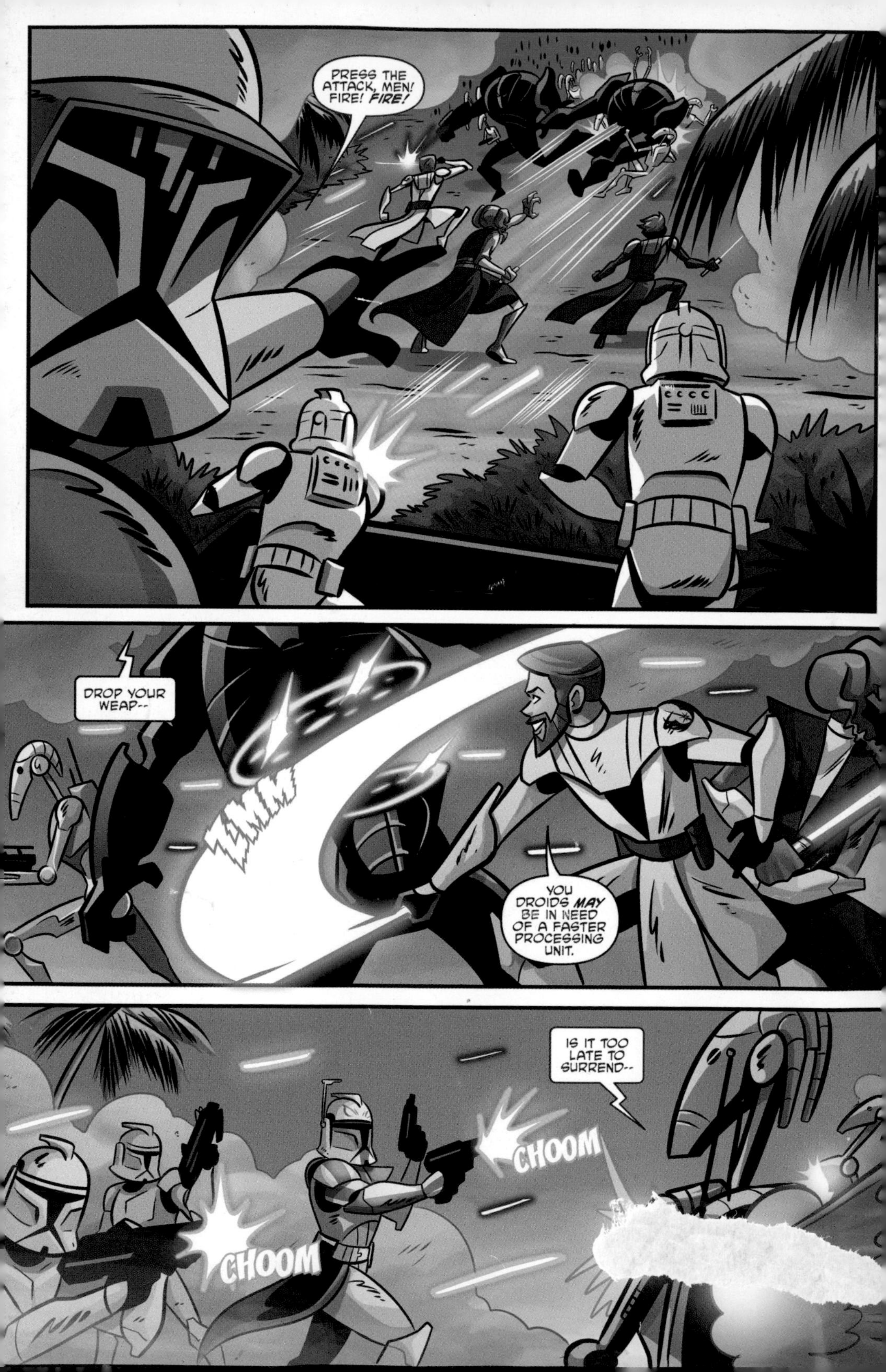
PRESS THE ATTACK, MEN! FIRE! *FIRE!*
DROP YOUR WEAP--
VMMM
YOU DROIDS *MAY* BE IN NEED OF A FASTER PROCESSING UNIT.
IS IT TOO LATE TO SURREND--
CHOOM
CHOOM

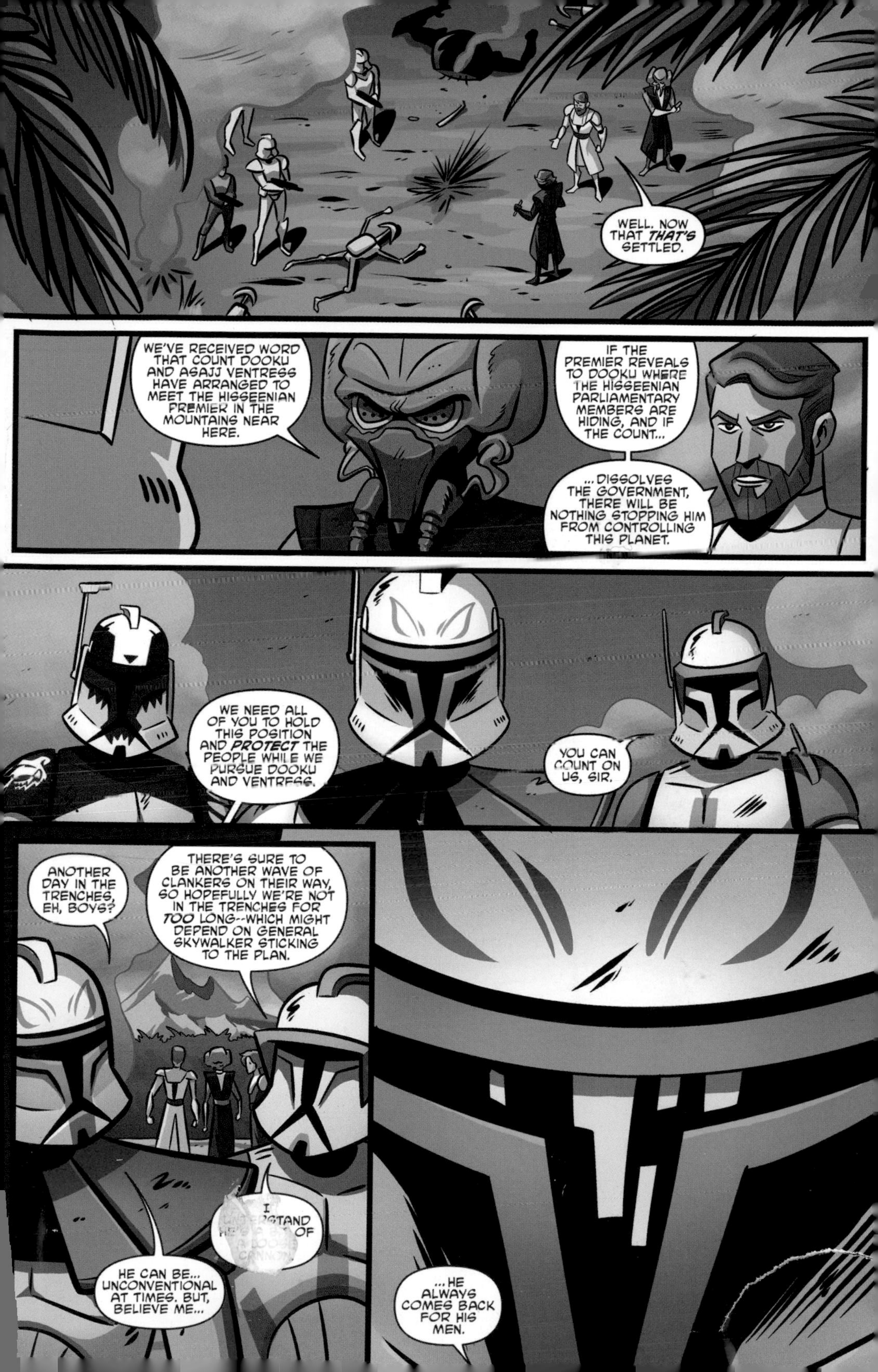
WELL. NOW THAT *THAT'S* SETTLED.
WE'VE RECEIVED WORD THAT COUNT DOOKU AND ASAJJ VENTRESS HAVE ARRANGED TO MEET THE HISSEENIAN PREMIER IN THE MOUNTAINS NEAR HERE.
IF THE PREMIER REVEALS TO DOOKU WHERE THE HISSEENIAN PARLIAMENTARY MEMBERS ARE HIDING, AND IF THE COUNT...
...DISSOLVES THE GOVERNMENT, THERE WILL BE NOTHING STOPPING HIM FROM CONTROLLING THIS PLANET.
WE NEED ALL OF YOU TO HOLD THIS POSITION AND *PROTECT* THE PEOPLE WHILE WE PURSUE DOOKU AND VENTRESS.
YOU CAN COUNT ON US, SIR.
ANOTHER DAY IN THE TRENCHES, EH, BOYS?
THERE'S SURE TO BE ANOTHER WAVE OF CLANKERS ON THEIR WAY, SO HOPEFULLY WE'RE NOT IN THE TRENCHES FOR *TOO* LONG--WHICH MIGHT DEPEND ON GENERAL SKYWALKER STICKING TO THE PLAN.
I UNDERSTAND HE'S A BIT OF A LOOSE CANNON.
HE CAN BE... UNCONVENTIONAL AT TIMES. BUT, BELIEVE ME...
...HE ALWAYS COMES BACK FOR HIS MEN.

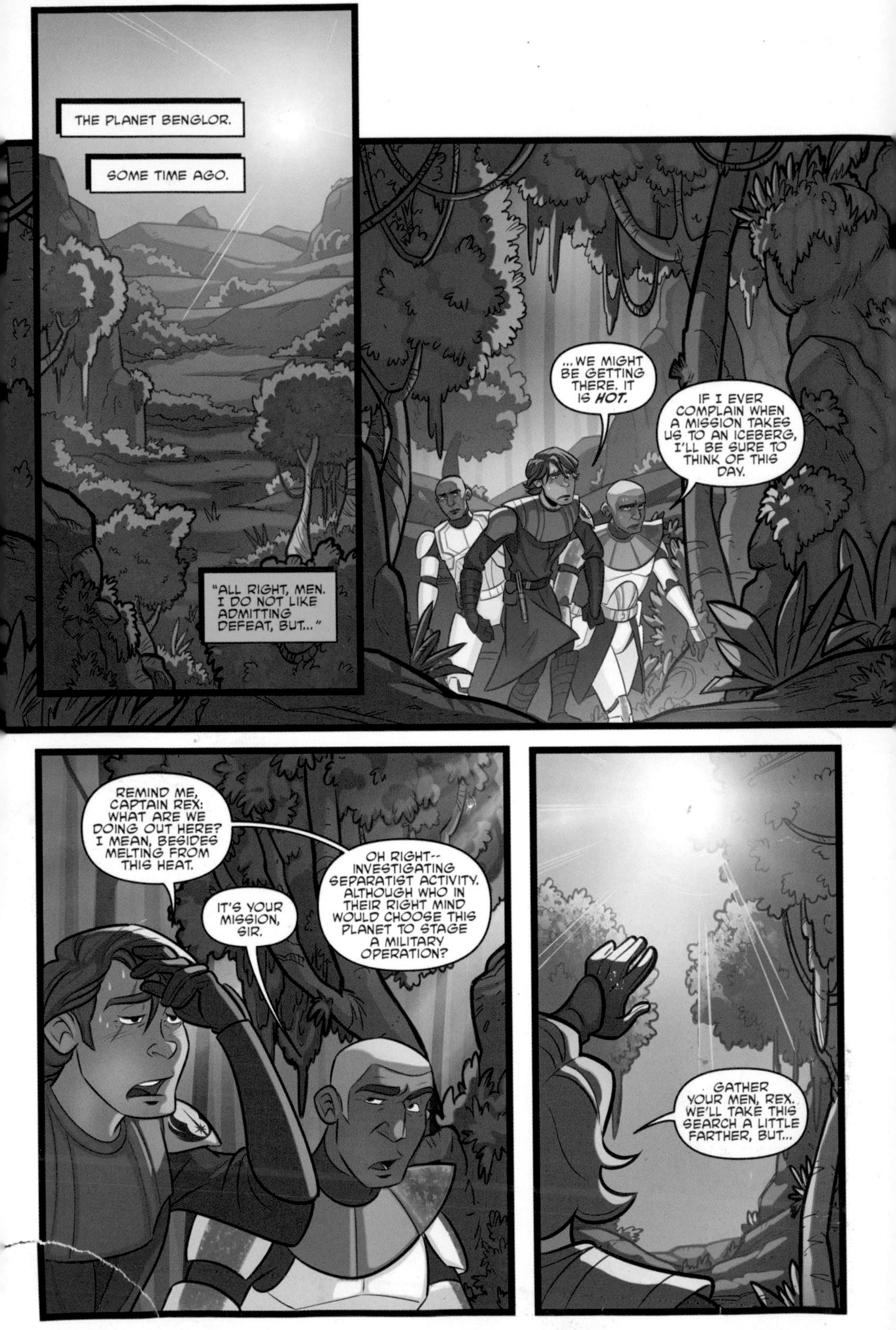
THE PLANET BENGLOR.
SOME TIME AGO.
"ALL RIGHT, MEN. I DO NOT LIKE ADMITTING DEFEAT, BUT..."
...WE MIGHT BE GETTING THERE. IT IS *HOT.*
IF I EVER COMPLAIN WHEN A MISSION TAKES US TO AN ICEBERG, I'LL BE SURE TO THINK OF THIS DAY.
REMIND ME, CAPTAIN REX: WHAT ARE WE DOING OUT HERE? I MEAN, BESIDES MELTING FROM THIS HEAT.
IT'S YOUR MISSION, SIR.
OH RIGHT-- INVESTIGATING SEPARATIST ACTIVITY. ALTHOUGH WHO IN THEIR RIGHT MIND WOULD CHOOSE THIS PLANET TO STAGE A MILITARY OPERATION?
GATHER YOUR MEN, REX. WE'LL TAKE THIS SEARCH A LITTLE FARTHER, BUT...

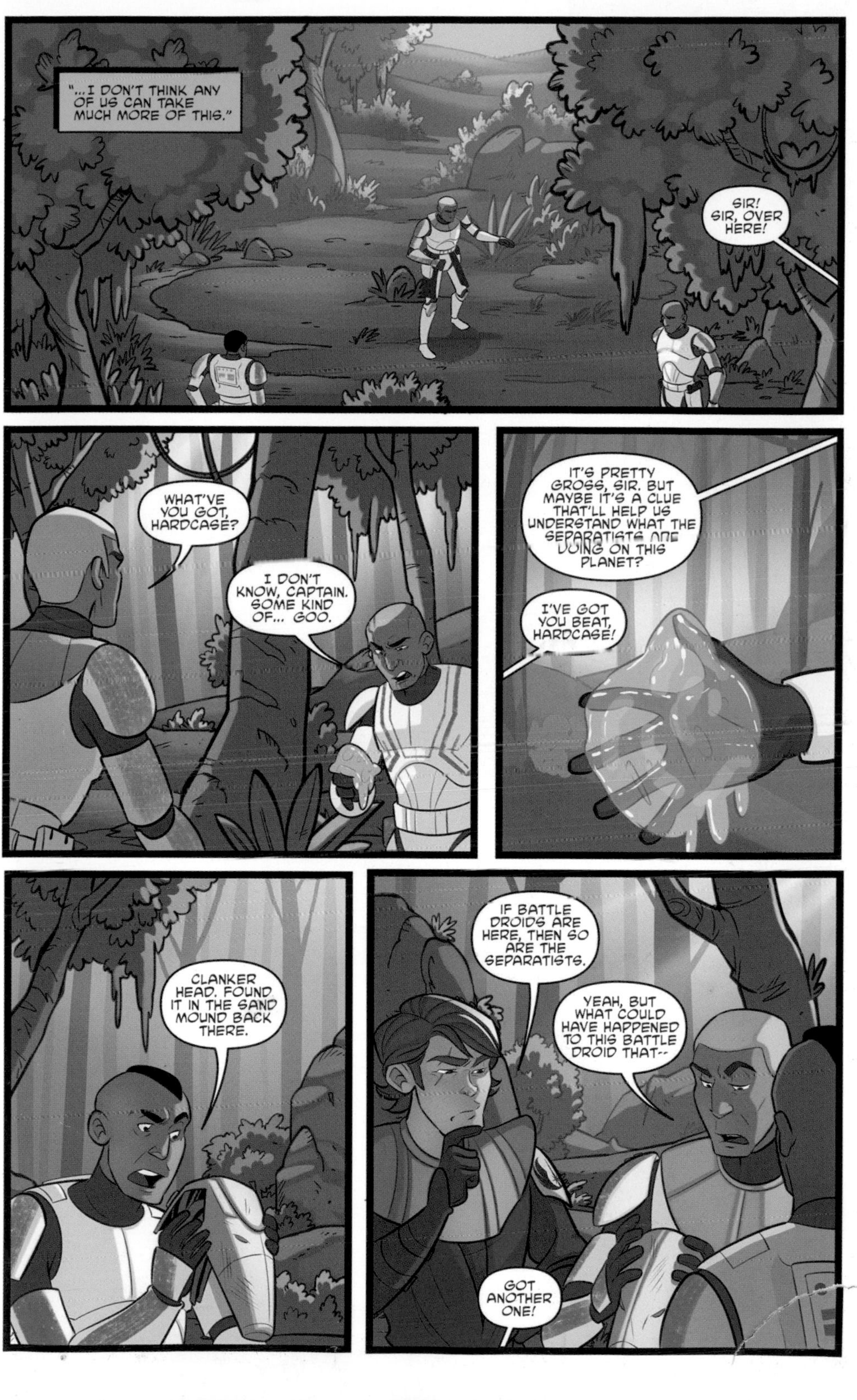
"...I DON'T THINK ANY OF US CAN TAKE MUCH MORE OF THIS."
SIR! SIR, OVER HERE!
WHAT'VE YOU GOT, HARDCASE?
I DON'T KNOW, CAPTAIN. SOME KIND OF... GOO.
IT'S PRETTY GROSS, SIR. BUT MAYBE IT'S A CLUE THAT'LL HELP US UNDERSTAND WHAT THE SEPARATISTS ARE DOING ON THIS PLANET?
I'VE GOT YOU BEAT, HARDCASE!
CLANKER HEAD. FOUND IT IN THE SAND MOUND BACK THERE.
IF BATTLE DROIDS ARE HERE, THEN SO ARE THE SEPARATISTS.
YEAH, BUT WHAT COULD HAVE HAPPENED TO THIS BATTLE DROID THAT--
GOT ANOTHER ONE!

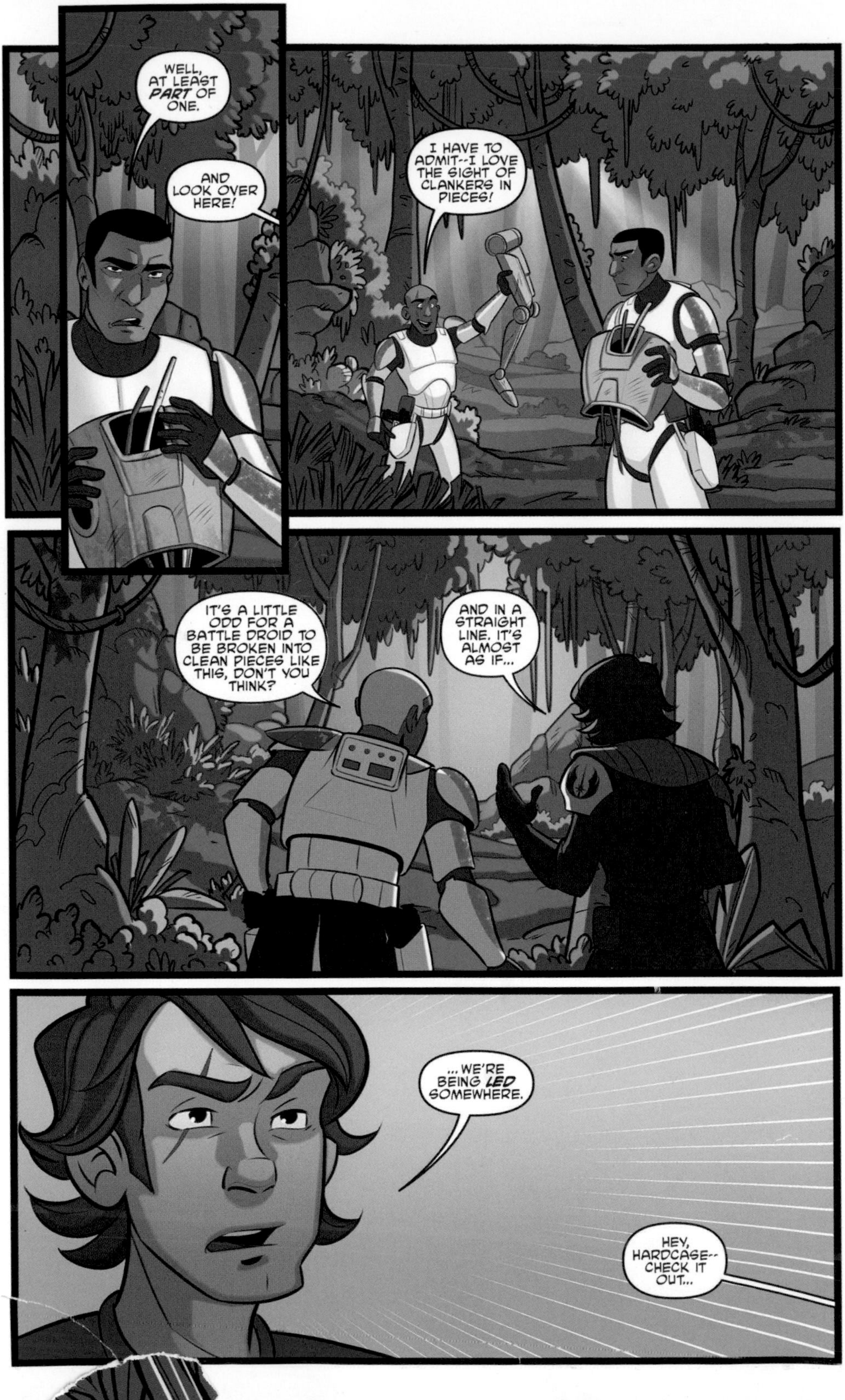
WELL, AT LEAST PART OF ONE.
AND LOOK OVER HERE!
I HAVE TO ADMIT--I LOVE THE SIGHT OF CLANKERS IN PIECES!
IT'S A LITTLE ODD FOR A BATTLE DROID TO BE BROKEN INTO CLEAN PIECES LIKE THIS, DON'T YOU THINK?
AND IN A STRAIGHT LINE. IT'S ALMOST AS IF...
...WE'RE BEING LED SOMEWHERE.
HEY, HARDCASE--CHECK IT OUT...

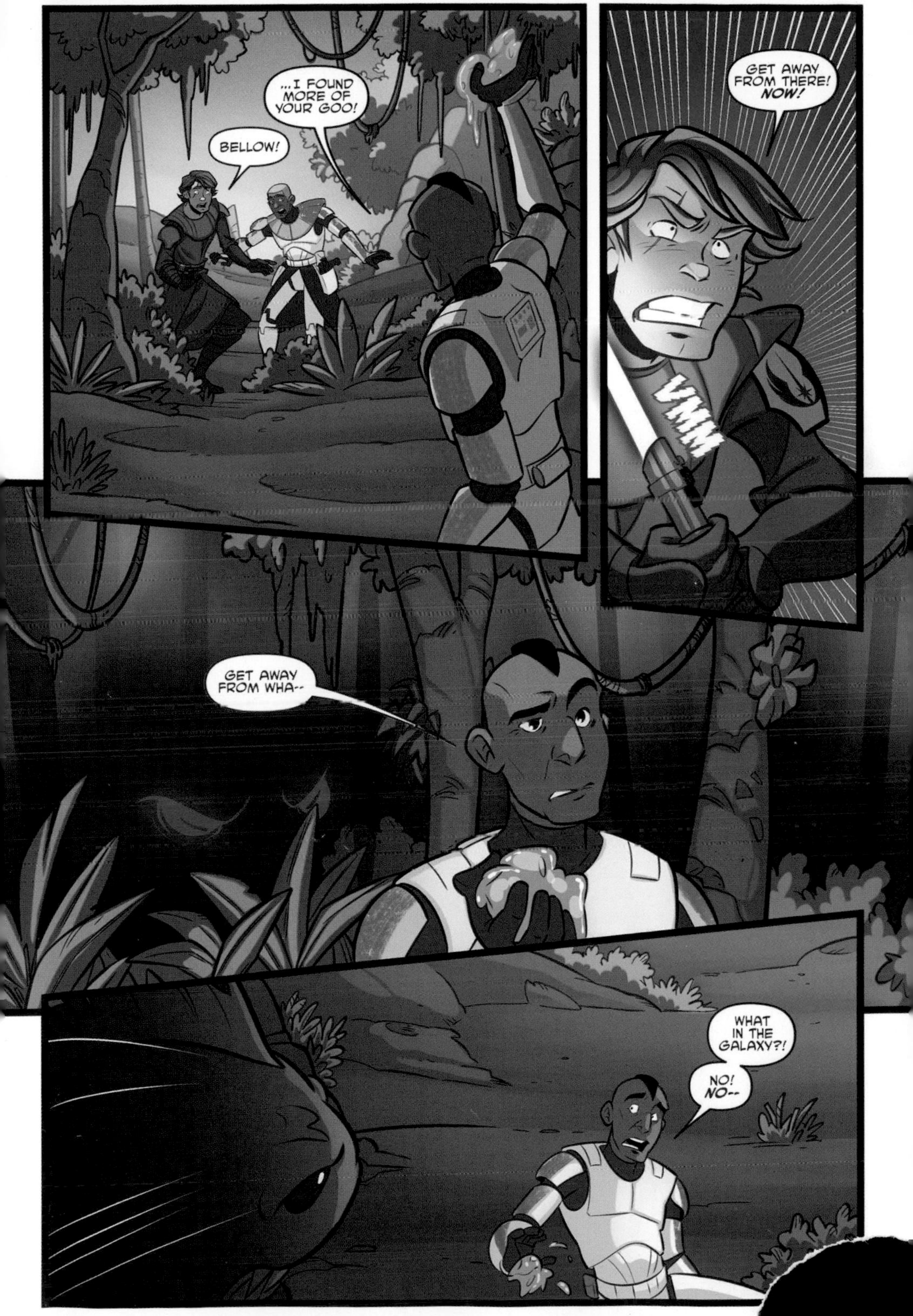
BELLOW!
...I FOUND MORE OF YOUR GOO!
GET AWAY FROM THERE! NOW!
VMM
GET AWAY FROM WHA--
WHAT IN THE GALAXY?!
NO! NO--

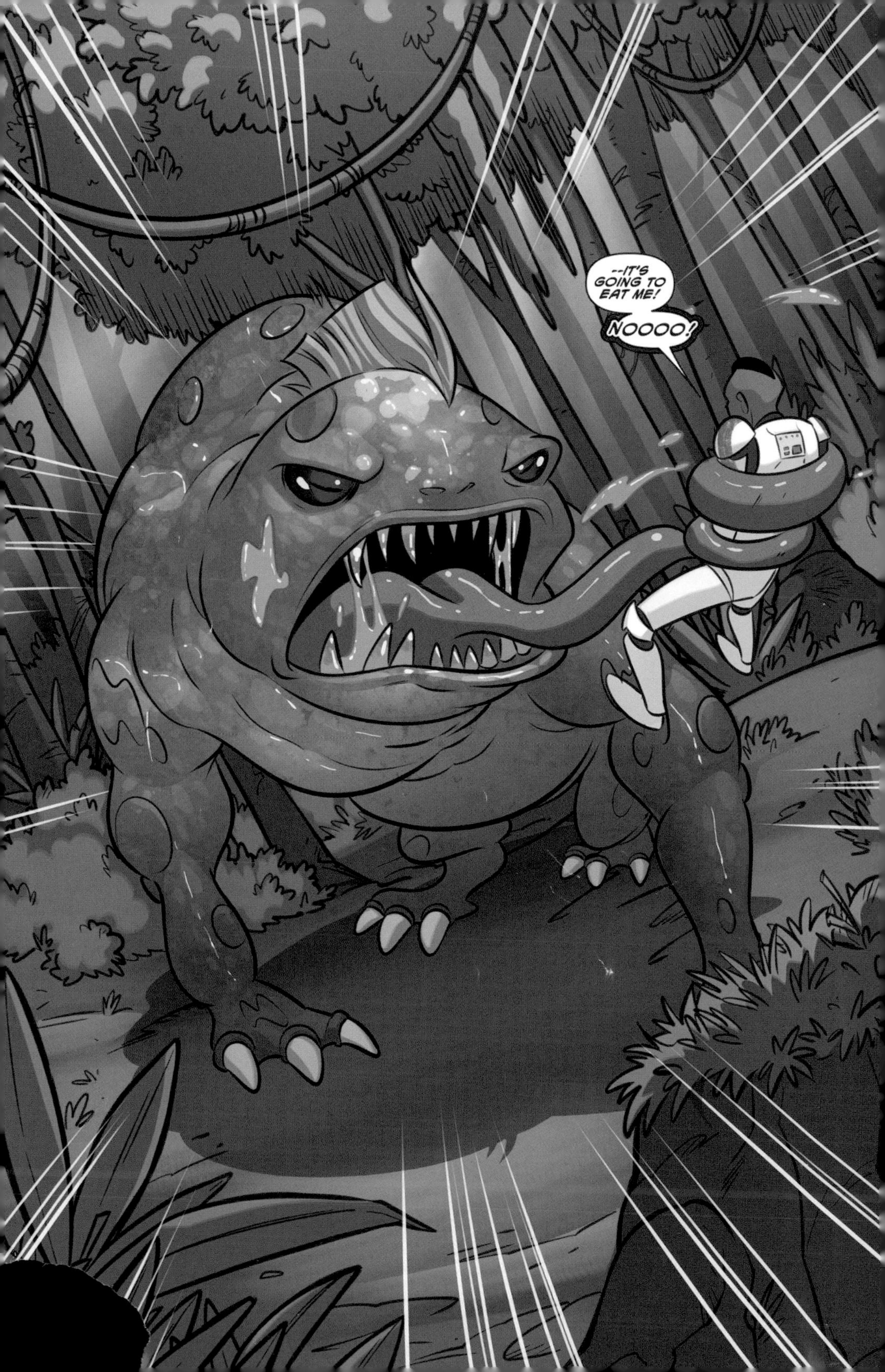
--IT'S GOING TO EAT ME!
NOOOO!

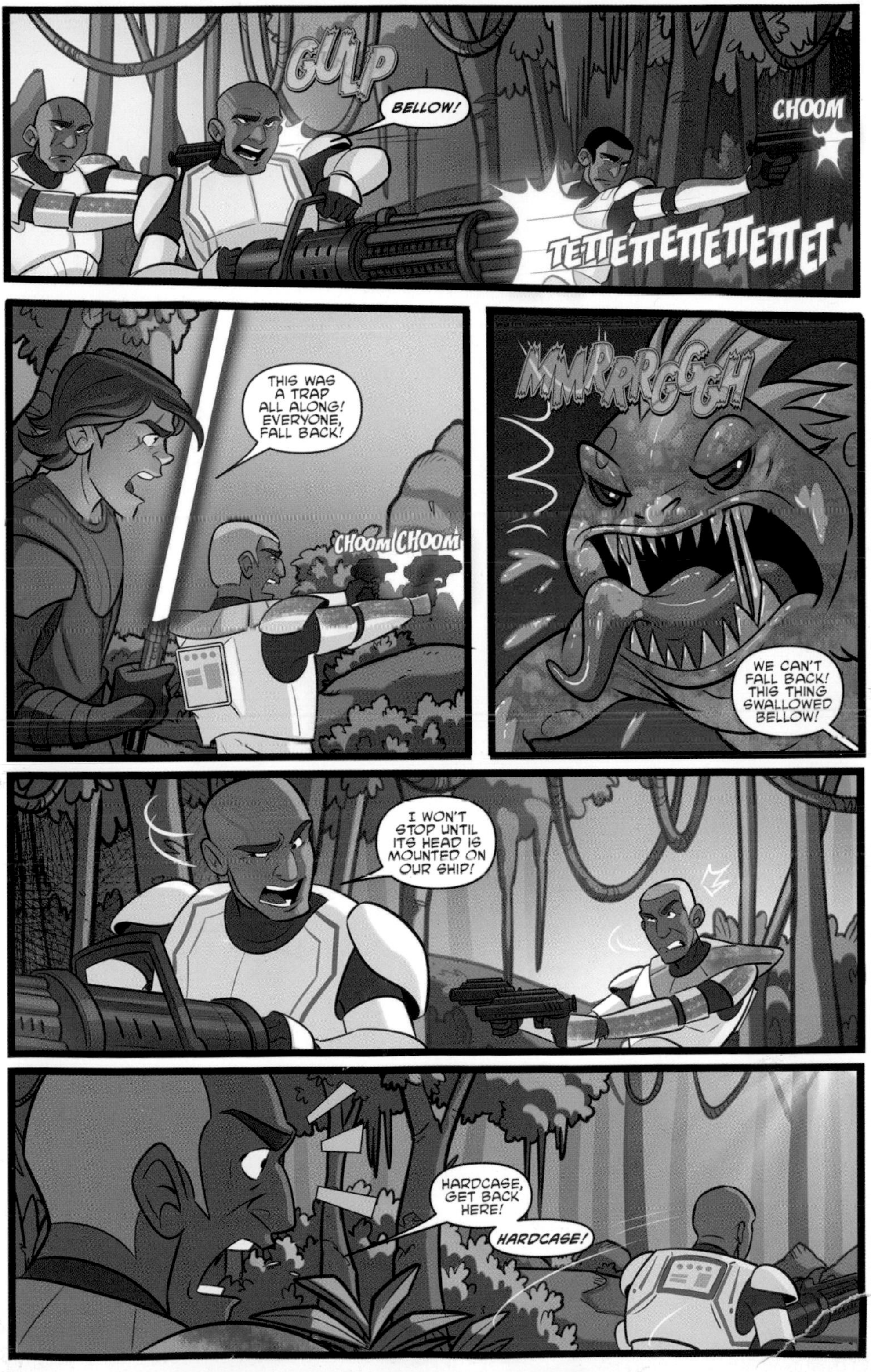
GULP
BELLOW!
CHOOM
TETTETTETTETTETTET
THIS WAS A TRAP ALL ALONG! EVERYONE, FALL BACK!
CHOOM CHOOM
MMRRRGGGH
WE CAN'T FALL BACK! THIS THING SWALLOWED BELLOW!
I WON'T STOP UNTIL ITS HEAD IS MOUNTED ON OUR SHIP!
HARDCASE, GET BACK HERE!
HARDCASE!

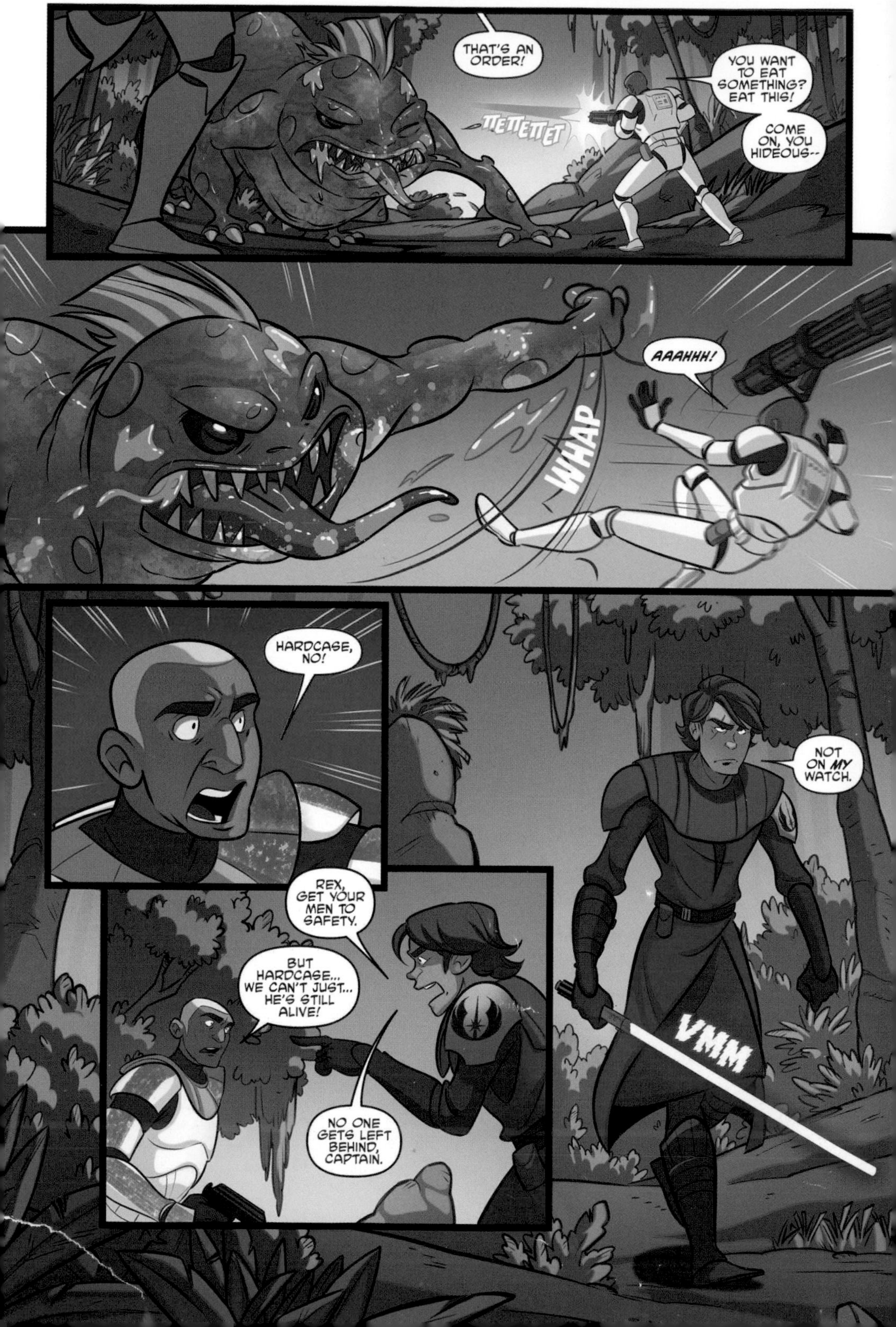
THAT'S AN ORDER!
YOU WANT TO EAT SOMETHING? EAT THIS!
TTETTETTET
COME ON, YOU HIDEOUS--
AAAHHH!
WHAP
HARDCASE, NO!
NOT ON MY WATCH.
VMM
REX, GET YOUR MEN TO SAFETY.
BUT HARDCASE... WE CAN'T JUST... HE'S STILL ALIVE!
NO ONE GETS LEFT BEHIND, CAPTAIN.

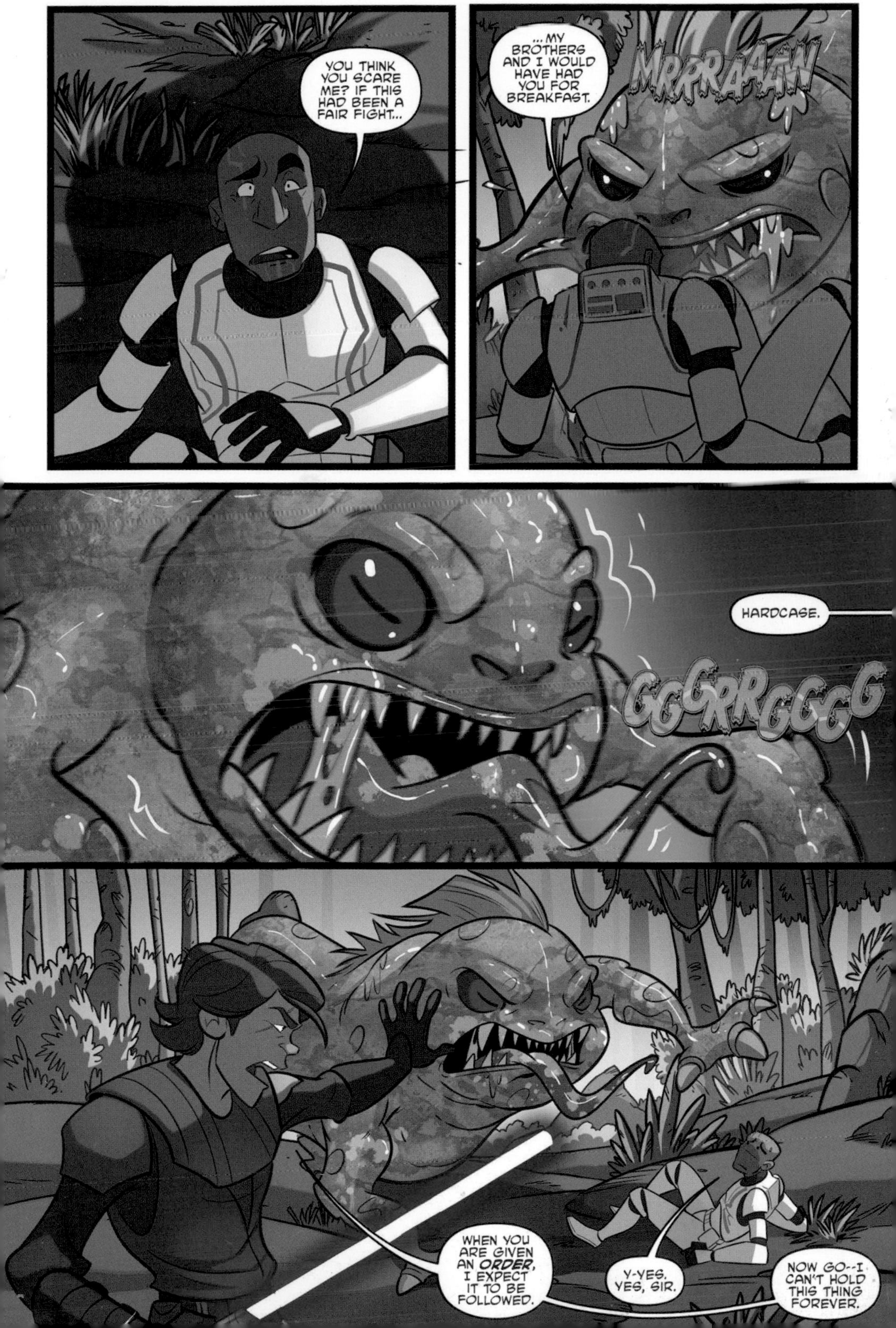
YOU THINK YOU SCARE ME? IF THIS HAD BEEN A FAIR FIGHT...
...MY BROTHERS AND I WOULD HAVE HAD YOU FOR BREAKFAST.
MRRRAAAW
HARDCASE.
GGGRRGGGG
WHEN YOU ARE GIVEN AN ORDER, I EXPECT IT TO BE FOLLOWED.
Y-YES. YES, SIR.
NOW GO--I CAN'T HOLD THIS THING FOREVER.

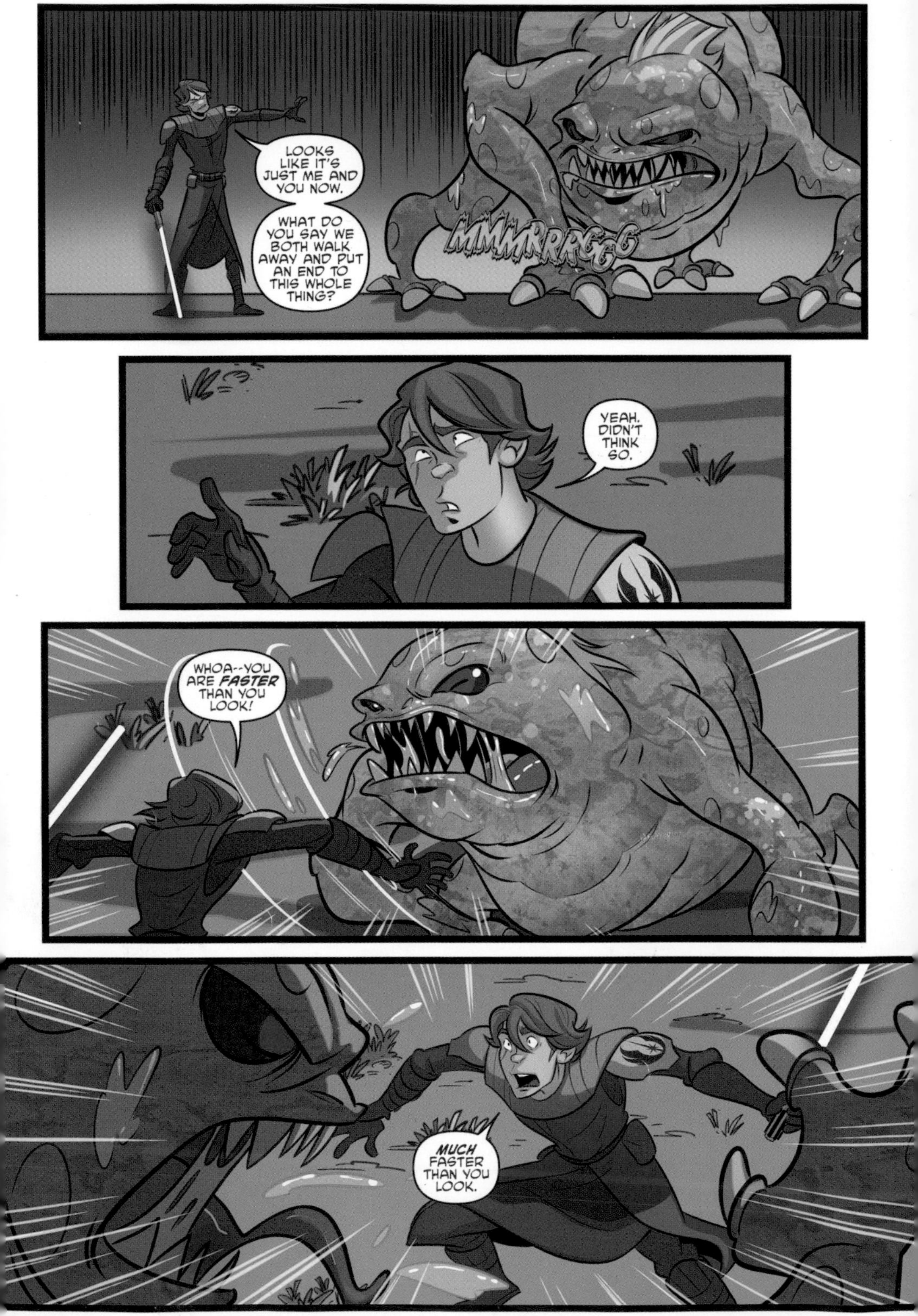
LOOKS LIKE IT'S JUST ME AND YOU NOW.
WHAT DO YOU SAY WE BOTH WALK AWAY AND PUT AN END TO THIS WHOLE THING?
MMMRRRGGG
YEAH. DIDN'T THINK SO.
WHOA--YOU ARE **FASTER** THAN YOU LOOK!
MUCH FASTER THAN YOU LOOK.

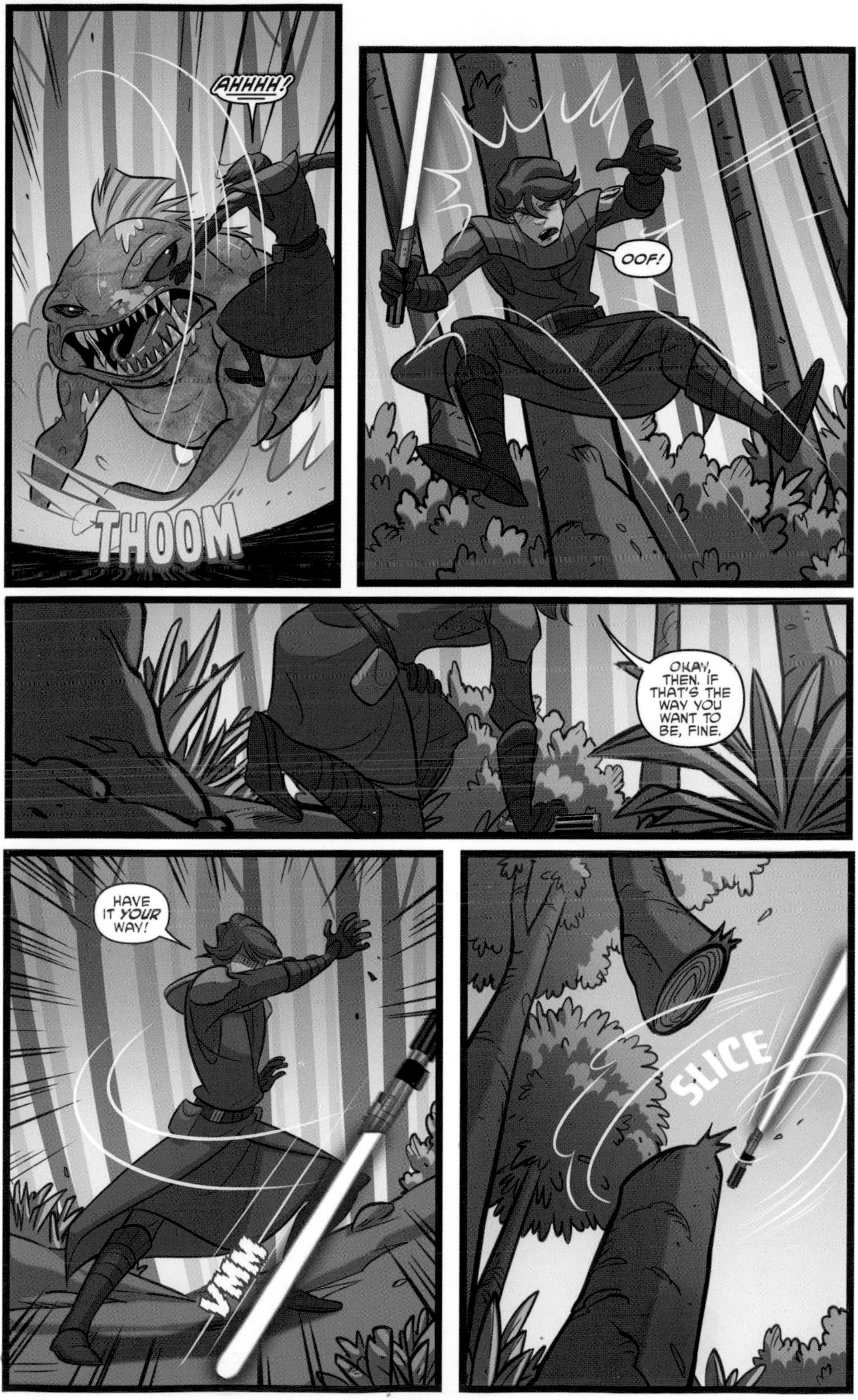
AHHHH!
THOOM
OOF!
OKAY, THEN. IF THAT'S THE WAY YOU WANT TO BE, FINE.
HAVE IT YOUR WAY!
VMM
SLICE

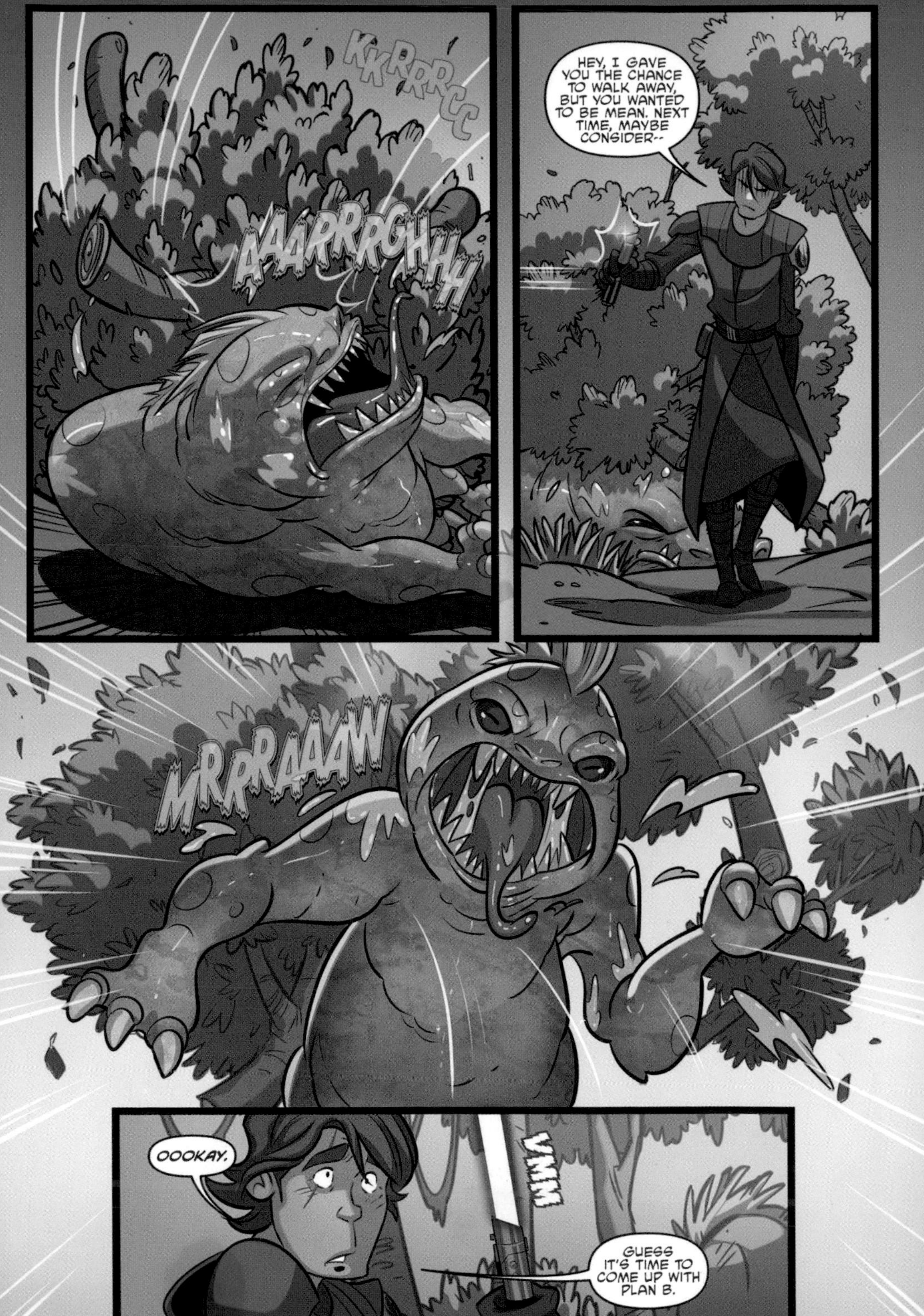
KKRRRCC
AAARRRGHHH
HEY, I GAVE YOU THE CHANCE TO WALK AWAY, BUT YOU WANTED TO BE MEAN. NEXT TIME, MAYBE CONSIDER--
MRRRAAAW
OOOKAY.
VMM
GUESS IT'S TIME TO COME UP WITH PLAN B.

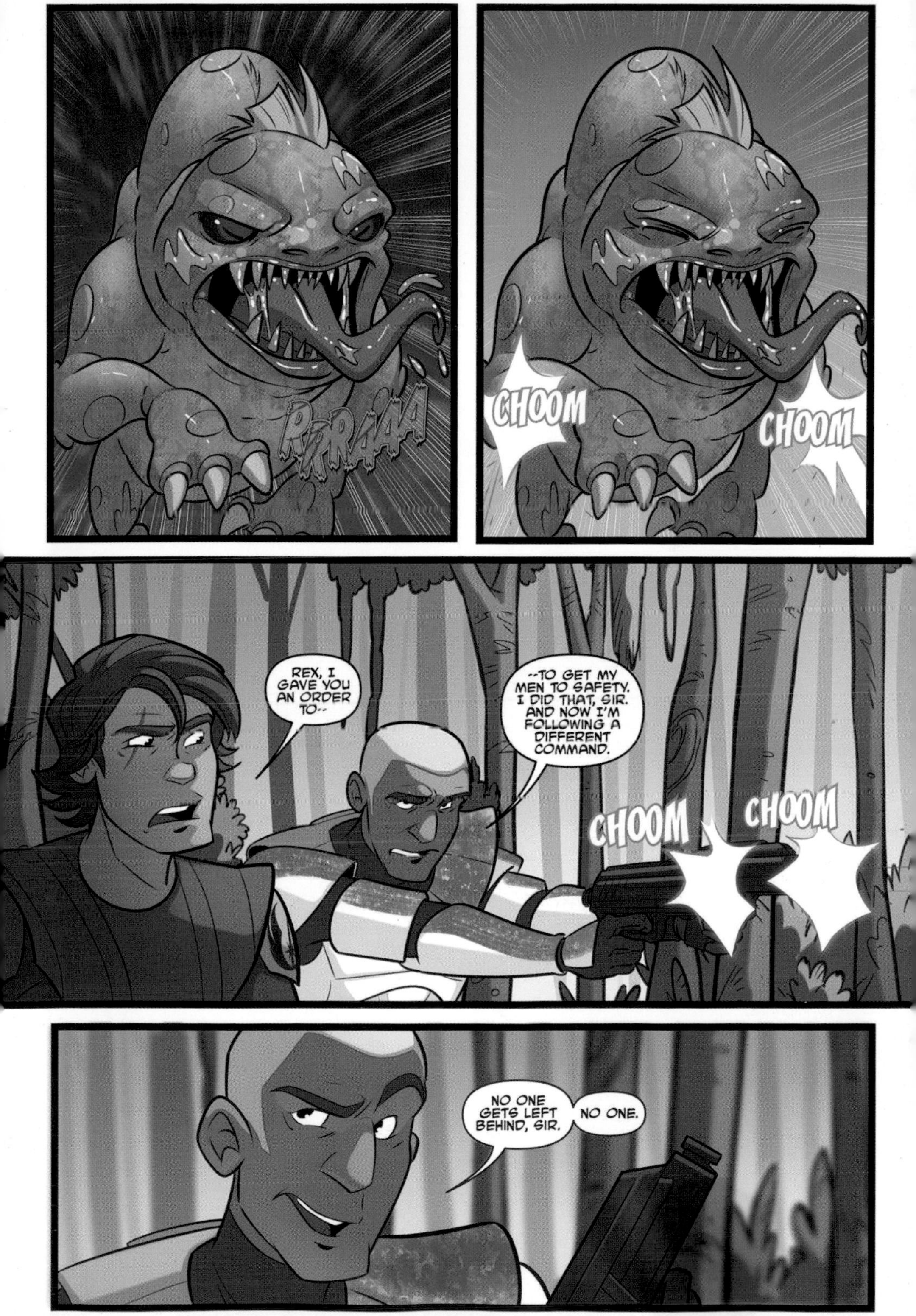
RRRAAA
CHOOM
CHOOM
REX, I GAVE YOU AN ORDER TO--
--TO GET MY MEN TO SAFETY. I DID THAT, SIR. AND NOW I'M FOLLOWING A DIFFERENT COMMAND.
CHOOM
CHOOM
NO ONE GETS LEFT BEHIND, SIR.
NO ONE.

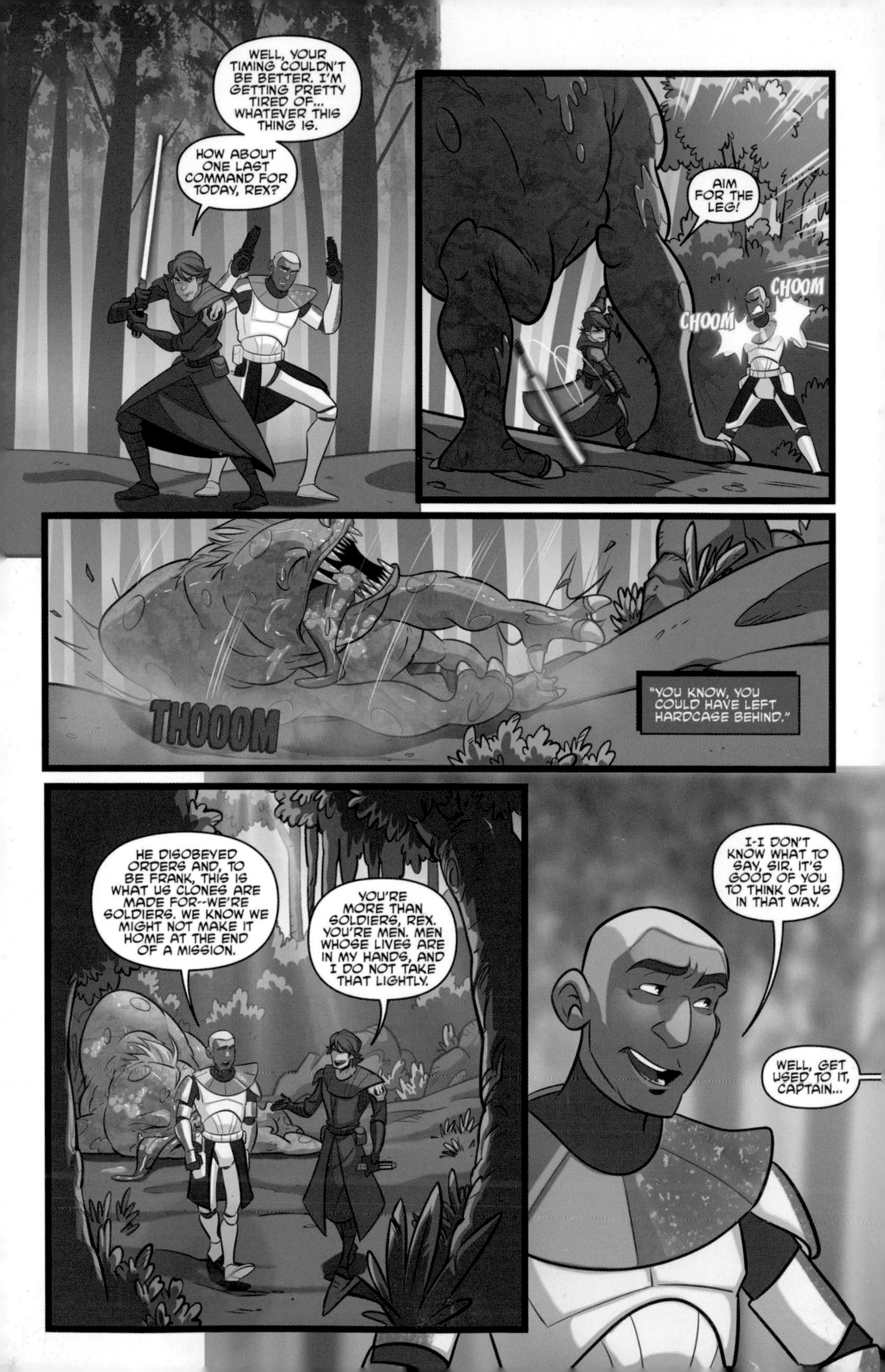
WELL, YOUR TIMING COULDN'T BE BETTER. I'M GETTING PRETTY TIRED OF... WHATEVER THIS THING IS.
HOW ABOUT ONE LAST COMMAND FOR TODAY, REX?
AIM FOR THE LEG!
CHOOM
CHOOM
THOOOM
"YOU KNOW, YOU COULD HAVE LEFT HARDCASE BEHIND."
HE DISOBEYED ORDERS AND, TO BE FRANK, THIS IS WHAT US CLONES ARE MADE FOR--WE'RE SOLDIERS. WE KNOW WE MIGHT NOT MAKE IT HOME AT THE END OF A MISSION.
YOU'RE MORE THAN SOLDIERS, REX. YOU'RE MEN. MEN WHOSE LIVES ARE IN MY HANDS, AND I DO NOT TAKE THAT LIGHTLY.
I-I DON'T KNOW WHAT TO SAY, SIR. IT'S GOOD OF YOU TO THINK OF US IN THAT WAY.
WELL, GET USED TO IT, CAPTAIN...

"...THAT'S HOW THINGS ARE UNDER MY COMMAND."

WELL, IT LOOKS LIKE WE COULD USE SOME OF SKYWALKER'S *DEDICATION* RIGHT ABOUT NOW, CAPTAIN...

CHOOM

CHOOM

...WE'VE GOT MORE COMPANY!

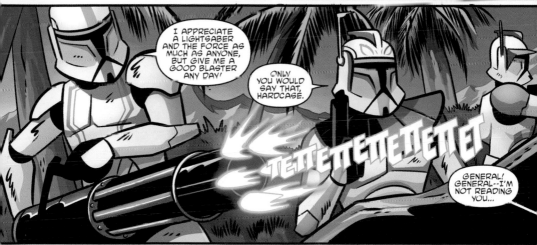

I APPRECIATE A LIGHTSABER AND THE FORCE AS MUCH AS ANYONE, BUT GIVE ME A GOOD BLASTER ANY DAY!

ONLY YOU WOULD SAY THAT, HARDCASE.

TETTETTETTETTET

GENERAL! GENERAL--I'M NOT READING YOU...

BOOST, WHAT IS IT?

WE'RE RECEIVING A TRANSMISSION FROM GENERAL PLO KOON, BUT... I CAN'T GET IT TO COME IN CLEARLY.

GET ME COMM--OLFFE, WE ⚡KKZZZKK⚡ NEED ⚡KKZZZKK⚡ TO--

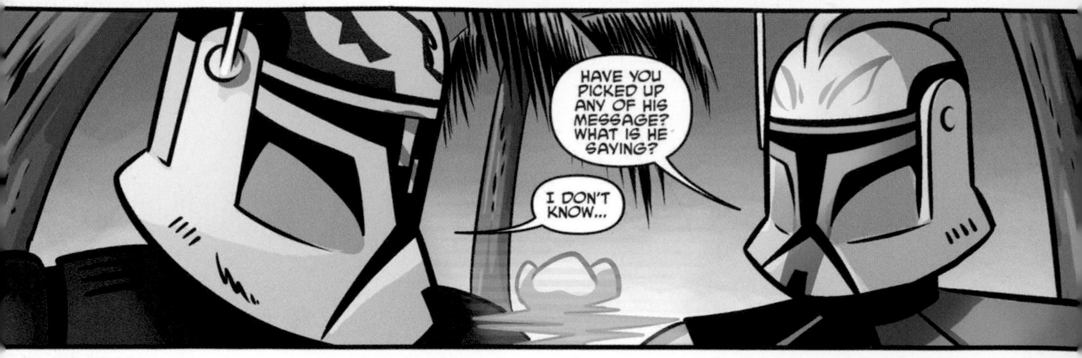
HAVE YOU PICKED UP ANY OF HIS MESSAGE? WHAT IS HE SAYING?
I DON'T KNOW...

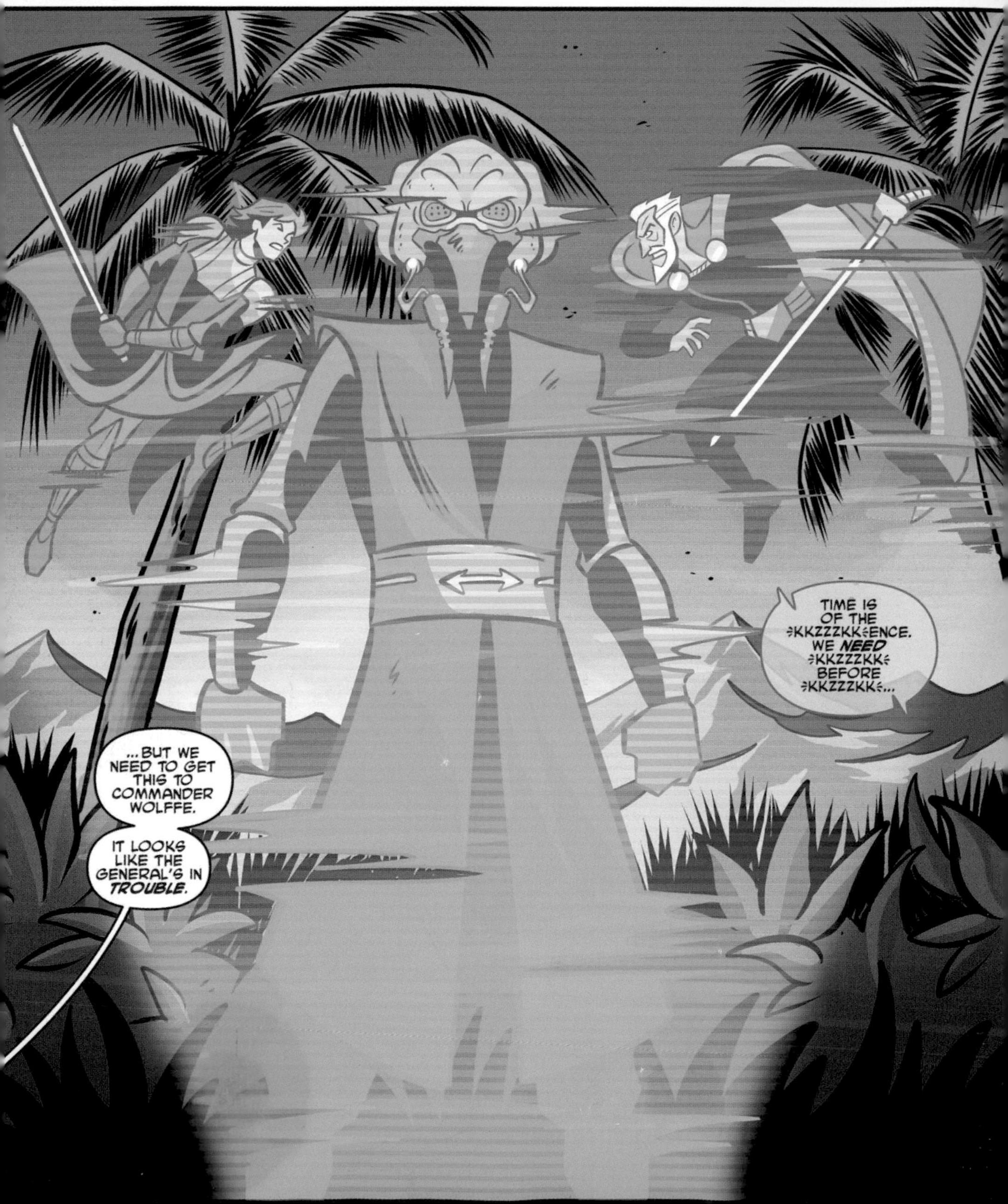
TIME IS OF THE ⚡KKZZZKK⚡ENCE. WE NEED ⚡KKZZZKK⚡ BEFORE ⚡KKZZZKK⚡...
...BUT WE NEED TO GET THIS TO COMMANDER WOLFFE.
IT LOOKS LIKE THE GENERAL'S IN TROUBLE.

2

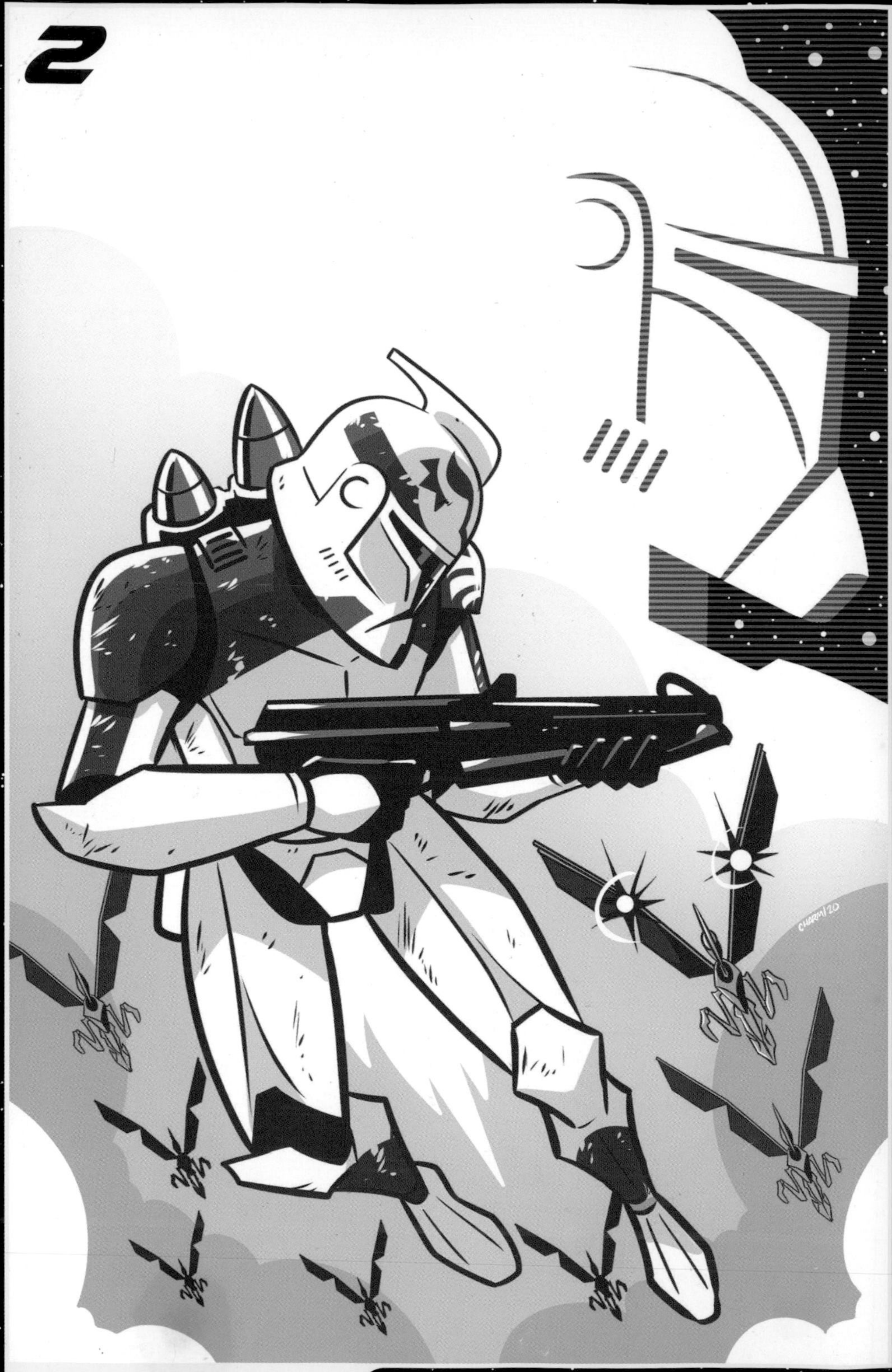

Art by Derek Charm

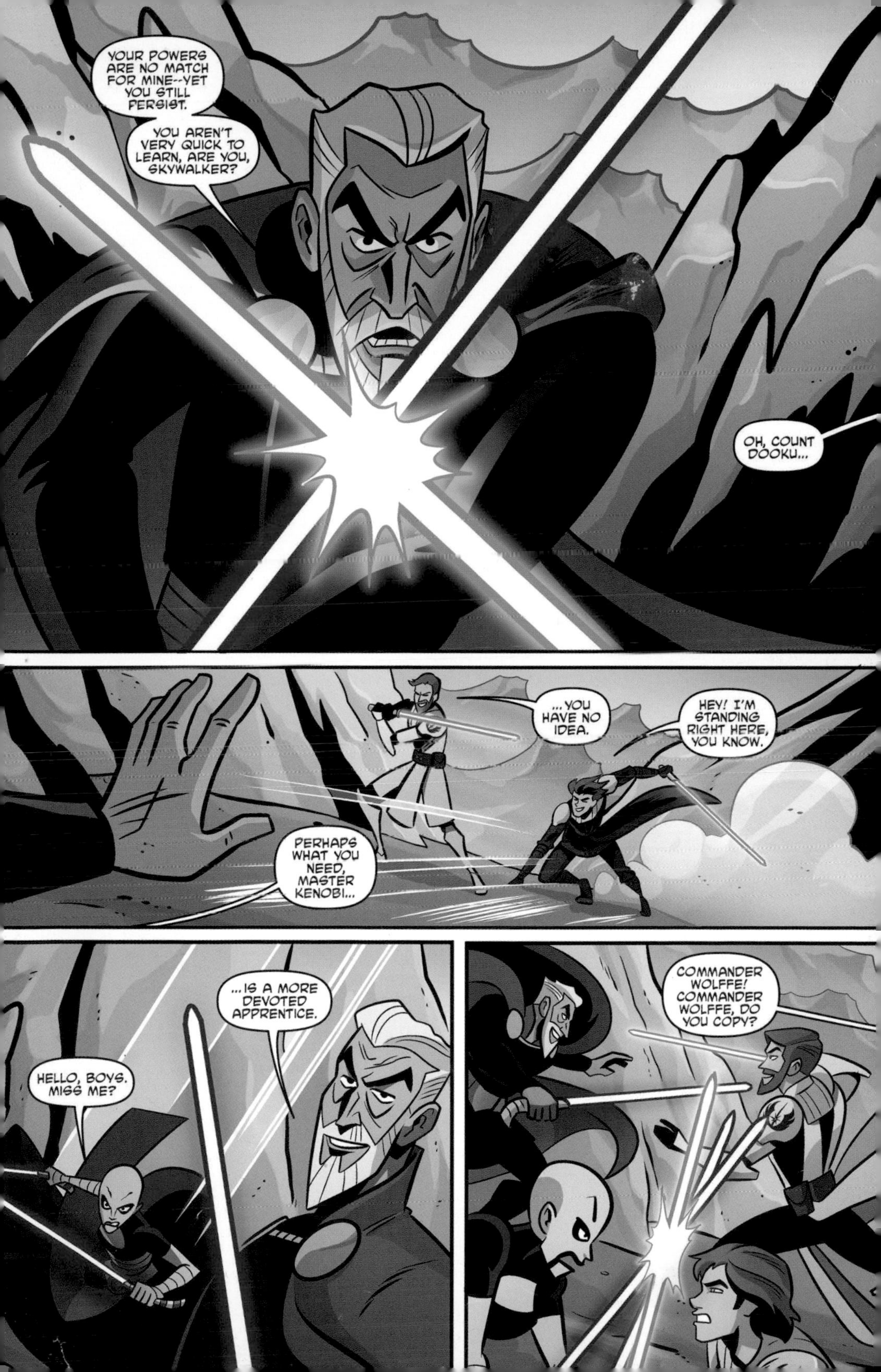
YOUR POWERS ARE NO MATCH FOR MINE--YET YOU STILL PERSIST.
YOU AREN'T VERY QUICK TO LEARN, ARE YOU, SKYWALKER?
OH, COUNT DOOKU...
...YOU HAVE NO IDEA.
HEY! I'M STANDING RIGHT HERE, YOU KNOW.
PERHAPS WHAT YOU NEED, MASTER KENOBI...
...IS A MORE DEVOTED APPRENTICE.
HELLO, BOYS. MISS ME?
COMMANDER WOLFFE! COMMANDER WOLFFE, DO YOU COPY?

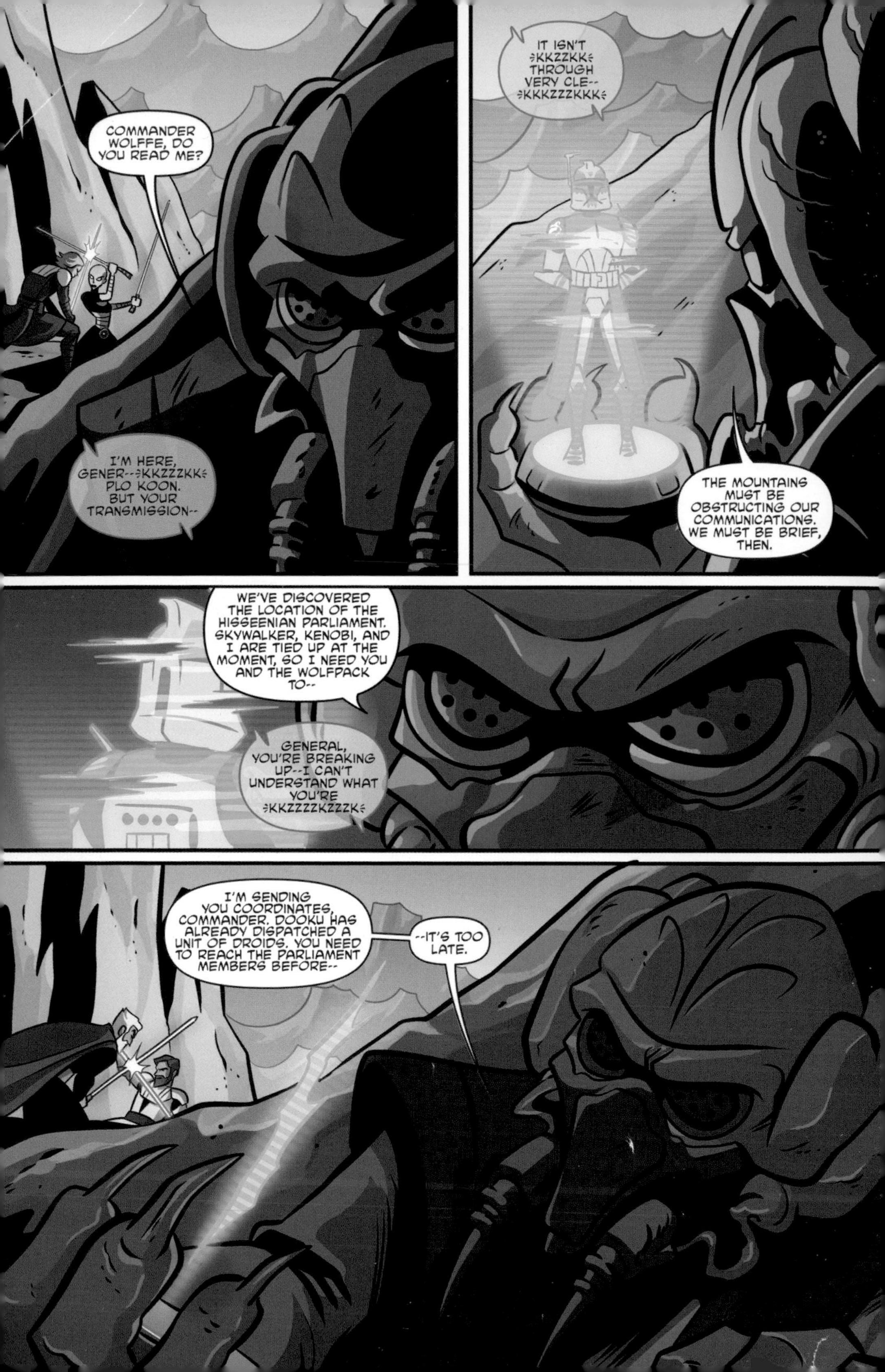
COMMANDER WOLFFE, DO YOU READ ME?
I'M HERE, GENER--⩩KKZZZKK⩩ PLO KOON. BUT YOUR TRANSMISSION--
IT ISN'T ⩩KKZZKK⩩ THROUGH VERY CLE-- ⩩KKKZZZKKK⩩
THE MOUNTAINS MUST BE OBSTRUCTING OUR COMMUNICATIONS. WE MUST BE BRIEF, THEN.
WE'VE DISCOVERED THE LOCATION OF THE HISSEENIAN PARLIAMENT. SKYWALKER, KENOBI, AND I ARE TIED UP AT THE MOMENT, SO I NEED YOU AND THE WOLFPACK TO--
GENERAL, YOU'RE BREAKING UP--I CAN'T UNDERSTAND WHAT YOU'RE ⩩KKZZZZKZZZK⩩
I'M SENDING YOU COORDINATES, COMMANDER. DOOKU HAS ALREADY DISPATCHED A UNIT OF DROIDS. YOU NEED TO REACH THE PARLIAMENT MEMBERS BEFORE--
--IT'S TOO LATE.

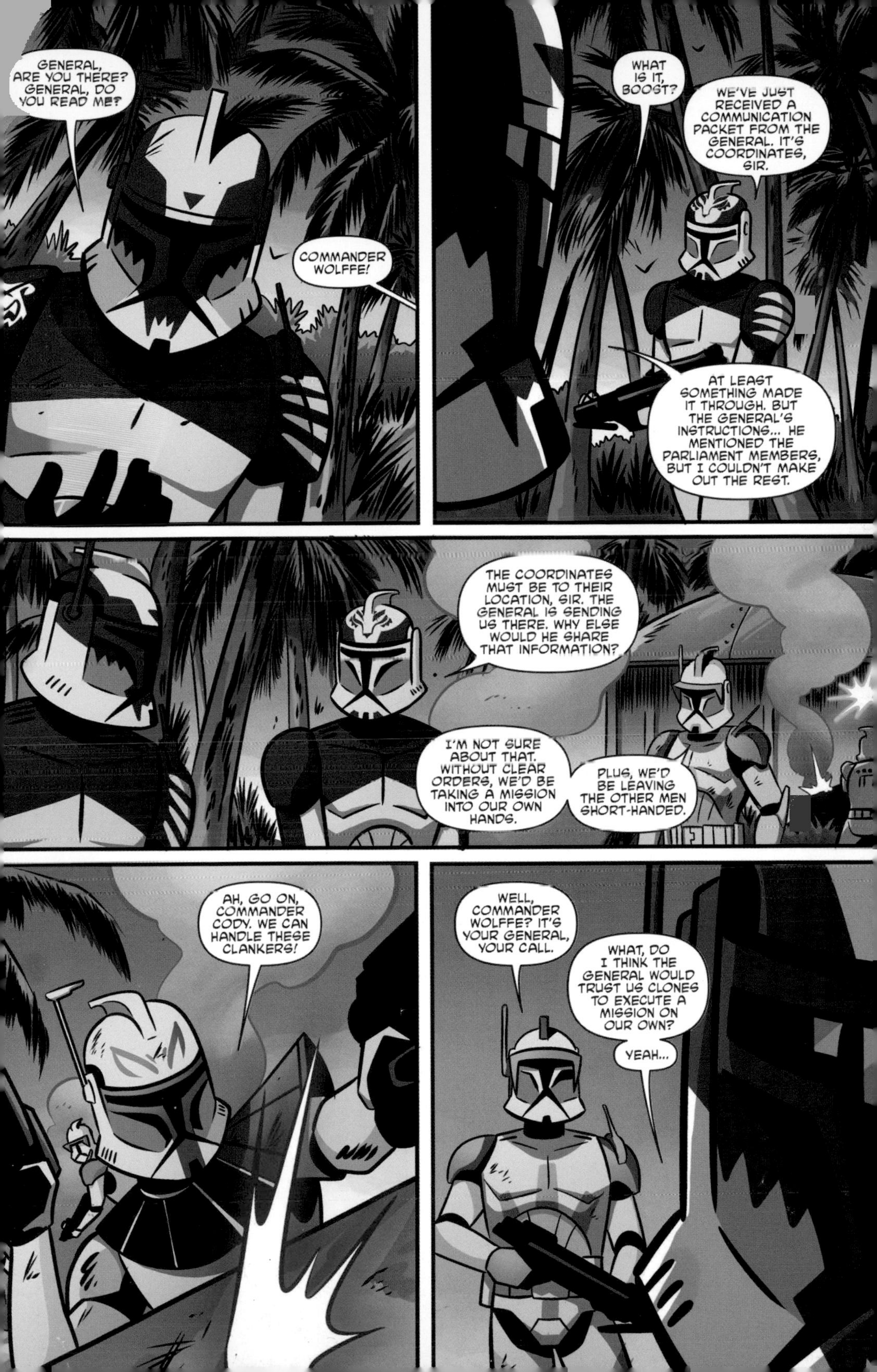
GENERAL, ARE YOU THERE? GENERAL, DO YOU READ ME?
COMMANDER WOLFFE!
WHAT IS IT, BOOST?
WE'VE JUST RECEIVED A COMMUNICATION PACKET FROM THE GENERAL. IT'S COORDINATES, SIR.
AT LEAST SOMETHING MADE IT THROUGH. BUT THE GENERAL'S INSTRUCTIONS... HE MENTIONED THE PARLIAMENT MEMBERS, BUT I COULDN'T MAKE OUT THE REST.
THE COORDINATES MUST BE TO THEIR LOCATION, SIR. THE GENERAL IS SENDING US THERE. WHY ELSE WOULD HE SHARE THAT INFORMATION?
I'M NOT SURE ABOUT THAT. WITHOUT CLEAR ORDERS, WE'D BE TAKING A MISSION INTO OUR OWN HANDS.
PLUS, WE'D BE LEAVING THE OTHER MEN SHORT-HANDED.
AH, GO ON, COMMANDER CODY. WE CAN HANDLE THESE CLANKERS!
WELL, COMMANDER WOLFFE? IT'S YOUR GENERAL, YOUR CALL.
WHAT, DO I THINK THE GENERAL WOULD TRUST US CLONES TO EXECUTE A MISSION ON OUR OWN?
YEAH...

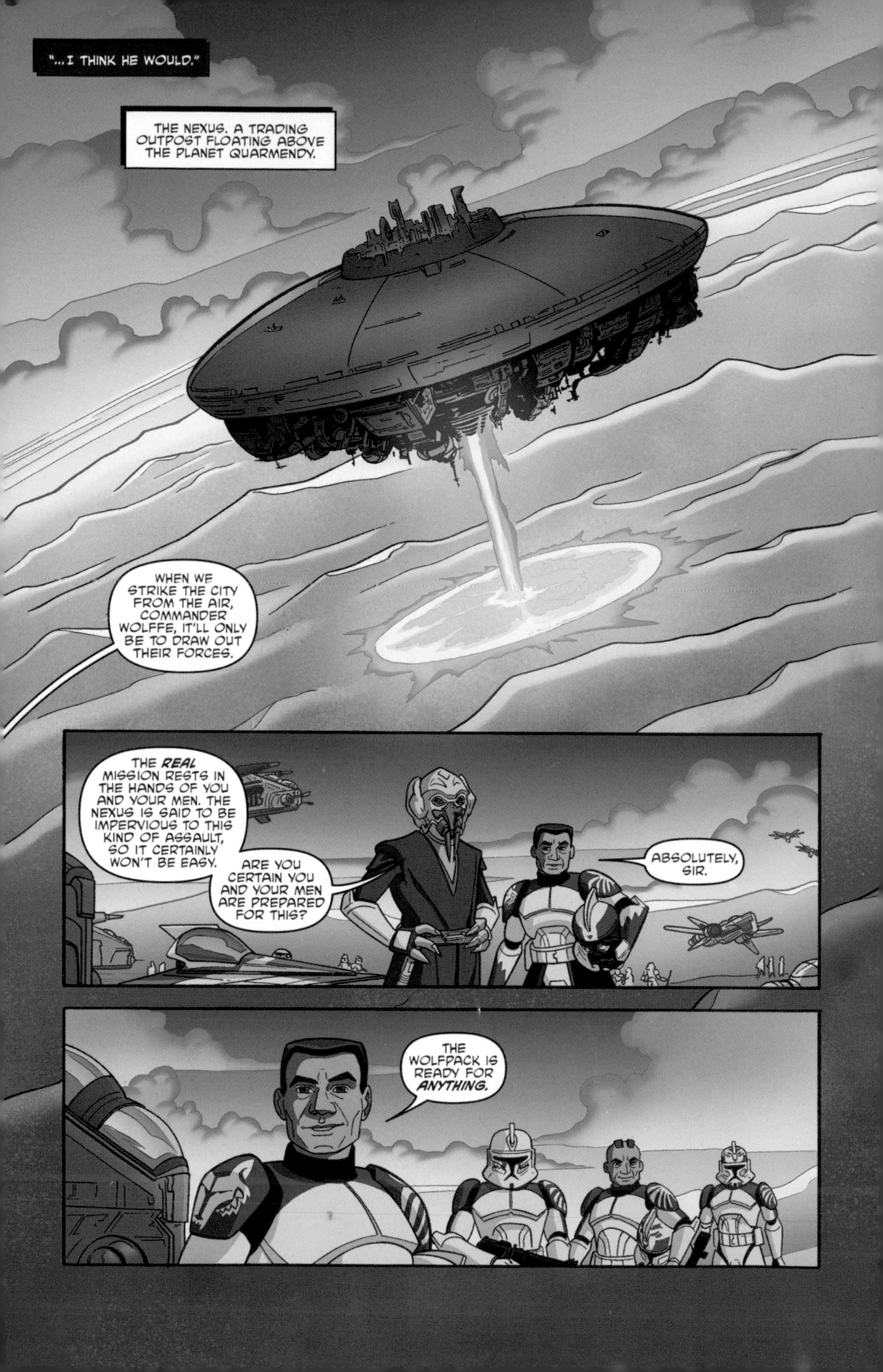
"...I THINK HE WOULD."
THE NEXUS. A TRADING OUTPOST FLOATING ABOVE THE PLANET QUARMENDY.
WHEN WE STRIKE THE CITY FROM THE AIR, COMMANDER WOLFFE, IT'LL ONLY BE TO DRAW OUT THEIR FORCES.
THE *REAL* MISSION RESTS IN THE HANDS OF YOU AND YOUR MEN. THE NEXUS IS SAID TO BE IMPERVIOUS TO THIS KIND OF ASSAULT, SO IT CERTAINLY WON'T BE EASY.
ARE YOU CERTAIN YOU AND YOUR MEN ARE PREPARED FOR THIS?
ABSOLUTELY, SIR.
THE WOLFPACK IS READY FOR *ANYTHING.*

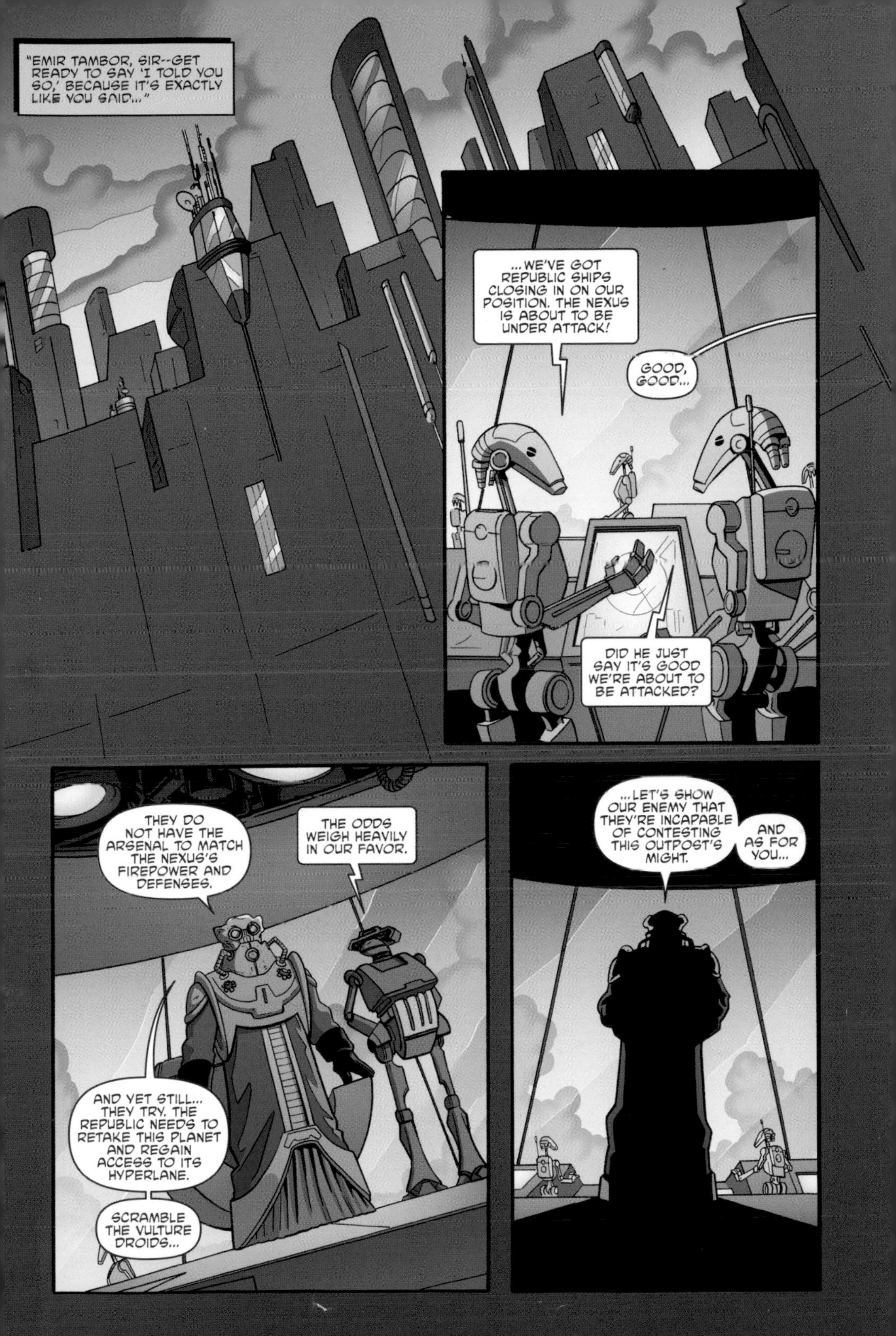
"EMIR TAMBOR, SIR--GET READY TO SAY 'I TOLD YOU SO,' BECAUSE IT'S EXACTLY LIKE YOU SAID..."
...WE'VE GOT REPUBLIC SHIPS CLOSING IN ON OUR POSITION. THE NEXUS IS ABOUT TO BE UNDER ATTACK!
GOOD, GOOD...
DID HE JUST SAY IT'S GOOD WE'RE ABOUT TO BE ATTACKED?
THEY DO NOT HAVE THE ARSENAL TO MATCH THE NEXUS'S FIREPOWER AND DEFENSES.
THE ODDS WEIGH HEAVILY IN OUR FAVOR.
AND YET STILL... THEY TRY. THE REPUBLIC NEEDS TO RETAKE THIS PLANET AND REGAIN ACCESS TO ITS HYPERLANE.
SCRAMBLE THE VULTURE DROIDS...
...LET'S SHOW OUR ENEMY THAT THEY'RE INCAPABLE OF CONTESTING THIS OUTPOST'S MIGHT.
AND AS FOR YOU...

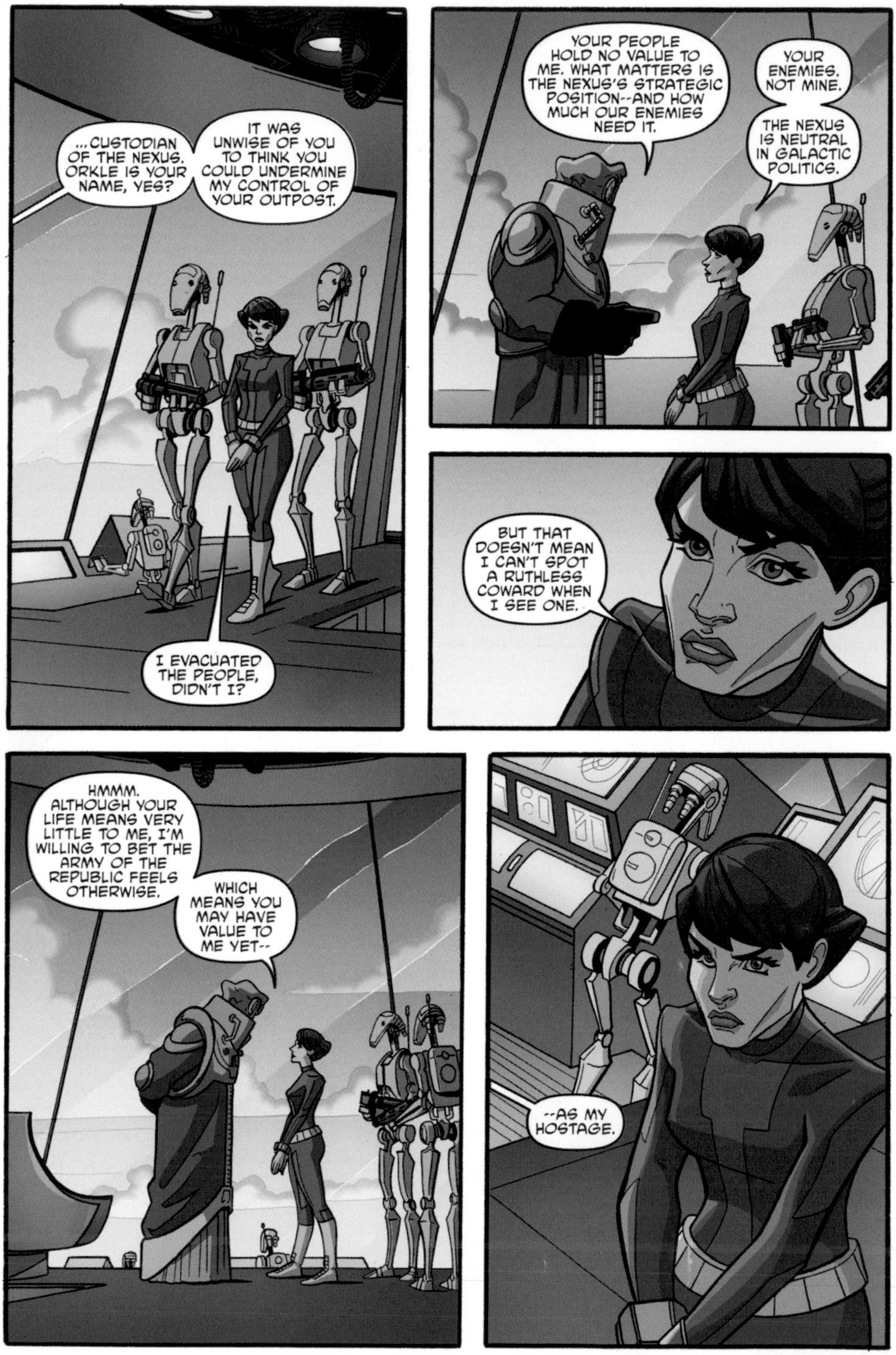
...CUSTODIAN OF THE NEXUS. ORKLE IS YOUR NAME, YES?
IT WAS UNWISE OF YOU TO THINK YOU COULD UNDERMINE MY CONTROL OF YOUR OUTPOST.
I EVACUATED THE PEOPLE, DIDN'T I?
YOUR PEOPLE HOLD NO VALUE TO ME. WHAT MATTERS IS THE NEXUS'S STRATEGIC POSITION--AND HOW MUCH OUR ENEMIES NEED IT.
YOUR ENEMIES. NOT MINE.
THE NEXUS IS NEUTRAL IN GALACTIC POLITICS.
BUT THAT DOESN'T MEAN I CAN'T SPOT A RUTHLESS COWARD WHEN I SEE ONE.
HMMM. ALTHOUGH YOUR LIFE MEANS VERY LITTLE TO ME, I'M WILLING TO BET THE ARMY OF THE REPUBLIC FEELS OTHERWISE.
WHICH MEANS YOU MAY HAVE VALUE TO ME YET--
--AS MY HOSTAGE.

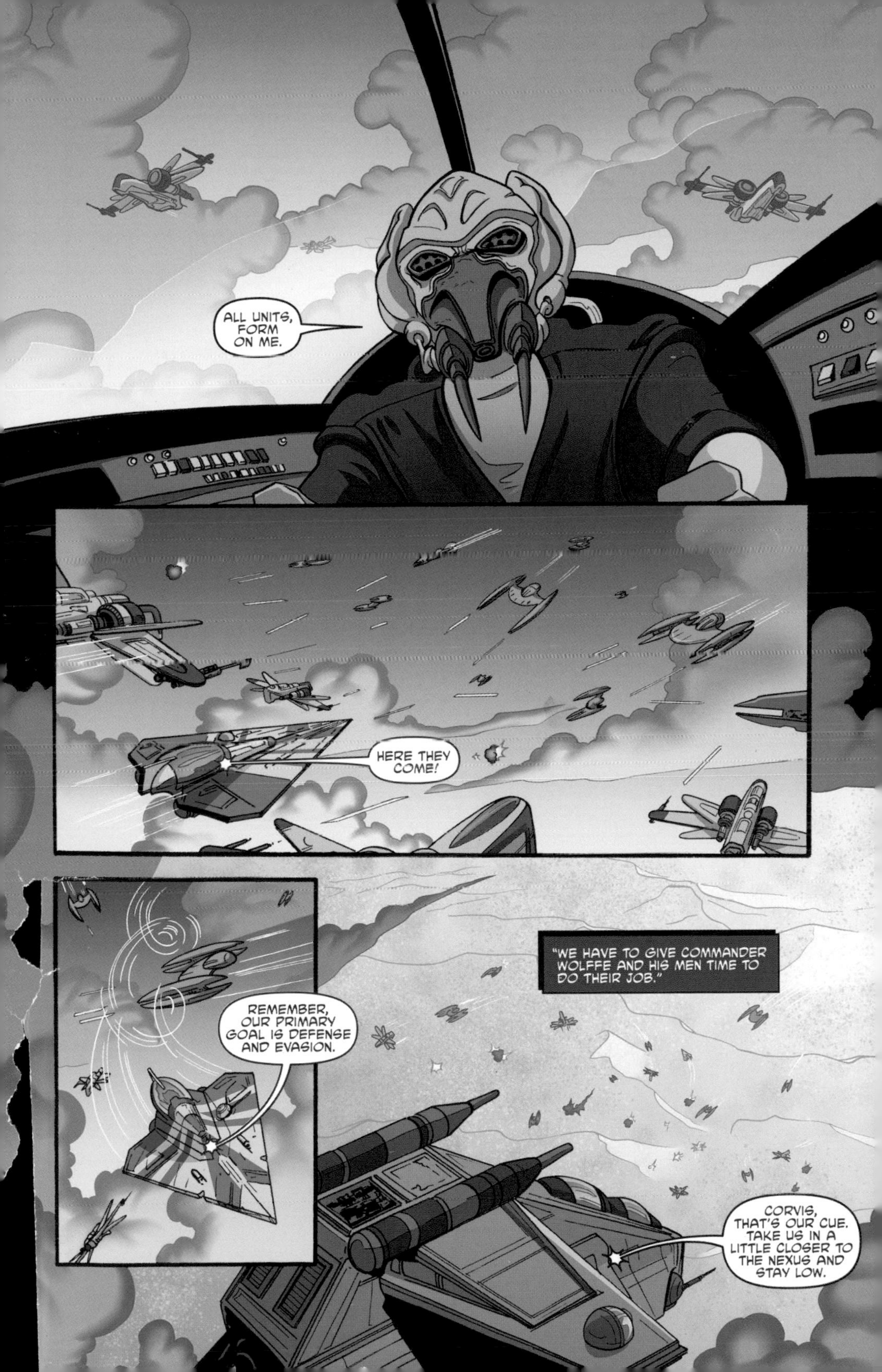
ALL UNITS, FORM ON ME.
HERE THEY COME!
REMEMBER, OUR PRIMARY GOAL IS DEFENSE AND EVASION.
"WE HAVE TO GIVE COMMANDER WOLFFE AND HIS MEN TIME TO DO THEIR JOB."
CORVIS, THAT'S OUR CUE. TAKE US IN A LITTLE CLOSER TO THE NEXUS AND STAY LOW.

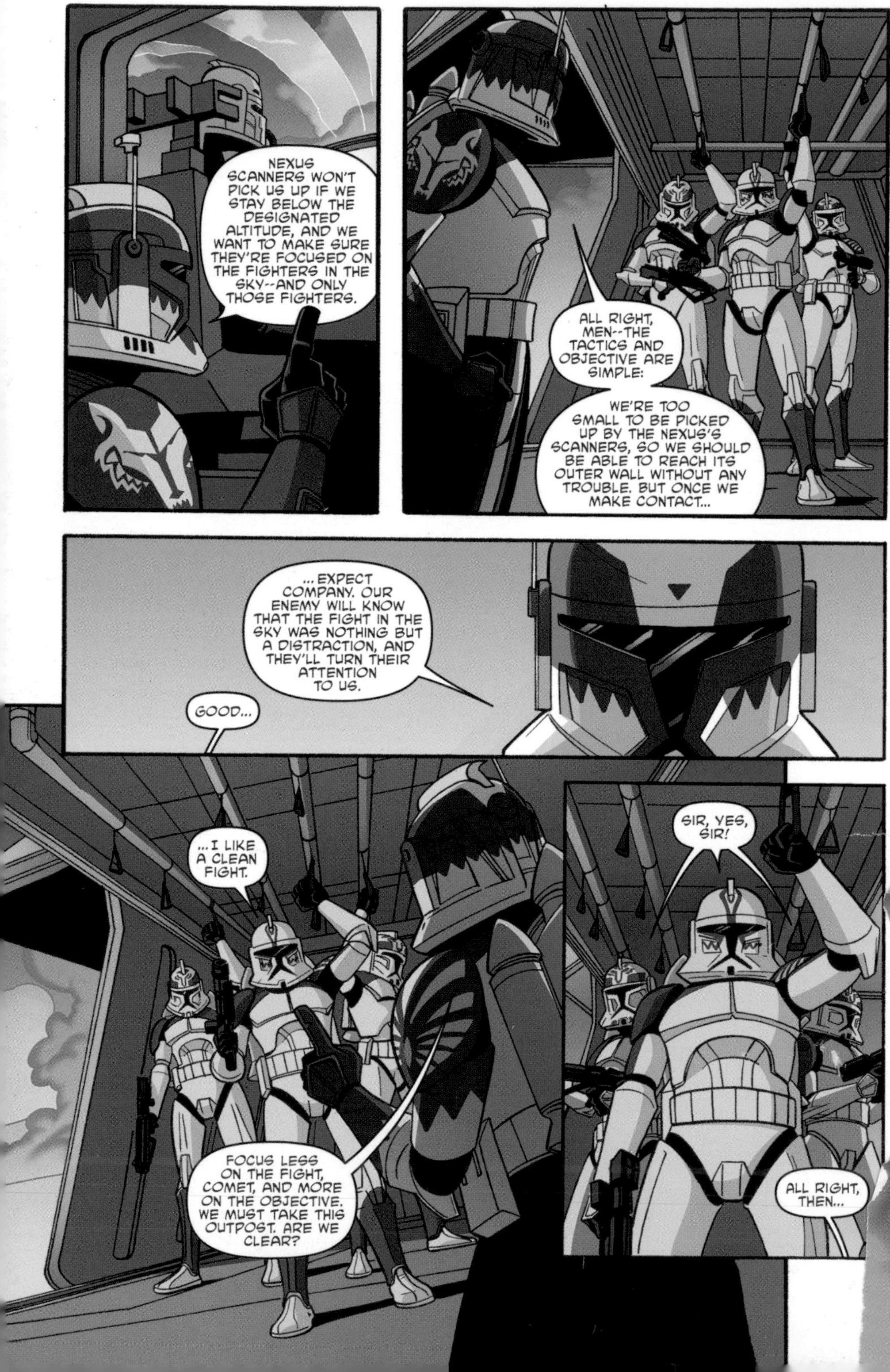
NEXUS SCANNERS WON'T PICK US UP IF WE STAY BELOW THE DESIGNATED ALTITUDE, AND WE WANT TO MAKE SURE THEY'RE FOCUSED ON THE FIGHTERS IN THE SKY--AND ONLY THOSE FIGHTERS.
ALL RIGHT, MEN--THE TACTICS AND OBJECTIVE ARE SIMPLE:
WE'RE TOO SMALL TO BE PICKED UP BY THE NEXUS'S SCANNERS, SO WE SHOULD BE ABLE TO REACH ITS OUTER WALL WITHOUT ANY TROUBLE. BUT ONCE WE MAKE CONTACT...
...EXPECT COMPANY. OUR ENEMY WILL KNOW THAT THE FIGHT IN THE SKY WAS NOTHING BUT A DISTRACTION, AND THEY'LL TURN THEIR ATTENTION TO US.
GOOD...
...I LIKE A CLEAN FIGHT.
FOCUS LESS ON THE FIGHT, COMET, AND MORE ON THE OBJECTIVE. WE MUST TAKE THIS OUTPOST. ARE WE CLEAR?
SIR, YES, SIR!
ALL RIGHT, THEN...

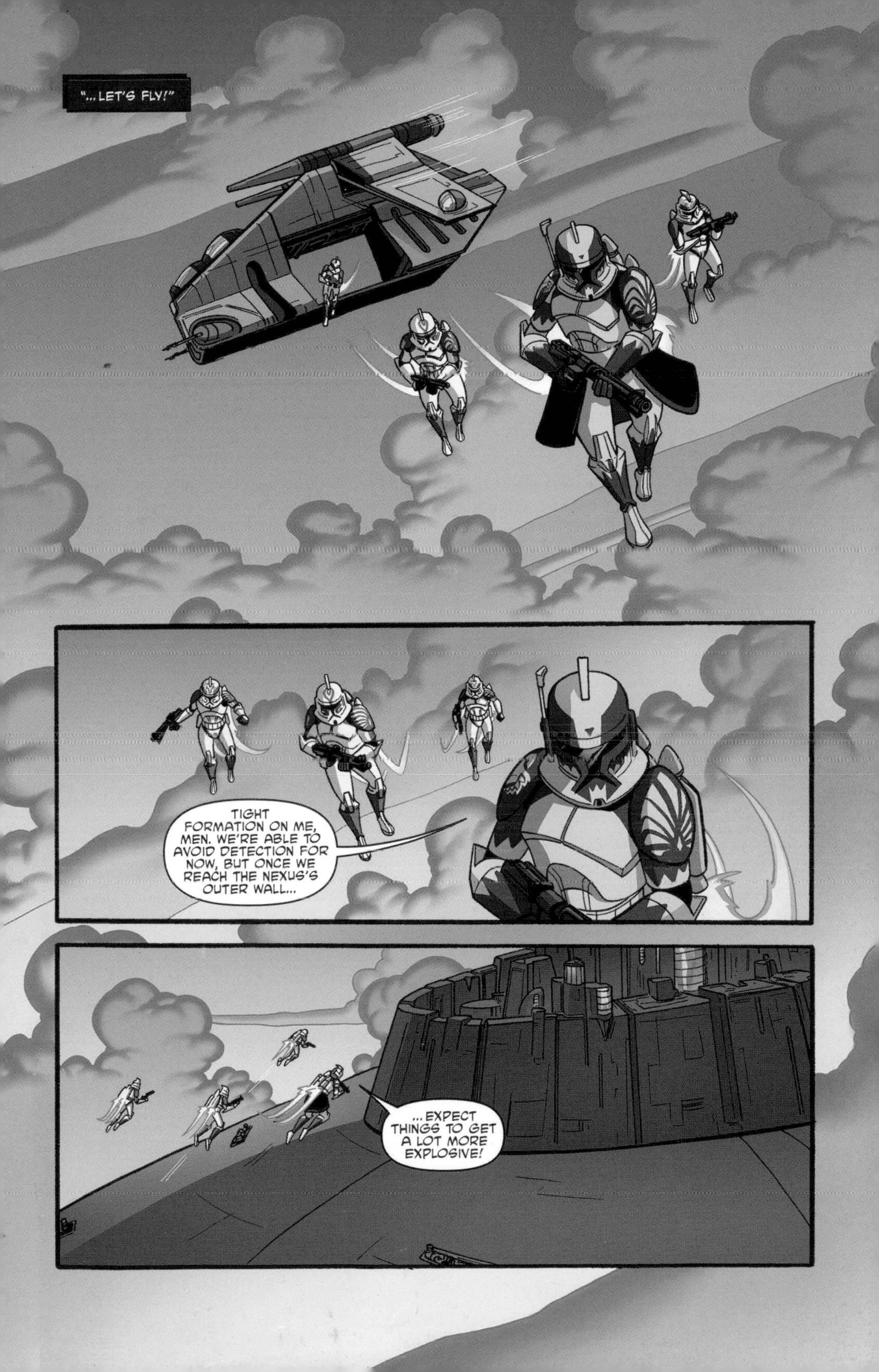
"...LET'S FLY!"
TIGHT FORMATION ON ME, MEN. WE'RE ABLE TO AVOID DETECTION FOR NOW, BUT ONCE WE REACH THE NEXUS'S OUTER WALL...
...EXPECT THINGS TO GET A LOT MORE EXPLOSIVE!

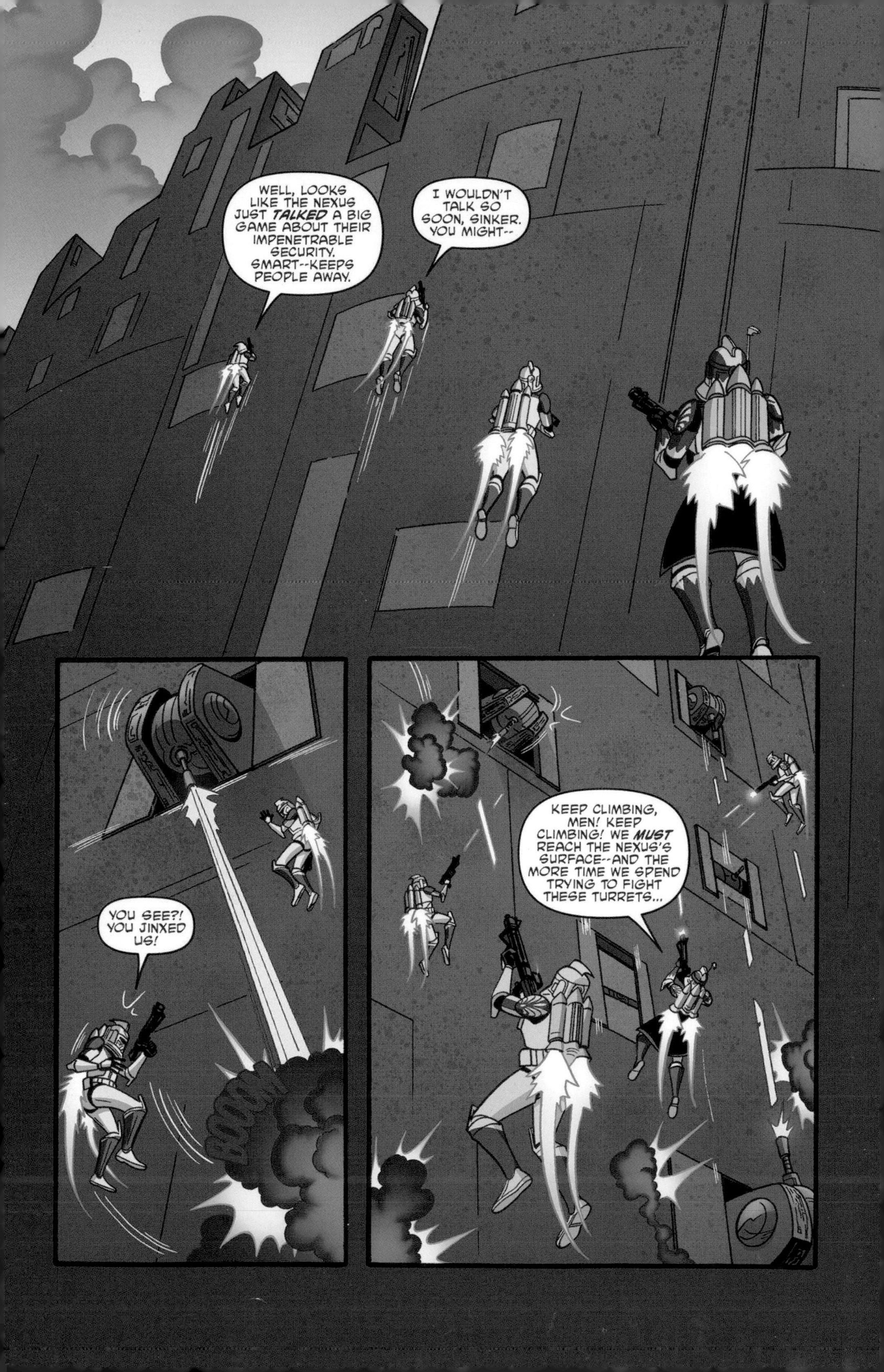
WELL, LOOKS LIKE THE NEXUS JUST TALKED A BIG GAME ABOUT THEIR IMPENETRABLE SECURITY. SMART--KEEPS PEOPLE AWAY.
I WOULDN'T TALK SO SOON, SINKER. YOU MIGHT--
YOU SEE?! YOU JINXED US!
KEEP CLIMBING, MEN! KEEP CLIMBING! WE MUST REACH THE NEXUS'S SURFACE--AND THE MORE TIME WE SPEND TRYING TO FIGHT THESE TURRETS...

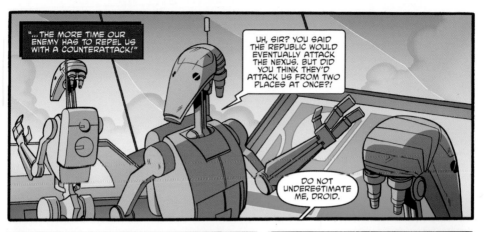

"...THE MORE TIME OUR ENEMY HAS TO REPEL US WITH A COUNTERATTACK!"

UH, SIR? YOU SAID THE REPUBLIC WOULD EVENTUALLY ATTACK THE NEXUS. BUT DID YOU THINK THEY'D ATTACK US FROM TWO PLACES AT ONCE?!

DO NOT UNDERESTIMATE ME, DROID.

THERE'S NOTHING THE ENEMY CAN THROW AT US THAT THIS STATION, AND OUR FORCES, CANNOT HANDLE.

BUT WE WOULDN'T WANT THEM THINKING THEY STAND A CHANCE AGAINST OUR MIGHT.

SEND OUR SPECIAL FORCE TO GREET OUR FRIENDS.

AND LET'S SEE THIS INCURSION ENDED.

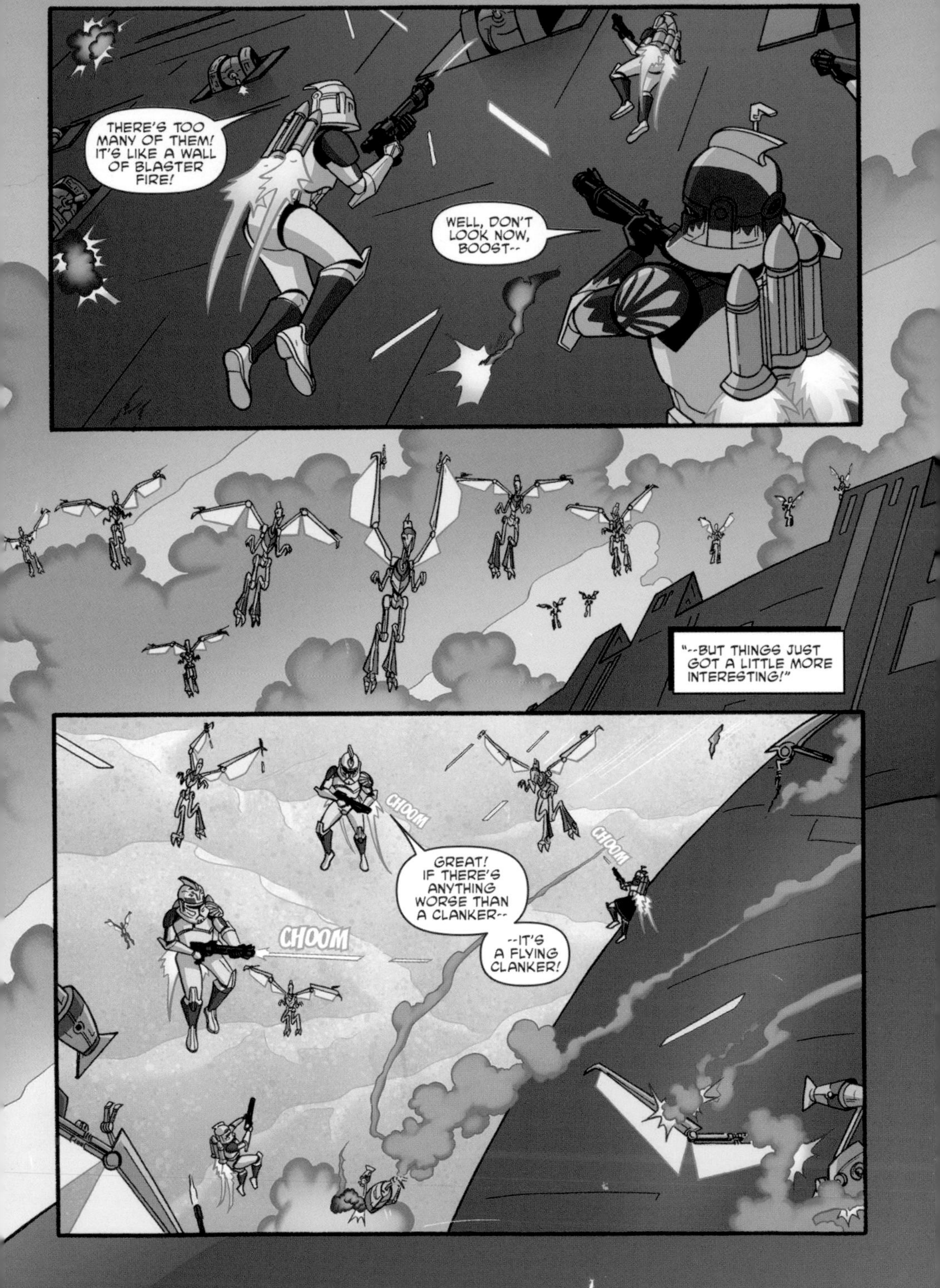
THERE'S TOO MANY OF THEM! IT'S LIKE A WALL OF BLASTER FIRE!
WELL, DON'T LOOK NOW, BOOST--
"--BUT THINGS JUST GOT A LITTLE MORE INTERESTING!"
CHOOM
CHOOM
CHOOM
GREAT! IF THERE'S ANYTHING WORSE THAN A CLANKER--
--IT'S A FLYING CLANKER!

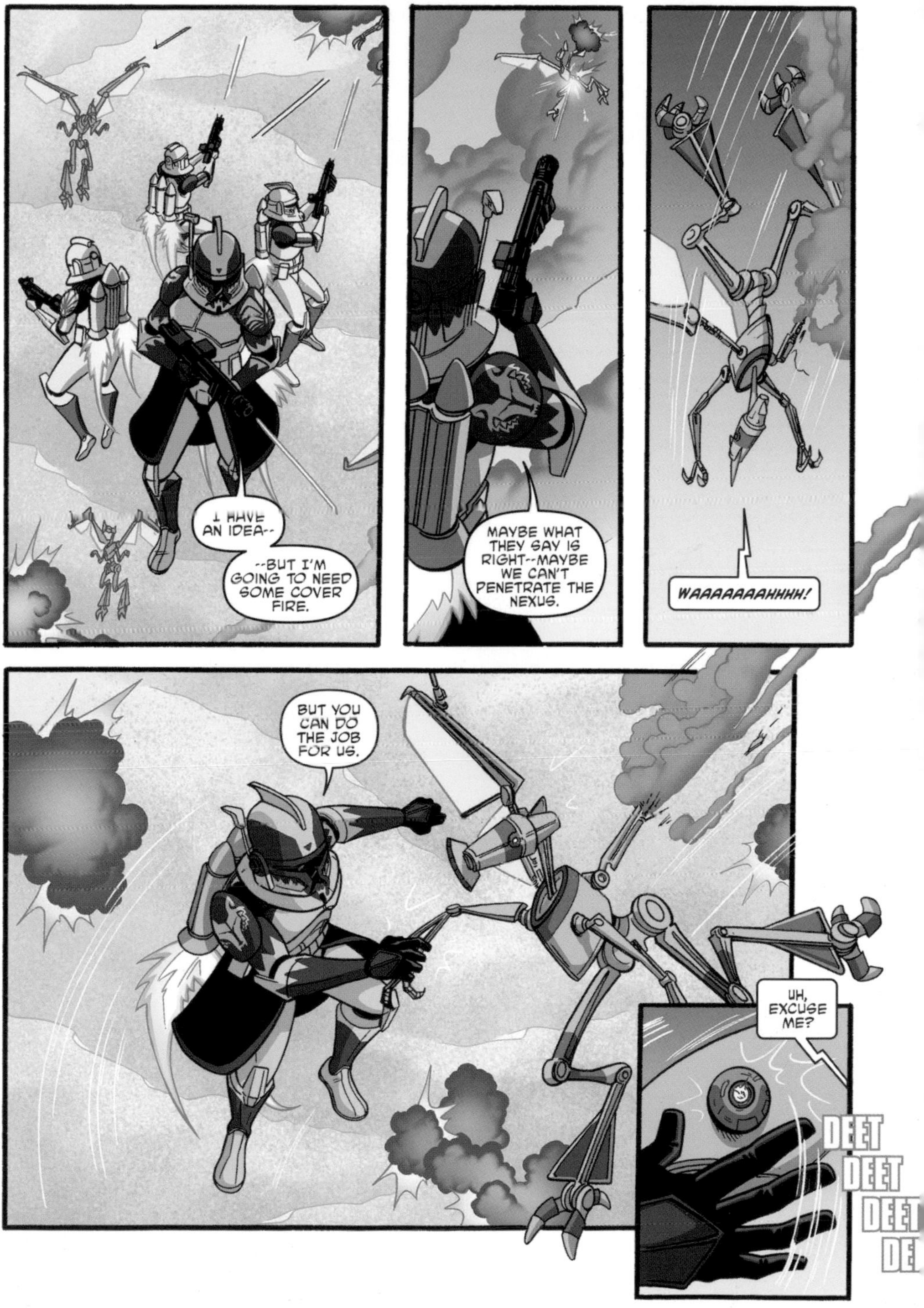
I HAVE AN IDEA--
--BUT I'M GOING TO NEED SOME COVER FIRE.
MAYBE WHAT THEY SAY IS RIGHT--MAYBE WE CAN'T PENETRATE THE NEXUS.
WAAAAAAAHHHH!
BUT YOU CAN DO THE JOB FOR US.
UH, EXCUSE ME?
DEET
DEET
DEET
DE

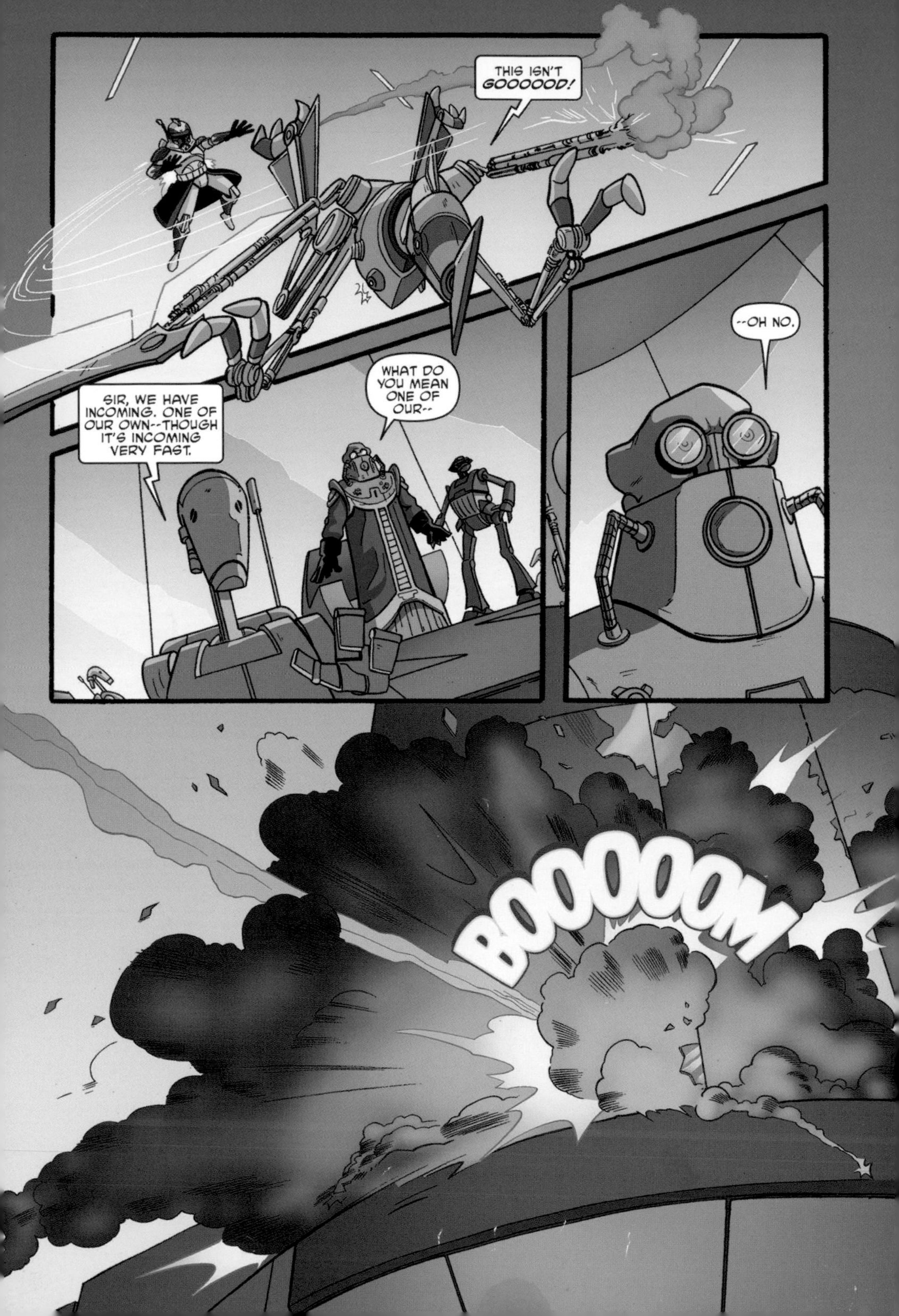
THIS ISN'T GOOOOOD!
SIR, WE HAVE INCOMING. ONE OF OUR OWN--THOUGH IT'S INCOMING VERY FAST.
WHAT DO YOU MEAN ONE OF OUR--
--OH NO.
BOOOOOM

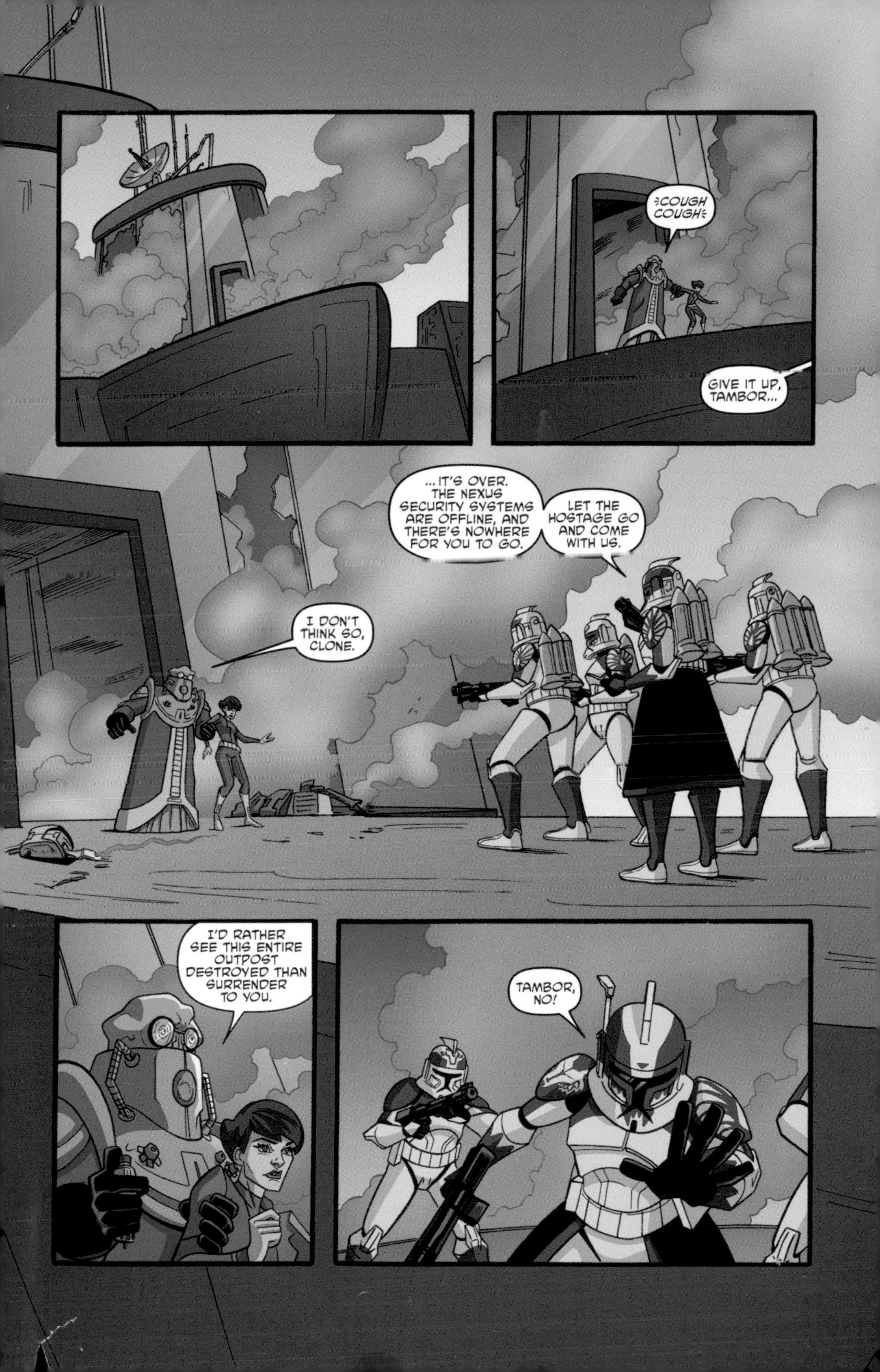
COUGH COUGH
GIVE IT UP, TAMBOR...
...IT'S OVER. THE NEXUS SECURITY SYSTEMS ARE OFFLINE, AND THERE'S NOWHERE FOR YOU TO GO.
LET THE HOSTAGE GO AND COME WITH US.
I DON'T THINK SO, CLONE.
I'D RATHER SEE THIS ENTIRE OUTPOST DESTROYED THAN SURRENDER TO YOU.
TAMBOR, NO!

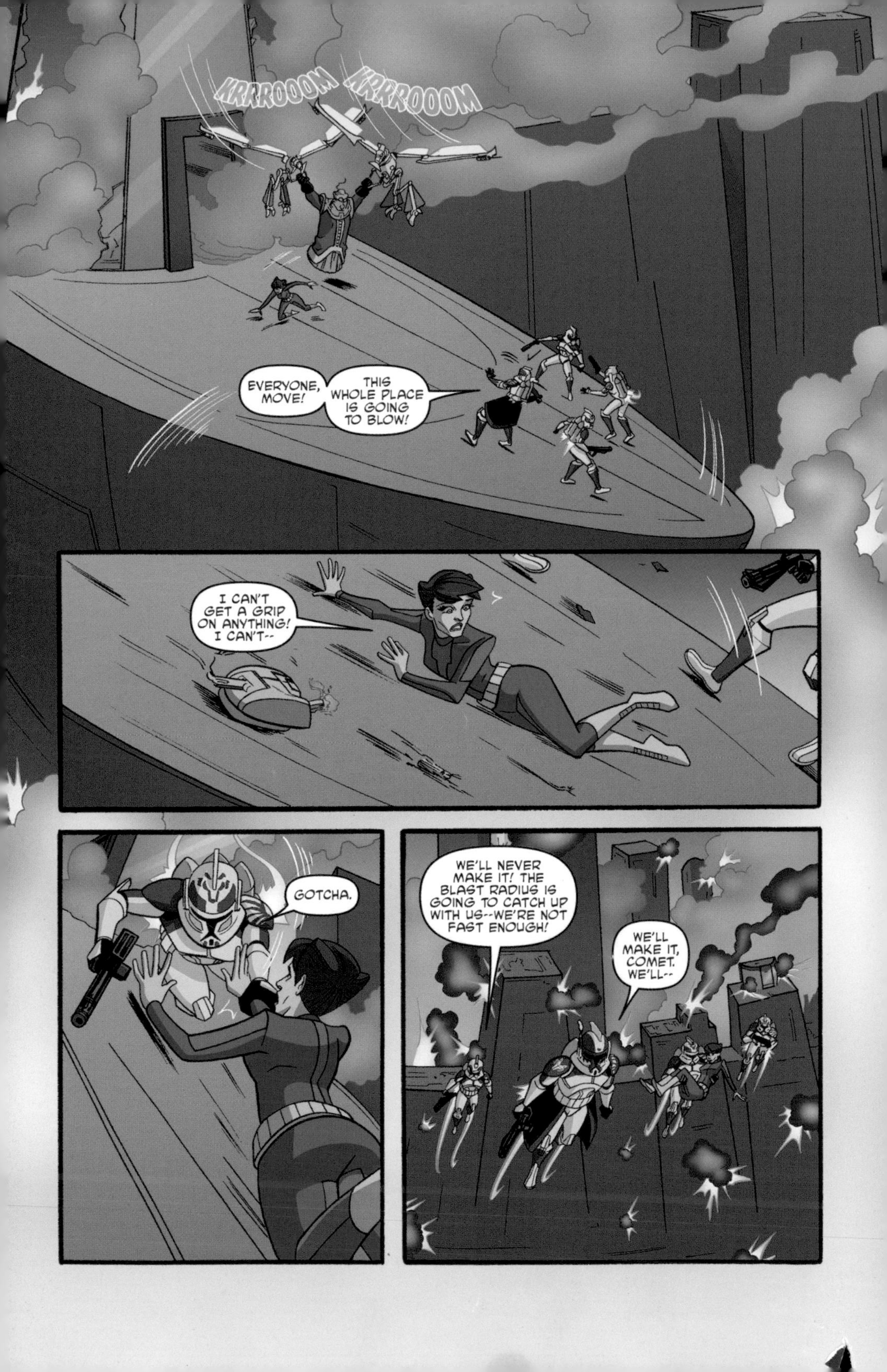
KRRROOOM KRRROOOM
EVERYONE, MOVE!
THIS WHOLE PLACE IS GOING TO BLOW!
I CAN'T GET A GRIP ON ANYTHING! I CAN'T--
GOTCHA.
WE'LL NEVER MAKE IT! THE BLAST RADIUS IS GOING TO CATCH UP WITH US--WE'RE NOT FAST ENOUGH!
WE'LL MAKE IT, COMET. WE'LL--

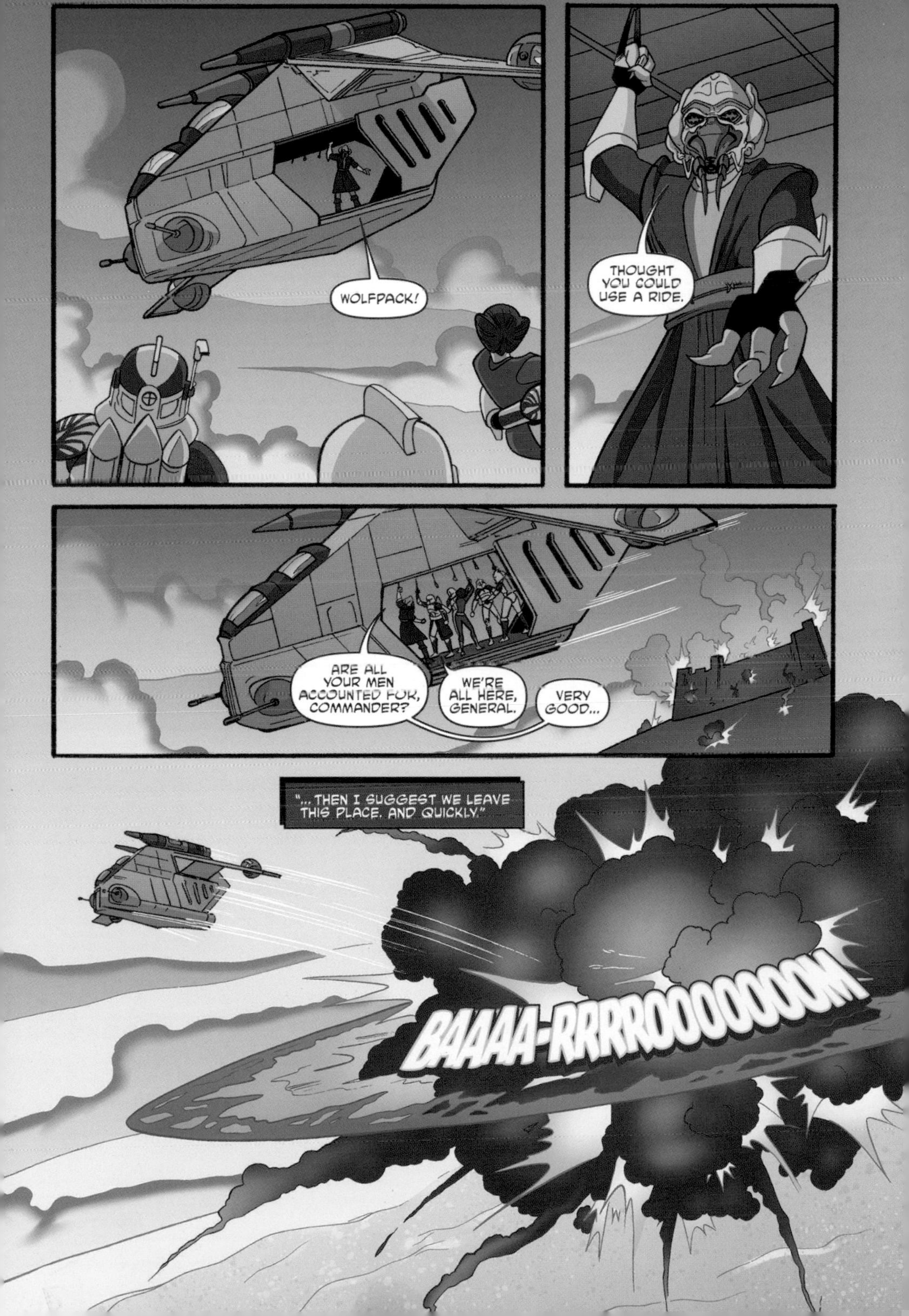
WOLFPACK!
THOUGHT YOU COULD USE A RIDE.
ARE ALL YOUR MEN ACCOUNTED FOR, COMMANDER?
WE'RE ALL HERE, GENERAL.
VERY GOOD...
"...THEN I SUGGEST WE LEAVE THIS PLACE. AND QUICKLY."
BAAAA-RRRROOOOOOOM

GENERAL, I... I HOPE YOU ACCEPT MY APOLOGIES.

THE NEXUS, IT--ITS DESTRUCTION WAS NOT PART OF THE MISSION.

WE FAILED YOU, SIR. I FAILED YOU.

IS THAT HOW YOU SEE IT, COMMANDER? BECAUSE WHEN I LOOK AROUND...

...I SEE YOUR ENTIRE UNIT ACCOUNTED FOR. I SEE THE ONE HOSTAGE RESCUED AND UNHARMED.

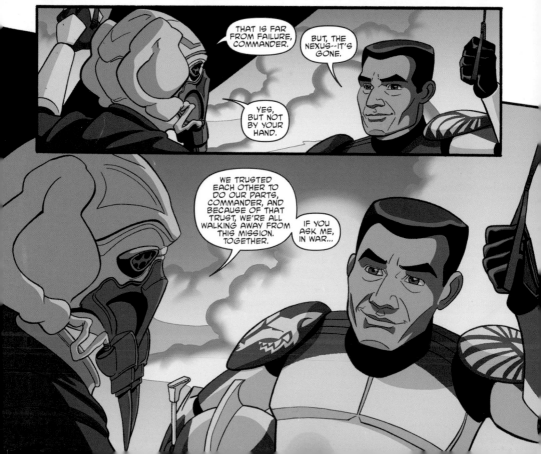

THAT IS FAR FROM FAILURE, COMMANDER.

BUT, THE NEXUS--IT'S GONE.

YES, BUT NOT BY YOUR HAND.

WE TRUSTED EACH OTHER TO DO OUR PARTS, COMMANDER, AND BECAUSE OF THAT TRUST, WE'RE ALL WALKING AWAY FROM THIS MISSION. TOGETHER.

IF YOU ASK ME, IN WAR...

"...YOU CAN'T HOPE FOR MUCH GREATER."

WELL, COMMANDER WOLFFE, IT'S A GOOD THING THE GENERAL TRUSTS YOU. I'VE GOT SOMETHING HERE.

YOU WERE RIGHT ABOUT THOSE COORDINATES. TAKE A LOOK FOR YOURSELF, JUST UP AHEAD, IN THE CLEARING.

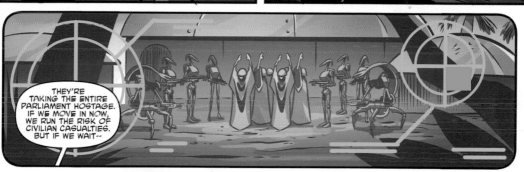

THEY'RE TAKING THE ENTIRE PARLIAMENT HOSTAGE. IF WE MOVE IN NOW, WE RUN THE RISK OF CIVILIAN CASUALTIES. BUT IF WE WAIT--

--WE MIGHT NOT GET ANOTHER CHANCE.

THE SEPARATISTS HAVE NO REGARD FOR INNOCENT LIFE. THEY DON'T CARE WHO WALKS AWAY FROM WAR AND WHO DOESN'T.

THAT'S WHY WE MOVE ON THEM NOW, COMMANDER...

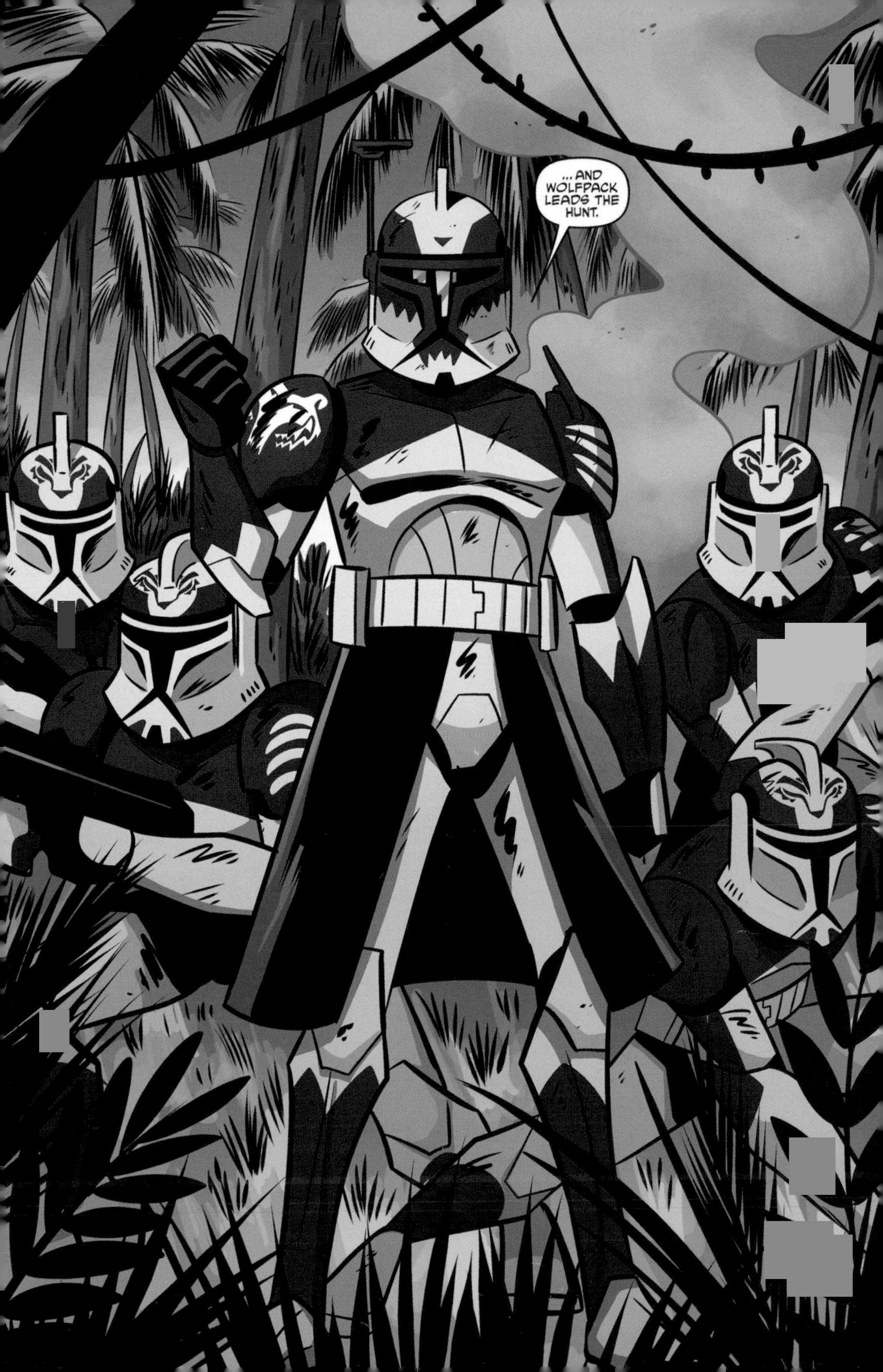
...AND WOLFPACK LEADS THE HUNT.

3

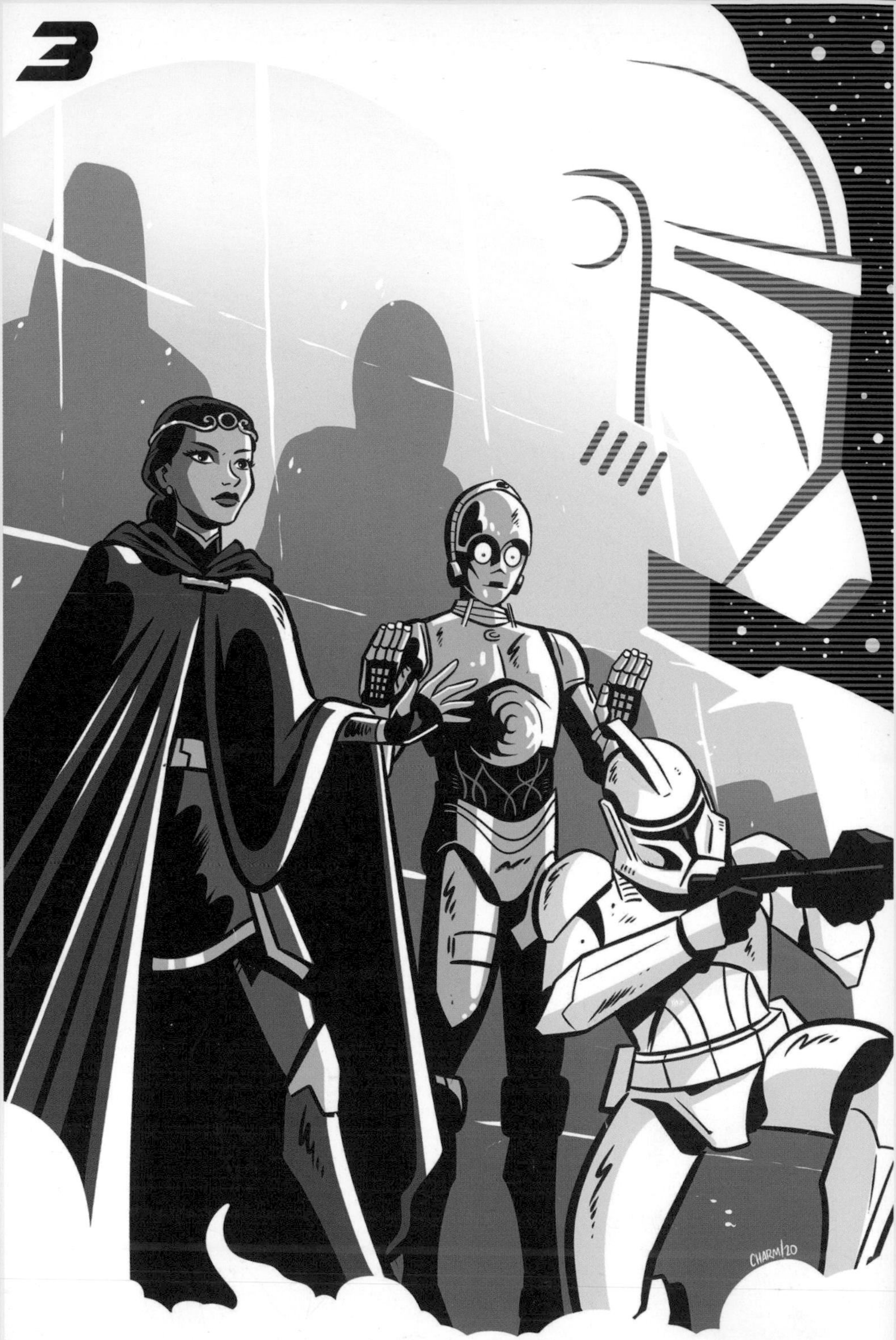
CHARM/20

Art by Derek Charm

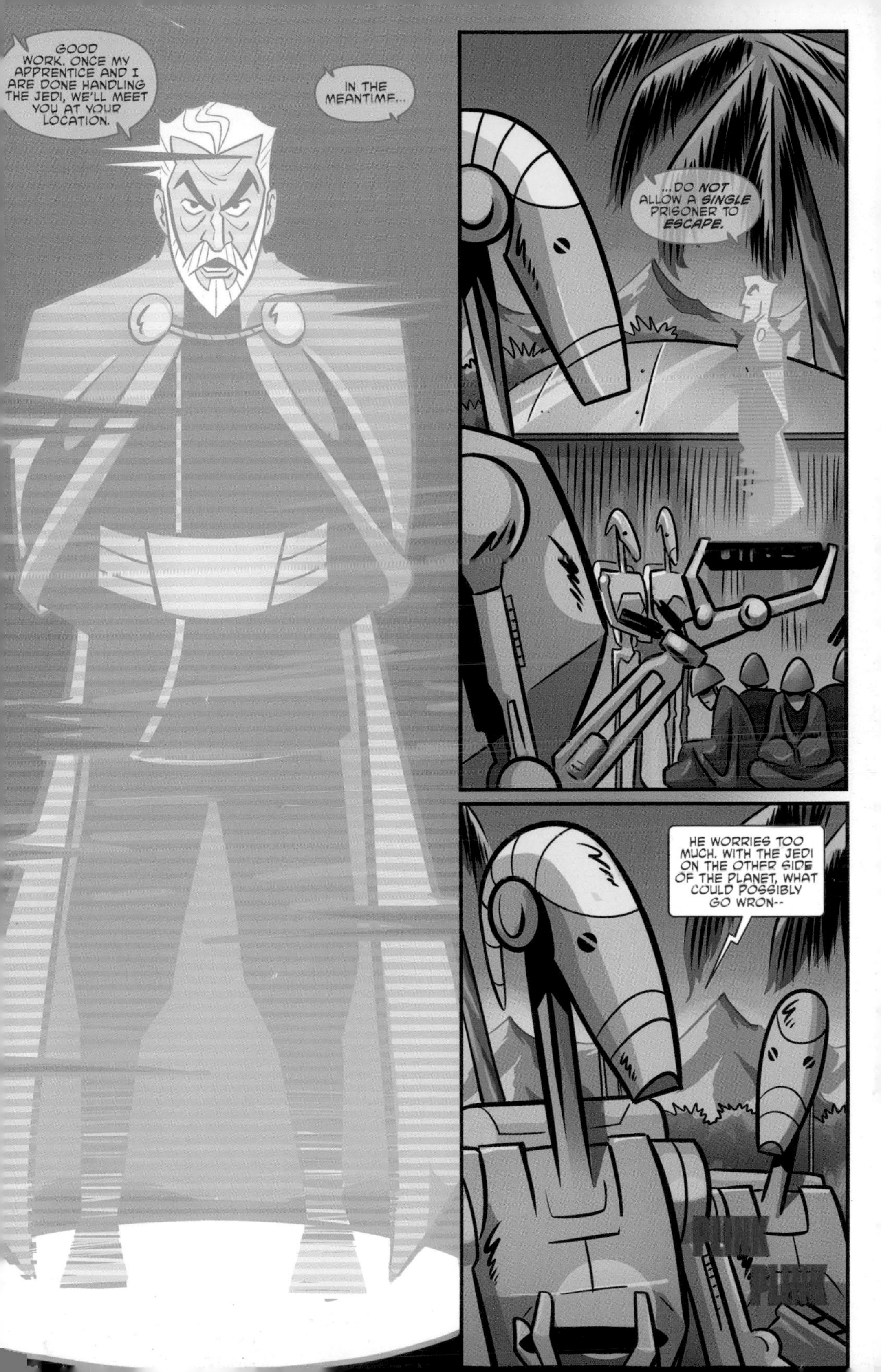
GOOD WORK. ONCE MY APPRENTICE AND I ARE DONE HANDLING THE JEDI, WE'LL MEET YOU AT YOUR LOCATION.
IN THE MEANTIME...
...DO NOT ALLOW A SINGLE PRISONER TO ESCAPE.
HE WORRIES TOO MUCH. WITH THE JEDI ON THE OTHER SIDE OF THE PLANET, WHAT COULD POSSIBLY GO WRON--

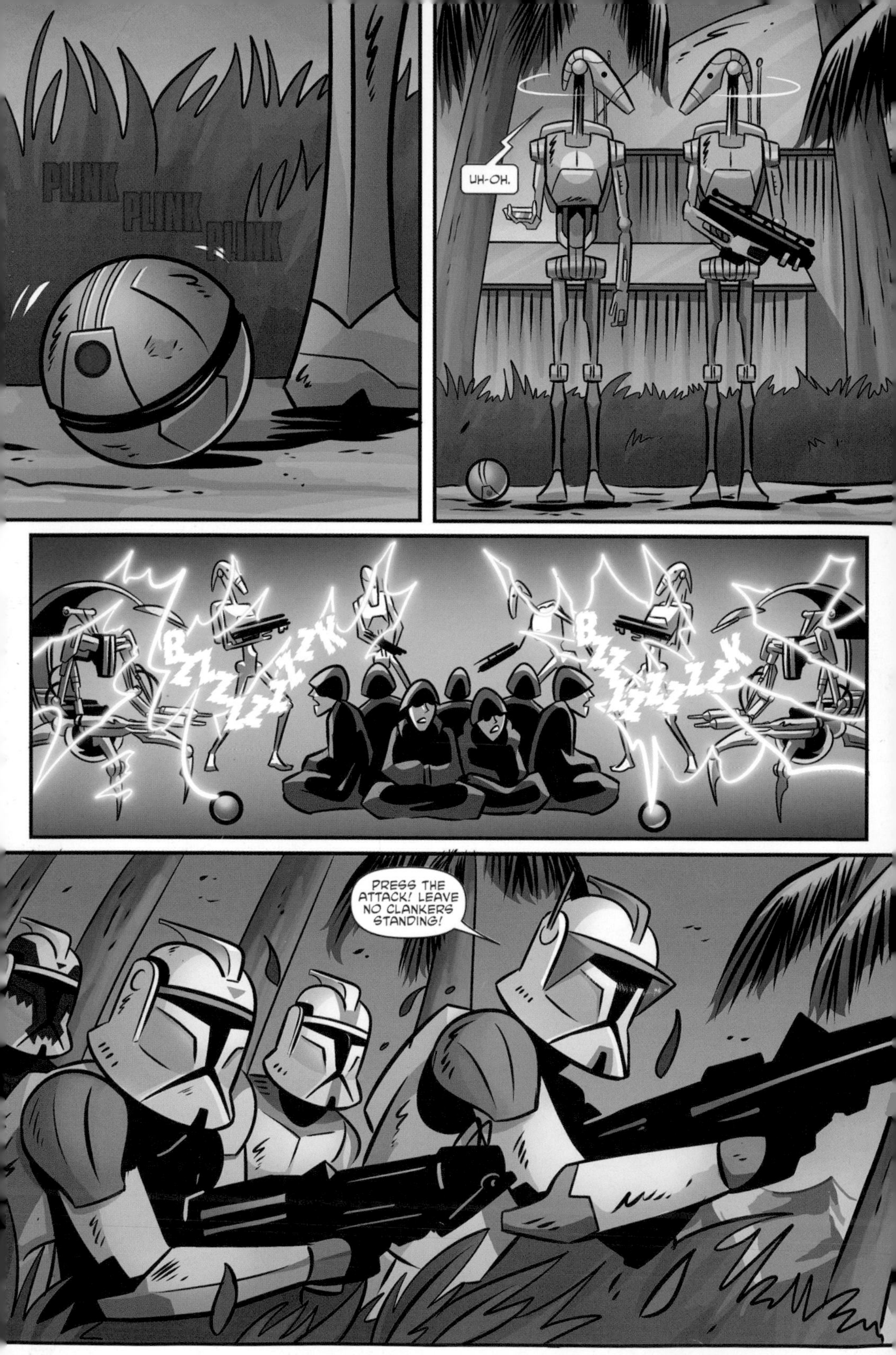
PLINK
PLINK
PLINK
UH-OH.
BZZZZZZZK
BZZZZZZZK
PRESS THE ATTACK! LEAVE NO CLANKERS STANDING!

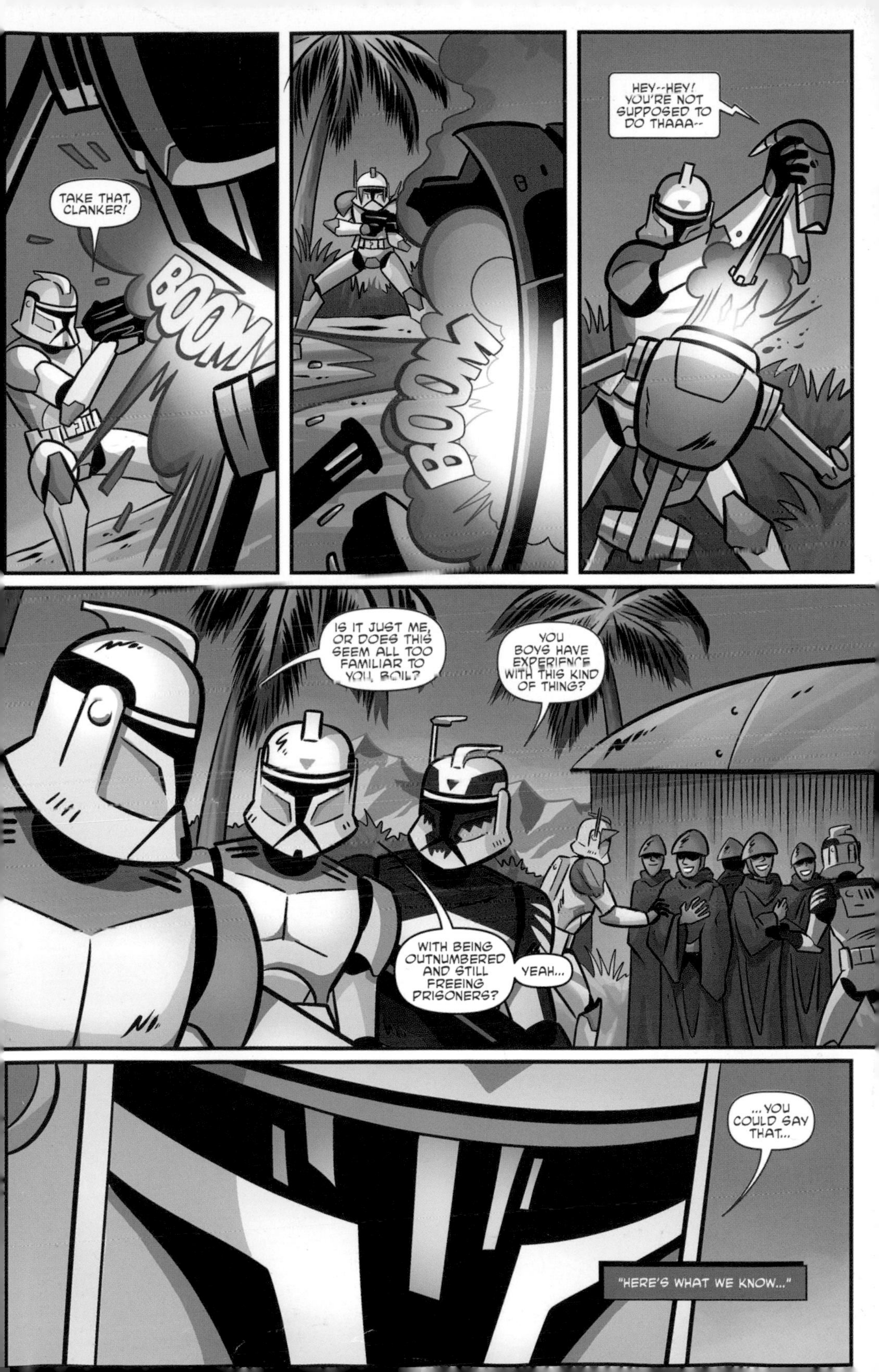
TAKE THAT, CLANKER!
BOOM
BOOM
HEY--HEY! YOU'RE NOT SUPPOSED TO DO THAAA--
IS IT JUST ME, OR DOES THIS SEEM ALL TOO FAMILIAR TO YOU, BOIL?
YOU BOYS HAVE EXPERIENCE WITH THIS KIND OF THING?
WITH BEING OUTNUMBERED AND STILL FREEING PRISONERS?
YEAH...
...YOU COULD SAY THAT...
"HERE'S WHAT WE KNOW..."

...AND I'LL WARN YOU IN ADVANCE, WHAT WE KNOW--IT *ISN'T* PROMISING.

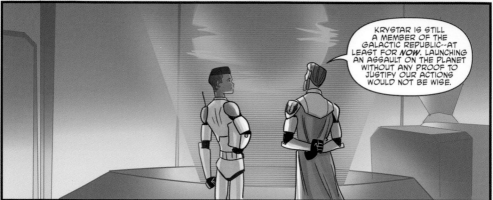

KRYSTAR IS STILL A MEMBER OF THE GALACTIC REPUBLIC--AT LEAST FOR *NOW*. LAUNCHING AN ASSAULT ON THE PLANET WITHOUT ANY PROOF TO JUSTIFY OUR ACTIONS WOULD NOT BE WISE.

BUT GENERAL KENOBI, THESE ARE OUR *BROTHERS* WE'RE TALKING ABOUT. IF THEY'RE BEING SECRETLY HELD AS PRISONERS OF WAR, WE *MUST* DO SOMETHING ABOUT IT.

I SHARE YOUR CONCERN, COMMANDER CODY. BUT I DO BELIEVE A MORE *SUBTLE* TACTIC IS IN ORDER.

SENATOR AMIDALA...?

WORD ABOUT THE CLONE POWs CAME TO ME FROM MY LONGTIME FRIEND VISHAR KOSS, A REPRESENTATIVE FROM KRYSTAR. SHE NOT ONLY ALERTED ME TO THE SITUATION...

...BUT SHE *ALSO* PROVIDED ME WITH VALUABLE INTEL.

THE KRYSTAR PALACE IS LOCATED HERE, AT THE HEART OF THE PLANET'S HABITABLE ZONE.

ACCORDING TO MY FRIEND, THE LOCAL REGENT HAS CONSTRUCTED A COMPOUND--IN SECRET--NOT FAR FROM THE PALACE.

A SECRET COMPOUND? WELL, *THAT* DOESN'T SEEM AT *ALL* SUSPICIOUS.

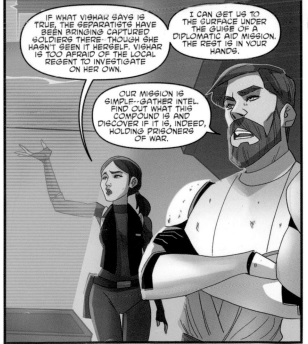

IF WHAT VISHAR SAYS IS TRUE, THE SEPARATISTS HAVE BEEN BRINGING CAPTURED SOLDIERS THERE--THOUGH SHE HASN'T SEEN IT HERSELF. VISHAR IS TOO AFRAID OF THE LOCAL REGENT TO INVESTIGATE ON HER OWN.

I CAN GET US TO THE SURFACE UNDER THE GUISE OF A DIPLOMATIC AID MISSION. THE REST IS IN YOUR HANDS.

OUR MISSION IS SIMPLE--GATHER INTEL. FIND OUT WHAT THIS COMPOUND IS AND DISCOVER IF IT IS, INDEED, HOLDING PRISONERS OF WAR.

AND IF KRYSTAR *IS* HOLDING REPUBLIC SOLDIERS PRISONER...

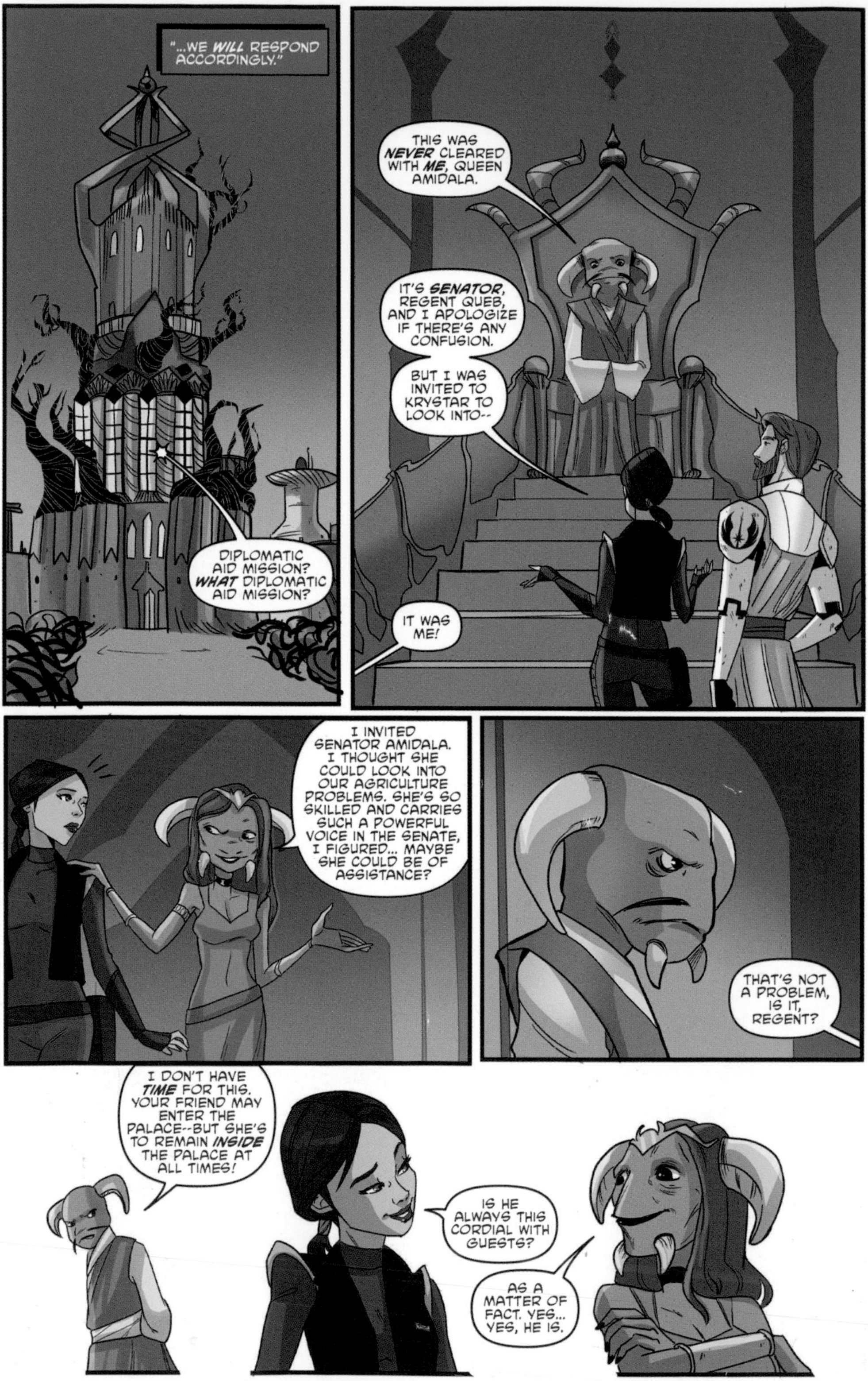
"...WE *WILL* RESPOND ACCORDINGLY."
DIPLOMATIC AID MISSION? *WHAT* DIPLOMATIC AID MISSION?
THIS WAS *NEVER* CLEARED WITH *ME*, QUEEN AMIDALA.
IT'S *SENATOR*, REGENT QUEB, AND I APOLOGIZE IF THERE'S ANY CONFUSION.
BUT I WAS INVITED TO KRYSTAR TO LOOK INTO--
IT WAS ME!
I INVITED SENATOR AMIDALA. I THOUGHT SHE COULD LOOK INTO OUR AGRICULTURE PROBLEMS. SHE'S SO SKILLED AND CARRIES SUCH A POWERFUL VOICE IN THE SENATE, I FIGURED... MAYBE SHE COULD BE OF ASSISTANCE?
THAT'S NOT A PROBLEM, IS IT, REGENT?
I DON'T HAVE *TIME* FOR THIS. YOUR FRIEND MAY ENTER THE PALACE--BUT SHE'S TO REMAIN *INSIDE* THE PALACE AT ALL TIMES!
IS HE ALWAYS THIS CORDIAL WITH GUESTS?
AS A MATTER OF FACT. YES... YES, HE IS.

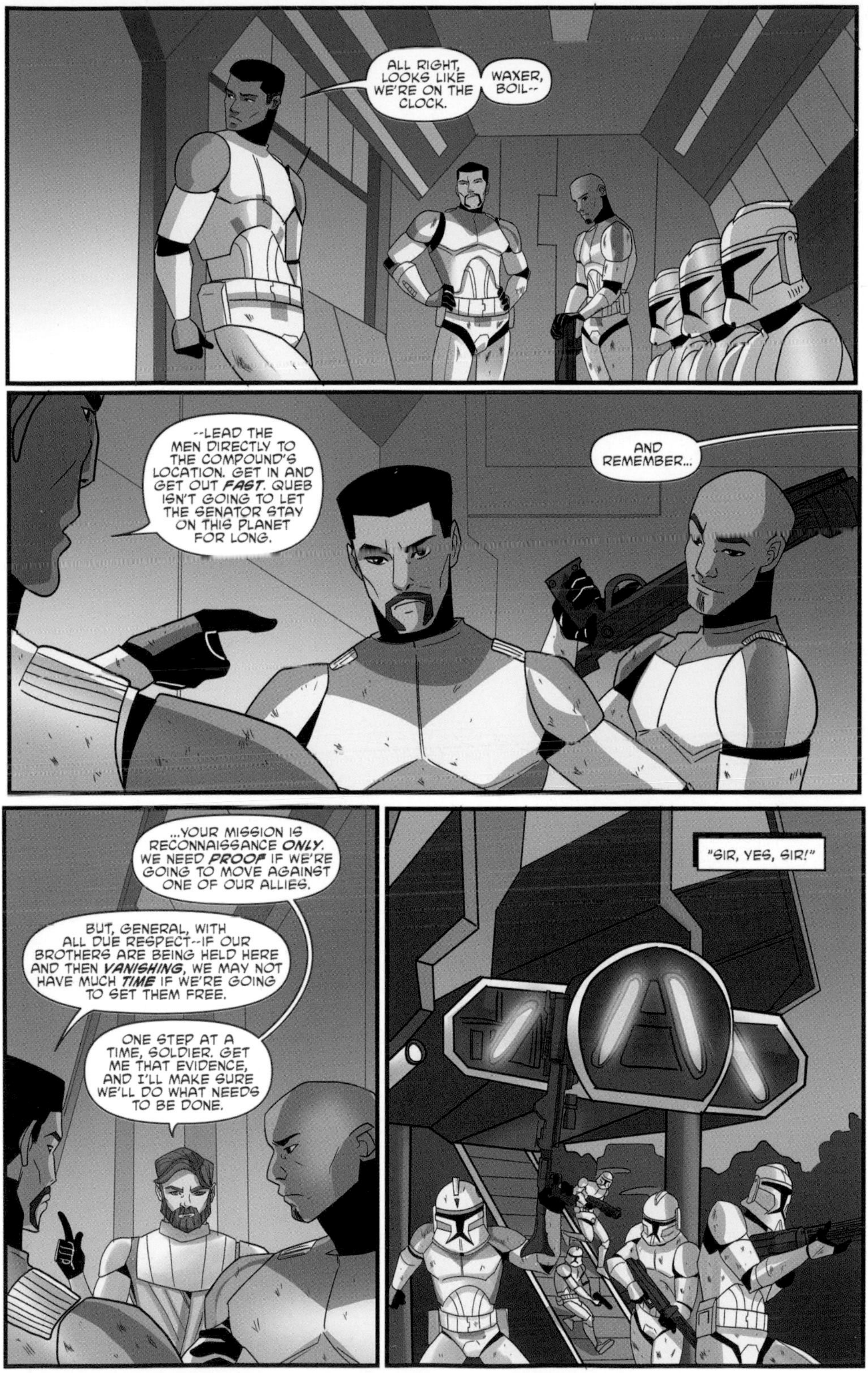
ALL RIGHT, LOOKS LIKE WE'RE ON THE CLOCK.
WAXER, BOIL--
--LEAD THE MEN DIRECTLY TO THE COMPOUND'S LOCATION. GET IN AND GET OUT FAST. QUEB ISN'T GOING TO LET THE SENATOR STAY ON THIS PLANET FOR LONG.
AND REMEMBER...
...YOUR MISSION IS RECONNAISSANCE ONLY. WE NEED PROOF IF WE'RE GOING TO MOVE AGAINST ONE OF OUR ALLIES.
BUT, GENERAL, WITH ALL DUE RESPECT--IF OUR BROTHERS ARE BEING HELD HERE AND THEN VANISHING, WE MAY NOT HAVE MUCH TIME IF WE'RE GOING TO SET THEM FREE.
ONE STEP AT A TIME, SOLDIER. GET ME THAT EVIDENCE, AND I'LL MAKE SURE WE'LL DO WHAT NEEDS TO BE DONE.
"SIR, YES, SIR!"

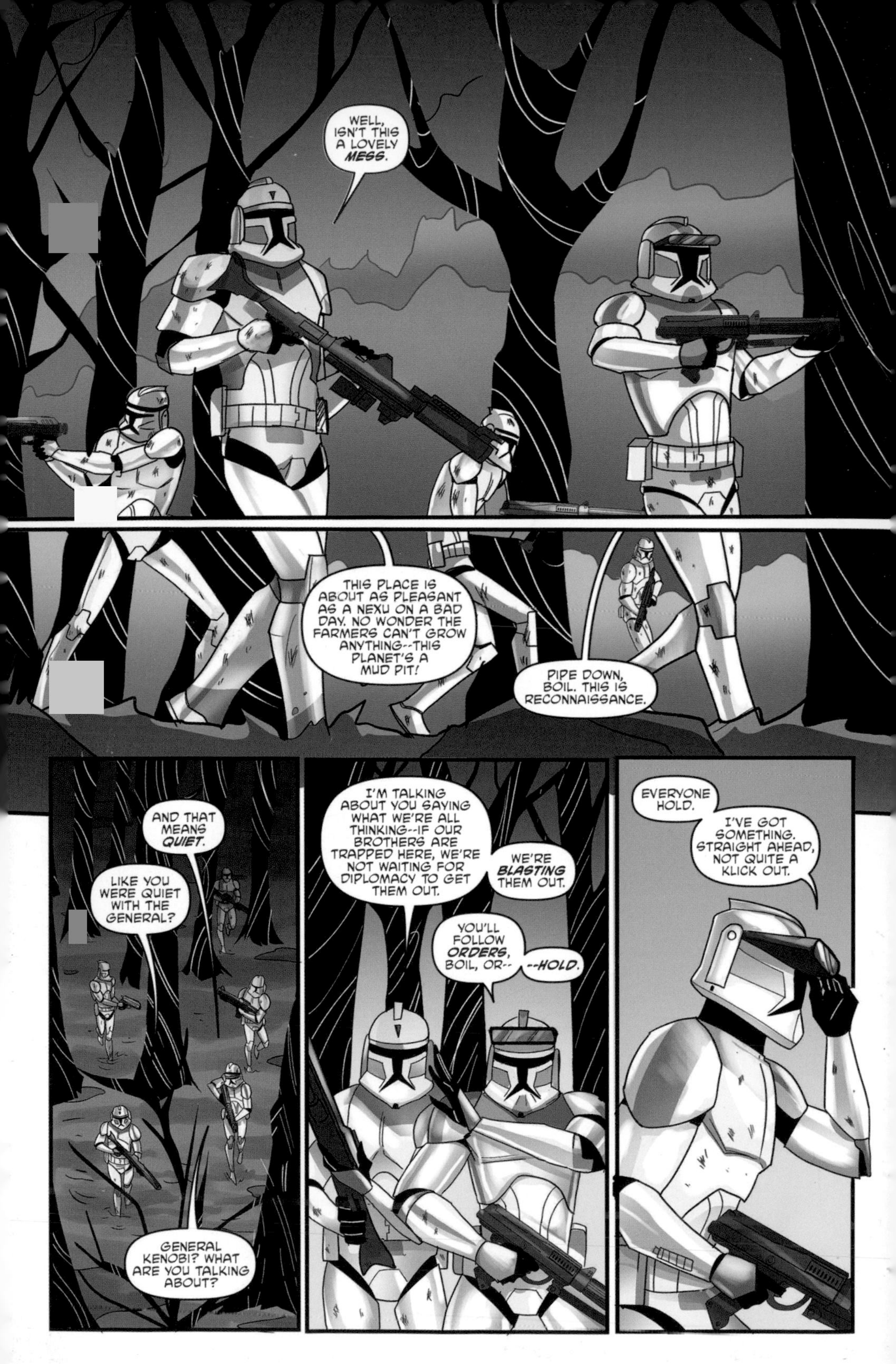
WELL, ISN'T THIS A LOVELY *MESS*.
THIS PLACE IS ABOUT AS PLEASANT AS A NEXU ON A BAD DAY. NO WONDER THE FARMERS CAN'T GROW ANYTHING--THIS PLANET'S A MUD PIT!
PIPE DOWN, BOIL. THIS IS RECONNAISSANCE.
AND THAT MEANS *QUIET*.
LIKE YOU WERE QUIET WITH THE GENERAL?
GENERAL KENOBI? WHAT ARE YOU TALKING ABOUT?
I'M TALKING ABOUT YOU SAYING WHAT WE'RE ALL THINKING--IF OUR BROTHERS ARE TRAPPED HERE, WE'RE NOT WAITING FOR DIPLOMACY TO GET THEM OUT.
WE'RE *BLASTING* THEM OUT.
YOU'LL FOLLOW *ORDERS*, BOIL, OR--
--*HOLD*.
EVERYONE HOLD.
I'VE GOT SOMETHING. STRAIGHT AHEAD, NOT QUITE A KLICK OUT.

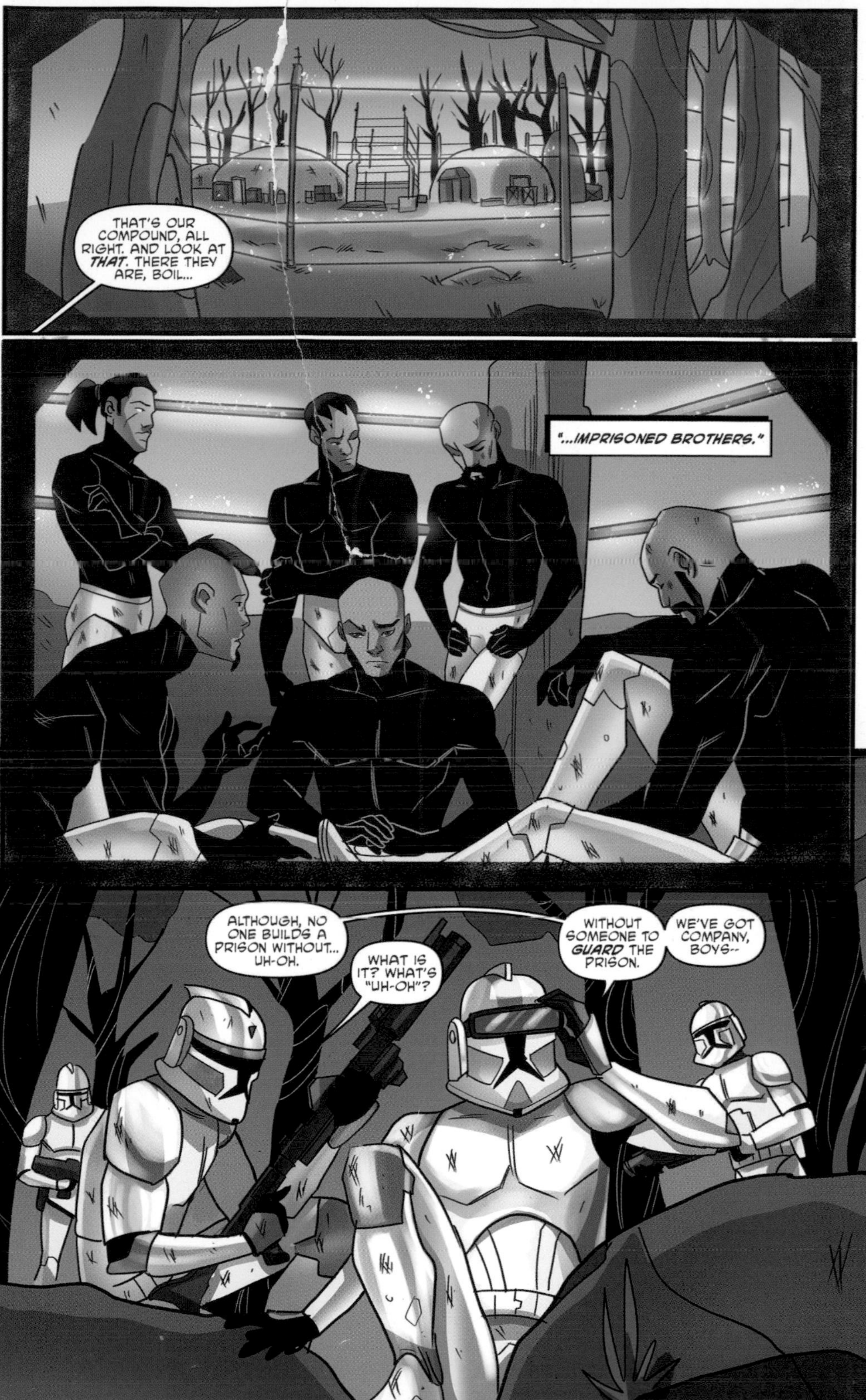
THAT'S OUR COMPOUND, ALL RIGHT. AND LOOK AT THAT. THERE THEY ARE, BOIL...
"...IMPRISONED BROTHERS."
ALTHOUGH, NO ONE BUILDS A PRISON WITHOUT... UH-OH.
WHAT IS IT? WHAT'S "UH-OH"?
WITHOUT SOMEONE TO GUARD THE PRISON.
WE'VE GOT COMPANY, BOYS--

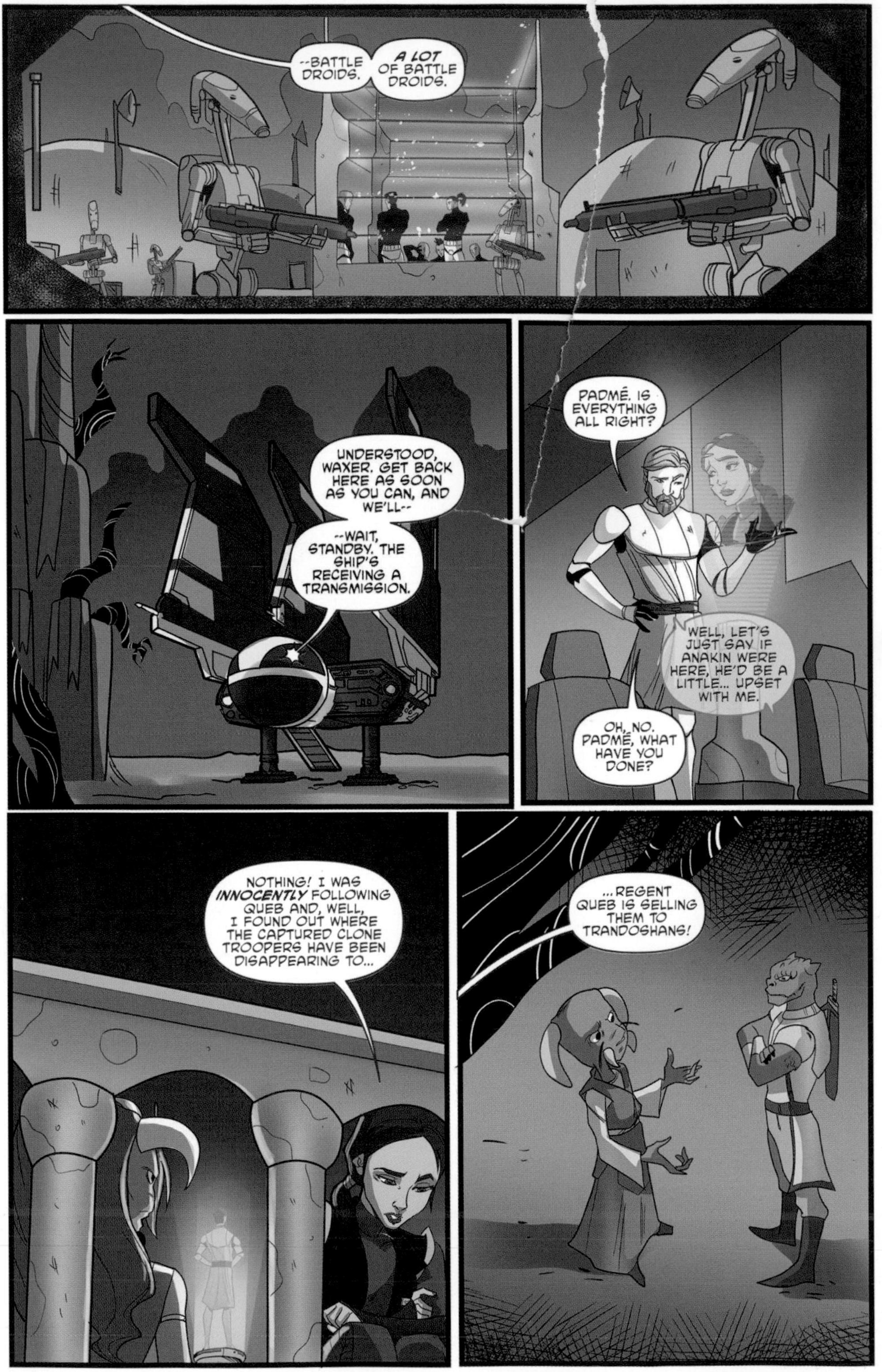
--BATTLE DROIDS.
A LOT OF BATTLE DROIDS.
UNDERSTOOD, WAXER. GET BACK HERE AS SOON AS YOU CAN, AND WE'LL--
--WAIT, STANDBY. THE SHIP'S RECEIVING A TRANSMISSION.
PADMÉ. IS EVERYTHING ALL RIGHT?
WELL, LET'S JUST SAY IF ANAKIN WERE HERE, HE'D BE A LITTLE... UPSET WITH ME.
OH, NO. PADMÉ, WHAT HAVE YOU DONE?
NOTHING! I WAS INNOCENTLY FOLLOWING QUEB AND, WELL, I FOUND OUT WHERE THE CAPTURED CLONE TROOPERS HAVE BEEN DISAPPEARING TO...
...REGENT QUEB IS SELLING THEM TO TRANDOSHANS!

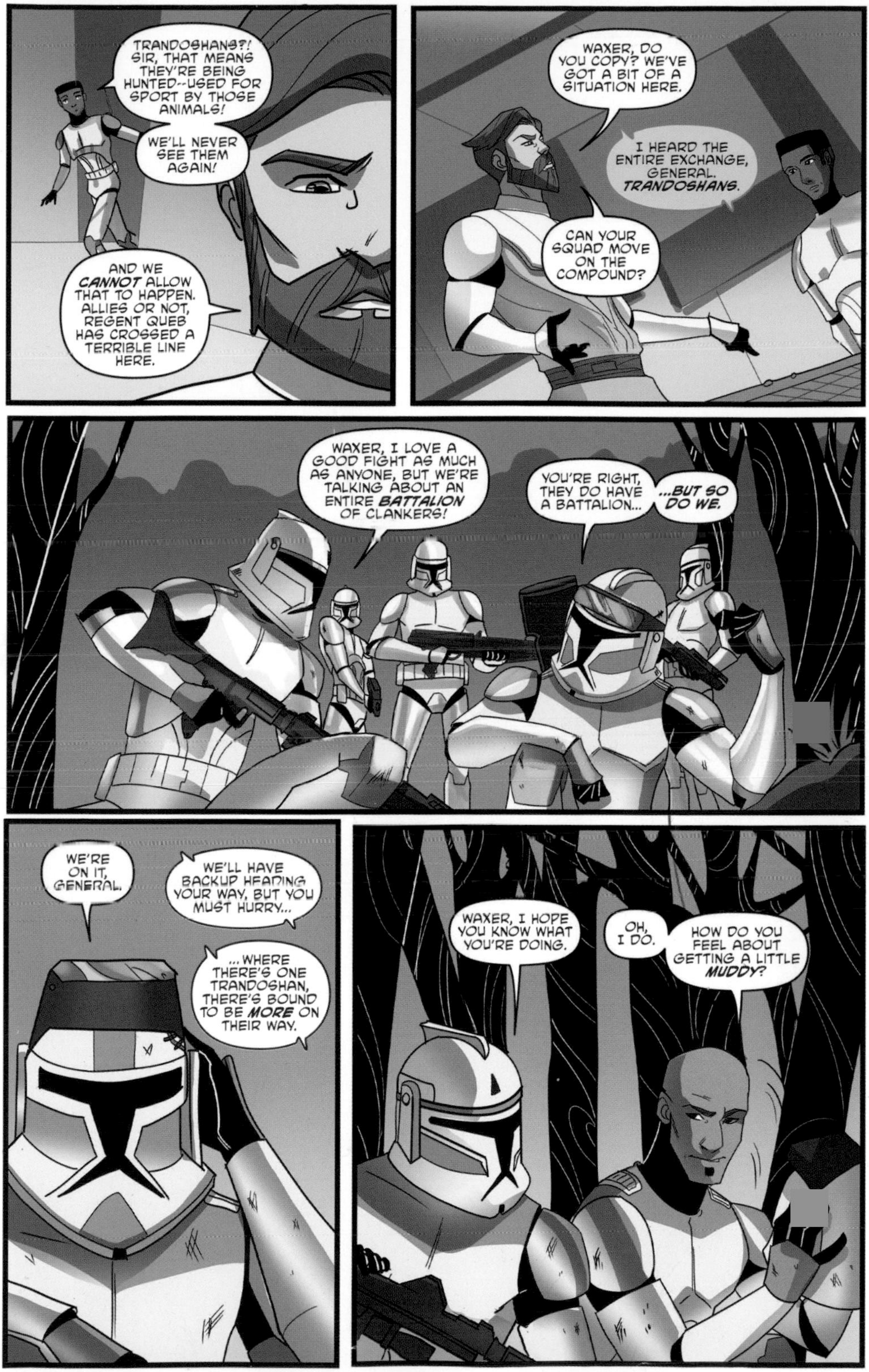
TRANDOSHANS?! SIR, THAT MEANS THEY'RE BEING HUNTED--USED FOR SPORT BY THOSE ANIMALS!
WE'LL NEVER SEE THEM AGAIN!
AND WE *CANNOT* ALLOW THAT TO HAPPEN. ALLIES OR NOT, REGENT QUEB HAS CROSSED A TERRIBLE LINE HERE.
WAXER, DO YOU COPY? WE'VE GOT A BIT OF A SITUATION HERE.
I HEARD THE ENTIRE EXCHANGE, GENERAL. *TRANDOSHANS*.
CAN YOUR SQUAD MOVE ON THE COMPOUND?
WAXER, I LOVE A GOOD FIGHT AS MUCH AS ANYONE, BUT WE'RE TALKING ABOUT AN ENTIRE *BATTALION* OF CLANKERS!
YOU'RE RIGHT, THEY DO HAVE A BATTALION...
...BUT SO DO WE.
WE'RE ON IT, GENERAL.
WE'LL HAVE BACKUP HEADING YOUR WAY, BUT YOU MUST HURRY...
...WHERE THERE'S ONE TRANDOSHAN, THERE'S BOUND TO BE *MORE* ON THEIR WAY.
WAXER, I HOPE YOU KNOW WHAT YOU'RE DOING.
OH, I DO.
HOW DO YOU FEEL ABOUT GETTING A LITTLE *MUDDY?*

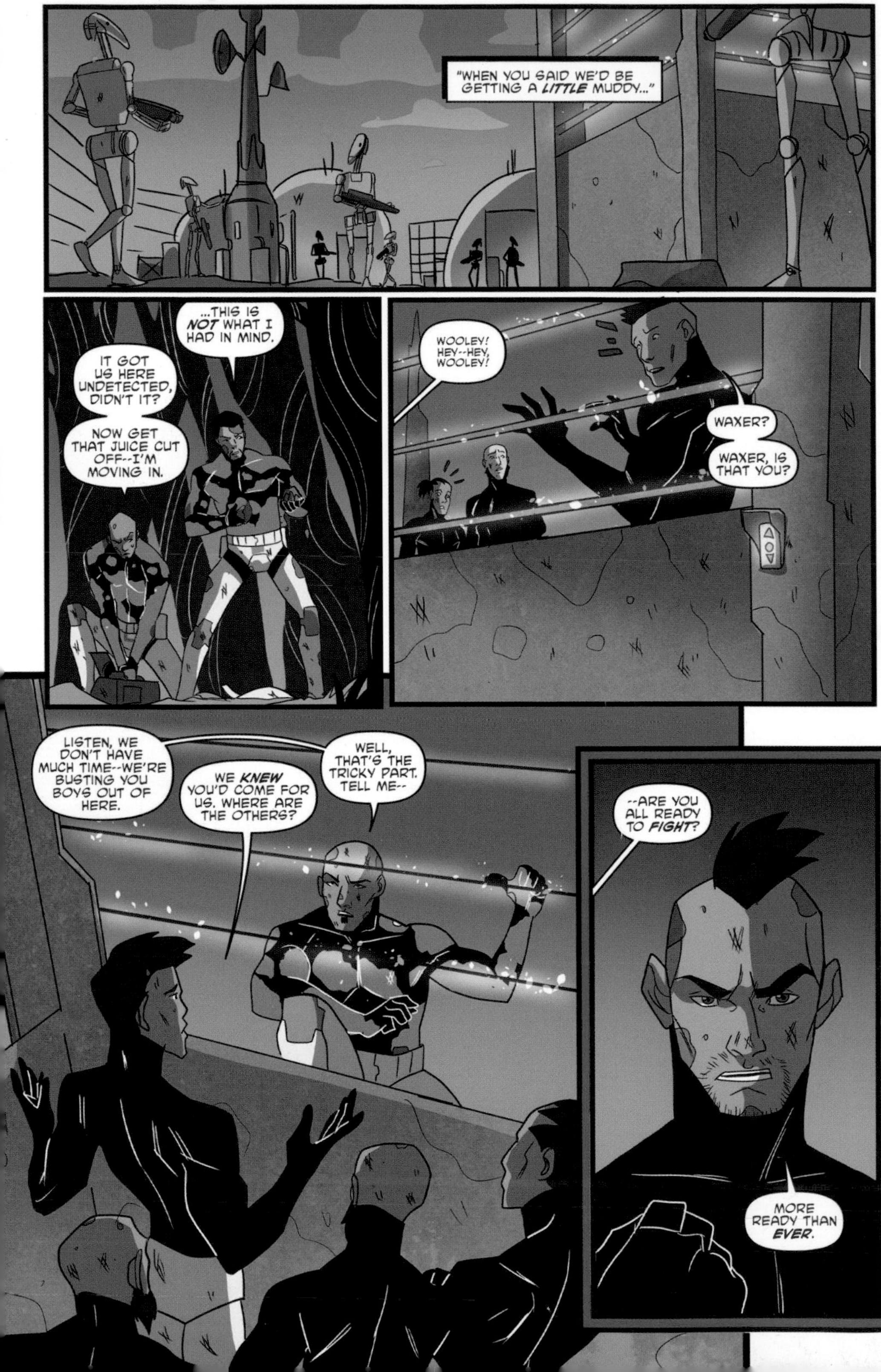
"WHEN YOU SAID WE'D BE GETTING A *LITTLE* MUDDY..."
...THIS IS *NOT* WHAT I HAD IN MIND.
IT GOT US HERE UNDETECTED, DIDN'T IT?
NOW GET THAT JUICE CUT OFF--I'M MOVING IN.
WOOLEY! HEY--HEY, WOOLEY!
WAXER?
WAXER, IS THAT YOU?
LISTEN, WE DON'T HAVE MUCH TIME--WE'RE BUSTING YOU BOYS OUT OF HERE.
WE *KNEW* YOU'D COME FOR US. WHERE ARE THE OTHERS?
WELL, THAT'S THE TRICKY PART. TELL ME--
--ARE YOU ALL READY TO *FIGHT*?
MORE READY THAN *EVER*.

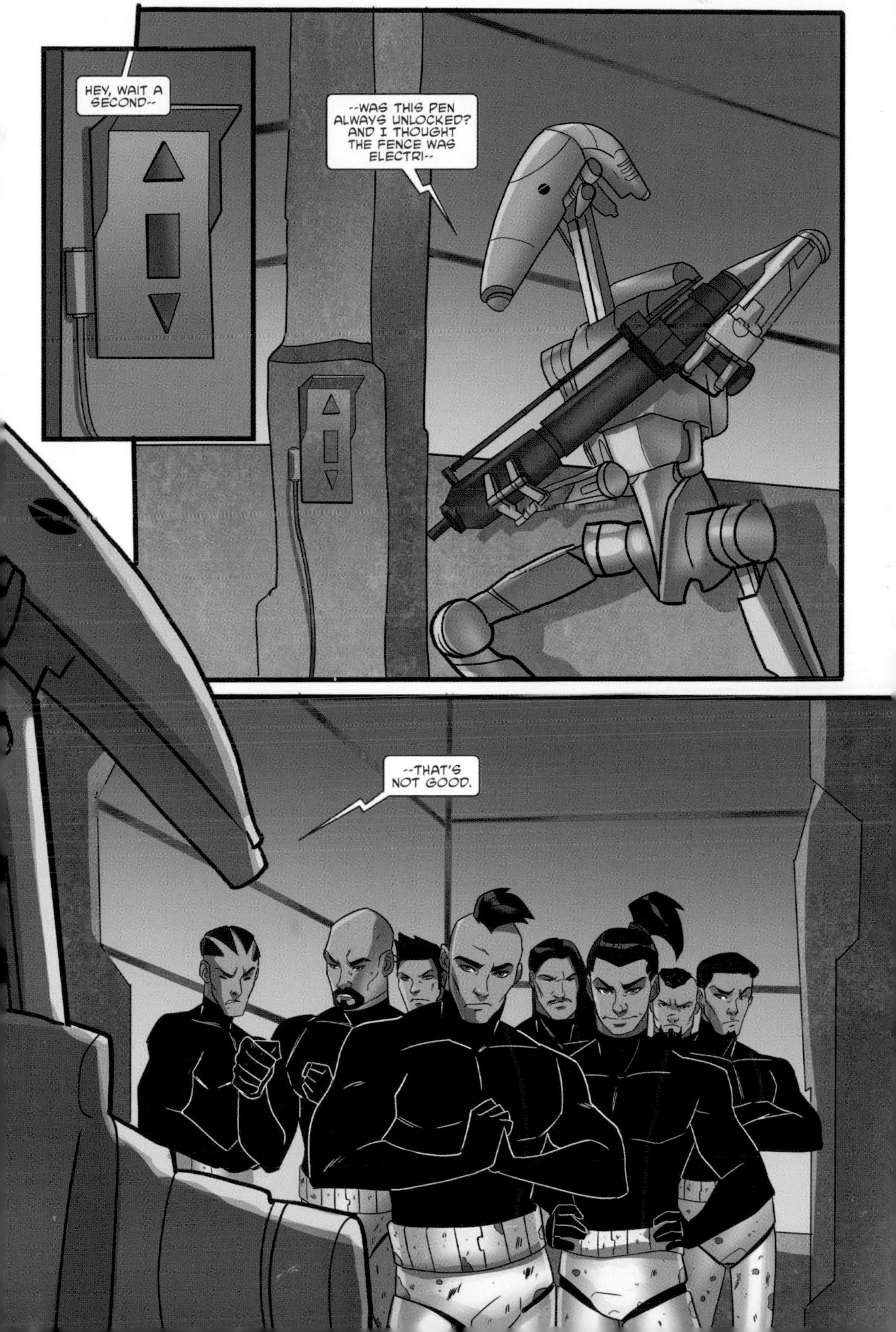
HEY, WAIT A SECOND--
--WAS THIS PEN ALWAYS UNLOCKED? AND I THOUGHT THE FENCE WAS ELECTRI--
--THAT'S NOT GOOD.

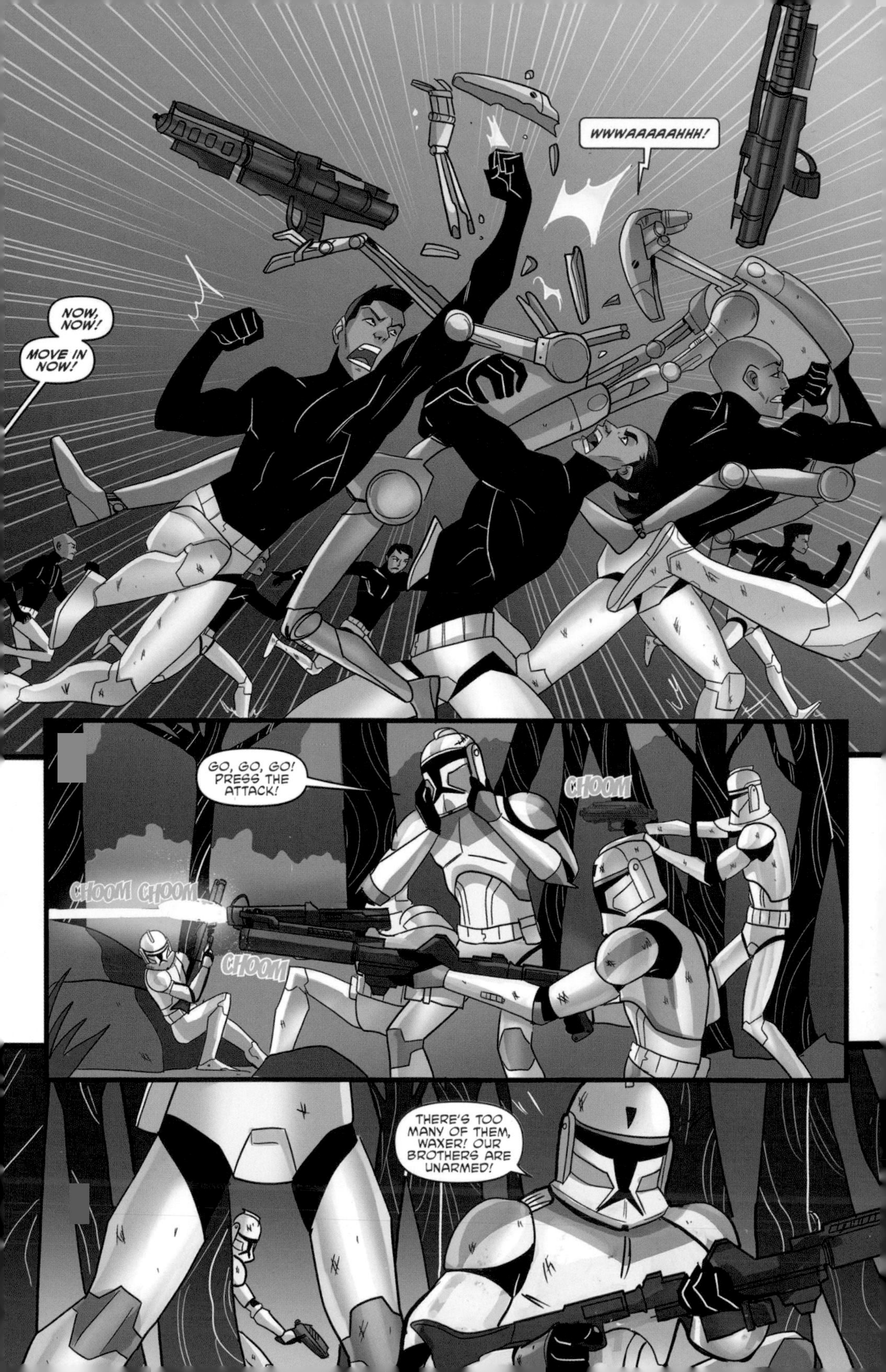
WWWAAAAAHHH!
NOW, NOW!
MOVE IN NOW!
GO, GO, GO! PRESS THE ATTACK!
CHOOM
CHOOM CHOOM
CHOOM
THERE'S TOO MANY OF THEM, WAXER! OUR BROTHERS ARE UNARMED!

THEY'RE BEING OVERWHELM--
CHOOM
CHOOM
CHOOM
LOOKS LIKE YOU BOYS CAN USE A HAND.
CHOOM
CHOOM

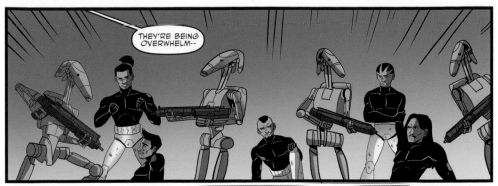

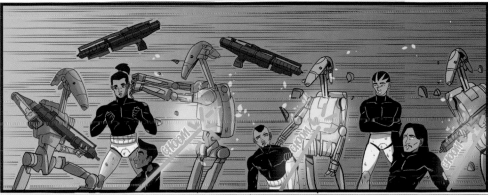

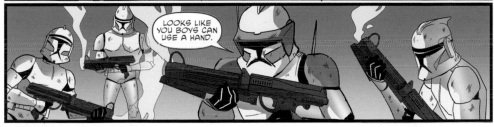

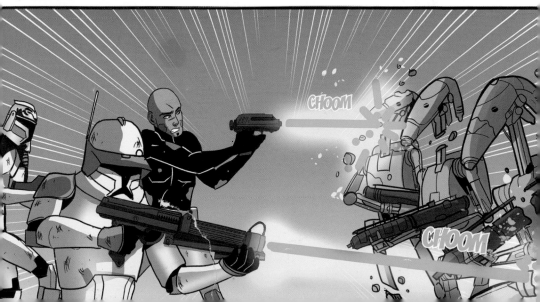

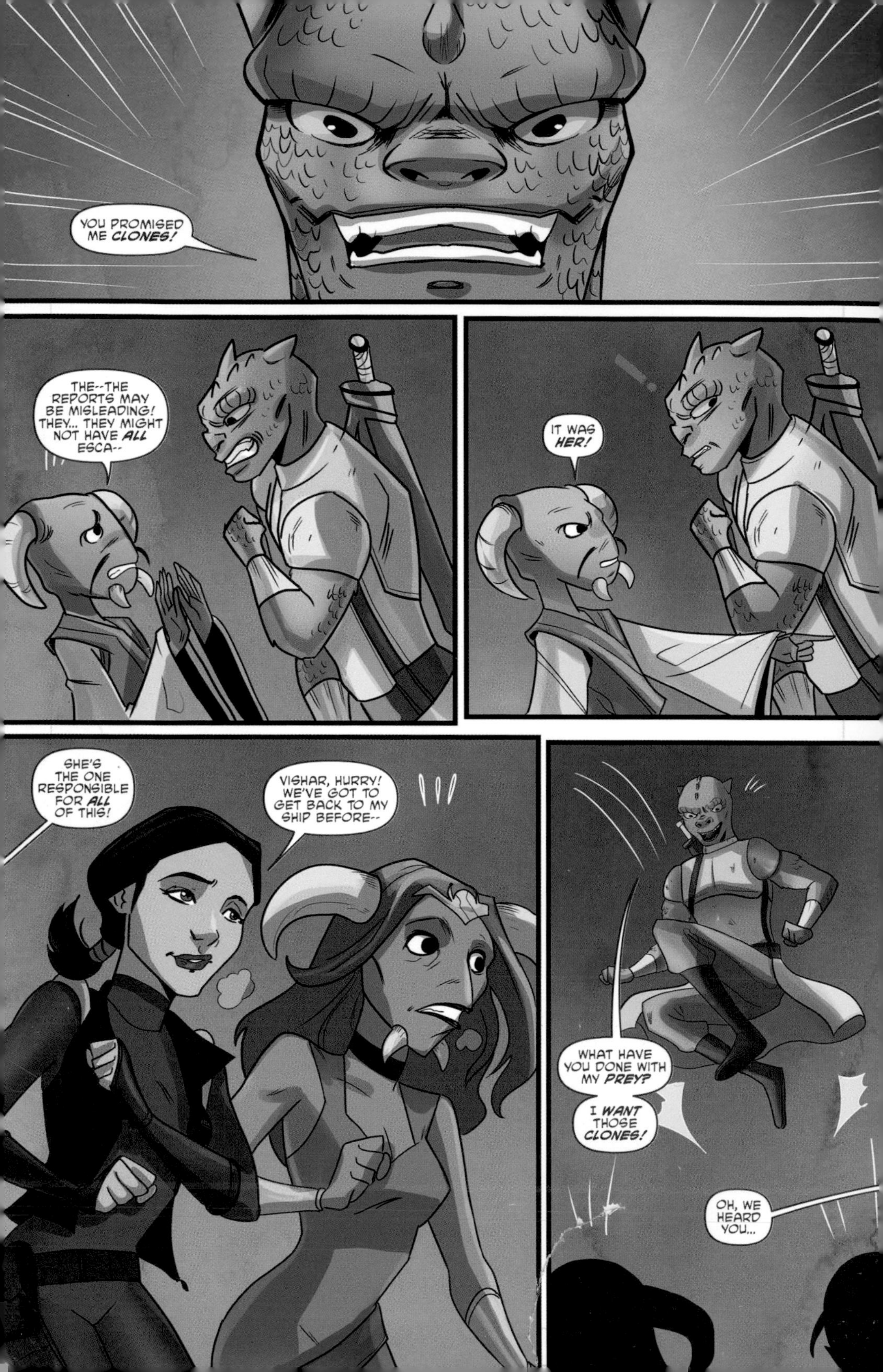
YOU PROMISED ME CLONES!
THE--THE REPORTS MAY BE MISLEADING! THEY... THEY MIGHT NOT HAVE ALL ESCA--
IT WAS HER!
SHE'S THE ONE RESPONSIBLE FOR ALL OF THIS!
VISHAR, HURRY! WE'VE GOT TO GET BACK TO MY SHIP BEFORE--
WHAT HAVE YOU DONE WITH MY PREY?
I WANT THOSE CLONES!
OH, WE HEARD YOU...

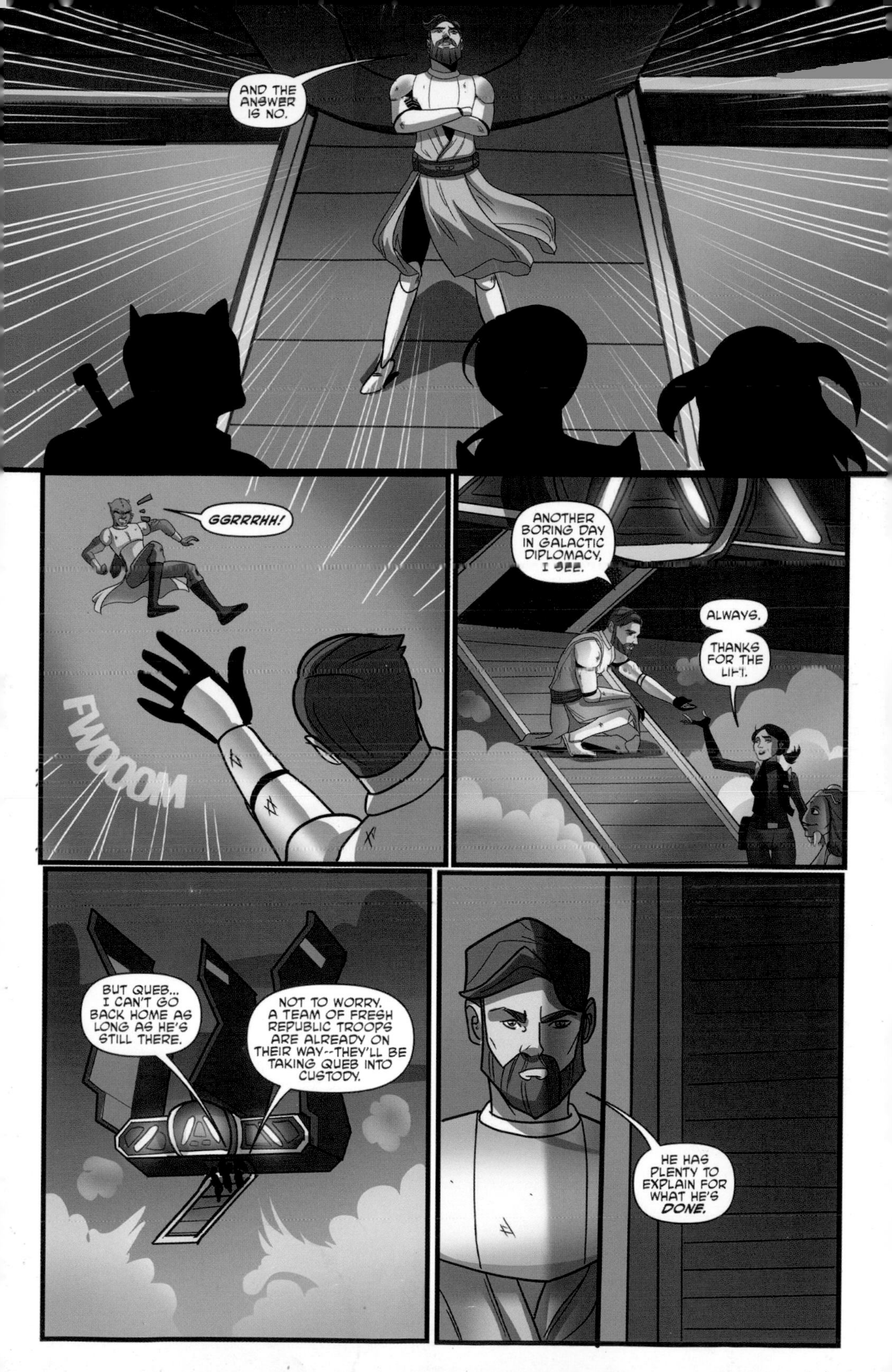
AND THE ANSWER IS NO.
GGRRRHH!
FWOOOM
ANOTHER BORING DAY IN GALACTIC DIPLOMACY, I SEE.
ALWAYS.
THANKS FOR THE LIFT.
BUT QUEB... I CAN'T GO BACK HOME AS LONG AS HE'S STILL THERE.
NOT TO WORRY. A TEAM OF FRESH REPUBLIC TROOPS ARE ALREADY ON THEIR WAY--THEY'LL BE TAKING QUEB INTO CUSTODY.
HE HAS PLENTY TO EXPLAIN FOR WHAT HE'S *DONE.*

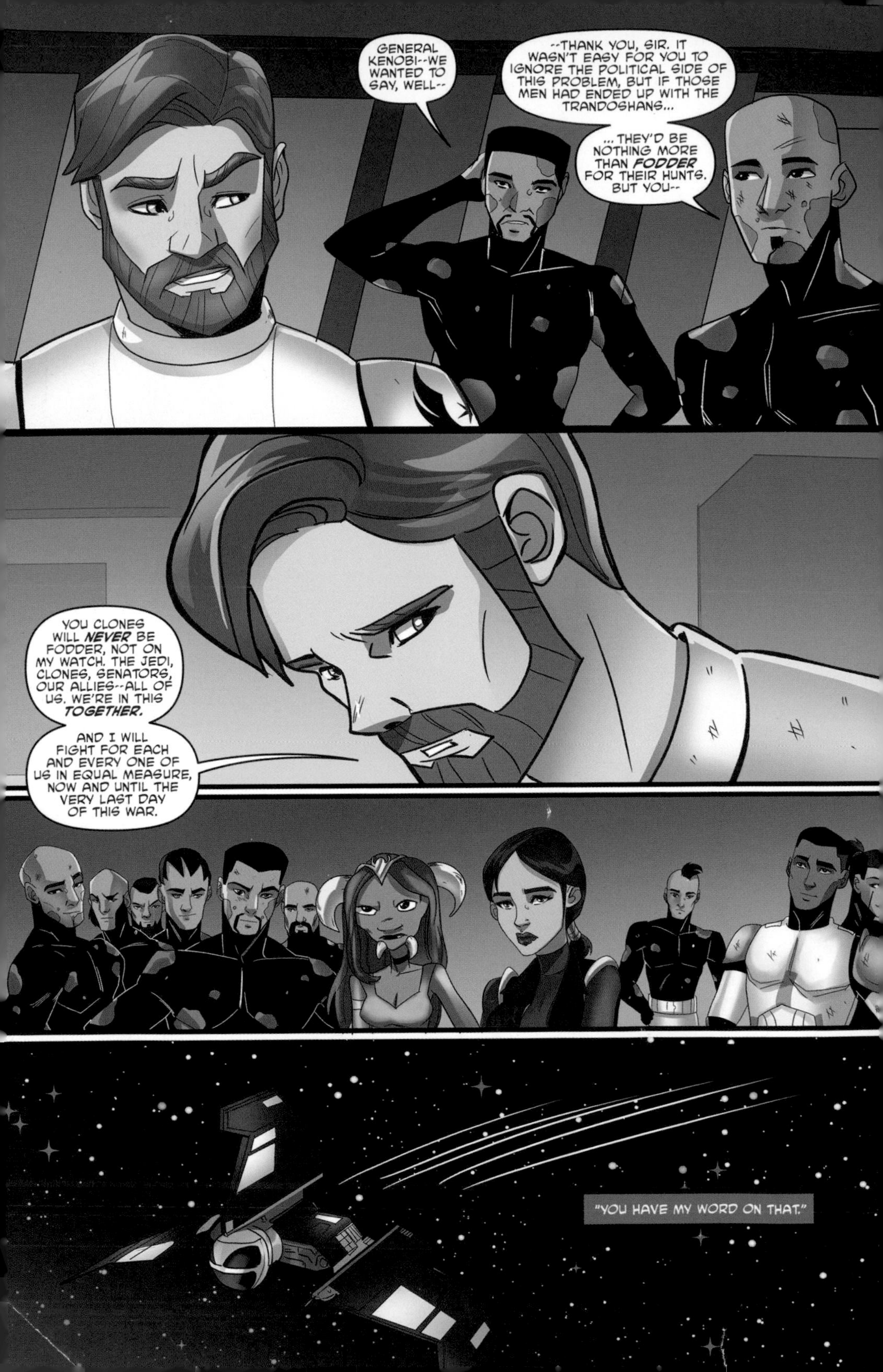
GENERAL KENOBI--WE WANTED TO SAY, WELL--
--THANK YOU, SIR. IT WASN'T EASY FOR YOU TO IGNORE THE POLITICAL SIDE OF THIS PROBLEM, BUT IF THOSE MEN HAD ENDED UP WITH THE TRANDOSHANS...
...THEY'D BE NOTHING MORE THAN FODDER FOR THEIR HUNTS. BUT YOU--
YOU CLONES WILL NEVER BE FODDER, NOT ON MY WATCH. THE JEDI, CLONES, SENATORS, OUR ALLIES--ALL OF US. WE'RE IN THIS TOGETHER.
AND I WILL FIGHT FOR EACH AND EVERY ONE OF US IN EQUAL MEASURE, NOW AND UNTIL THE VERY LAST DAY OF THIS WAR.
"YOU HAVE MY WORD ON THAT."

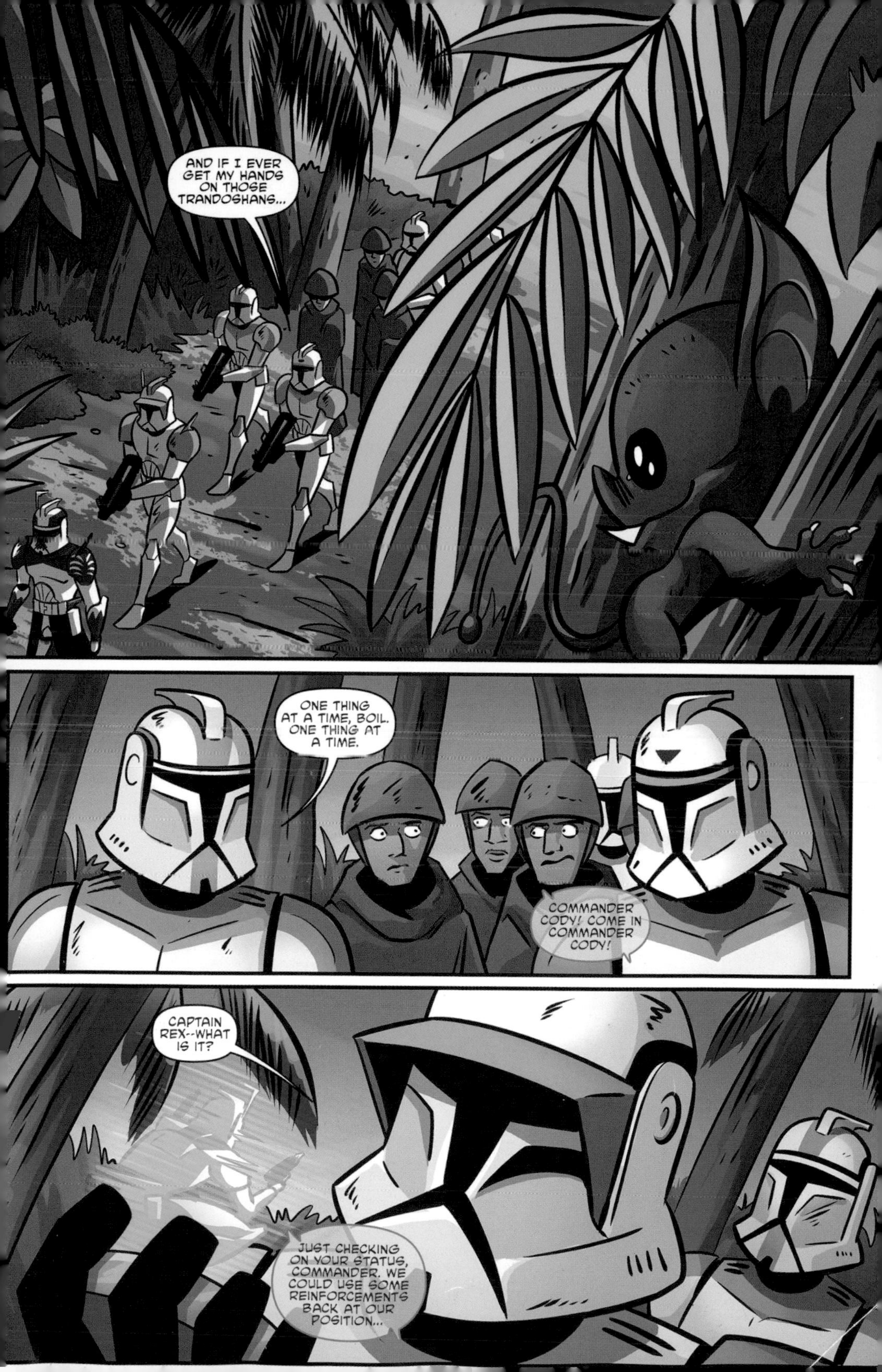
AND IF I EVER GET MY HANDS ON THOSE TRANDOSHANS...
ONE THING AT A TIME, BOIL. ONE THING AT A TIME.
COMMANDER CODY! COME IN COMMANDER CODY!
CAPTAIN REX--WHAT IS IT?
JUST CHECKING ON YOUR STATUS, COMMANDER. WE COULD USE SOME REINFORCEMENTS BACK AT OUR POSITION...

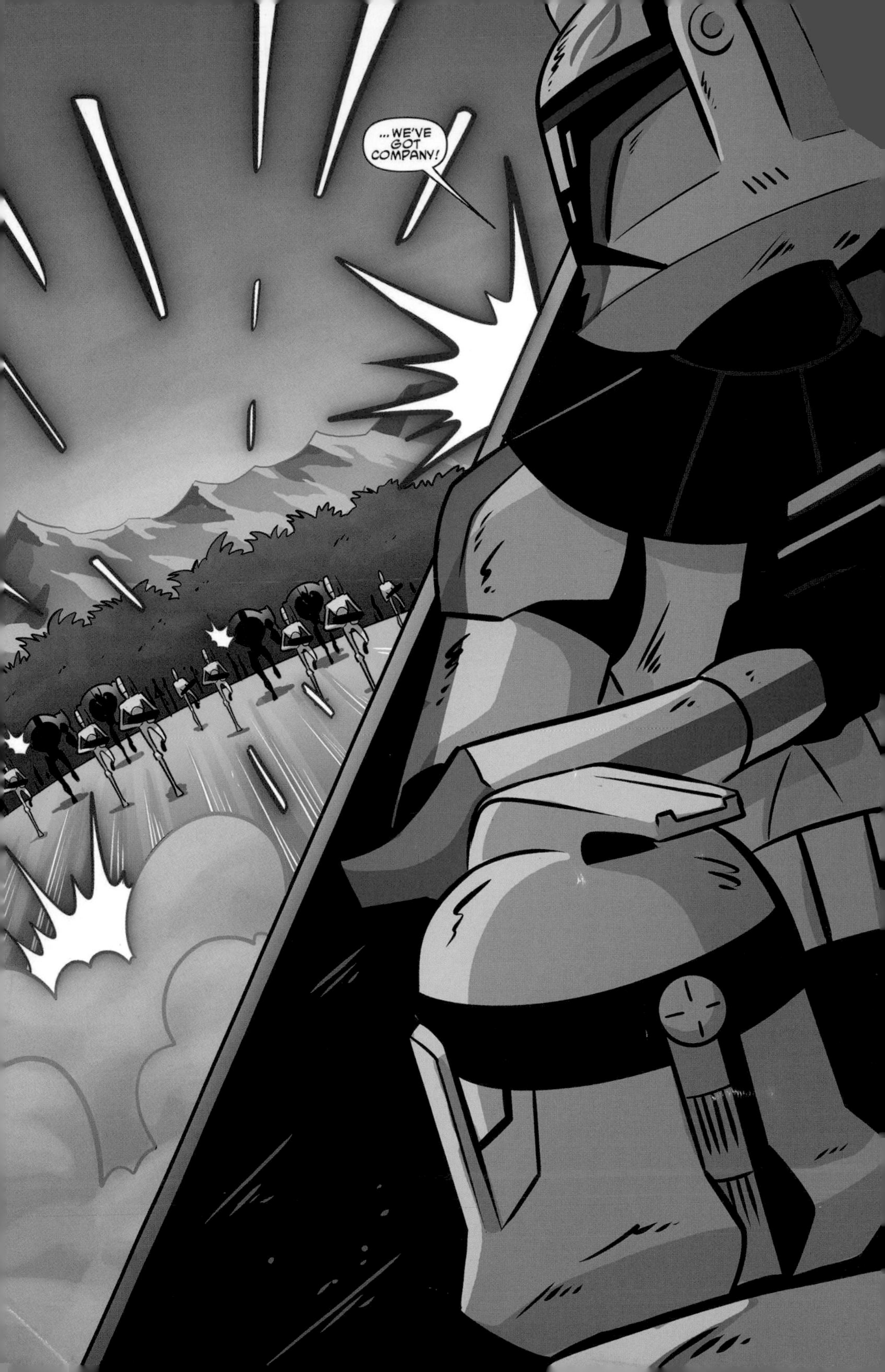
...WE'VE GOT COMPANY!

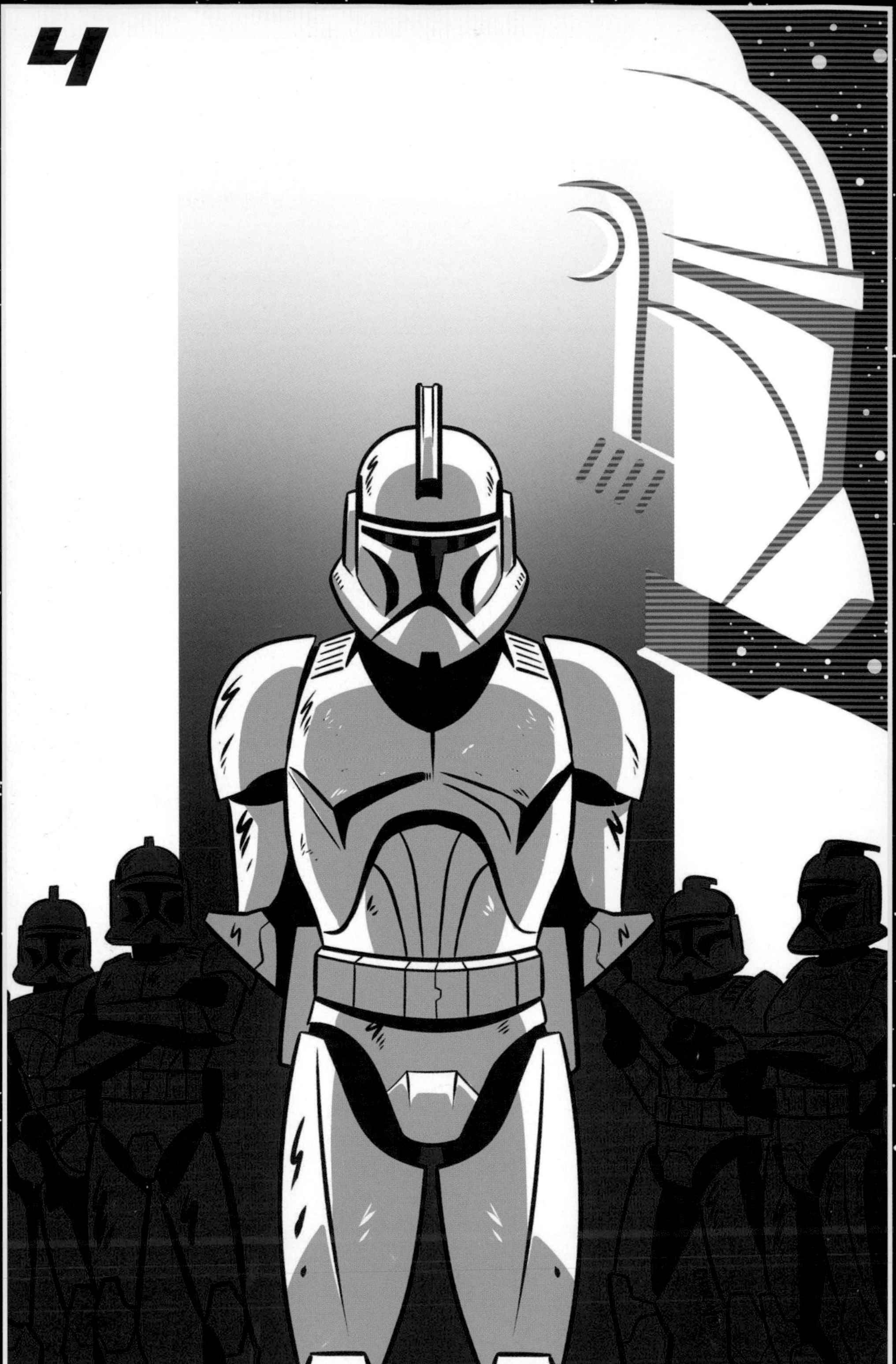
4

Art by Derek Charm

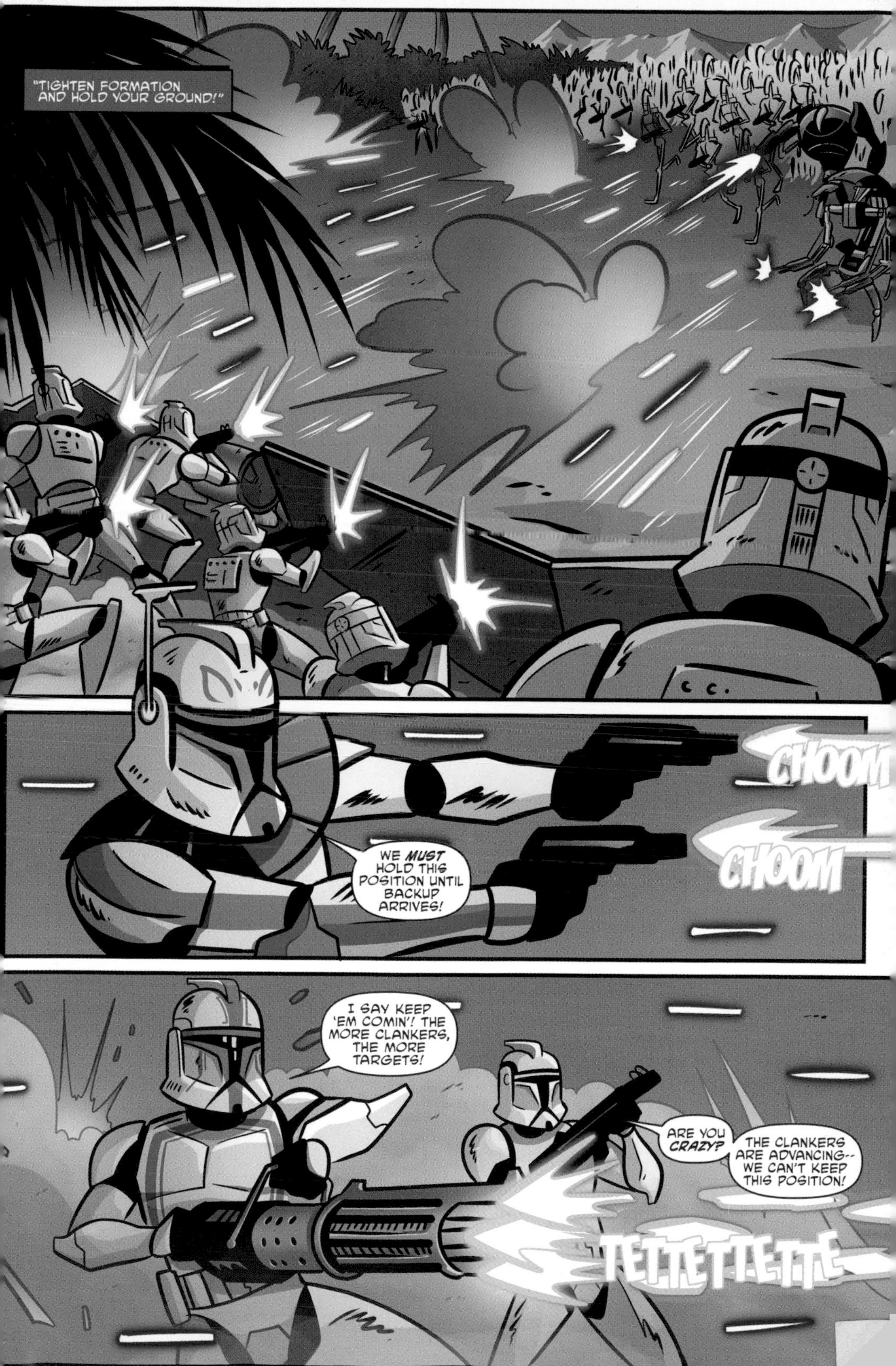
"TIGHTEN FORMATION AND HOLD YOUR GROUND!"
WE MUST HOLD THIS POSITION UNTIL BACKUP ARRIVES!
CHOOM
CHOOM
I SAY KEEP 'EM COMIN'! THE MORE CLANKERS, THE MORE TARGETS!
ARE YOU CRAZY?
THE CLANKERS ARE ADVANCING-- WE CAN'T KEEP THIS POSITION!
TETTETTETTE

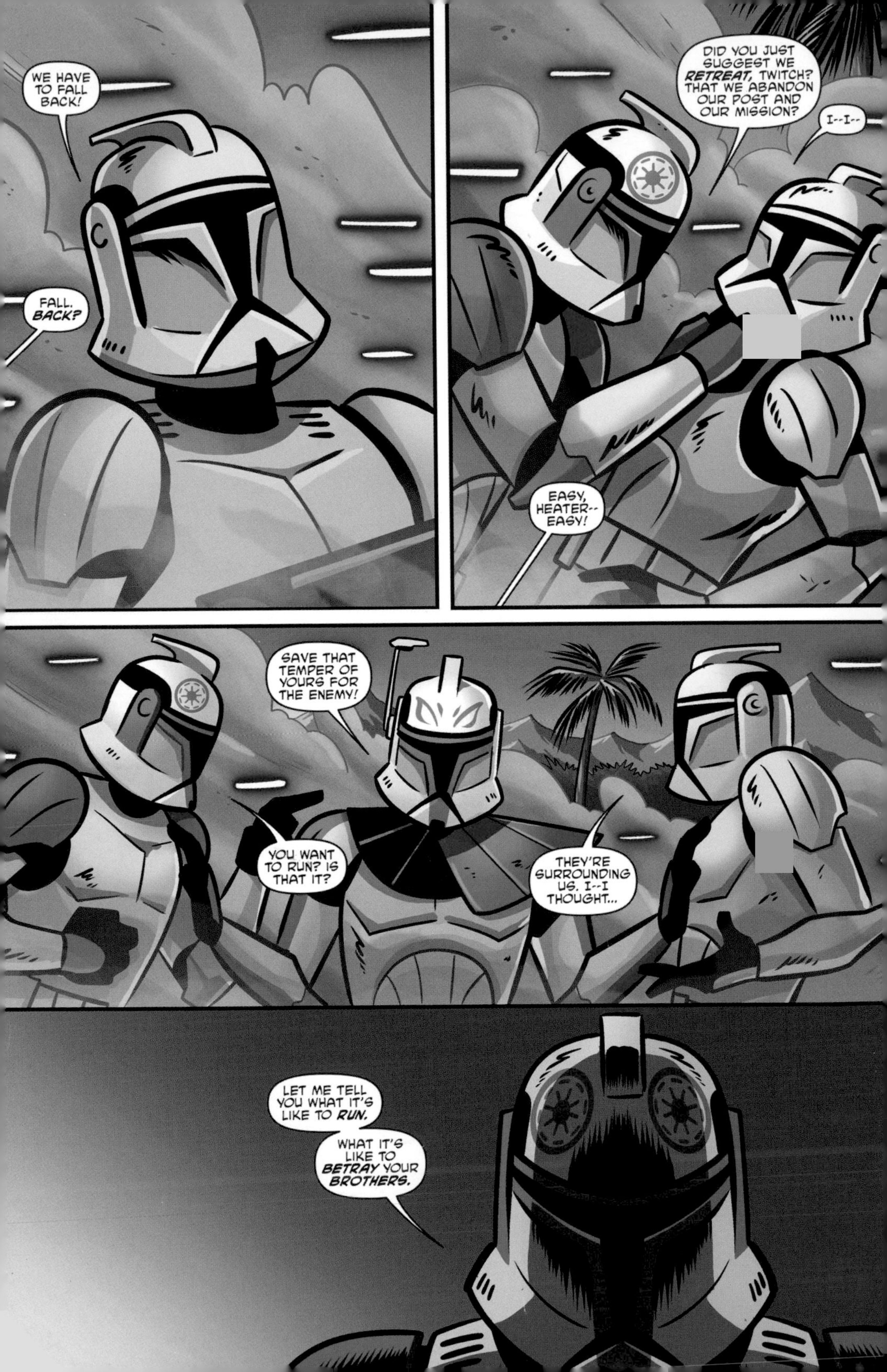
WE HAVE TO FALL BACK!
FALL. BACK?
DID YOU JUST SUGGEST WE RETREAT, TWITCH? THAT WE ABANDON OUR POST AND OUR MISSION?
I--I--
EASY, HEATER-- EASY!
SAVE THAT TEMPER OF YOURS FOR THE ENEMY!
YOU WANT TO RUN? IS THAT IT?
THEY'RE SURROUNDING US. I--I THOUGHT...
LET ME TELL YOU WHAT IT'S LIKE TO RUN.
WHAT IT'S LIKE TO BETRAY YOUR BROTHERS.

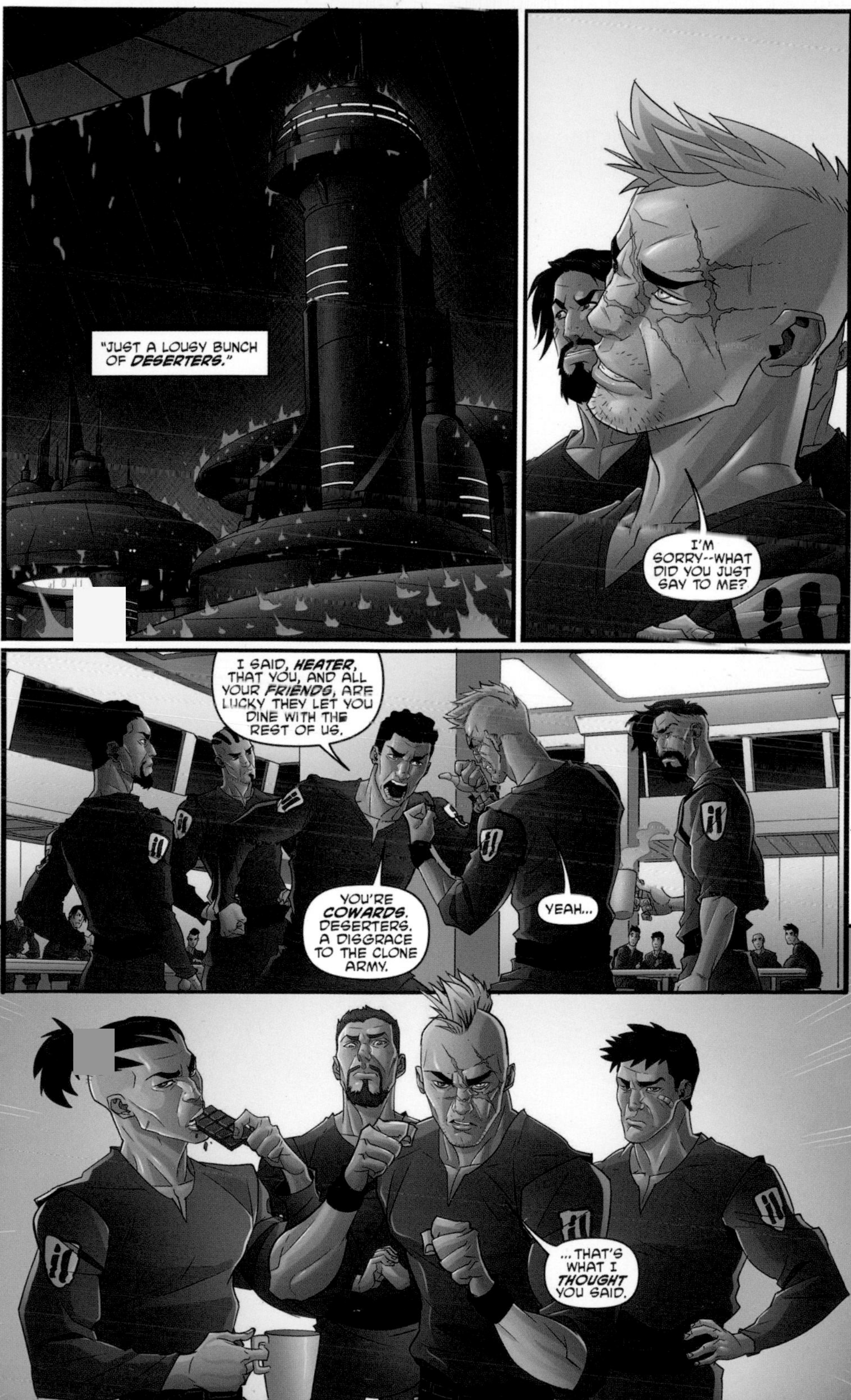
"JUST A LOUSY BUNCH OF *DESERTERS.*"
I'M SORRY--WHAT DID YOU JUST SAY TO ME?
I SAID, *HEATER*, THAT YOU, AND ALL YOUR *FRIENDS*, ARE LUCKY THEY LET YOU DINE WITH THE REST OF US.
YOU'RE *COWARDS*. DESERTERS. A DISGRACE TO THE CLONE ARMY.
YEAH...
...THAT'S WHAT I *THOUGHT* YOU SAID.

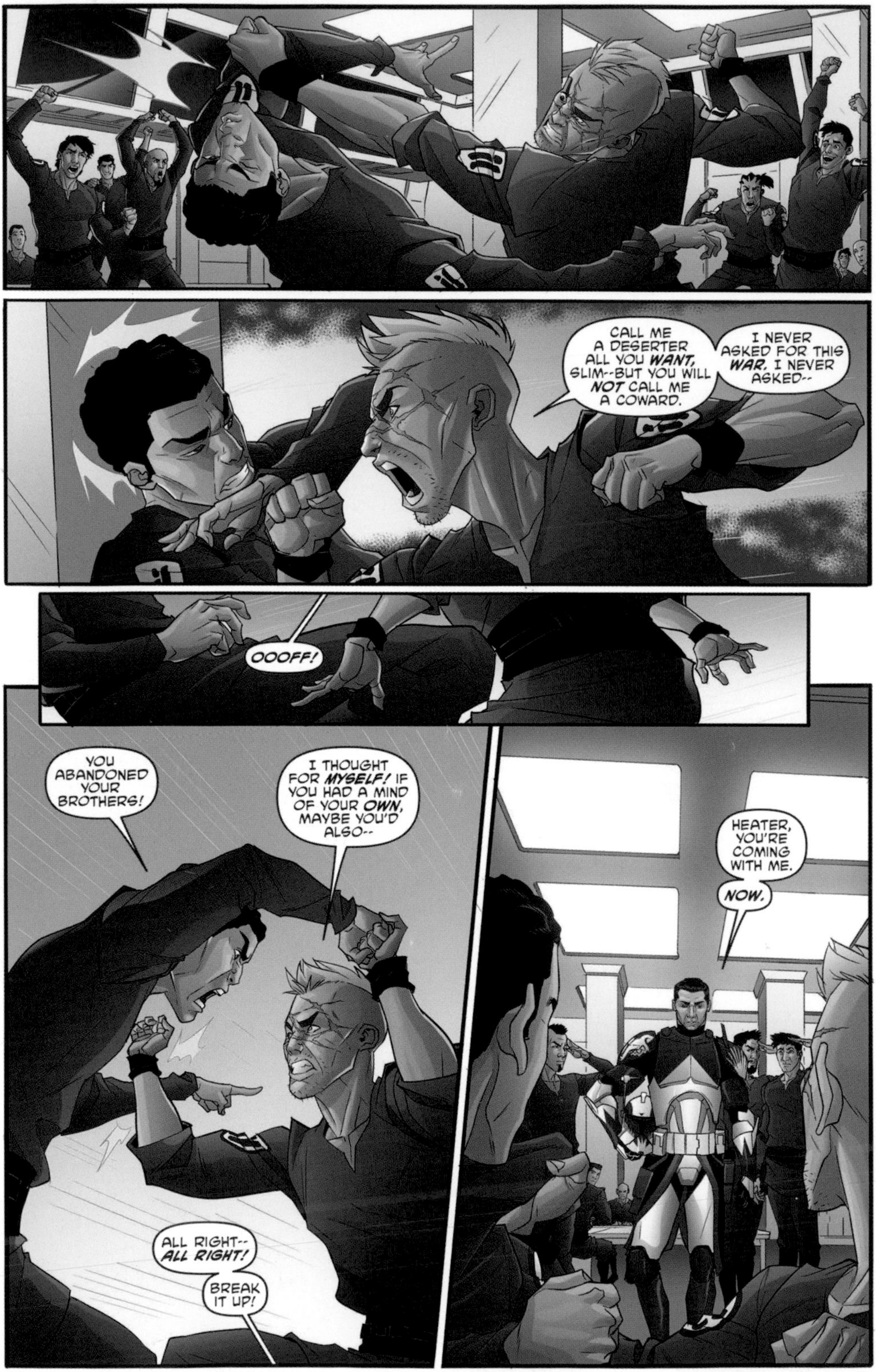
CALL ME A DESERTER ALL YOU *WANT,* SLIM--BUT YOU WILL *NOT* CALL ME A COWARD.
I NEVER ASKED FOR THIS *WAR.* I NEVER ASKED--
OOOFF!
YOU ABANDONED YOUR BROTHERS!
I THOUGHT FOR *MYSELF!* IF YOU HAD A MIND OF YOUR *OWN,* MAYBE YOU'D ALSO--
ALL RIGHT-- *ALL RIGHT!*
BREAK IT UP!
HEATER, YOU'RE COMING WITH ME.
NOW.

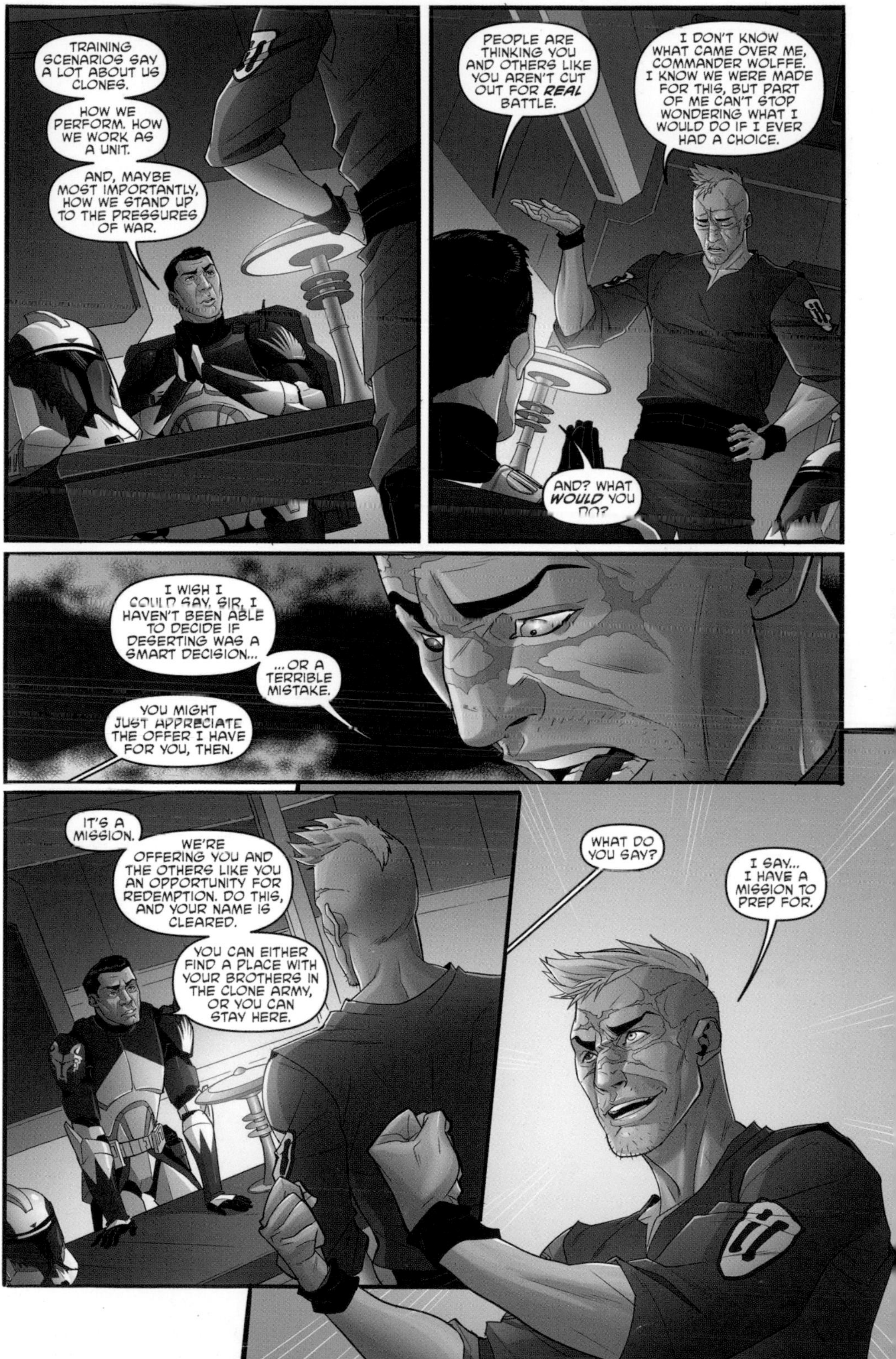
TRAINING SCENARIOS SAY A LOT ABOUT US CLONES.
HOW WE PERFORM. HOW WE WORK AS A UNIT.
AND, MAYBE MOST IMPORTANTLY, HOW WE STAND UP TO THE PRESSURES OF WAR.
PEOPLE ARE THINKING YOU AND OTHERS LIKE YOU AREN'T CUT OUT FOR *REAL* BATTLE.
I DON'T KNOW WHAT CAME OVER ME, COMMANDER WOLFFE. I KNOW WE WERE MADE FOR THIS, BUT PART OF ME CAN'T STOP WONDERING WHAT I WOULD DO IF I EVER HAD A CHOICE.
AND? WHAT ***WOULD*** YOU DO?
I WISH I COULD SAY, SIR. I HAVEN'T BEEN ABLE TO DECIDE IF DESERTING WAS A SMART DECISION...
...OR A TERRIBLE MISTAKE.
YOU MIGHT JUST APPRECIATE THE OFFER I HAVE FOR YOU, THEN.
IT'S A MISSION.
WE'RE OFFERING YOU AND THE OTHERS LIKE YOU AN OPPORTUNITY FOR REDEMPTION. DO THIS, AND YOUR NAME IS CLEARED.
YOU CAN EITHER FIND A PLACE WITH YOUR BROTHERS IN THE CLONE ARMY, OR YOU CAN STAY HERE.
WHAT DO YOU SAY?
I SAY... I HAVE A MISSION TO PREP FOR.

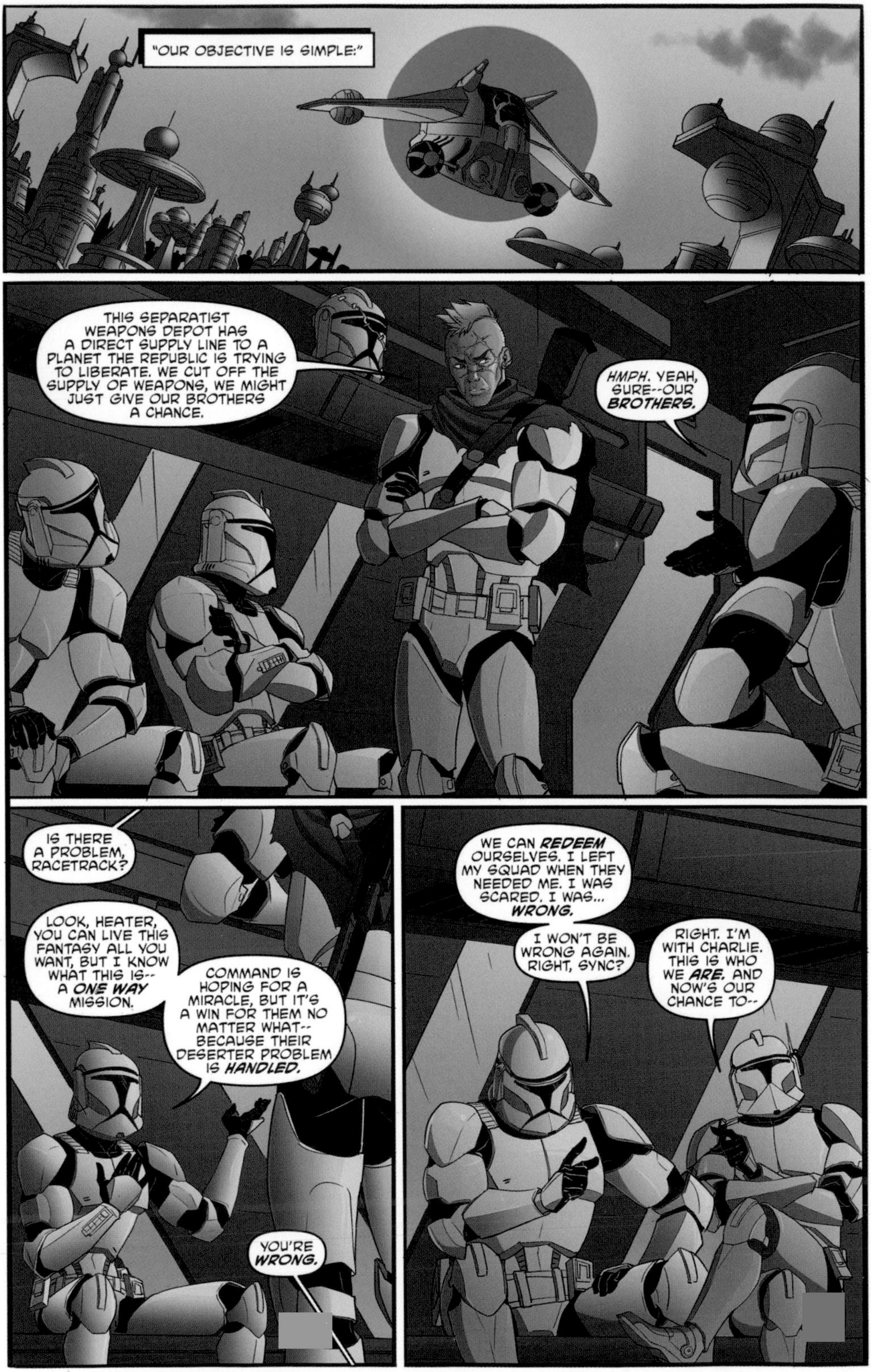
"OUR OBJECTIVE IS SIMPLE:"
THIS SEPARATIST WEAPONS DEPOT HAS A DIRECT SUPPLY LINE TO A PLANET THE REPUBLIC IS TRYING TO LIBERATE. WE CUT OFF THE SUPPLY OF WEAPONS, WE MIGHT JUST GIVE OUR BROTHERS A CHANCE.
HMPH. YEAH, SURE--OUR BROTHERS.
IS THERE A PROBLEM, RACETRACK?
LOOK, HEATER, YOU CAN LIVE THIS FANTASY ALL YOU WANT, BUT I KNOW WHAT THIS IS-- A ONE WAY MISSION.
COMMAND IS HOPING FOR A MIRACLE, BUT IT'S A WIN FOR THEM NO MATTER WHAT-- BECAUSE THEIR DESERTER PROBLEM IS HANDLED.
YOU'RE WRONG.
WE CAN REDEEM OURSELVES. I LEFT MY SQUAD WHEN THEY NEEDED ME. I WAS SCARED. I WAS... WRONG.
I WON'T BE WRONG AGAIN. RIGHT, SYNC?
RIGHT. I'M WITH CHARLIE. THIS IS WHO WE ARE. AND NOW'S OUR CHANCE TO--

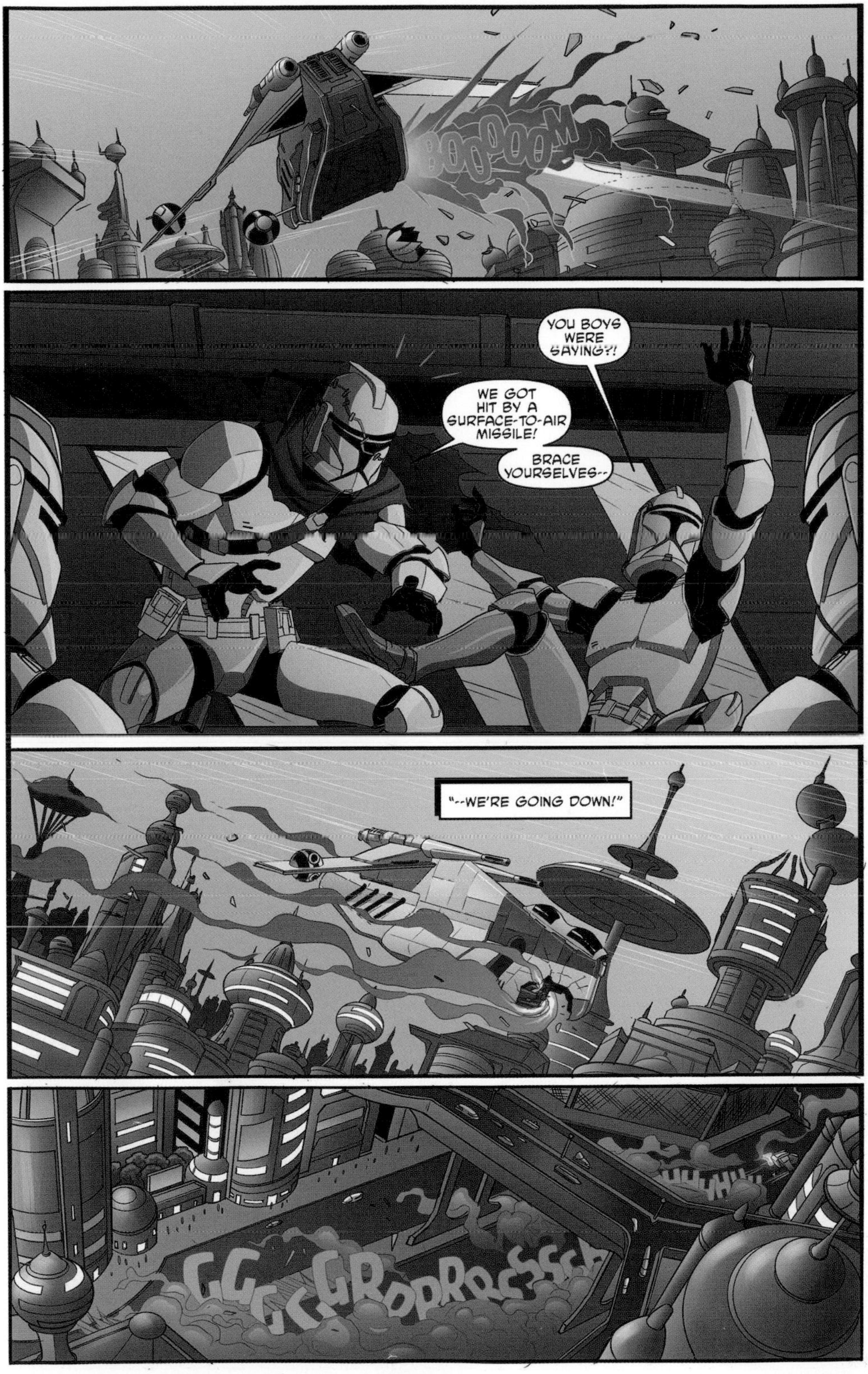
BOOOOOOM
YOU BOYS WERE SAYING?!
WE GOT HIT BY A SURFACE-TO-AIR MISSILE!
BRACE YOURSELVES--
"--WE'RE GOING DOWN!"
GGGGGRDRRRSSSSA

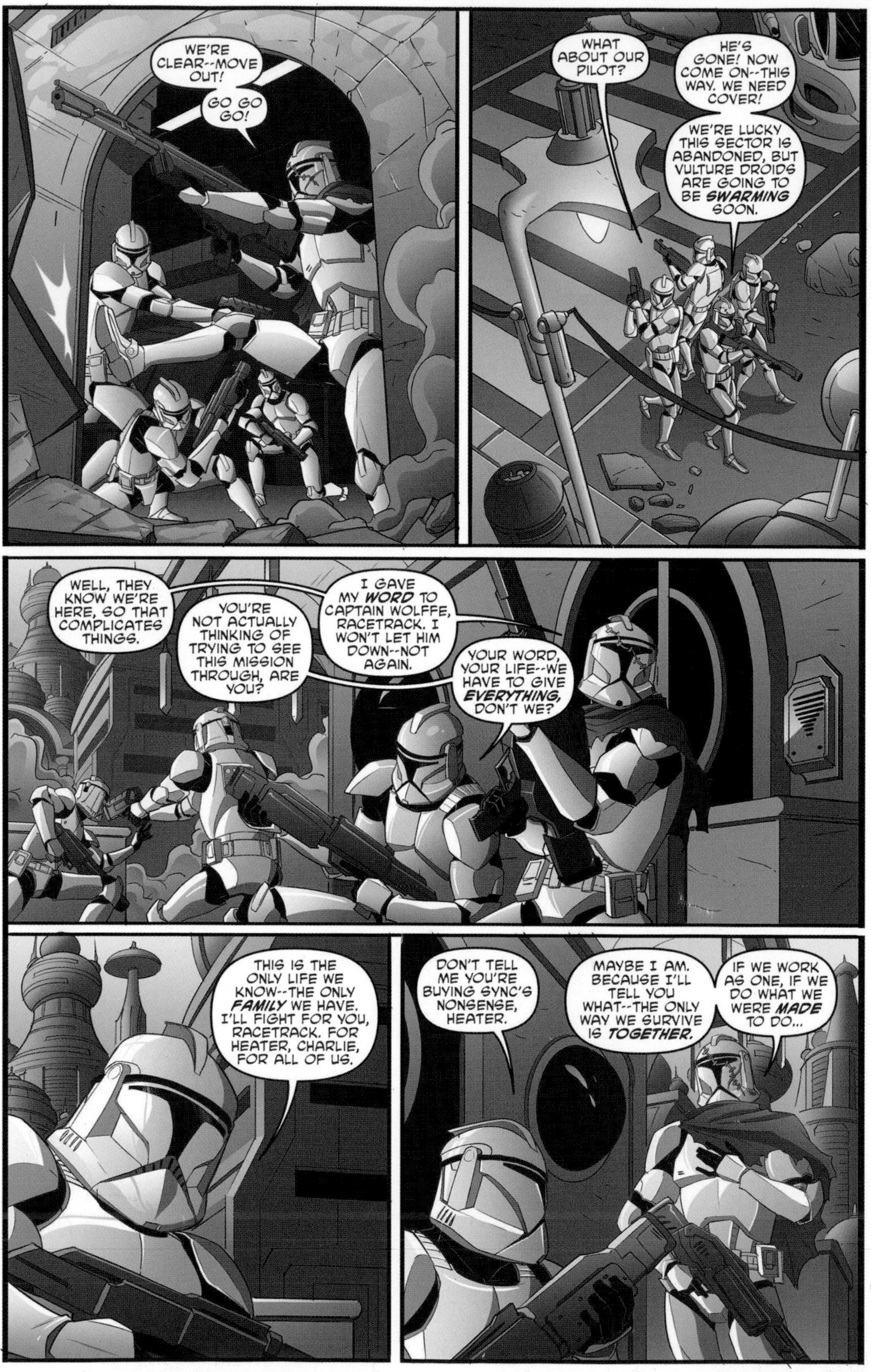
WE'RE CLEAR--MOVE OUT!
GO GO GO!
WHAT ABOUT OUR PILOT?
HE'S GONE! NOW COME ON--THIS WAY. WE NEED COVER!
WE'RE LUCKY THIS SECTOR IS ABANDONED, BUT VULTURE DROIDS ARE GOING TO BE *SWARMING* SOON.
WELL, THEY KNOW WE'RE HERE, SO THAT COMPLICATES THINGS.
YOU'RE NOT ACTUALLY THINKING OF TRYING TO SEE THIS MISSION THROUGH, ARE YOU?
I GAVE MY *WORD* TO CAPTAIN WOLFFE, RACETRACK. I WON'T LET HIM DOWN--NOT AGAIN.
YOUR WORD, YOUR LIFE--WE HAVE TO GIVE *EVERYTHING,* DON'T WE?
THIS IS THE ONLY LIFE WE KNOW--THE ONLY *FAMILY* WE HAVE. I'LL FIGHT FOR YOU, RACETRACK. FOR HEATER, CHARLIE, FOR ALL OF US.
DON'T TELL ME YOU'RE BUYING SYNC'S NONSENSE, HEATER.
MAYBE I AM. BECAUSE I'LL TELL YOU WHAT--THE ONLY WAY WE SURVIVE IS *TOGETHER.*
IF WE WORK AS ONE, IF WE DO WHAT WE WERE *MADE* TO DO...

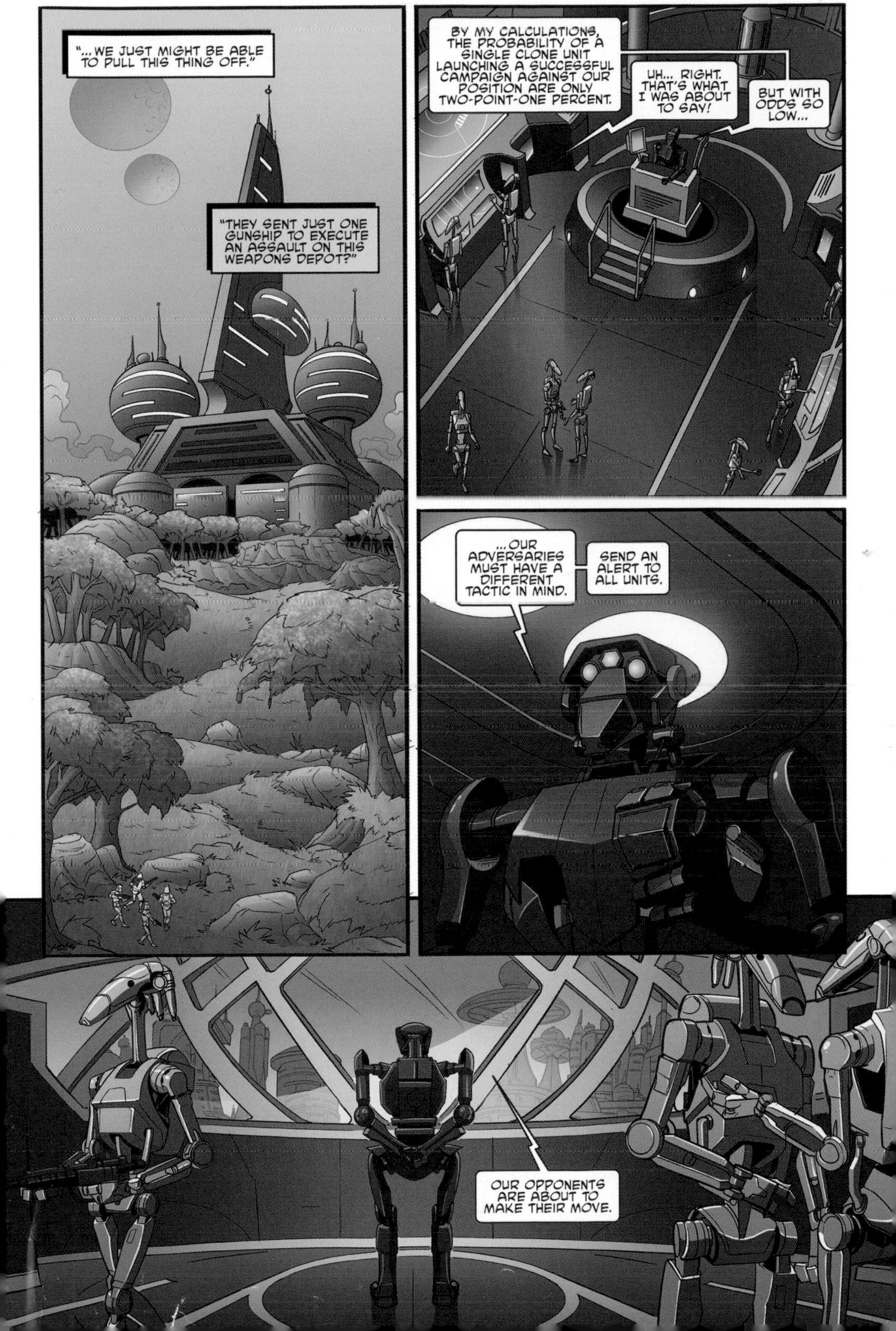
"...WE JUST MIGHT BE ABLE TO PULL THIS THING OFF."
"THEY SENT JUST ONE GUNSHIP TO EXECUTE AN ASSAULT ON THIS WEAPONS DEPOT?"
BY MY CALCULATIONS, THE PROBABILITY OF A SINGLE CLONE UNIT LAUNCHING A SUCCESSFUL CAMPAIGN AGAINST OUR POSITION ARE ONLY TWO-POINT-ONE PERCENT.
UH... RIGHT. THAT'S WHAT I WAS ABOUT TO SAY!
BUT WITH ODDS SO LOW...
...OUR ADVERSARIES MUST HAVE A DIFFERENT TACTIC IN MIND.
SEND AN ALERT TO ALL UNITS.
OUR OPPONENTS ARE ABOUT TO MAKE THEIR MOVE.

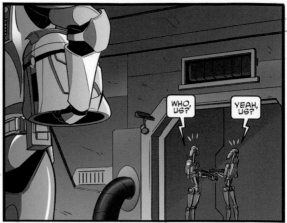

CAN'T BELIEVE I'M DOING THIS.

HEY, YOU! YOU DROIDS!

WHO, US?

YEAH, US?

YEAH, YOU, I'M FROM THE REPUBLIC GUNSHIP THAT CRASHED. I'M THE ONLY SURVIVOR, AND I'M HERE TO NEGOTIATE THE TERMS OF MY SURRENDER.

WE DON'T NEGOTIATE SURRENDER.

WE DON'T KNOW HOW!

WELL, HERE--TAKE THESE.

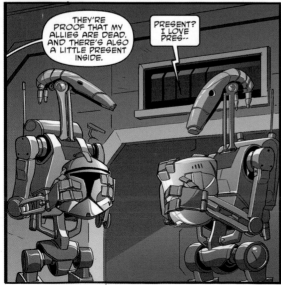

THEY'RE PROOF THAT MY ALLIES ARE DEAD. AND THERE'S ALSO A LITTLE PRESENT INSIDE.

PRESENT? I LOVE PRES--

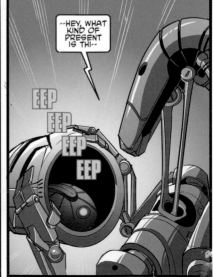

--HEY, WHAT KIND OF PRESENT IS THI--

EEP
EEP
EEP
EEP

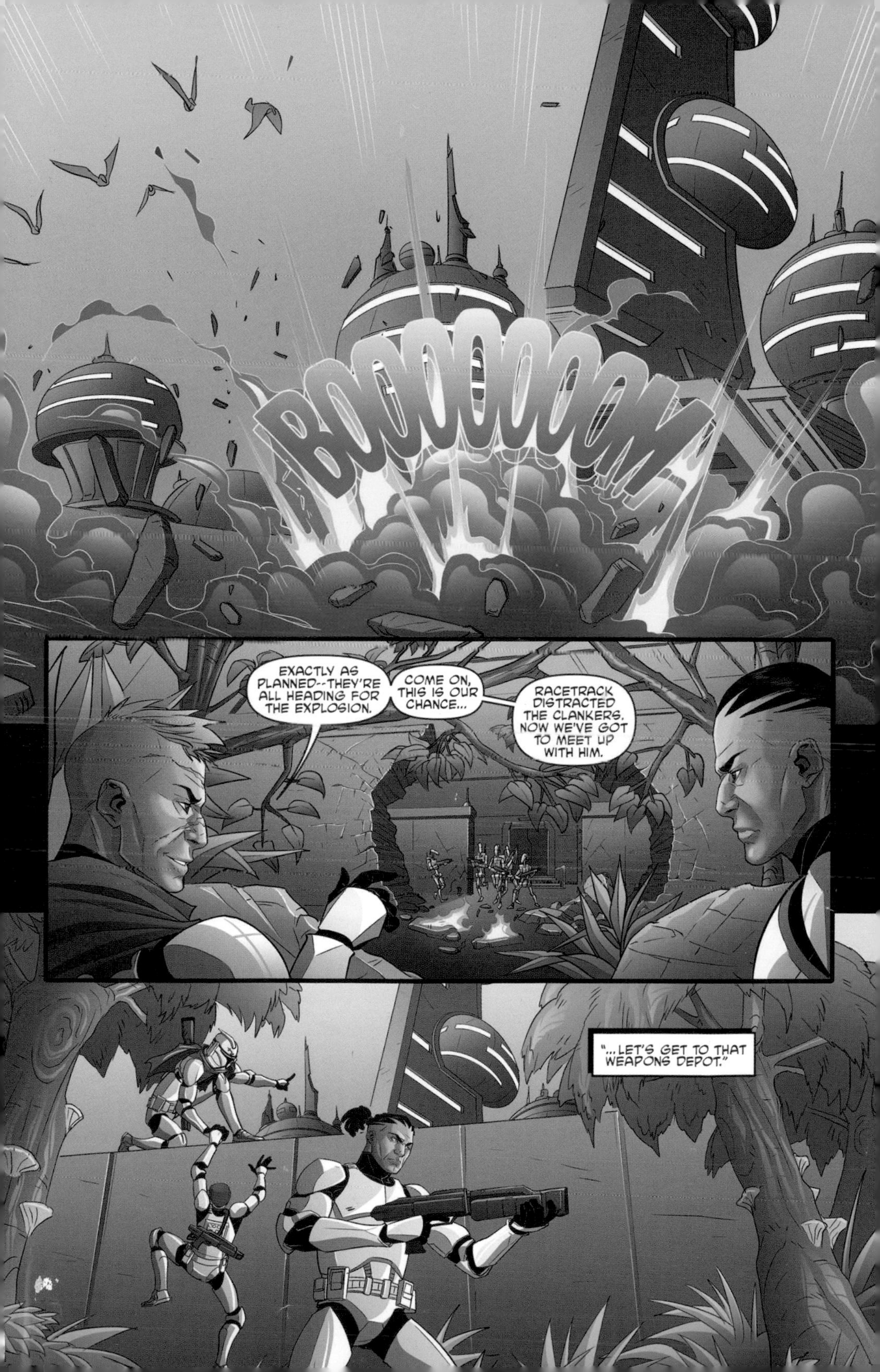
BOOOOOOM
EXACTLY AS PLANNED--THEY'RE ALL HEADING FOR THE EXPLOSION.
COME ON, THIS IS OUR CHANCE...
RACETRACK DISTRACTED THE CLANKERS. NOW WE'VE GOT TO MEET UP WITH HIM.
"...LET'S GET TO THAT WEAPONS DEPOT."

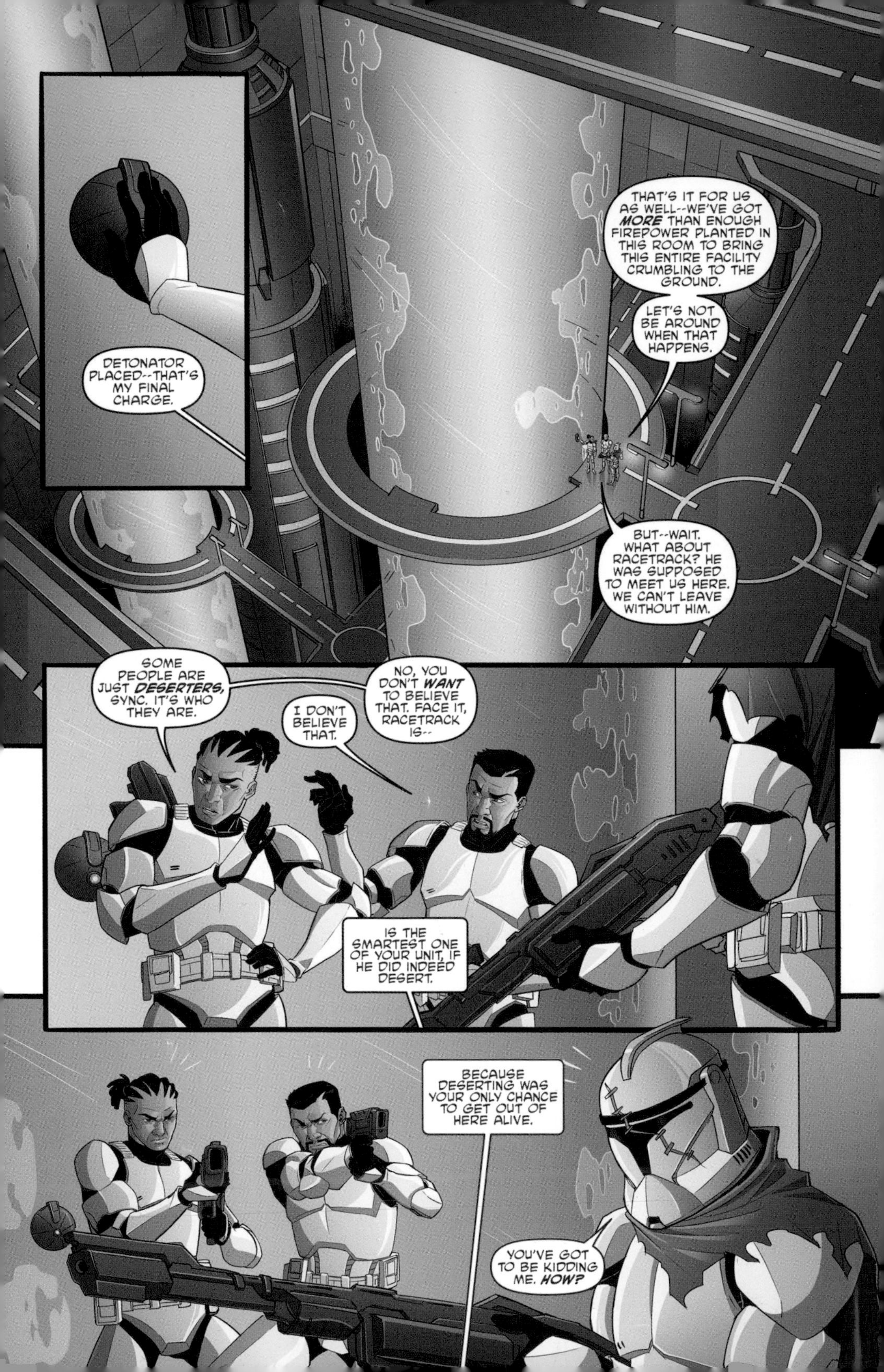
DETONATOR PLACED--THAT'S MY FINAL CHARGE.
THAT'S IT FOR US AS WELL--WE'VE GOT **MORE** THAN ENOUGH FIREPOWER PLANTED IN THIS ROOM TO BRING THIS ENTIRE FACILITY CRUMBLING TO THE GROUND.
LET'S NOT BE AROUND WHEN THAT HAPPENS.
BUT--WAIT. WHAT ABOUT RACETRACK? HE WAS SUPPOSED TO MEET US HERE. WE CAN'T LEAVE WITHOUT HIM.
SOME PEOPLE ARE JUST **DESERTERS,** SYNC. IT'S WHO THEY ARE.
I DON'T BELIEVE THAT.
NO, YOU DON'T **WANT** TO BELIEVE THAT. FACE IT, RACETRACK IS--
IS THE SMARTEST ONE OF YOUR UNIT, IF HE DID INDEED DESERT.
BECAUSE DESERTING WAS YOUR ONLY CHANCE TO GET OUT OF HERE ALIVE.
YOU'VE GOT TO BE KIDDING ME. **HOW?**

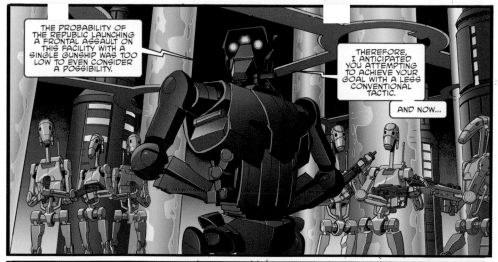

THE PROBABILITY OF THE REPUBLIC LAUNCHING A FRONTAL ASSAULT ON THIS FACILITY WITH A SINGLE GUNSHIP WAS TOO LOW TO EVEN CONSIDER A POSSIBILITY.

THEREFORE, I ANTICIPATED YOU ATTEMPTING TO ACHIEVE YOUR GOAL WITH A LESS CONVENTIONAL TACTIC.

AND NOW...

...YOU WILL SURRENDER.

OR DIE.

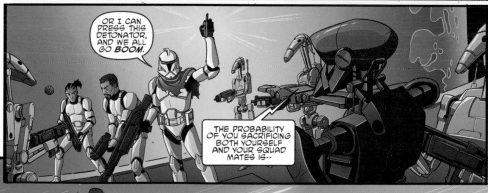

OR I CAN PRESS THIS DETONATOR, AND WE ALL GO *BOOM*.

THE PROBABILITY OF YOU SACRIFICING BOTH YOURSELF AND YOUR SQUAD MATES IS--

CHOOM

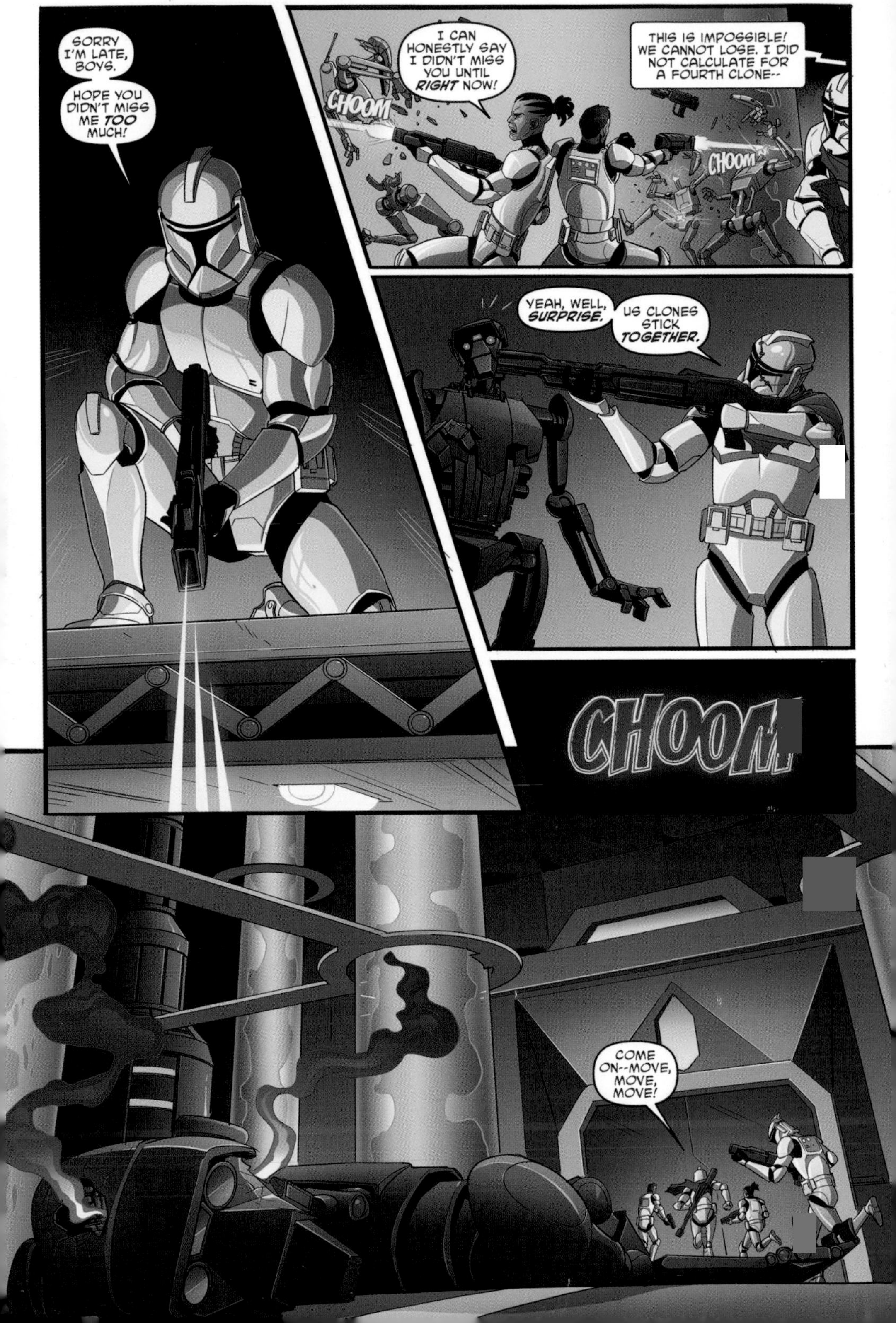
SORRY I'M LATE, BOYS.
HOPE YOU DIDN'T MISS ME *TOO* MUCH!
I CAN HONESTLY SAY I DIDN'T MISS YOU UNTIL *RIGHT* NOW!
CHOOM
THIS IS IMPOSSIBLE! WE CANNOT LOSE. I DID NOT CALCULATE FOR A FOURTH CLONE--
CHOOM
YEAH, WELL, *SURPRISE.*
US CLONES STICK *TOGETHER.*
COME ON--MOVE, MOVE, MOVE!

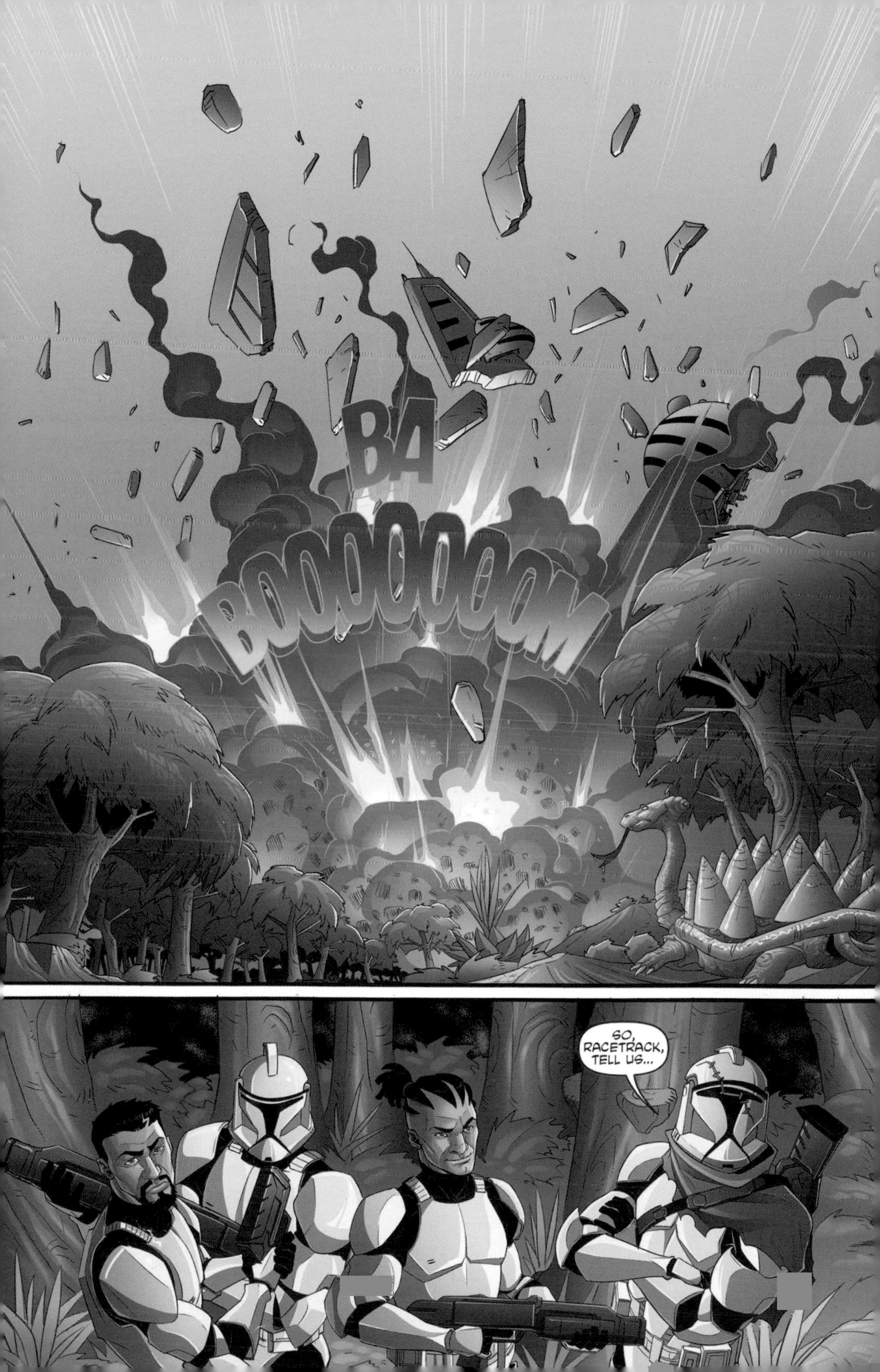
BA
BOOOOOOOM
SO, RACETRACK, TELL US...

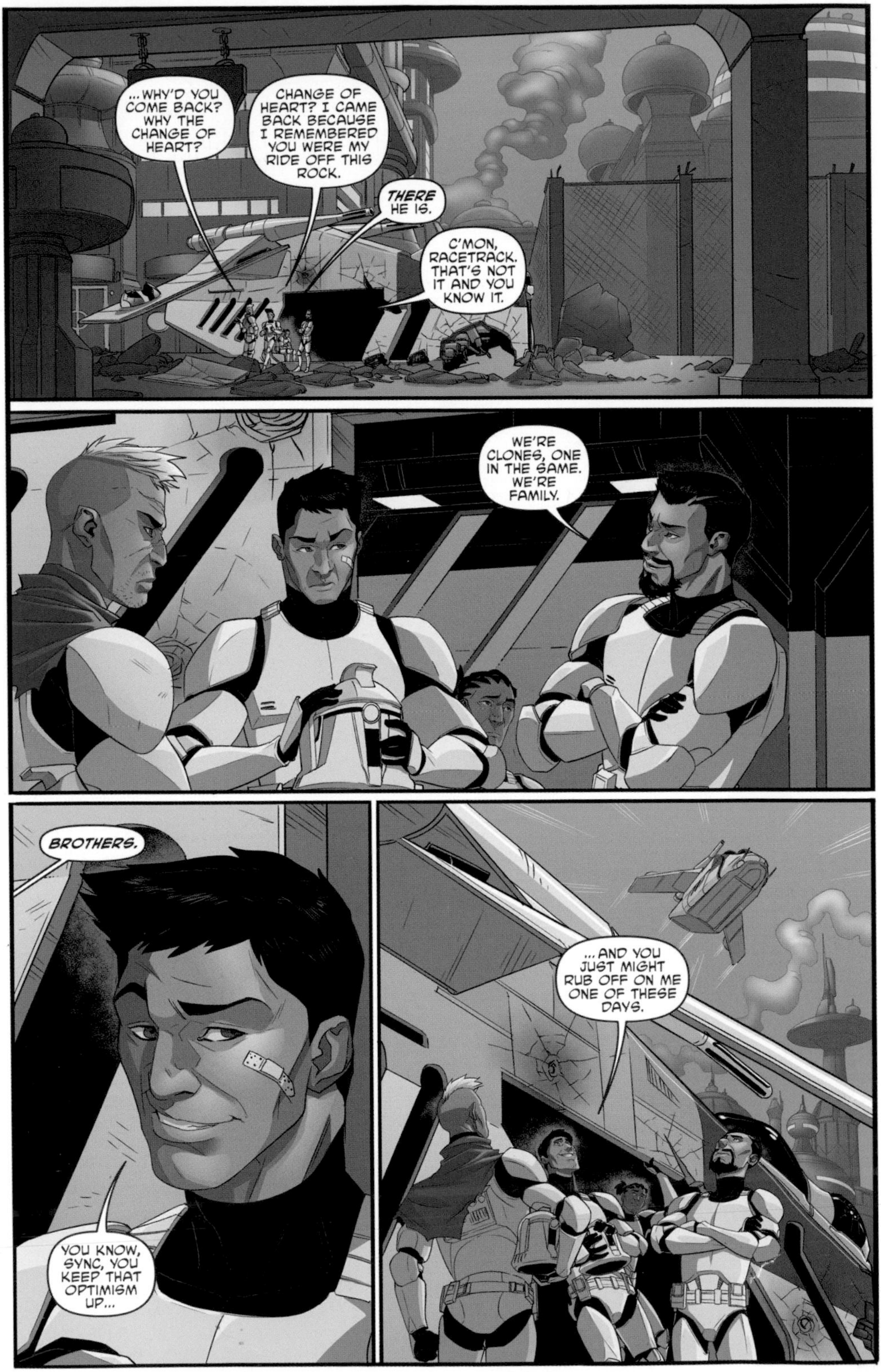
...WHY'D YOU COME BACK? WHY THE CHANGE OF HEART?
CHANGE OF HEART? I CAME BACK BECAUSE I REMEMBERED YOU WERE MY RIDE OFF THIS ROCK.
THERE HE IS.
C'MON, RACETRACK. THAT'S NOT IT AND YOU KNOW IT.
WE'RE CLONES, ONE IN THE SAME. WE'RE FAMILY.
BROTHERS.
YOU KNOW, SYNC, YOU KEEP THAT OPTIMISM UP...
...AND YOU JUST MIGHT RUB OFF ON ME ONE OF THESE DAYS.

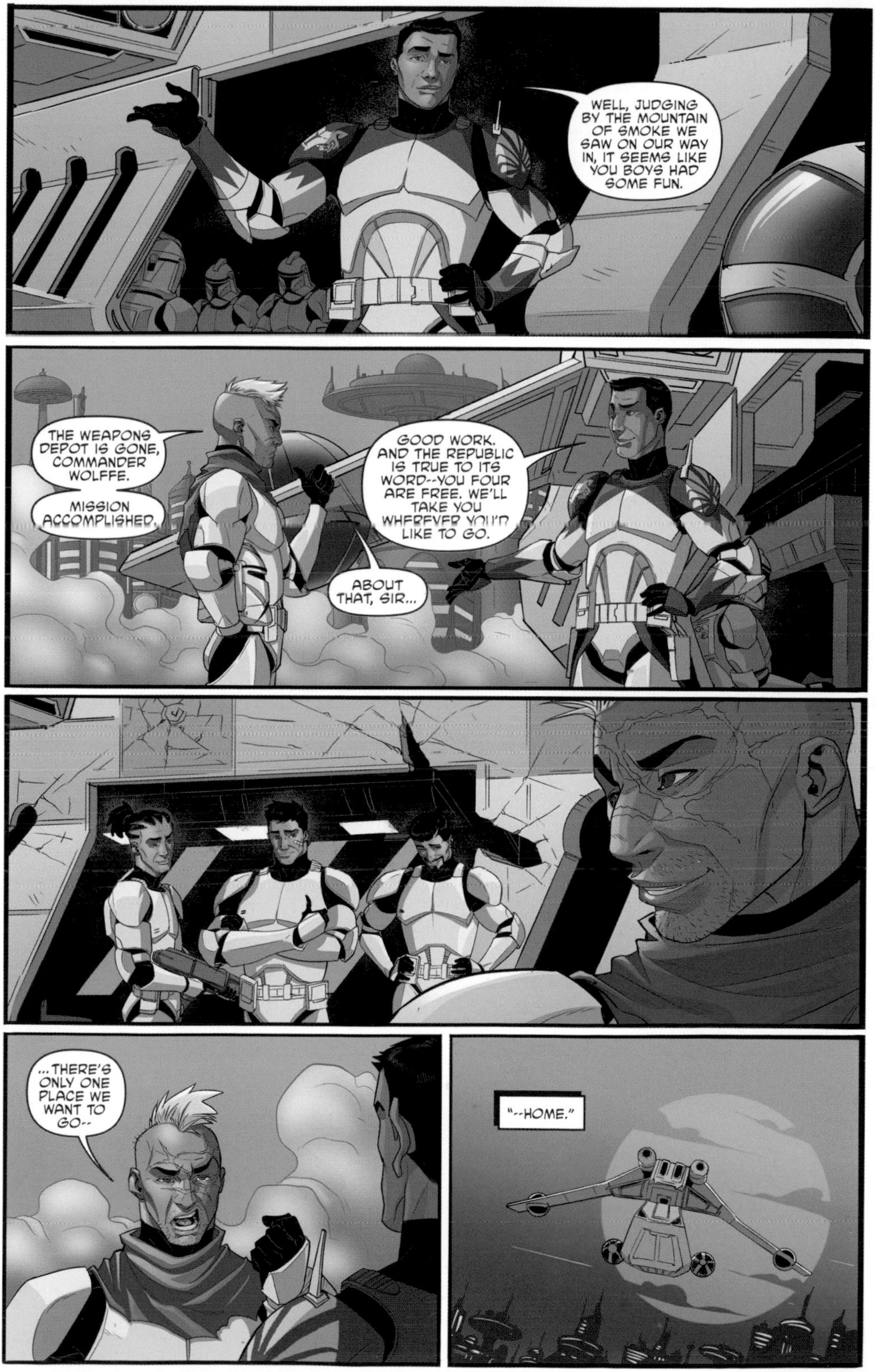
WELL, JUDGING BY THE MOUNTAIN OF SMOKE WE SAW ON OUR WAY IN, IT SEEMS LIKE YOU BOYS HAD SOME FUN.
THE WEAPONS DEPOT IS GONE, COMMANDER WOLFFE.
MISSION ACCOMPLISHED.
GOOD WORK. AND THE REPUBLIC IS TRUE TO ITS WORD--YOU FOUR ARE FREE. WE'LL TAKE YOU WHEREVER YOU'D LIKE TO GO.
ABOUT THAT, SIR...
...THERE'S ONLY ONE PLACE WE WANT TO GO--
"--HOME."

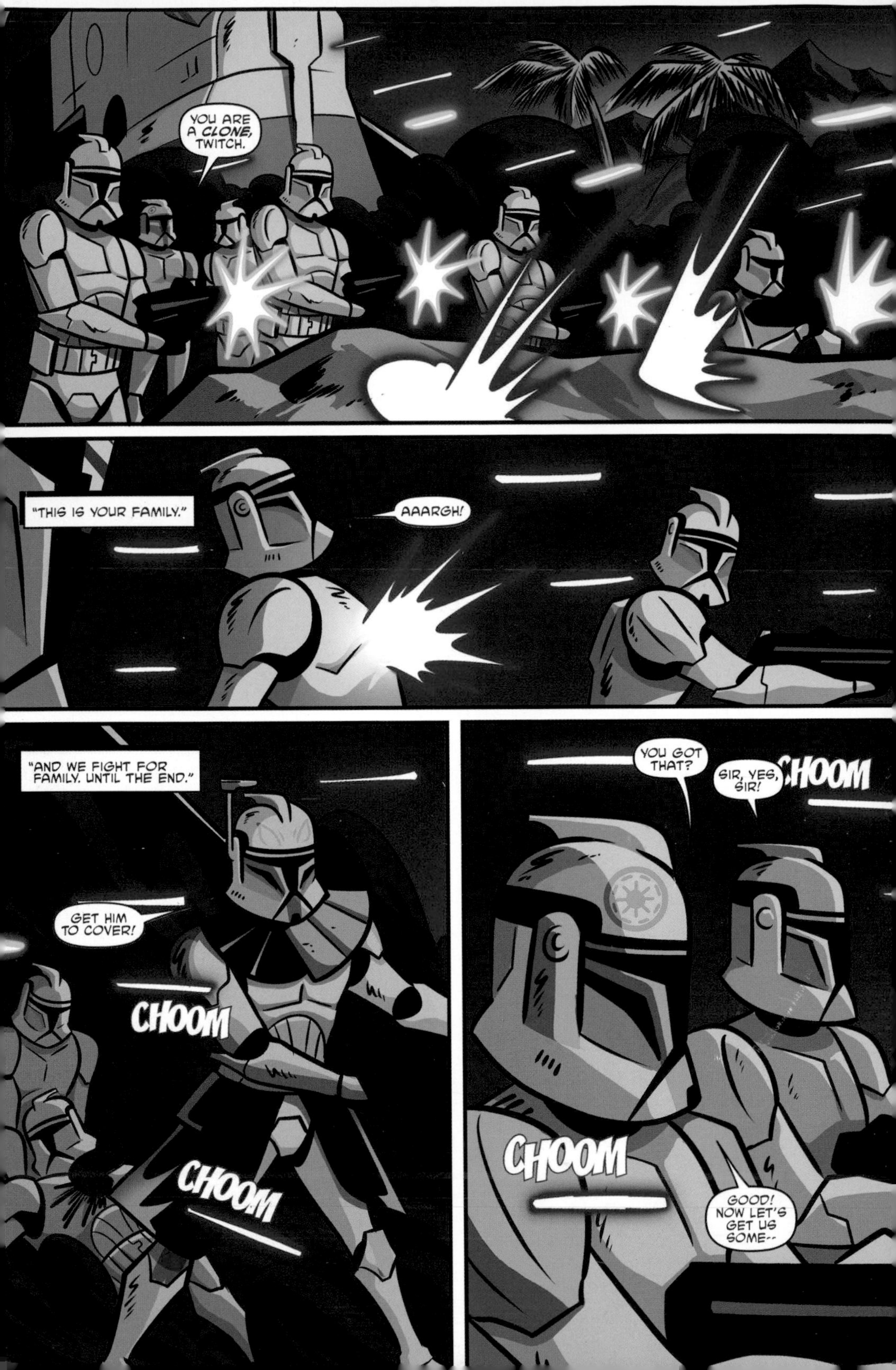
YOU ARE A CLONE, TWITCH.
"THIS IS YOUR FAMILY."
AAARGH!
"AND WE FIGHT FOR FAMILY. UNTIL THE END."
GET HIM TO COVER!
CHOOM
CHOOM
YOU GOT THAT?
SIR, YES, SIR!
CHOOM
CHOOM
GOOD! NOW LET'S GET US SOME--

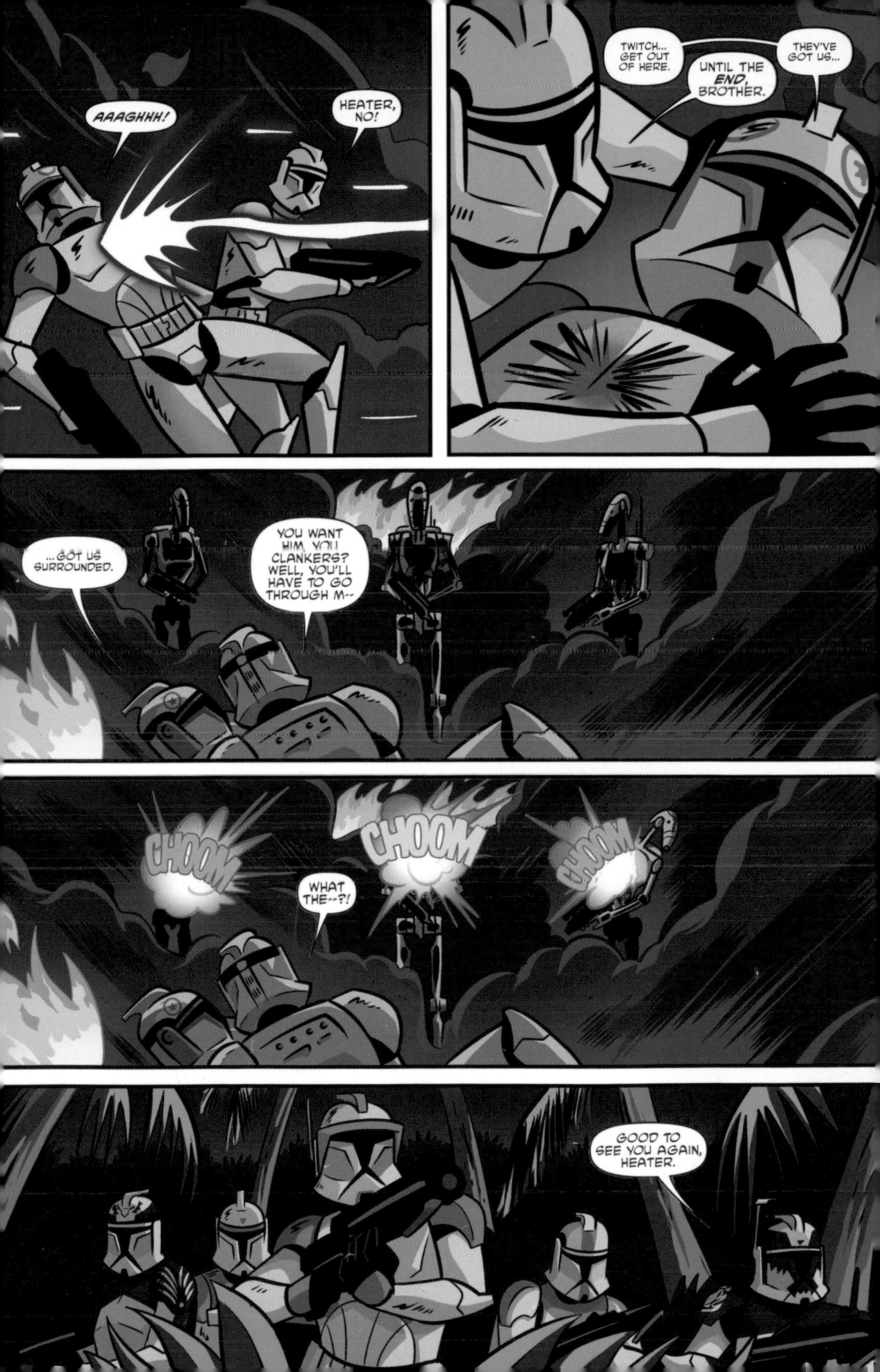
AAAGHHH!
HEATER, NO!
TWITCH... GET OUT OF HERE.
UNTIL THE END, BROTHER.
THEY'VE GOT US...
...GOT US SURROUNDED.
YOU WANT HIM, YOU CLANKERS? WELL, YOU'LL HAVE TO GO THROUGH M--
CHOOM
CHOOM
CHOOM
WHAT THE--?!
GOOD TO SEE YOU AGAIN, HEATER.

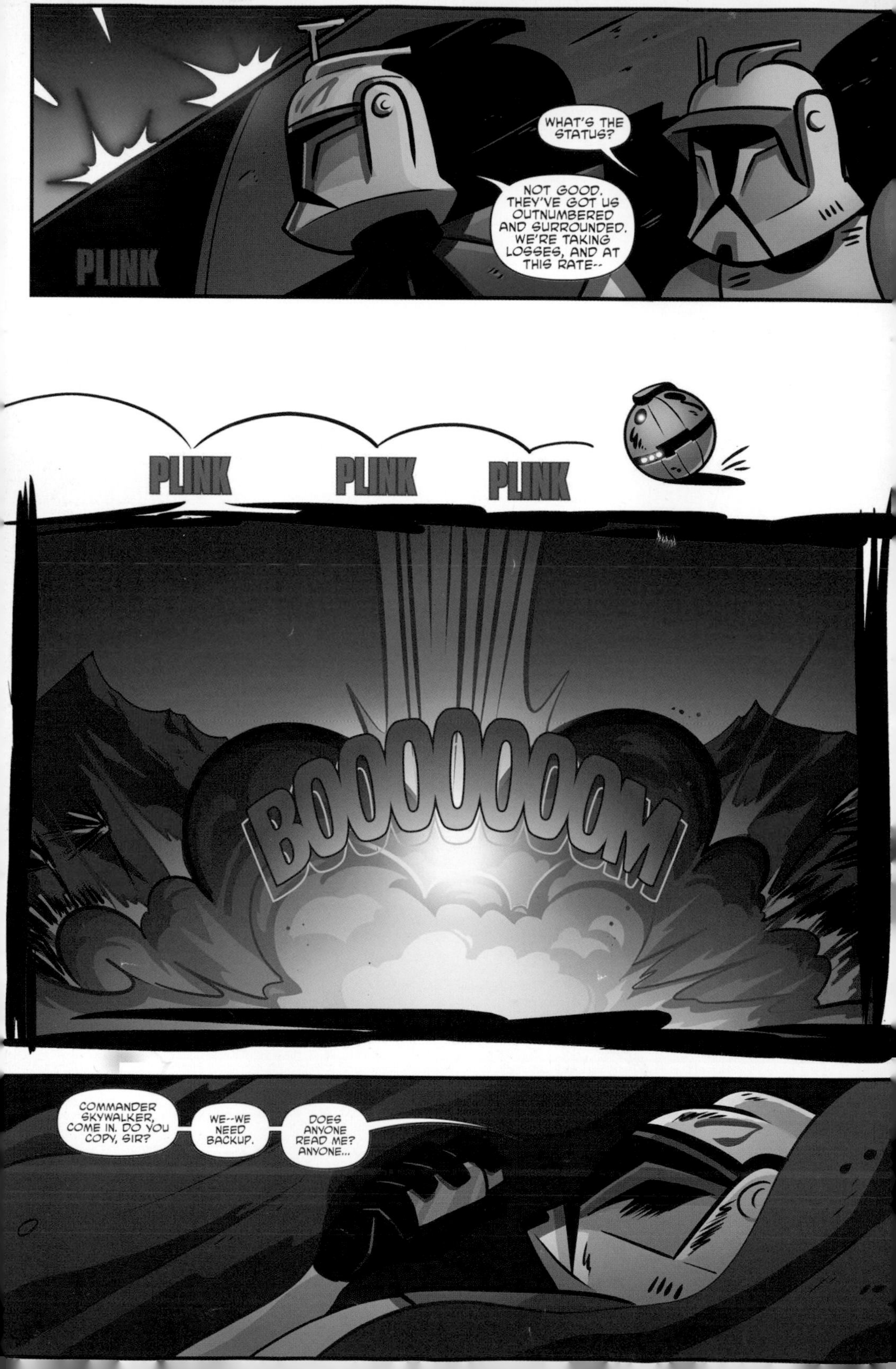
WHAT'S THE STATUS?
NOT GOOD. THEY'VE GOT US OUTNUMBERED AND SURROUNDED. WE'RE TAKING LOSSES, AND AT THIS RATE--
PLINK
PLINK
PLINK
PLINK
BOOOOOOOM
COMMANDER SKYWALKER, COME IN. DO YOU COPY, SIR?
WE--WE NEED BACKUP.
DOES ANYONE READ ME? ANYONE...

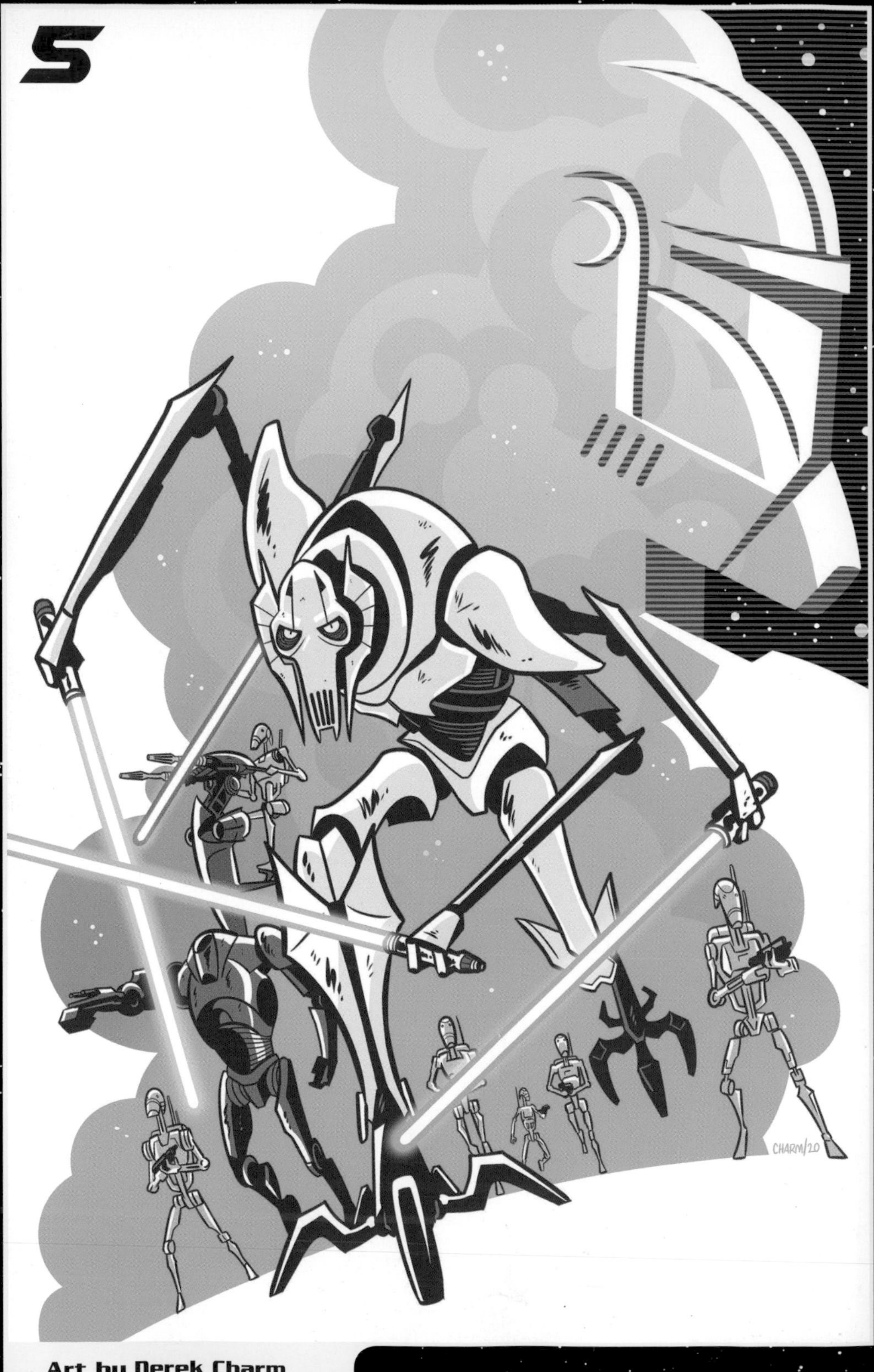
5
CHARM/20

Art by Derek Charm

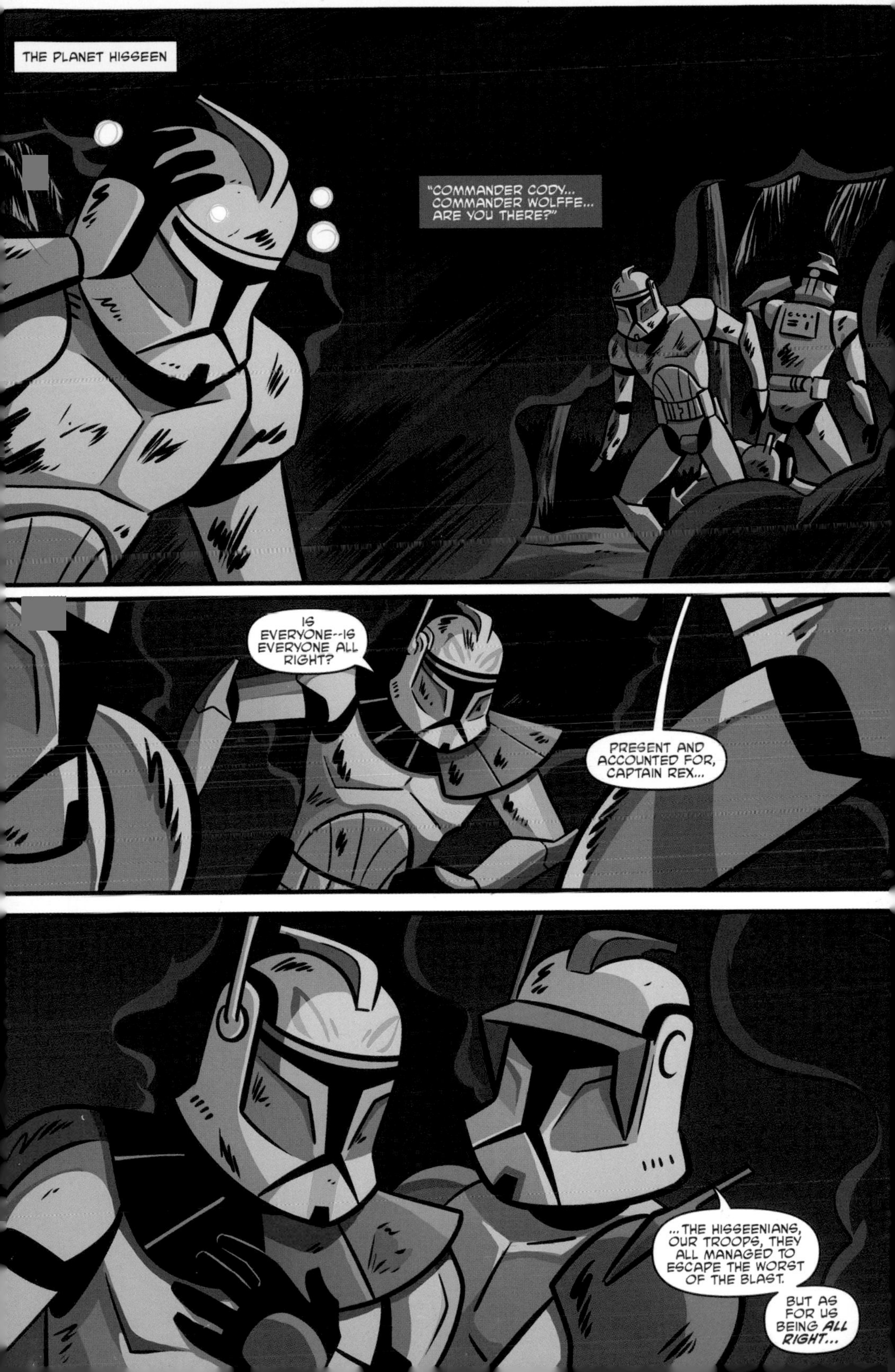
THE PLANET HISSEEN
"COMMANDER CODY... COMMANDER WOLFFE... ARE YOU THERE?"
IS EVERYONE--IS EVERYONE ALL RIGHT?
PRESENT AND ACCOUNTED FOR, CAPTAIN REX...
...THE HISSEENIANS, OUR TROOPS, THEY ALL MANAGED TO ESCAPE THE WORST OF THE BLAST.
BUT AS FOR US BEING *ALL RIGHT*...

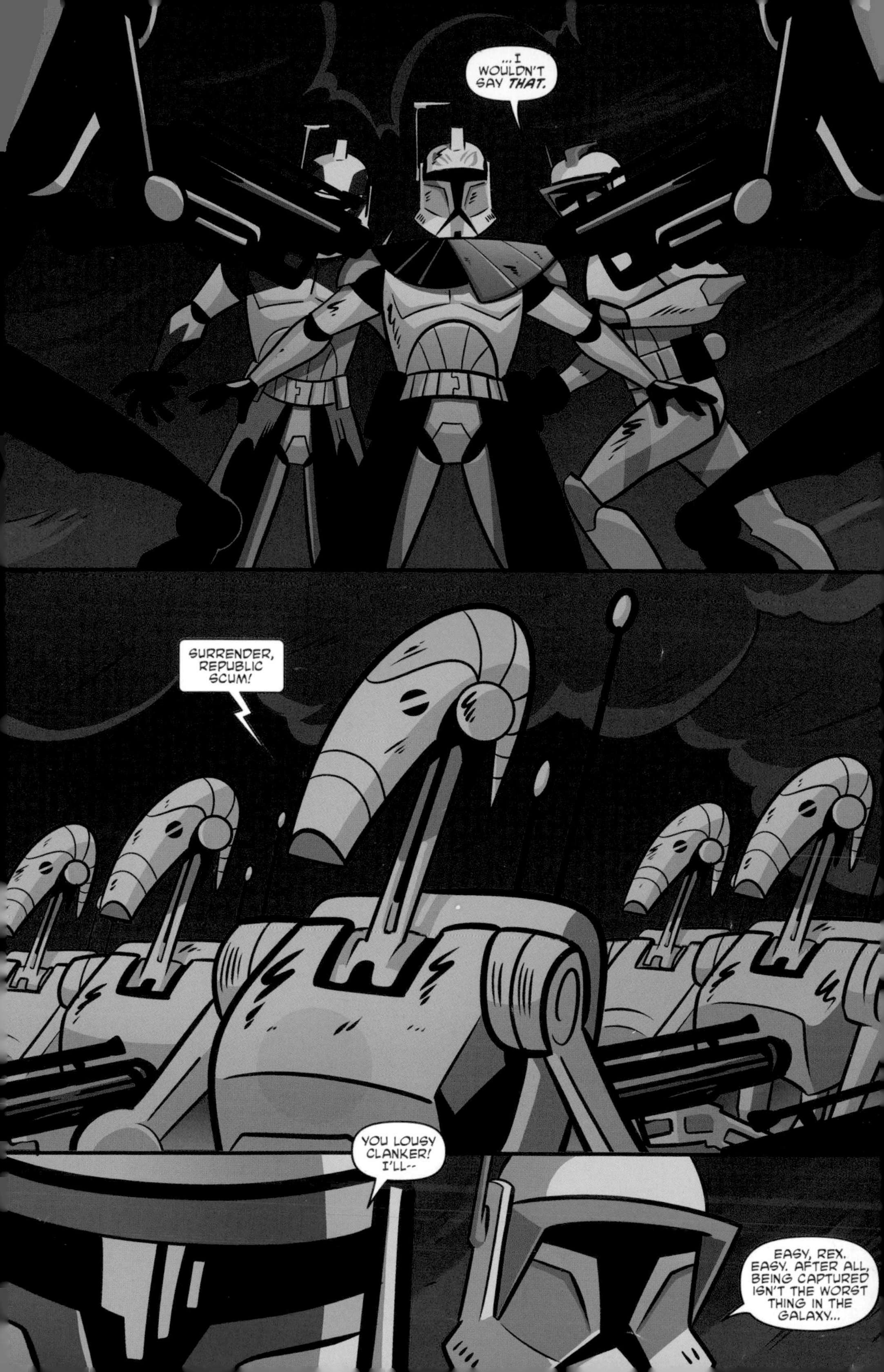
...I WOULDN'T SAY *THAT.*
SURRENDER, REPUBLIC SCUM!
YOU LOUSY CLANKER! I'LL--
EASY, REX. EASY. AFTER ALL, BEING CAPTURED ISN'T THE WORST THING IN THE GALAXY...

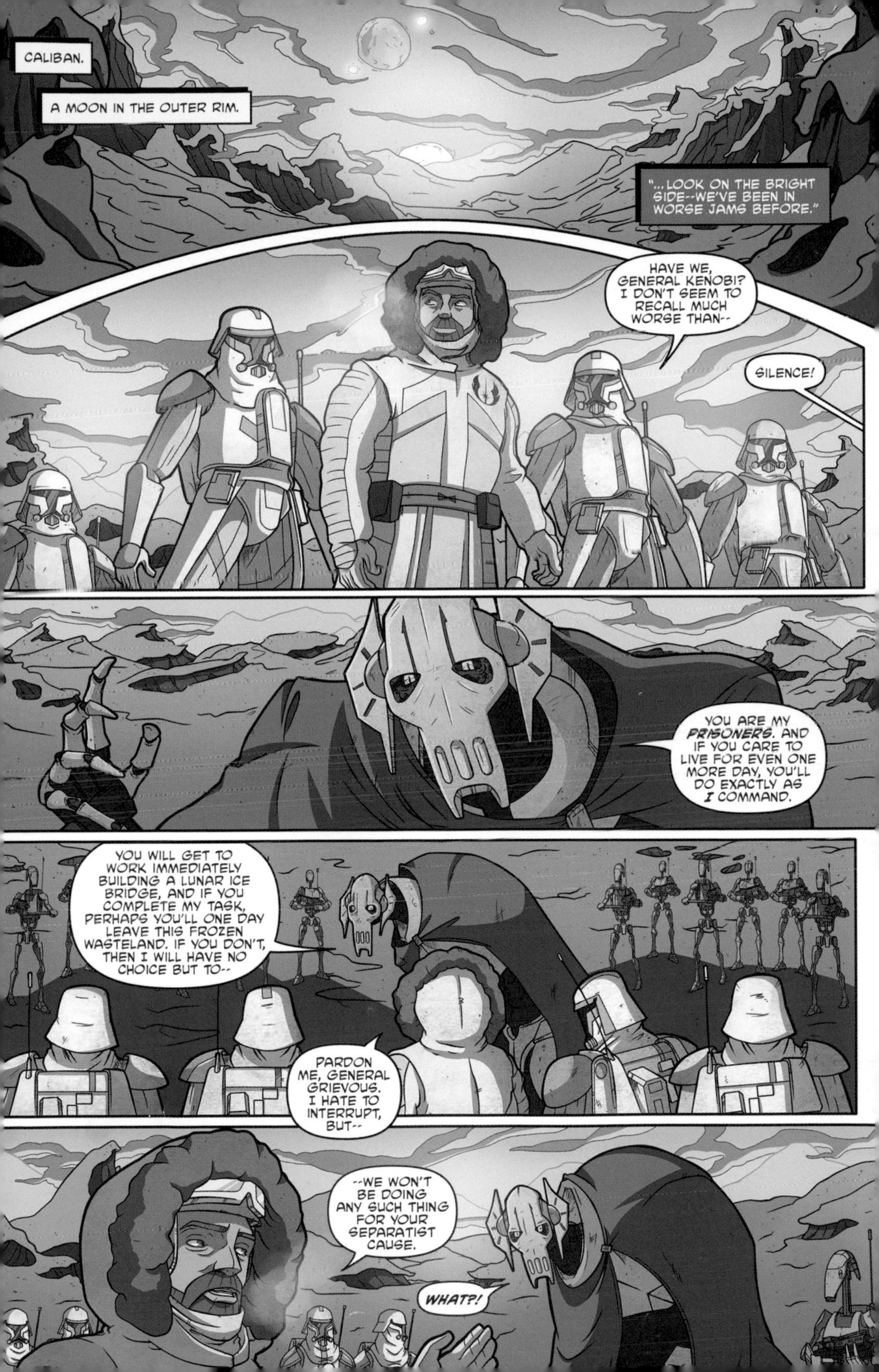
CALIBAN.
A MOON IN THE OUTER RIM.
"...LOOK ON THE BRIGHT SIDE--WE'VE BEEN IN WORSE JAMS BEFORE."
HAVE WE, GENERAL KENOBI? I DON'T SEEM TO RECALL MUCH WORSE THAN--
SILENCE!
YOU ARE MY PRISONERS. AND IF YOU CARE TO LIVE FOR EVEN ONE MORE DAY, YOU'LL DO EXACTLY AS I COMMAND.
YOU WILL GET TO WORK IMMEDIATELY BUILDING A LUNAR ICE BRIDGE, AND IF YOU COMPLETE MY TASK, PERHAPS YOU'LL ONE DAY LEAVE THIS FROZEN WASTELAND. IF YOU DON'T, THEN I WILL HAVE NO CHOICE BUT TO--
PARDON ME, GENERAL GRIEVOUS. I HATE TO INTERRUPT, BUT--
--WE WON'T BE DOING ANY SUCH THING FOR YOUR SEPARATIST CAUSE.
WHAT?!

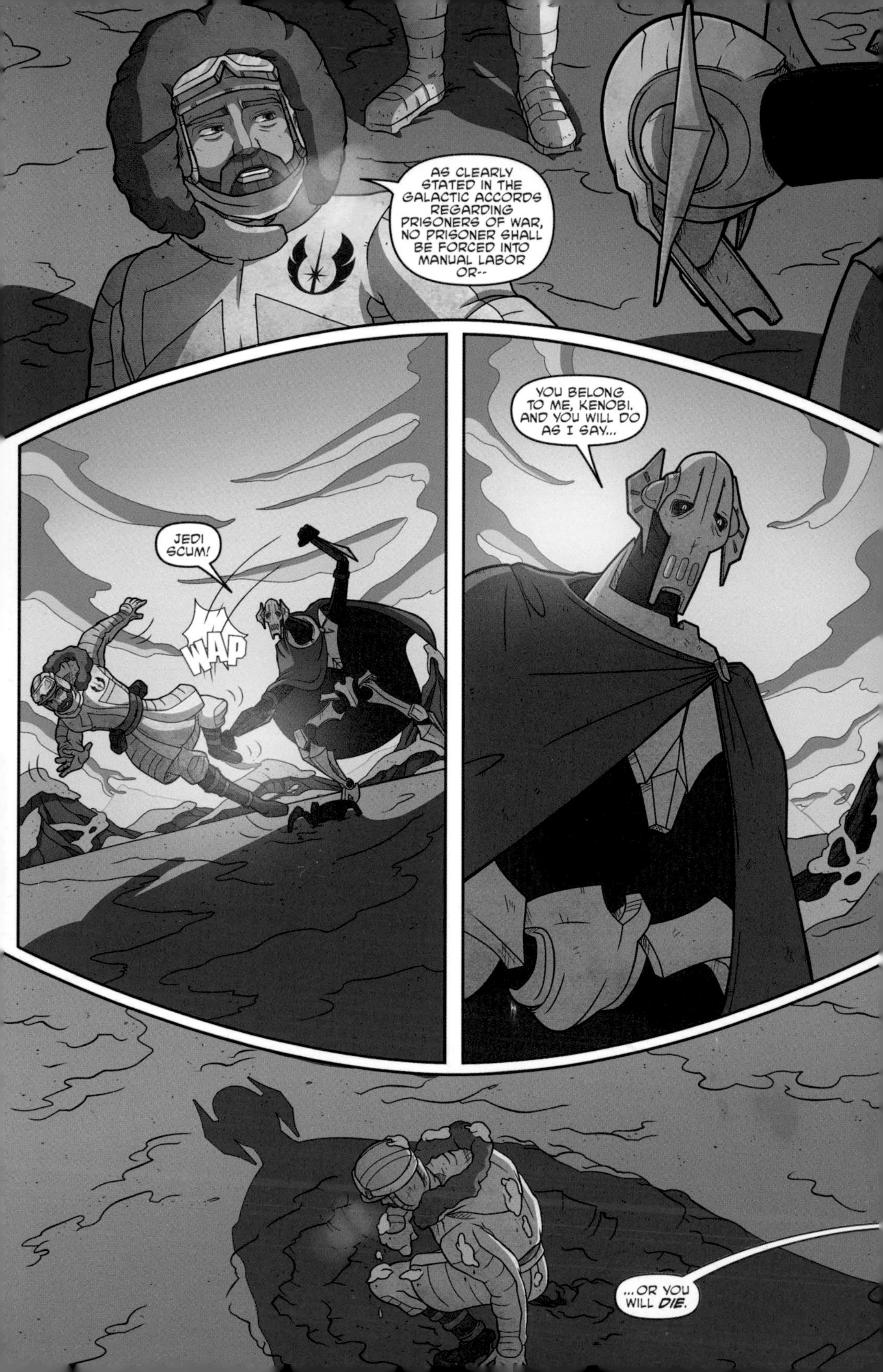
AS CLEARLY STATED IN THE GALACTIC ACCORDS REGARDING PRISONERS OF WAR, NO PRISONER SHALL BE FORCED INTO MANUAL LABOR OR--
JEDI SCUM!
WAP
YOU BELONG TO ME, KENOBI. AND YOU WILL DO AS I SAY...
...OR YOU WILL *DIE*.

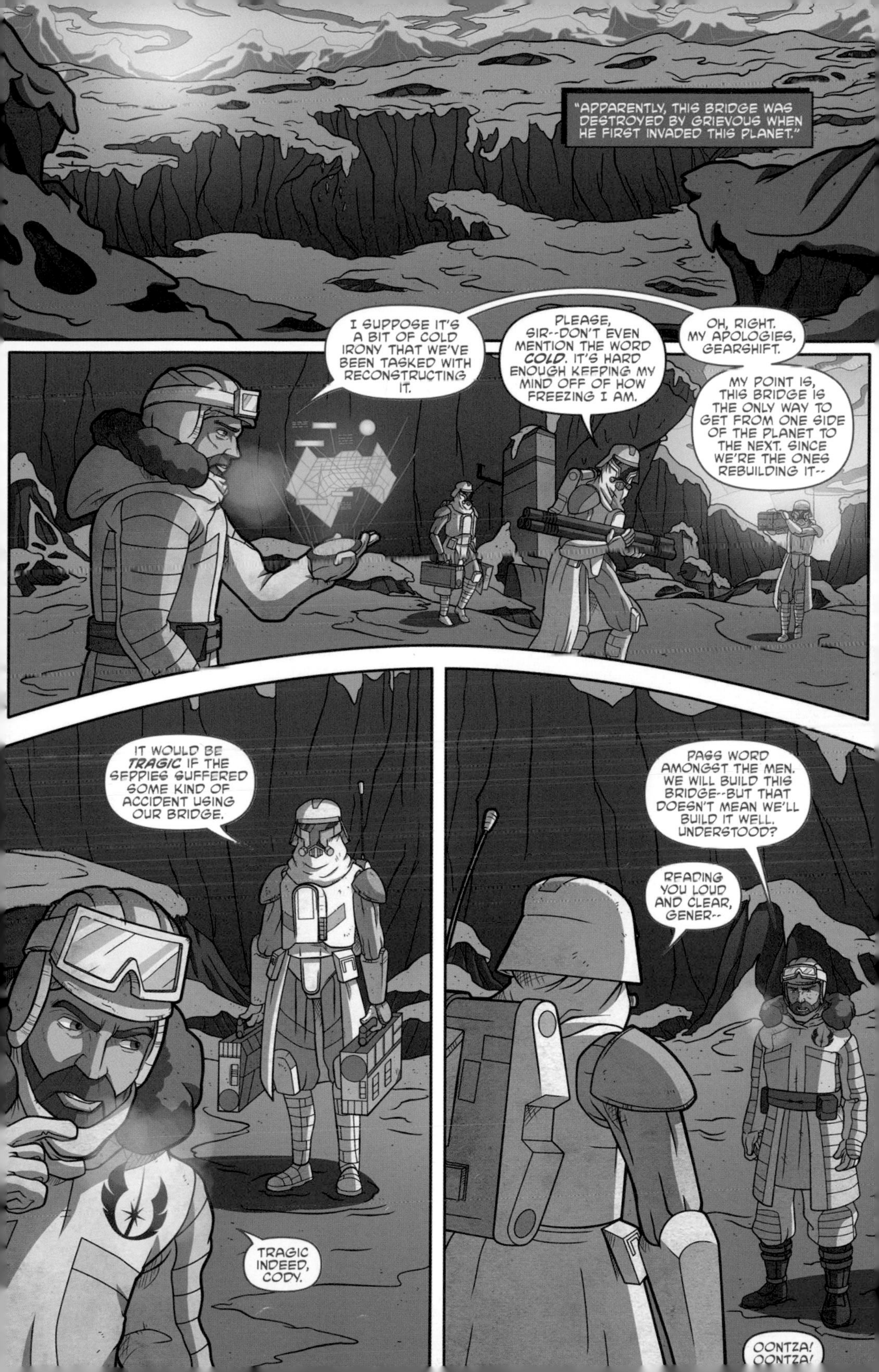
"APPARENTLY, THIS BRIDGE WAS DESTROYED BY GRIEVOUS WHEN HE FIRST INVADED THIS PLANET."
I SUPPOSE IT'S A BIT OF COLD IRONY THAT WE'VE BEEN TASKED WITH RECONSTRUCTING IT.
PLEASE, SIR--DON'T EVEN MENTION THE WORD COLD. IT'S HARD ENOUGH KEEPING MY MIND OFF OF HOW FREEZING I AM.
OH, RIGHT. MY APOLOGIES, GEARSHIFT.
MY POINT IS, THIS BRIDGE IS THE ONLY WAY TO GET FROM ONE SIDE OF THE PLANET TO THE NEXT. SINCE WE'RE THE ONES REBUILDING IT--
IT WOULD BE TRAGIC IF THE SEPPIES SUFFERED SOME KIND OF ACCIDENT USING OUR BRIDGE.
TRAGIC INDEED, CODY.
PASS WORD AMONGST THE MEN. WE WILL BUILD THIS BRIDGE--BUT THAT DOESN'T MEAN WE'LL BUILD IT WELL. UNDERSTOOD?
READING YOU LOUD AND CLEAR, GENER--
OONTZA! OONTZA!

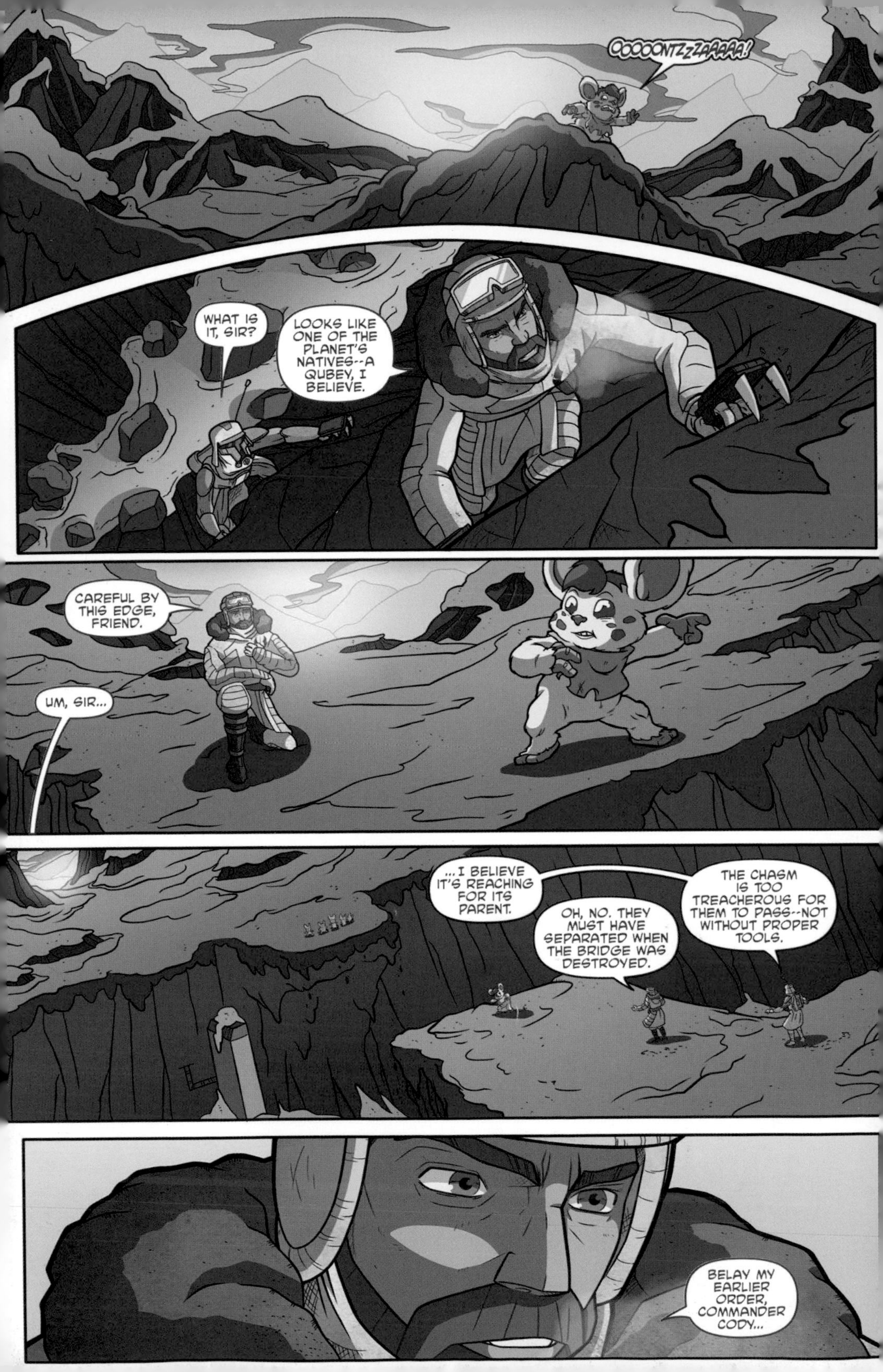
OOOOONTZZZAAAAA!
WHAT IS IT, SIR?
LOOKS LIKE ONE OF THE PLANET'S NATIVES--A QUBEY, I BELIEVE.
CAREFUL BY THIS EDGE, FRIEND.
UM, SIR...
...I BELIEVE IT'S REACHING FOR ITS PARENT.
OH, NO. THEY MUST HAVE SEPARATED WHEN THE BRIDGE WAS DESTROYED.
THE CHASM IS TOO TREACHEROUS FOR THEM TO PASS--NOT WITHOUT PROPER TOOLS.
BELAY MY EARLIER ORDER, COMMANDER CODY...

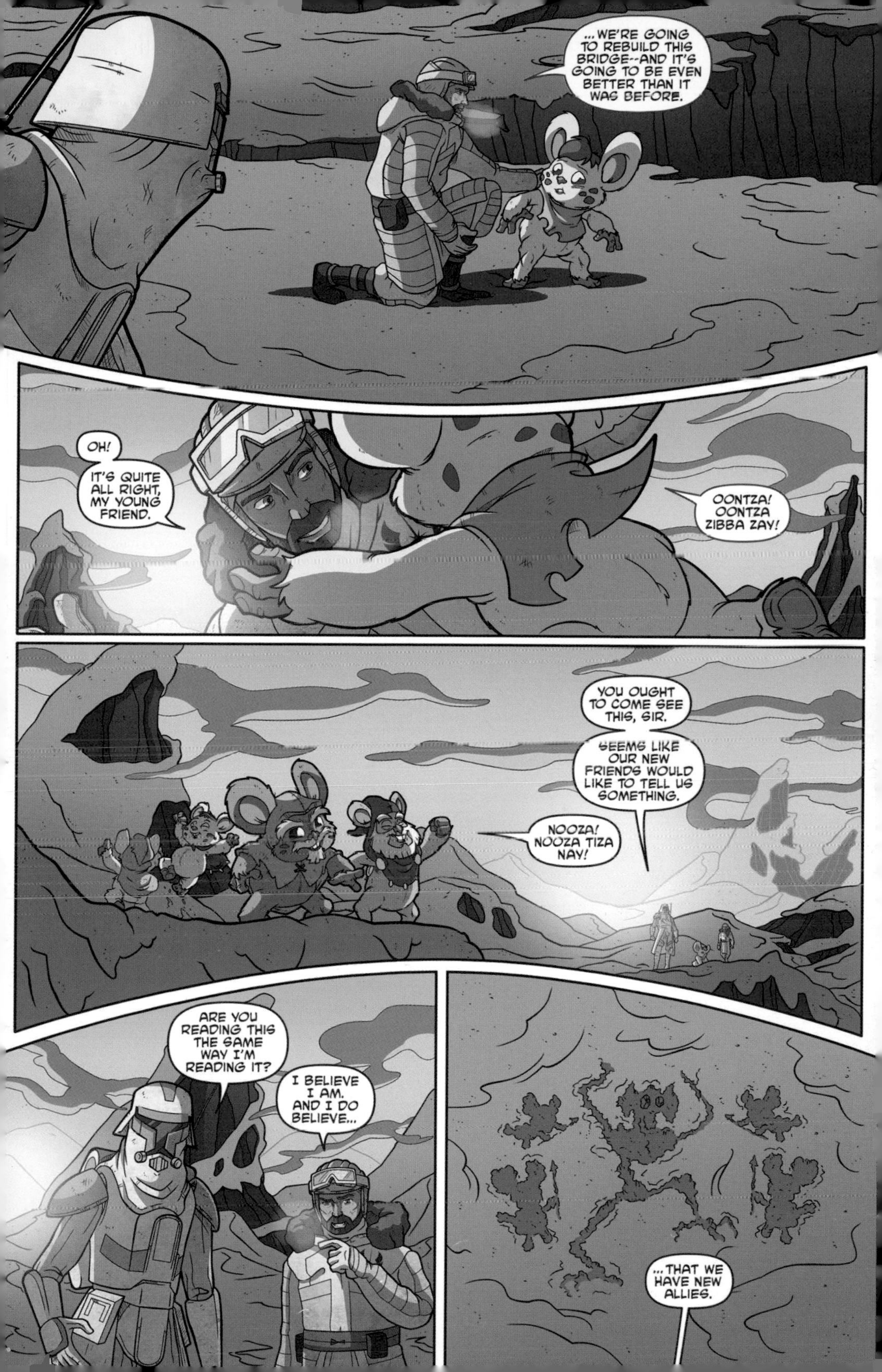
...WE'RE GOING TO REBUILD THIS BRIDGE--AND IT'S GOING TO BE EVEN BETTER THAN IT WAS BEFORE.
OH!
IT'S QUITE ALL RIGHT, MY YOUNG FRIEND.
OONTZA! OONTZA ZIBBA ZAY!
YOU OUGHT TO COME SEE THIS, SIR.
SEEMS LIKE OUR NEW FRIENDS WOULD LIKE TO TELL US SOMETHING.
NOOZA! NOOZA TIZA NAY!
ARE YOU READING THIS THE SAME WAY I'M READING IT?
I BELIEVE I AM. AND I DO BELIEVE...
...THAT WE HAVE NEW ALLIES.

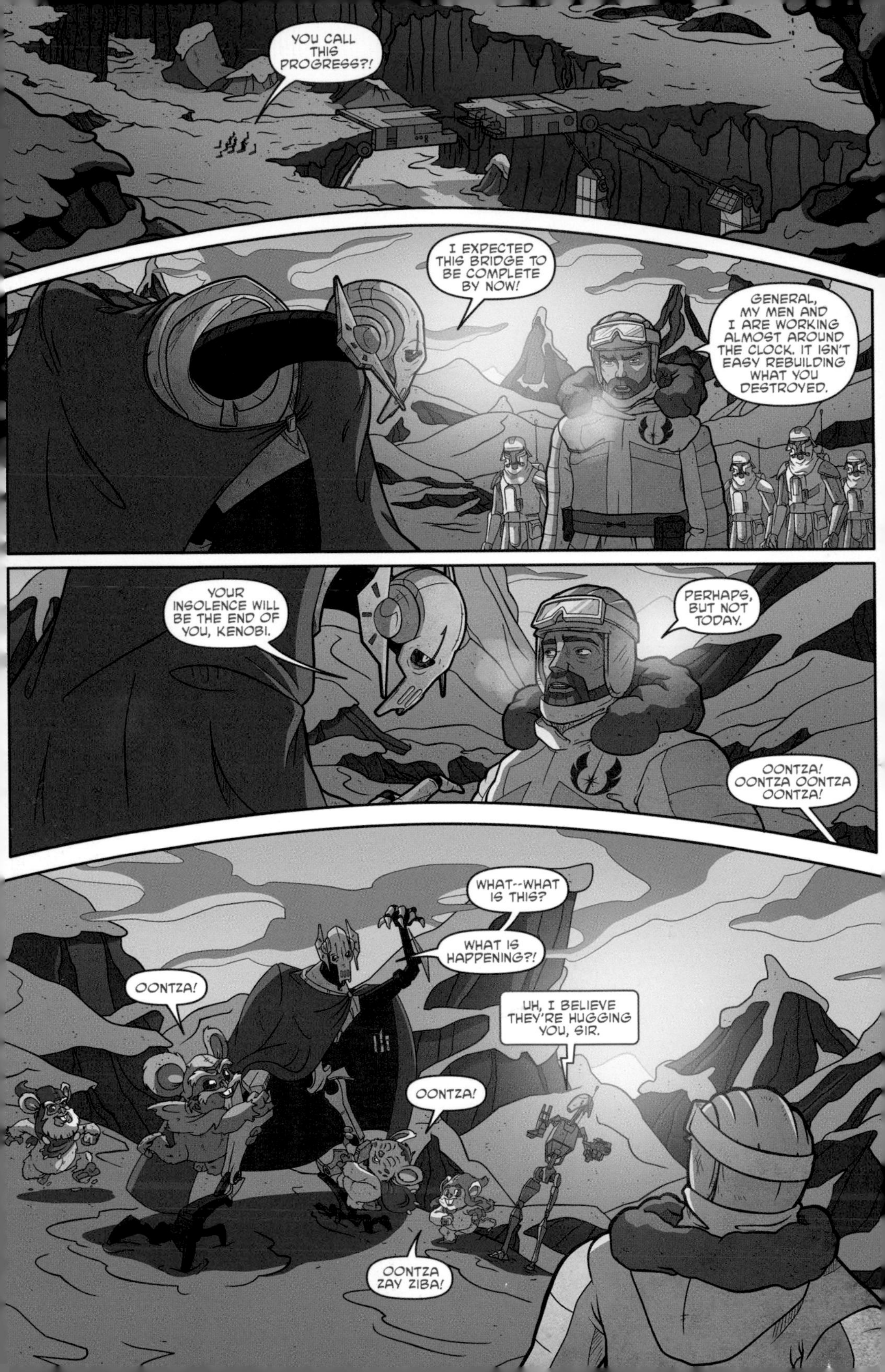
YOU CALL THIS PROGRESS?!
I EXPECTED THIS BRIDGE TO BE COMPLETE BY NOW!
GENERAL, MY MEN AND I ARE WORKING ALMOST AROUND THE CLOCK. IT ISN'T EASY REBUILDING WHAT YOU DESTROYED.
YOUR INSOLENCE WILL BE THE END OF YOU, KENOBI.
PERHAPS, BUT NOT TODAY.
OONTZA! OONTZA OONTZA OONTZA!
WHAT--WHAT IS THIS?
WHAT IS HAPPENING?!
OONTZA!
UH, I BELIEVE THEY'RE HUGGING YOU, SIR.
OONTZA!
OONTZA ZAY ZIBA!

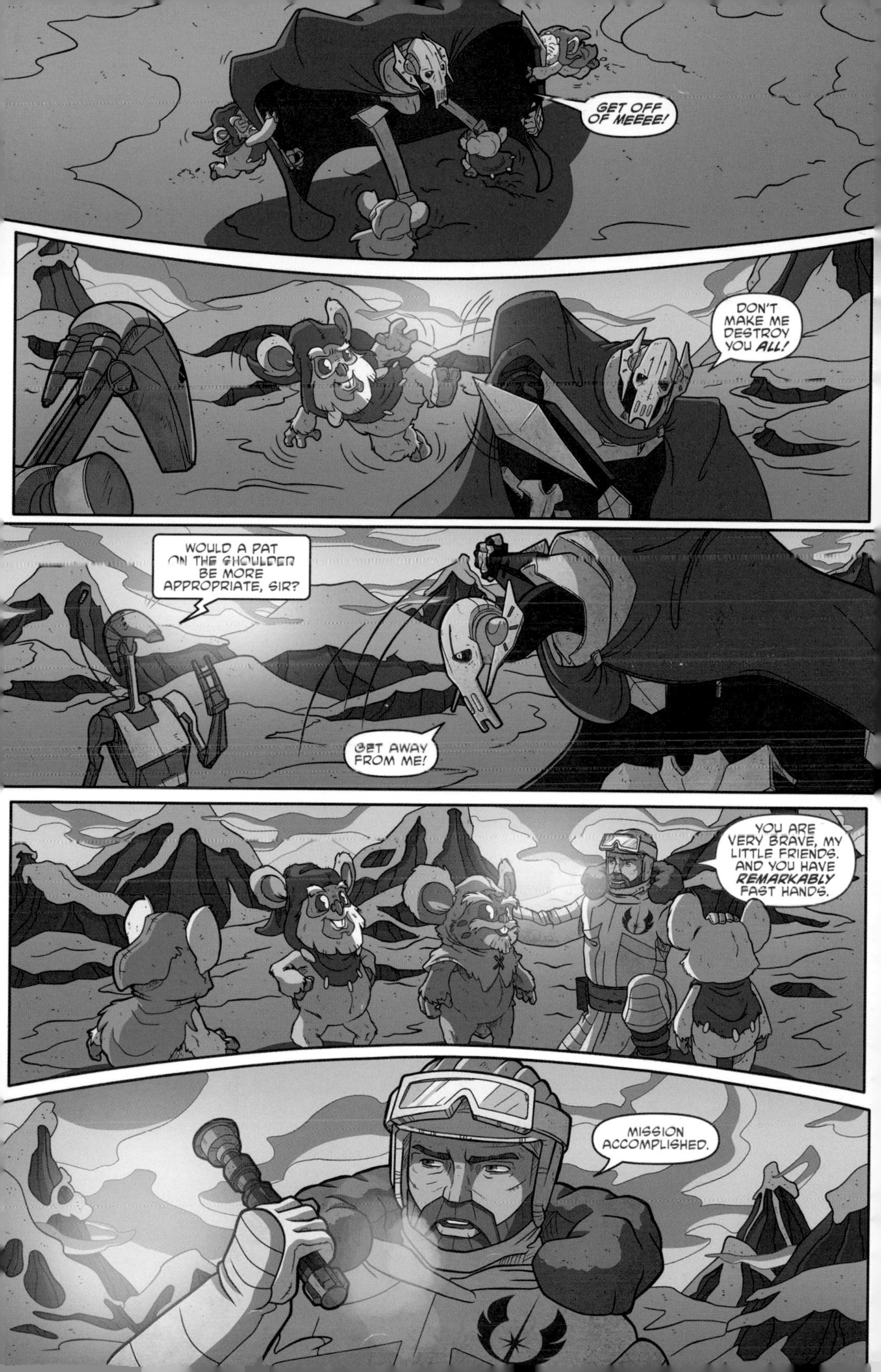
GET OFF OF MEEEE!
DON'T MAKE ME DESTROY YOU ALL!
WOULD A PAT ON THE SHOULDER BE MORE APPROPRIATE, SIR?
GET AWAY FROM ME!
YOU ARE VERY BRAVE, MY LITTLE FRIENDS. AND YOU HAVE REMARKABLY FAST HANDS.
MISSION ACCOMPLISHED.

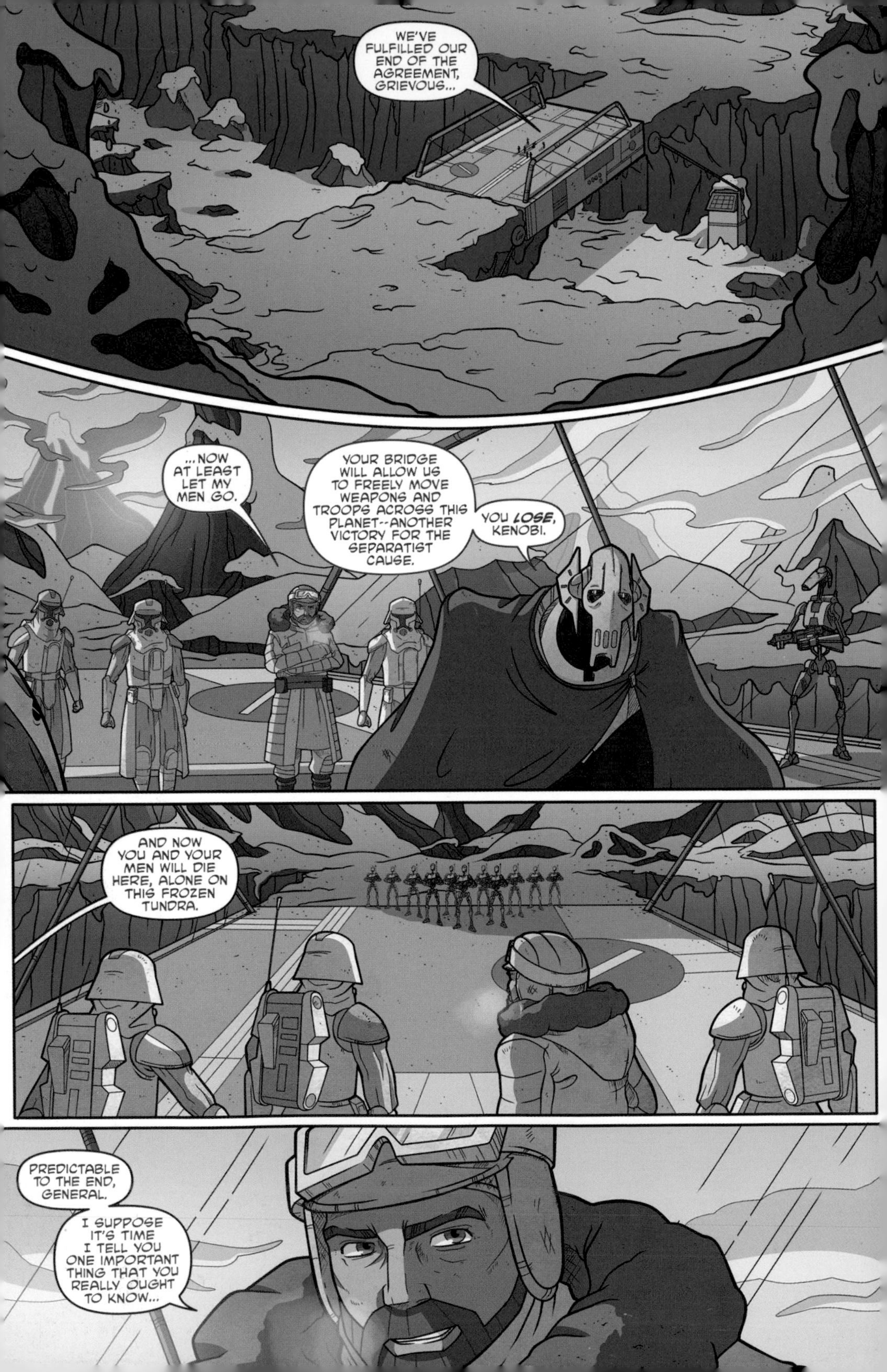
WE'VE FULFILLED OUR END OF THE AGREEMENT, GRIEVOUS...
...NOW AT LEAST LET MY MEN GO.
YOUR BRIDGE WILL ALLOW US TO FREELY MOVE WEAPONS AND TROOPS ACROSS THIS PLANET--ANOTHER VICTORY FOR THE SEPARATIST CAUSE.
YOU *LOSE*, KENOBI.
AND NOW YOU AND YOUR MEN WILL DIE HERE, ALONE ON THIS FROZEN TUNDRA.
PREDICTABLE TO THE END, GENERAL.
I SUPPOSE IT'S TIME I TELL YOU ONE IMPORTANT THING THAT YOU REALLY OUGHT TO KNOW...

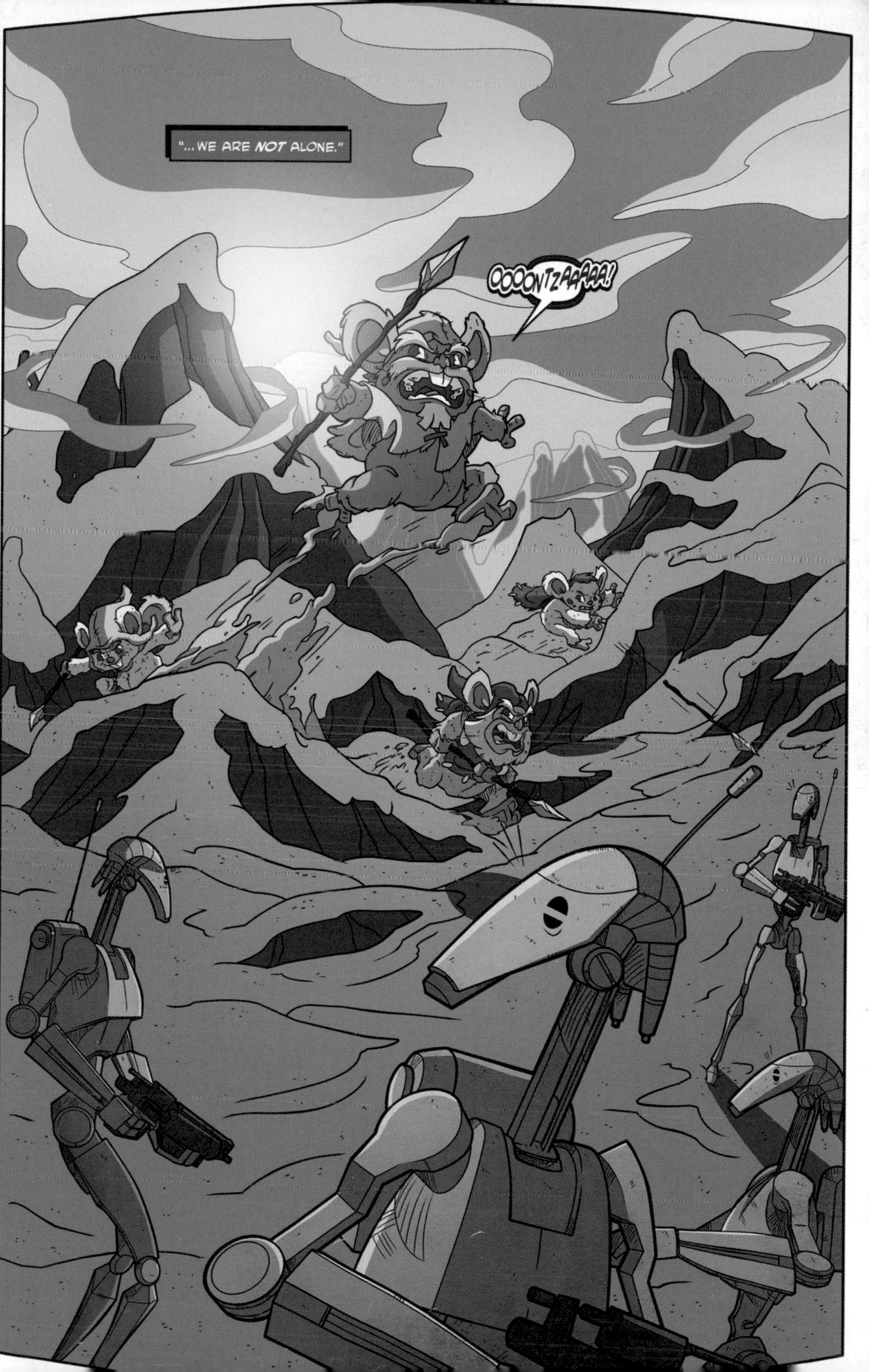
"...WE ARE NOT ALONE."
OOOONTZAAAAA!

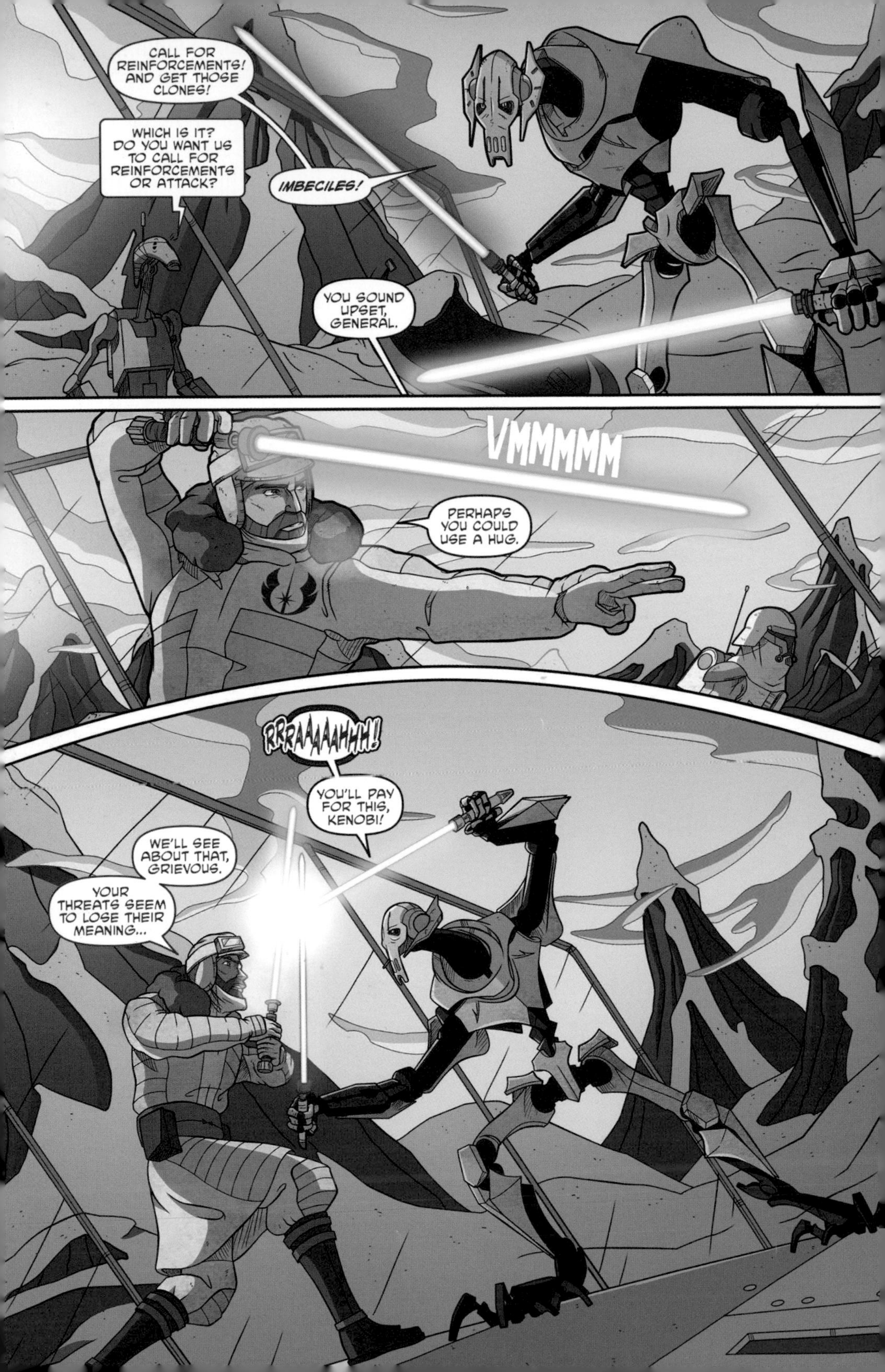
CALL FOR REINFORCEMENTS! AND GET THOSE CLONES!
WHICH IS IT? DO YOU WANT US TO CALL FOR REINFORCEMENTS OR ATTACK?
IMBECILES!
YOU SOUND UPSET, GENERAL.
VMMMMM
PERHAPS YOU COULD USE A HUG.
RRRAAAAAHHH!
YOU'LL PAY FOR THIS, KENOBI!
WE'LL SEE ABOUT THAT, GRIEVOUS.
YOUR THREATS SEEM TO LOSE THEIR MEANING...

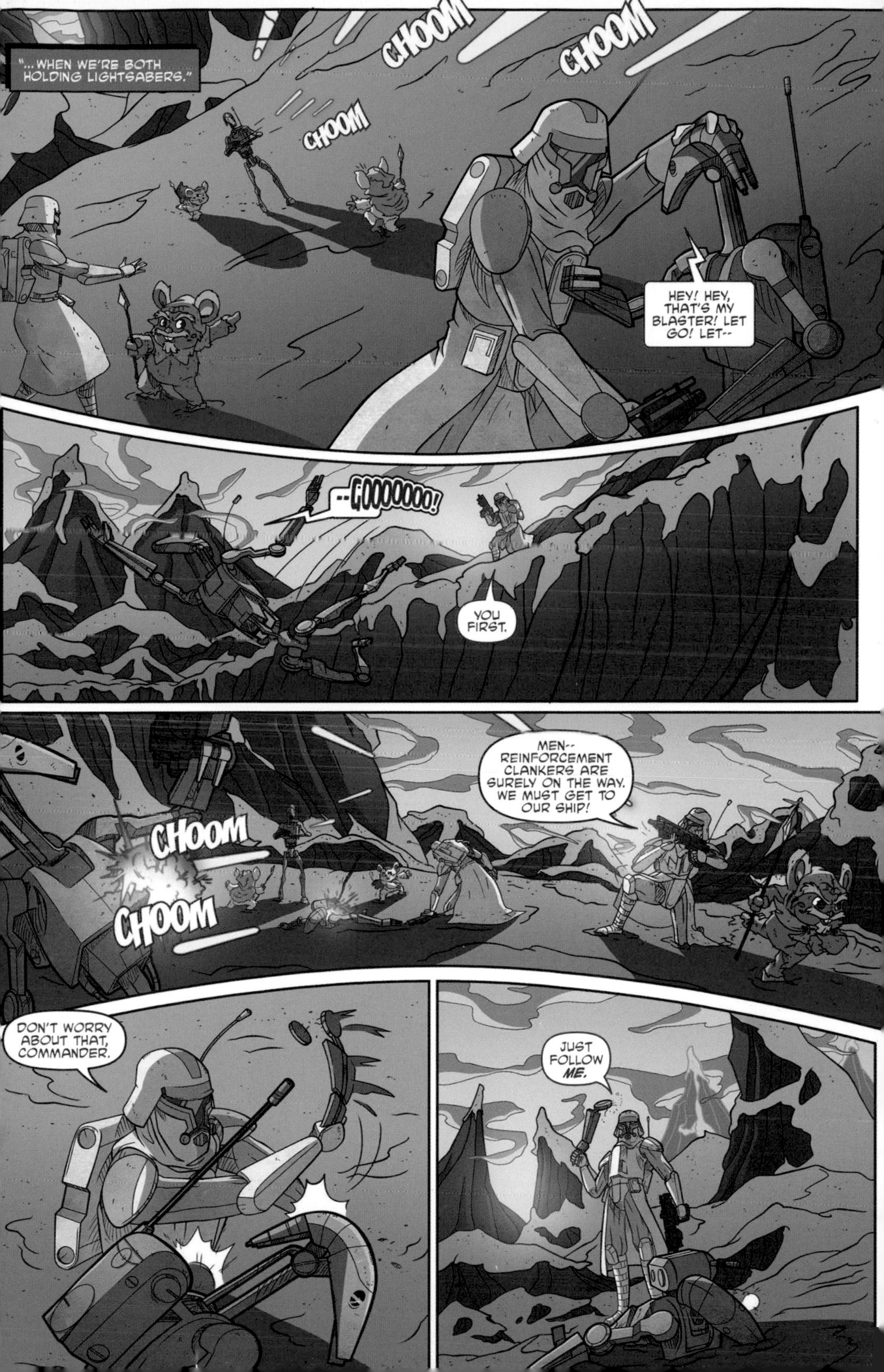
"...WHEN WE'RE BOTH HOLDING LIGHTSABERS."
CHOOM
CHOOM
CHOOM
HEY! HEY, THAT'S MY BLASTER! LET GO! LET--
--GOOOOOOO!
YOU FIRST.
MEN-- REINFORCEMENT CLANKERS ARE SURELY ON THE WAY. WE MUST GET TO OUR SHIP!
CHOOM
CHOOM
DON'T WORRY ABOUT THAT, COMMANDER.
JUST FOLLOW *ME.*

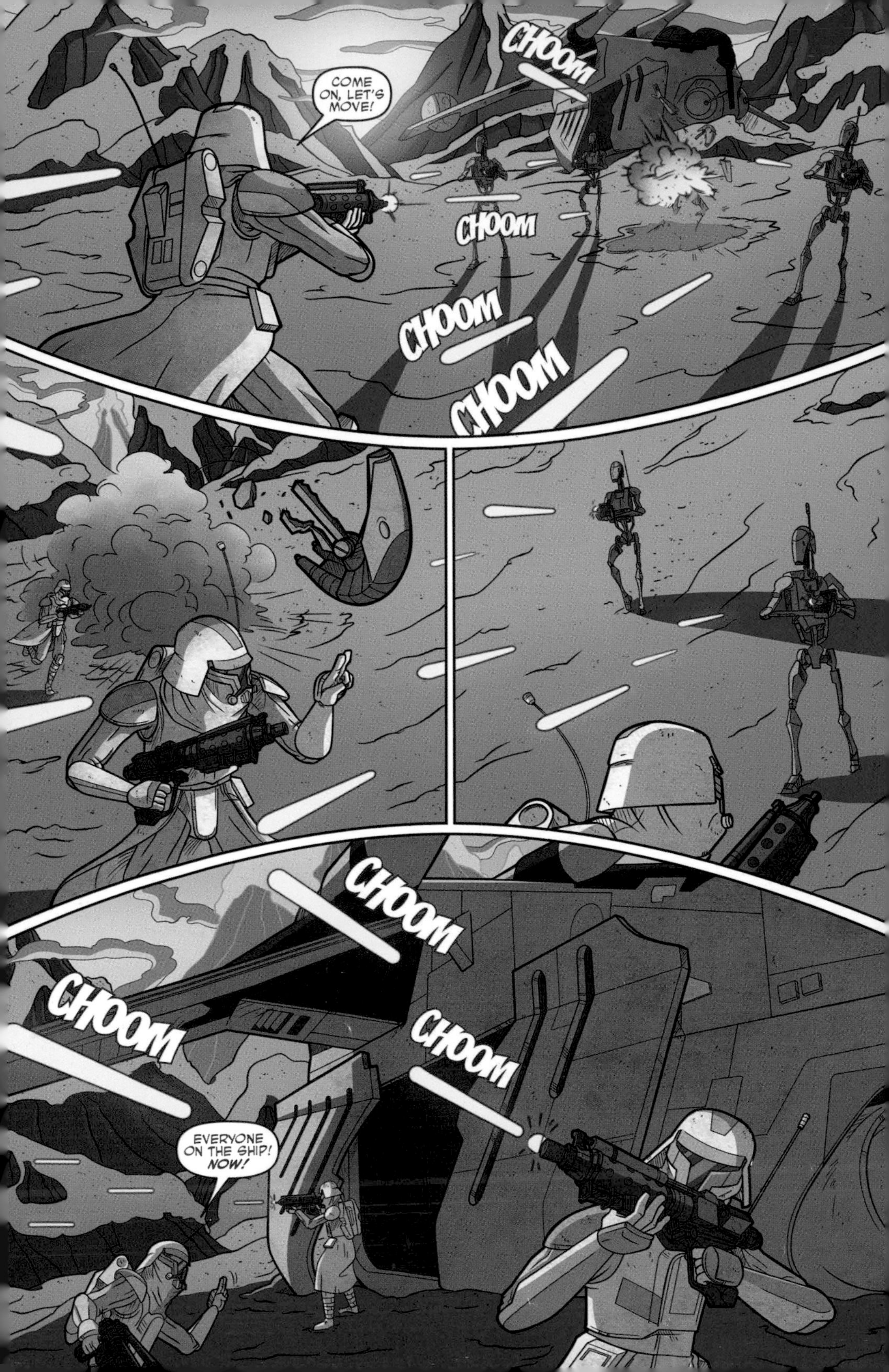
COME ON, LET'S MOVE!
CHOOM
CHOOM
CHOOM
CHOOM
CHOOM
CHOOM
CHOOM
CHOOM
EVERYONE ON THE SHIP! NOW!

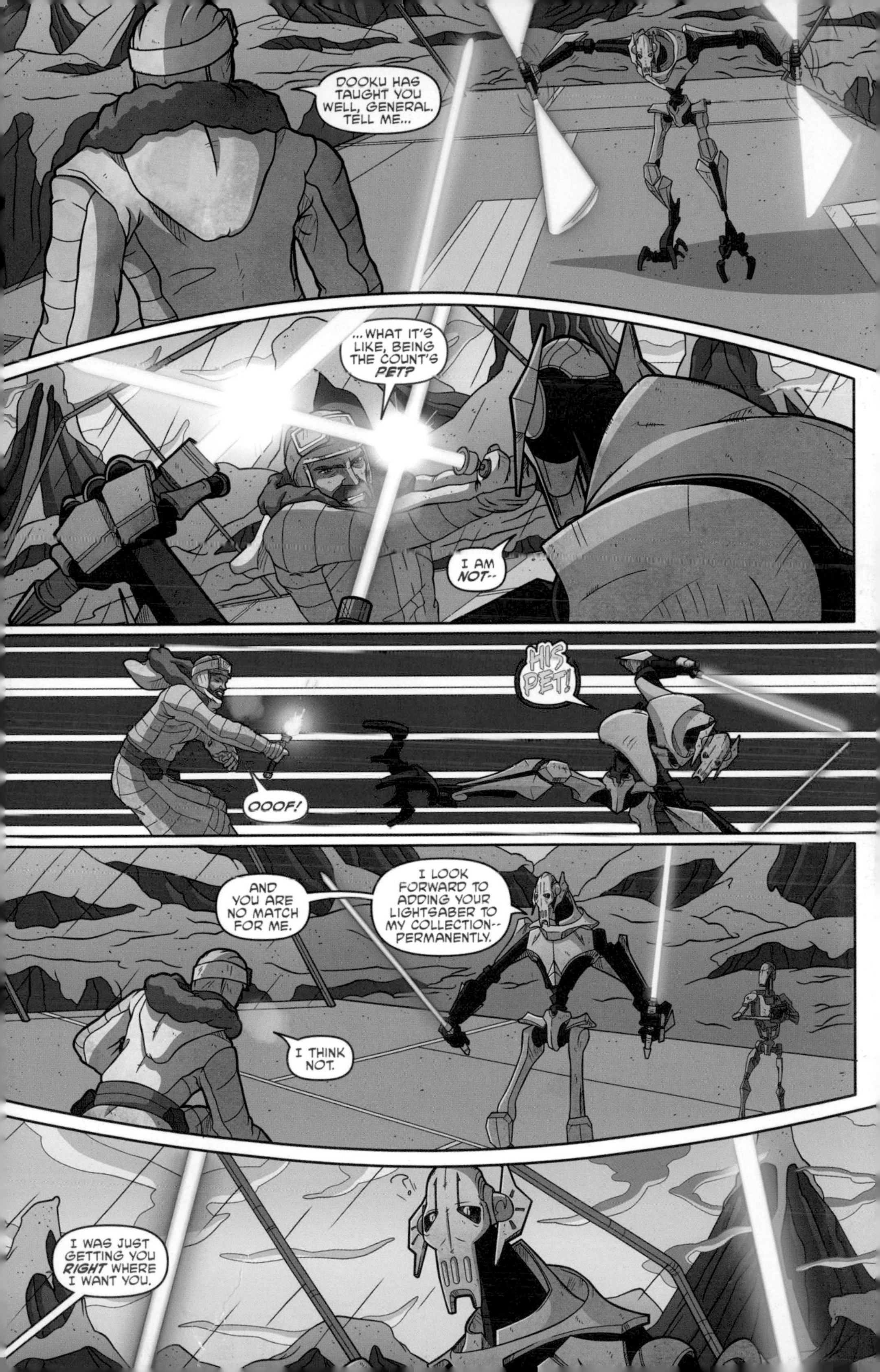
DOOKU HAS TAUGHT YOU WELL, GENERAL. TELL ME...
...WHAT IT'S LIKE, BEING THE COUNT'S *PET?*
I AM *NOT*--
HIS PET!
OOOF!
AND YOU ARE NO MATCH FOR ME.
I LOOK FORWARD TO ADDING YOUR LIGHTSABER TO MY COLLECTION--PERMANENTLY.
I THINK NOT.
?!
I WAS JUST GETTING YOU *RIGHT* WHERE I WANT YOU.

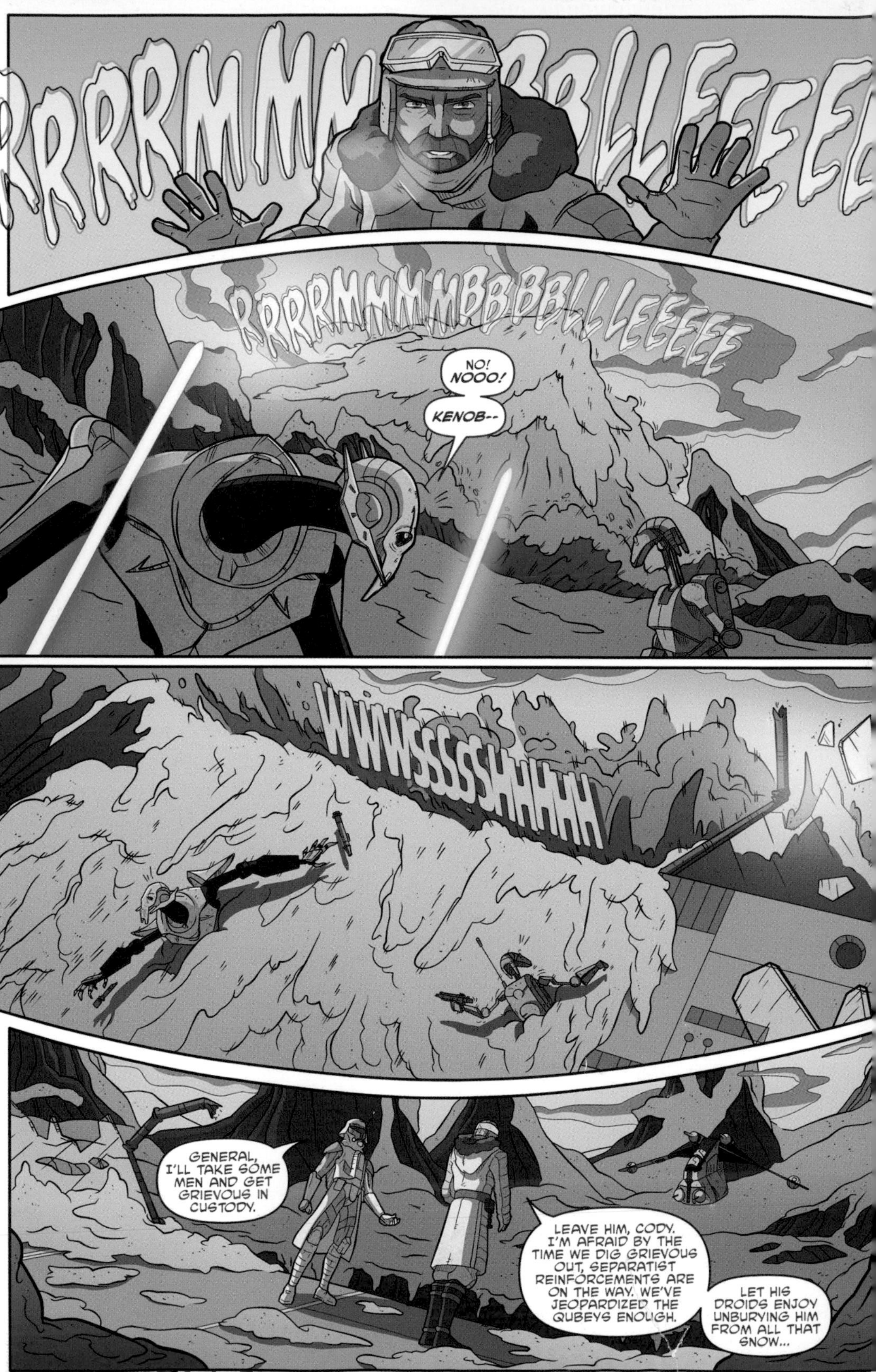
RRRRMMMMBBLLEEEEL
RRRRMMMMBBBBLLEEEEEE
NO! NOOO!
KENOB--
WWWSSSSHHHHH
GENERAL, I'LL TAKE SOME MEN AND GET GRIEVOUS IN CUSTODY.
LEAVE HIM, CODY. I'M AFRAID BY THE TIME WE DIG GRIEVOUS OUT, SEPARATIST REINFORCEMENTS ARE ON THE WAY. WE'VE JEOPARDIZED THE QUBEYS ENOUGH.
LET HIS DROIDS ENJOY UNBURYING HIM FROM ALL THAT SNOW...

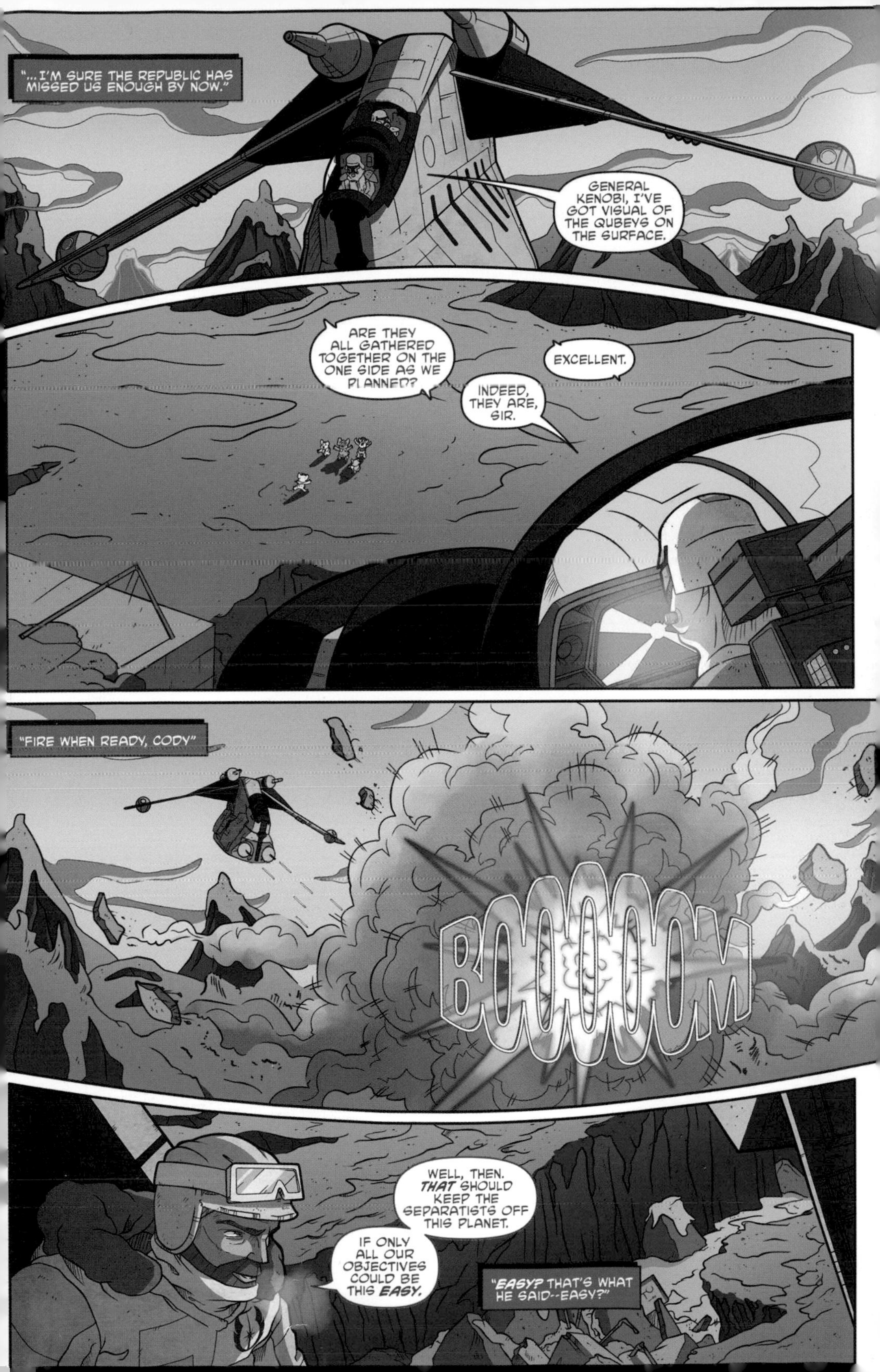
"...I'M SURE THE REPUBLIC HAS MISSED US ENOUGH BY NOW."
GENERAL KENOBI, I'VE GOT VISUAL OF THE QUBEYS ON THE SURFACE.
ARE THEY ALL GATHERED TOGETHER ON THE ONE SIDE AS WE PLANNED?
INDEED, THEY ARE, SIR.
EXCELLENT.
"FIRE WHEN READY, CODY"
BOOOOOOM
WELL, THEN. THAT SHOULD KEEP THE SEPARATISTS OFF THIS PLANET.
IF ONLY ALL OUR OBJECTIVES COULD BE THIS EASY.
"EASY? THAT'S WHAT HE SAID--EASY?"

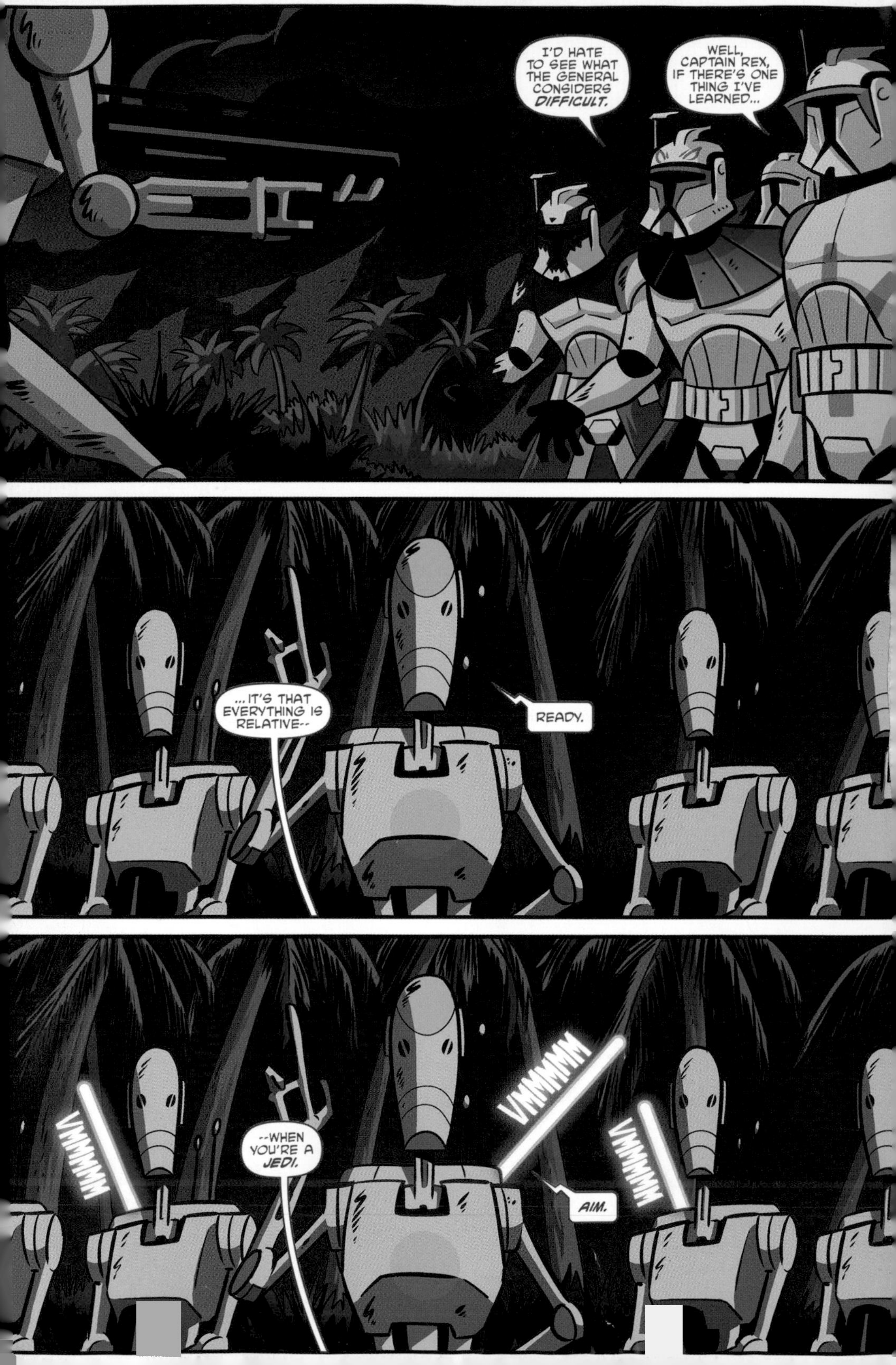
I'D HATE TO SEE WHAT THE GENERAL CONSIDERS *DIFFICULT.*
WELL, CAPTAIN REX, IF THERE'S ONE THING I'VE LEARNED...
...IT'S THAT EVERYTHING IS RELATIVE--
READY.
VMMMM
--WHEN YOU'RE A *JEDI.*
VMMMM
VMMMM
AIM.

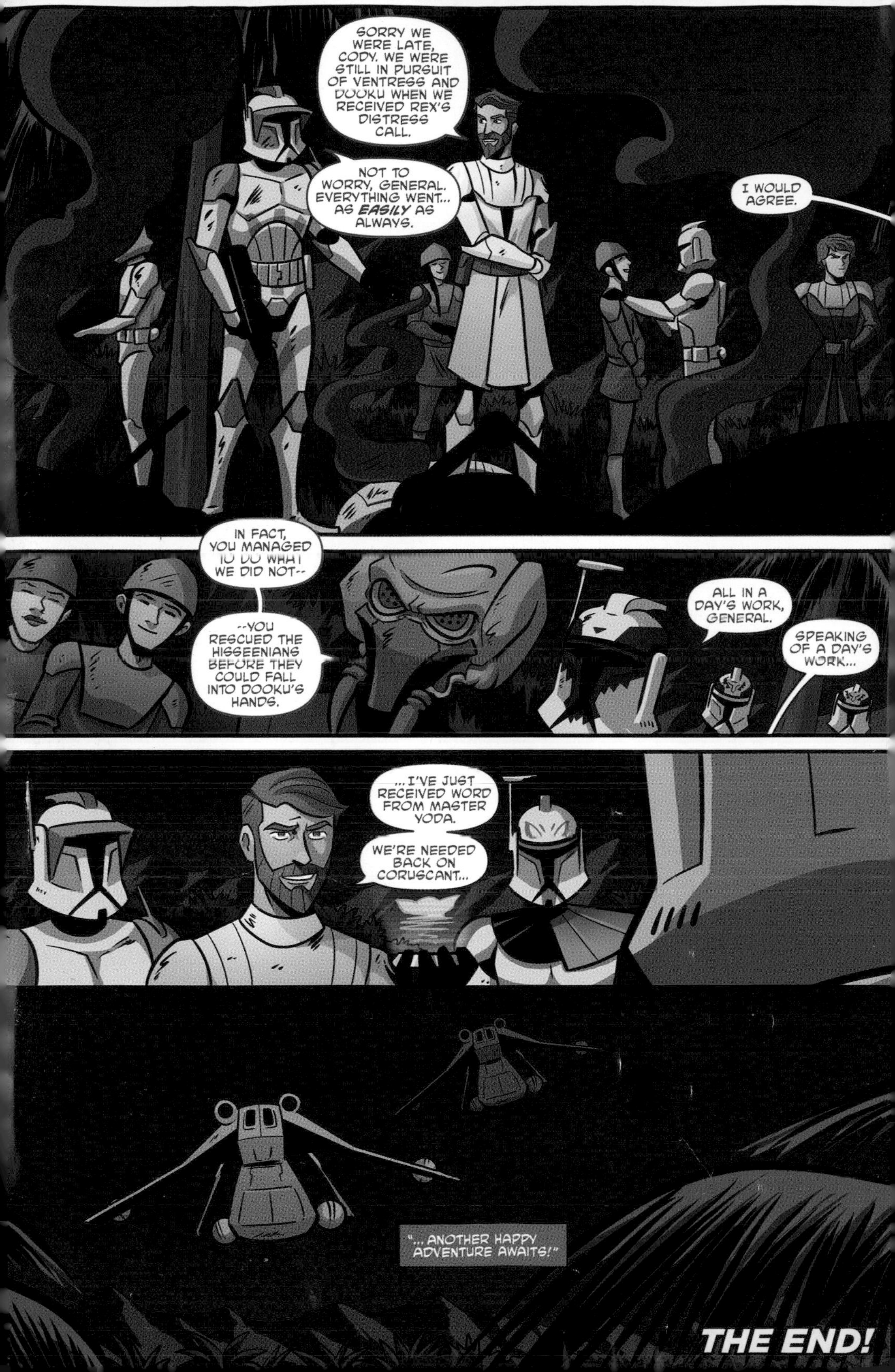
SORRY WE WERE LATE, CODY. WE WERE STILL IN PURSUIT OF VENTRESS AND DOOKU WHEN WE RECEIVED REX'S DISTRESS CALL.
NOT TO WORRY, GENERAL. EVERYTHING WENT... AS EASILY AS ALWAYS.
I WOULD AGREE.
IN FACT, YOU MANAGED TO DO WHAT WE DID NOT--
--YOU RESCUED THE HISSEENIANS BEFORE THEY COULD FALL INTO DOOKU'S HANDS.
ALL IN A DAY'S WORK, GENERAL.
SPEAKING OF A DAY'S WORK...
...I'VE JUST RECEIVED WORD FROM MASTER YODA.
WE'RE NEEDED BACK ON CORUSCANT...
"...ANOTHER HAPPY ADVENTURE AWAITS!"
THE END!

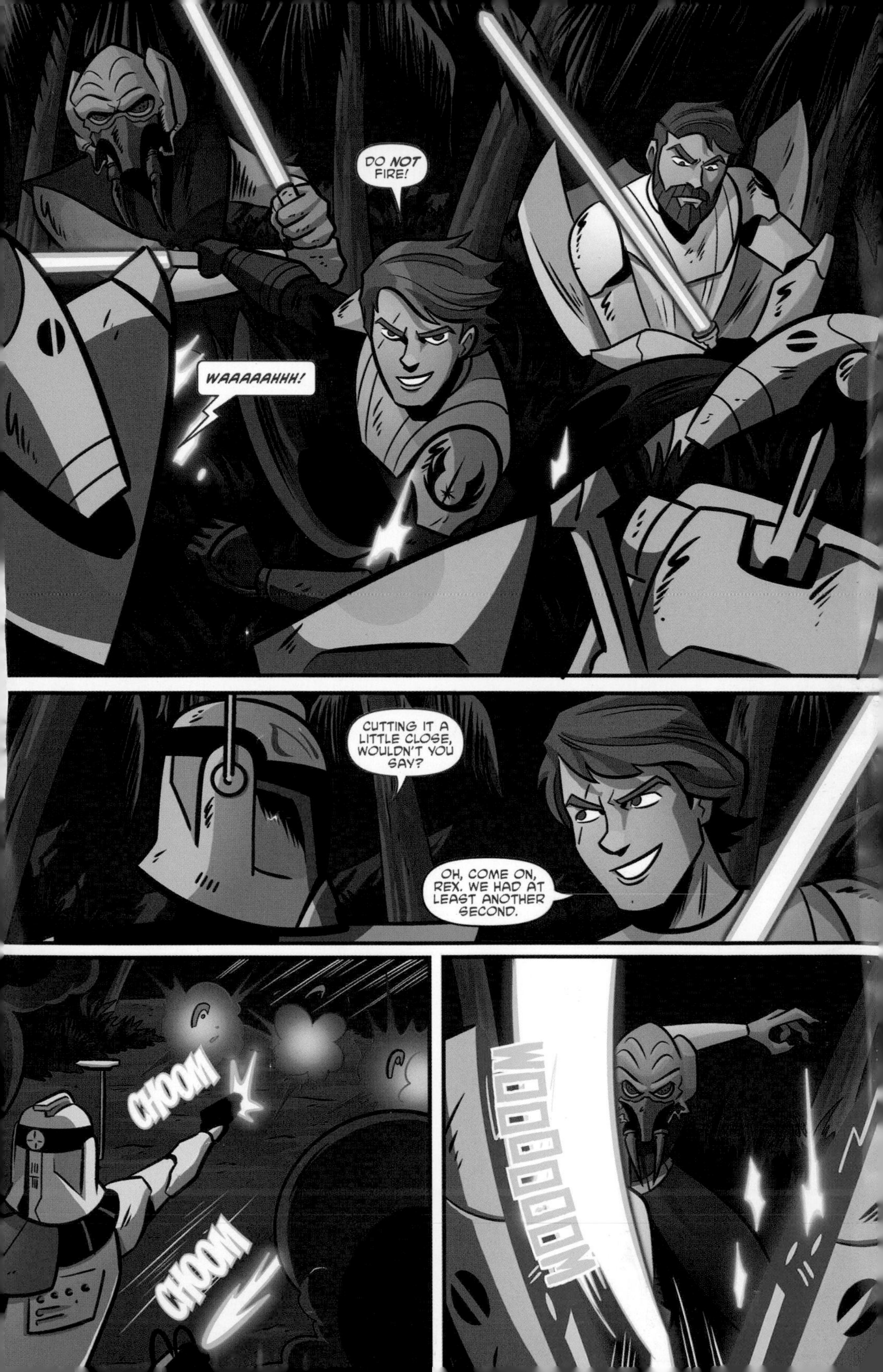
DO NOT FIRE!
WAAAAAHHH!
CUTTING IT A LITTLE CLOSE, WOULDN'T YOU SAY?
OH, COME ON, REX. WE HAD AT LEAST ANOTHER SECOND.
CHOOM
CHOOM
WOOOOOOOM!

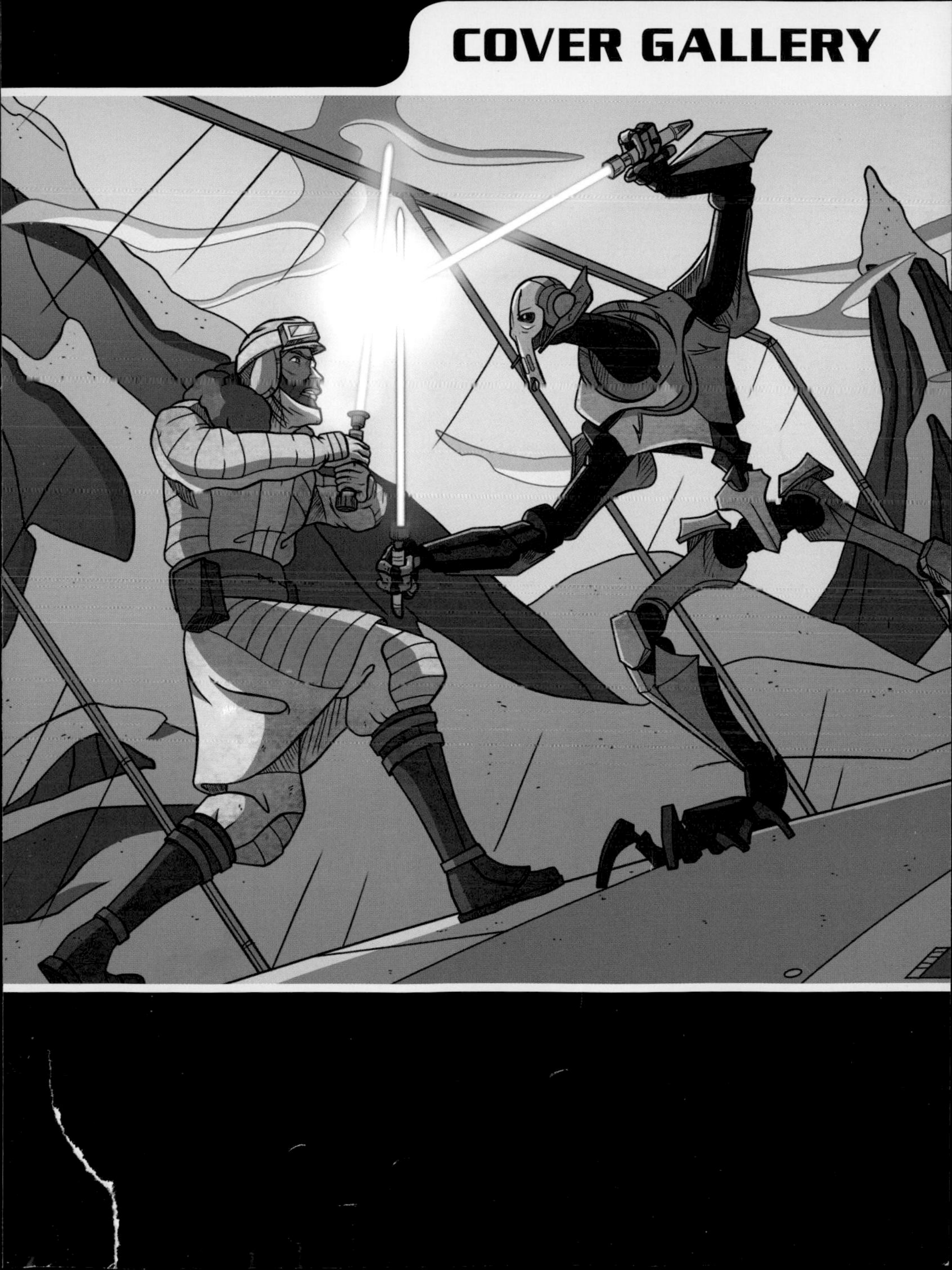

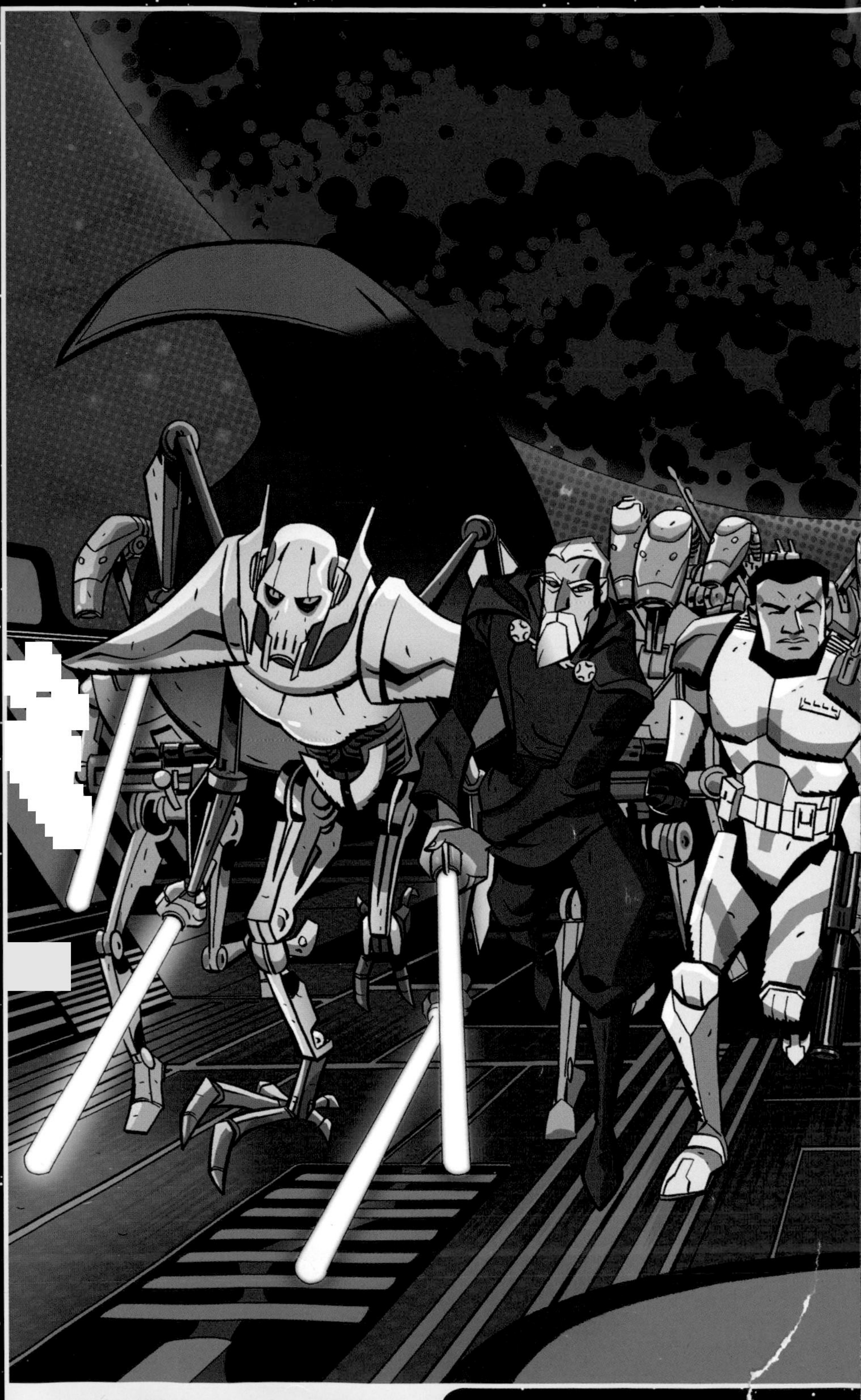

Art by Michael Avon Oeming

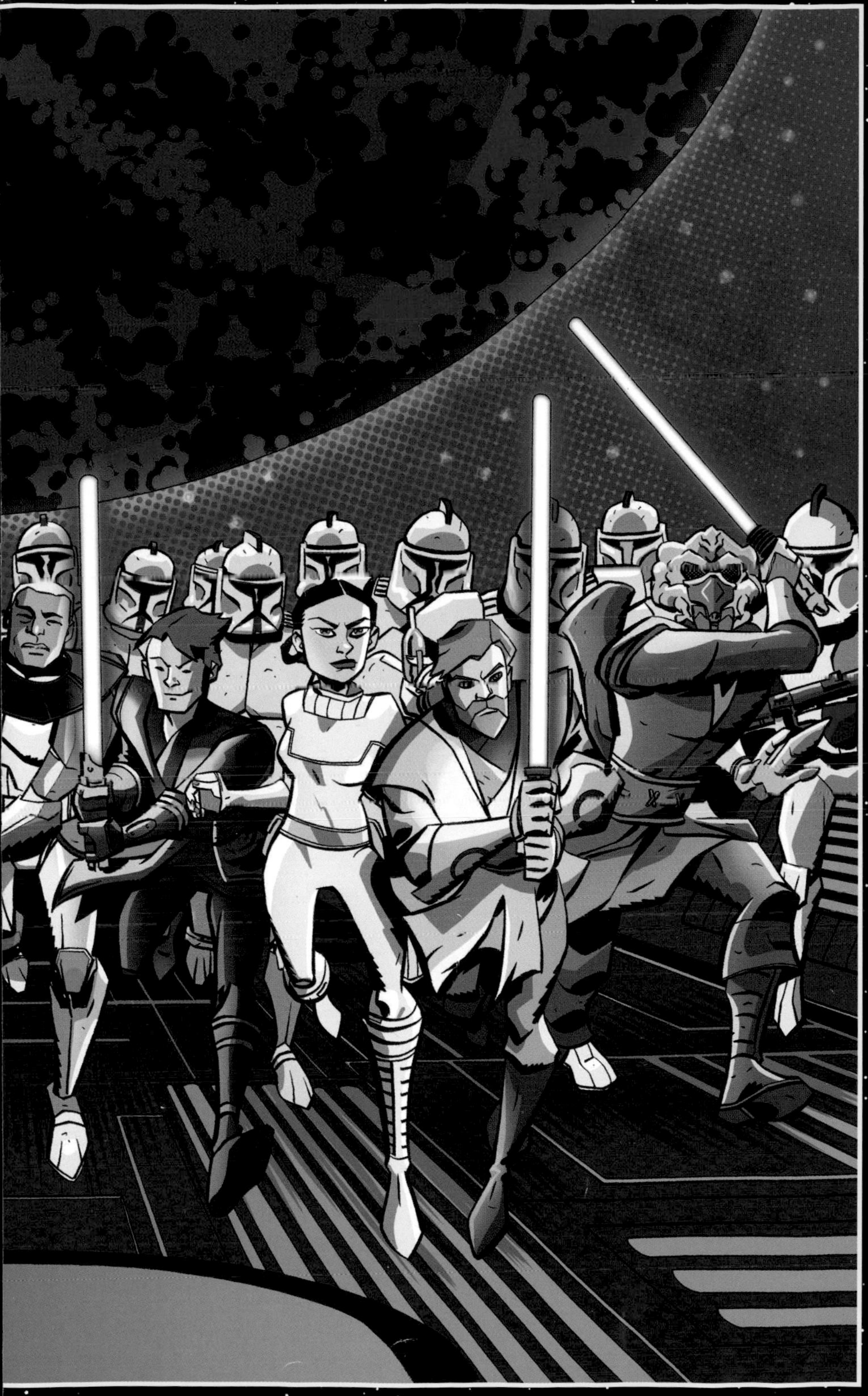

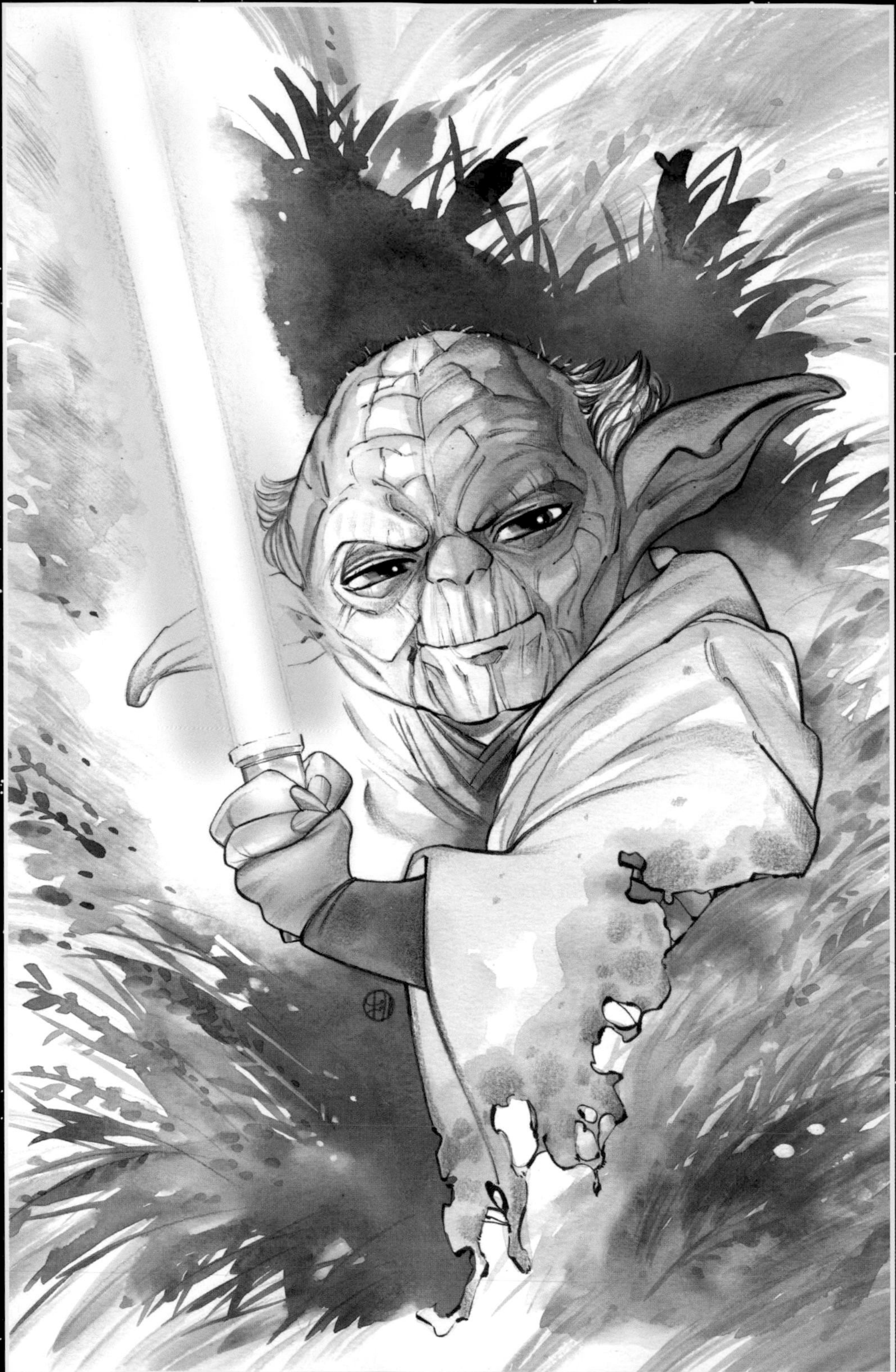

Art by Peach Momoko

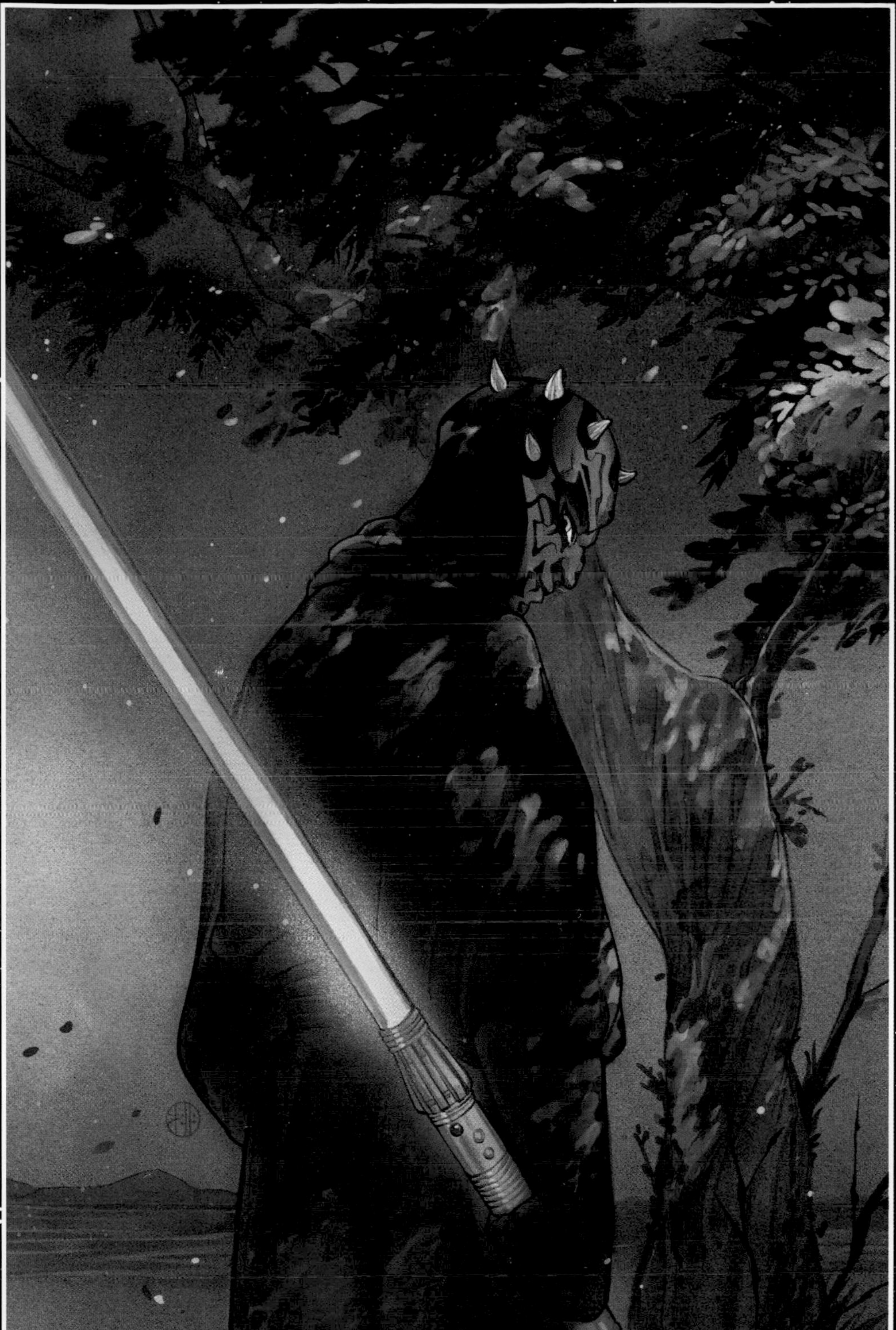

Art by Peach Momoko

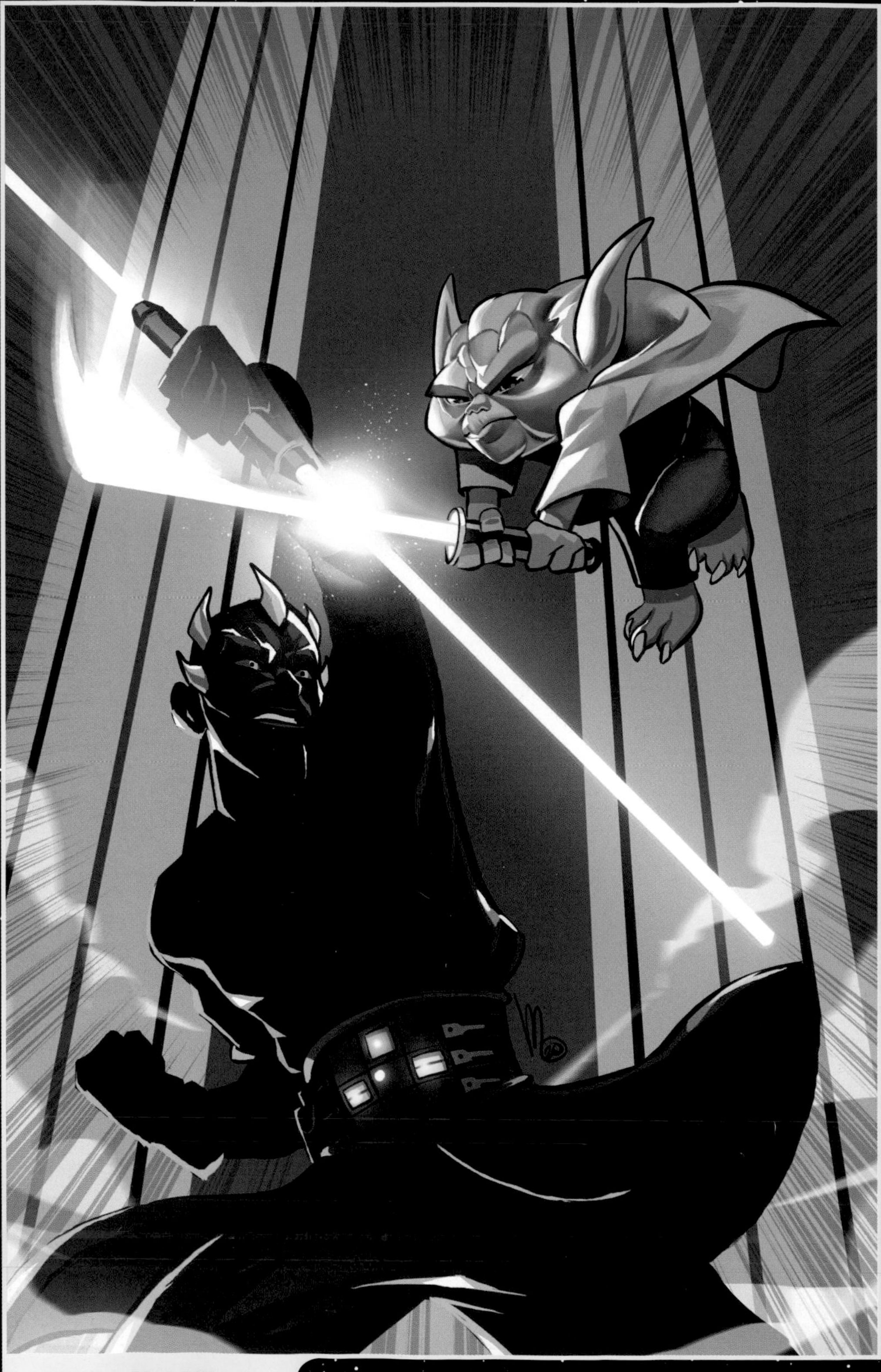

Art by Mel Milton

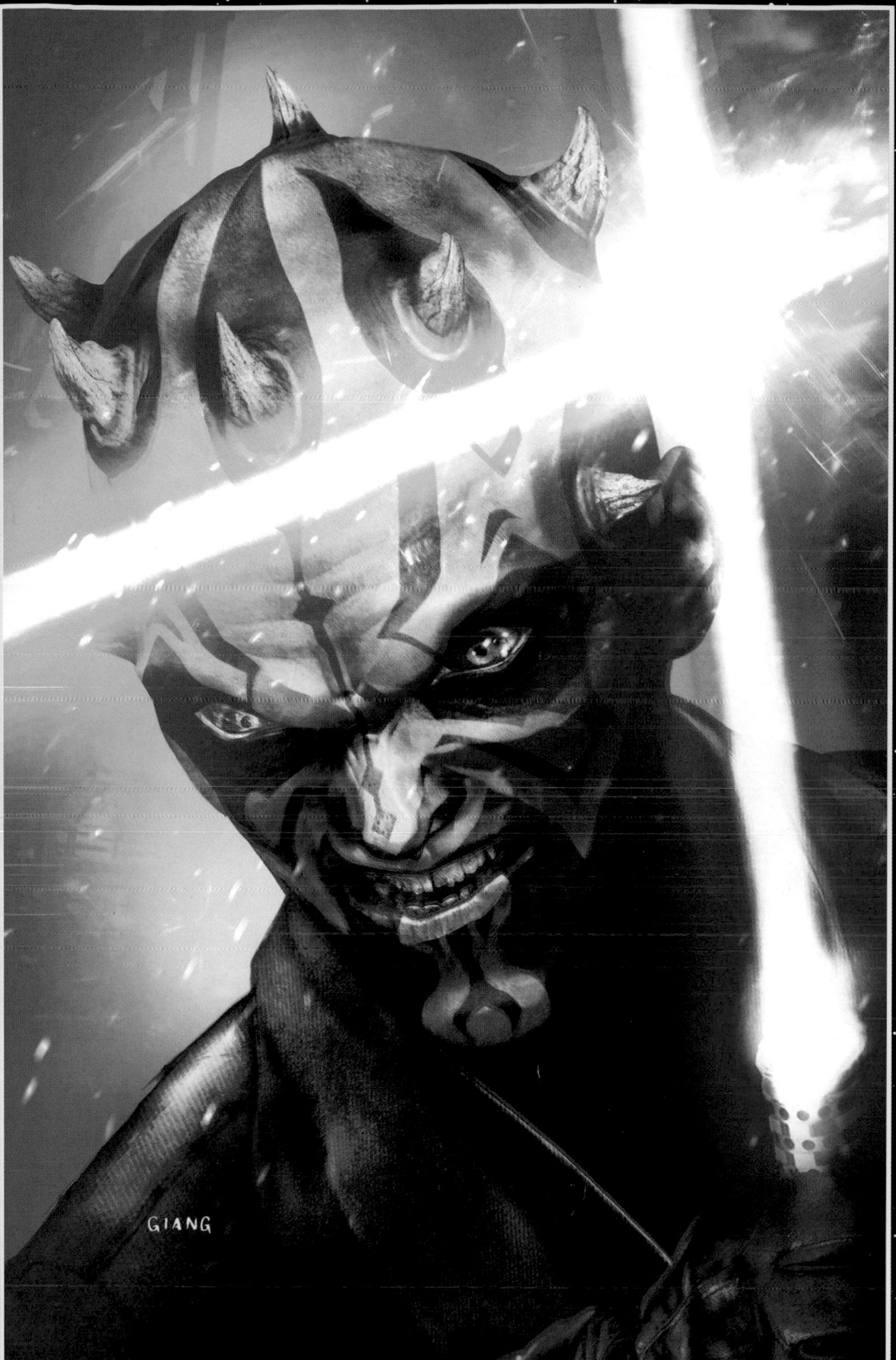
GIANG

Art by John Giang